THE DARK SIDE OF THE SKY

Also by Francesco Dimitri and available from Titan Books

THE BOOK OF HIDDEN THINGS

NEVER THE WIND

THE DARK SIDE OF THE SKY

FRANCESCO DIMITRI

TITAN BOOKS

The Dark Side of the Sky
Print edition ISBN: 9781803362786
E-book edition ISBN: 9781803363721

Published by Titan Books
A division of Titan Publishing Group Ltd
144 Southwark Street, London SE1 0UP
www.titanbooks.com

First edition: May 2024
10 9 8 7 6 5 4 3 2 1

This is a work of fiction. All of the characters, organizations, and events portrayed in this novel are either products of the author's imagination or are used fictitiously. Any resemblance to actual persons, living or dead (except for satirical purposes), is entirely coincidental.

A CIP catalogue record for this title is available from the British Library.

Printed and bound by CPI Group (UK) Ltd, Croydon, CR0 4YY.

Cosmology is a literary art.

Northrop Frye

1

OUR FEAST

THE BASTION

At dusk, we made a circle around the body.

Lila started on her drum, each beat a thunder in tune with our hearts. Charlie shook a tambourine with a clatter of fresh rain. Sam, an attention-seeker until his last breath, rose his head to the sky and howled. We'll never forget how Sam would howl; someone always howled back. We joined in, clapping our hands, beating our chests, humming. It was a cure for the gloom. We stomped our feet, we laughed, we swayed, we sung, Lila now drumming fast, Zoey and Mikka drumming with her. We were a family, we had each other's backs. We had to keep that in mind. We were a little tense – it was the first time we would taste human flesh.

The sky was orange, the land red and green, the winter grass soft underfoot. Our world was almost perfect. Yes, cracks were appearing, spreading fast, but we were young, each in our own way. Heartbreakingly beautiful. We were so young as to believe that we could just ignore the badness and the badness would go away.

Rebecca raised her arms, and the music wound down. When she beamed her full presence at you, you realised that you had been living in black and white, while she was tawny, blue and chestnut. She would paint you in bright colours too, if you listened to her. Everybody listened, friend or foe. You could love her or hate her, as some of us came to do, but you could not ignore her.

A journalist recently published a long-winded piece arguing that Becca's personal charm was a fabrication of lawyers and media outlets. The hack had never met her in person.

'This is a great day,' she said, 'and nothing great was ever easy.'

Her eyes were bloodshot, her lovely cheeks pale, her voice unsteady.

'And I…' she stopped. Our heartbeat stopped. We had never seen her falter, not once.

'Nothing great is ever easy,' she repeated, in a lower voice. 'We are gathered here tonight because of death, the greatest mystery, and the hardest one. It is a mystery we have already met. What is death?' she asked.

'A blank slate,' we answered immediately, as we should.

'What is death?' she asked again, in a louder voice.

And we answered: 'An opportunity.'

'What is death?' she asked for the third time, not quite shouting.

'A gift!' we shouted back.

That pleased her. 'And the truth of that gift is change. Imagine how dreadful it would be to be stuck in this one form for ever,' she said, touching her own face, and we thought that her face was lovely, not dreadful at all. 'To know only one body, only one sex, one race, one set of circumstances. If we didn't die, if the eyes we have now were open for ever, we would only see what they see, only that, and nothing more. We might be born rich and smart and gorgeous. We might have it good. But any river, no matter how pure, becomes a swamp when it stops flowing. Death is what keeps our river flowing.'

She paused, and we had time to think her words through. They told us nothing we didn't know, and yet, with Ric's body lying naked in the centre of our circle, they seemed to hint at some deeper truth.

The silence stretched to unsettling lengths. A sparrow landed on Ric's forehead to rest there a moment, then flew away. We listened to the wind and the birds, we breathed in the clean air. We wished Becca would start talking again.

On cue, she said, 'We may weep because Ric left us. I have spent the last day crying, and I am going to cry tomorrow, and for days to come. I am barely…' She stopped. 'I am barely able to get ahold of myself as it is. We may weep if we need; we may voice the pain we feel. *Give sorrow words*, Shakespeare said. *The grief that does not speak whispers the o'er-fraught heart and bids it break.*'

The mark of great thinkers: they are not afraid to use the words of others to put across their own message.

'But we should know why we mourn. Nothing sad happened to Ric. Something sad happened to *us*: we lost a dear friend, a guide. I will be missing him every day I have left to live. He will not be with me by the fireplace tonight. He will not touch the nape of my neck the way he used to do, he will not…' She paused again, and swallowed back her tears.

We were crying with her. We saw an Oddball hovering above us, a crow with a rat's head and the tiny hands of a mouse.

'So yes,' she said, after composing herself. 'We may cry, but we must know we cry for ourselves, rather than for him. There is no reason to cry for him.'

She brought a hand to her belt, where she had her working knife. She unsheathed it. We held our breath while she walked to the body.

'Jesus of Nazareth asked his disciples to eat of his body and drink of his blood, in token. It is not our custom to do things in token. What would Ric say?'

'Be real,' Lila answered. 'Be real to the end.'

'And hell, are we real.'

We stood in silence while the birds sung and there was a gentle scraping of metal against flesh. Becca chewed, and swallowed. Someone offered her a sip of water.

'Come, my friends,' she said.

We took our knives and swarmed on Ric.

Had he not died, we would be looking at a different story. A triumph, perhaps.

CHARLIE

It wasn't like now, when you can google the Bastion and see the pinewood, that spectacular beach, almost all of our faces. When Bertrand and I started looking into it, there were no photographs. What pics you could see on their Insta were attractive, but vague: thick myrtle on dunes, tattooed hands playing a theremin, a silhouette of a man (or perhaps it was a woman, you couldn't tell) skinny-dipping into moonlit dark waters. What did Becca and Ric look like? What kind of folks did they attract? Some people would wonder; only a fraction of them, as it happens, would be curious enough to investigate online; and only a fraction of those would go and see for themselves. Becca and Ric taught us, 'Fate is nature unfolding.'

ZOEY

Yeah, filling my application, I massaged the truth where the truth was sore, starting with my name and job. I could not disclose I was Zoey Lee, CEO of Soul Journey. We were perhaps not the biggest Mind, Body and Spirit festival in the world, but the best-known for sure. I'm not bragging; it is what it is. From Reiki to witchcraft to astrology, we covered the whole spectrum of woo-woo, with glitz.

Everybody in the industry knew SoulJo and everybody knew me and my partner (my *business* partner, that is), Janis Mackenzie. I thought the application was a gimmick to make people feel special while gathering info. I know better now, but at that time I'd have bet good money that the Bastion accepted everybody solvent, and that disclosing my identity would be the only surefire way to get rejected.

I wrote, *Zoey Pagano*.

CHARLIE

Bertrand and I sent our application on a blustery night. I remember every moment of it as if it isn't a memory, but something that is happening now. A part of me is still in Saint-Malo with Bertrand, checking the Open Feast's website on my phone. We are both naked under a rough woollen blanket, lying on a piece of cardboard as wind and rain rage against what passes for our window. But it is a memory after all. I am a different person now. I am in a different place.

I said something along the lines of: 'The glass could give up at any time.'

'It could.'

'It's wonderful.'

He kissed me and I curled up against him. Being happy is not like riding a bike; you *can* forget how to do it. Not so long before, Bertrand and I had lost faith we would ever remember, but here we were, against all odds.

ZOEY

'Are you using your real first name?' Janis asked.

She was sitting by my side on the perfectly round, perfectly white, Saarinen tulip table in my living room. We used to work like that, side by side.

'I need something I'll answer to instinctively. I'm not sure what to write down as my job though.'

'HR? It's generic enough.'

'They might check LinkedIn.'

'Good point. Landlady then? No social networks needed.'

'I just rent what I inherited. A quiet job, off the radar. Brilliant.'

To be clear, I'd not inherited a thing. What I had, I had fought tooth and nail for, starting with my apartment in Greenwich Village, New York. I loved it: I close my eyes and it is there, in all its swankiness. The living room was painted light green, with a window opening onto a leafy street. In a corner was an Arco floor lamp, with an Eames chair under its round metal shade. Framed on a wall was a Leonora Carrington limited print, the one with the woman in a white cloak and a halo of flames, or hair, around her head. On another wall was the promo poster of the first Soul Journey Festival that Janis and I produced: a white background, and at the centre, a black spiral, hand-drawn, from which different religious symbols (a crucifix, a rune, a pentacle, a half-moon with a star...) hung like small charms from a bracelet. It was an amateur's work that Janis made with input from me. The budget for that first festival had been non-existent, and we made do. The DIY aesthetic was key to our early success; now we had a hired agency making sure that the aesthetic kept a DIY feel.

CHARLIE

Bertrand and I had married (it was a small ceremony with only a handful of friends) on 19 January 2020. Yes – 2020, the year the Earth stood still. The winter wedding was Bertrand's idea. January sucks, he proclaimed, and we would set it right. From then on, January wouldn't be the unforgiving month of frost and fasting, it would be the month of our anniversary, a party time to shake off the winter blues. Bertrand could come across like a giant, over-eager puppy, but he was a thoughtful man.

What he wasn't – and me neither – is a seer. He could not know that in a matter of weeks the winter blues would be the last of our problems. The pandemic swept France along with the rest of the world, finding us completely unprepared, along with the rest of the world. Bertrand was a session saxophonist, I was a junior doctor, which meant that while his income dropped to zero from one day to the next, I found myself working all day, every day. Married life felt like war – until I got sick.

The public doesn't fully realise yet what a meat-grinder the pandemic was for people working in hospitals: we were called 'front-line' as if it were a metaphor, but it wasn't. We were in the trenches, keeping our heads low and praying enemy fire wouldn't hit us. The day I saw the two lines on my test was the day I had learnt a colleague of mine, the same age as me, with no pre-existing conditions, had passed. I saw those two lines and my body went cold with fear. I remember thinking, *I'm going to lose everything, oh my God, I'm going to lose everything.* The numbers were on my side; most people my age and with no conditions got out lightly, but fear hears no reason, and I felt I was done for.

Well – I was on my feet in four days, with nothing more than a little cough. Meanwhile though I'd passed the bug to Bertrand,

and it wasn't so easy for him. He spent two weeks in bed, and when he managed to kick that bastard illness out, it took his wind in revenge. Bertrand couldn't blow as much as three notes before getting short of breath. It was heart-rending to hear what muffled, pitiful wheezes he managed to produce, like an old lion whose vocal cords had been cut by some sadistic poacher.

I'm ashamed to say I was happy to go back to work. I knew I should have been by my husband's side, but I just couldn't see him so dejected. I became angry so as not to feel guilty – *somebody* had to bring money home, right? Bertrand sensed I was running away, but he couldn't say much, because it was true that we had rent to pay. It was a bad time, which left us exhausted, penniless, all too ready to snap at each other.

'It's a miracle we stayed together,' Bertrand would say later, with a large grin, when he was in an especially good mood. Which happened a lot, after we got to the other end of it. With patience, his wind came back, the world started to spin again. Not only did we stay together, but we rebuilt our relationship, our whole life, from scratch, and a fine life it was at that. We were right to be proud, both of us.

ZOEY

'Look, they're asking for a personal essay.'

Janis touched her loop earrings. 'Only two hundred words.' She read the question aloud. '*Describe your biggest fear: what keeps you awake at night? What is it that makes you feel desperate, and helpless?*' She paused. 'These guys are intense.'

'Say it. They're nuts.'

'Some call us that too.'

'Yeah, no, it's different.'

'So, tell me, Zoey, my friend, who's your bogeyman?'

'Like hell I'm going to tell the competition.'

I started writing some bullshit on spiders, then I deleted it. On the off chance the Bastion folks actually *read* the application, I thought, they'd want some juice. *Strangers,* I wrote. I went on about how little understood I was, how mistrustful of new people, and ended with a flourish about finding succour in books. The shy-bookish-girl act is an evergreen; three-quarters of the Soul Journey audience fancied themselves romantic introverts, to justify their being narcissist assholes. *Stories are my escape hatch,* I wrote. *Doors onto better worlds.* That crap on stories being doors never failed to make a workshop audience nod thoughtfully. Trust a cliché and it will take you places.

Janis said I was a monster, laughing.

CHARLIE

A blast of rain rattled the window like a convict beating on his cell's bars.

'First thing we get is a new window,' Bertrand said.

'We can afford a good one straight away – if we get on a diet of crackers and tap water for two months.'

He laughed, called me one of our private names, and kissed me on the tip of my nose. We were penniless again by that point, but in a completely different way. As of that day, we owned a home, a one-bedroom flat in a nice part of town. IKEA furniture (including a bed) was coming soon. We had a mortgage and the means to repay it. There was little left at the end of the month, but there was *something.* We were not flush, but who was, after the plague?

We were okay. We had seen through the bad times and now we had every intention of enjoying the good ones, on a budget.

Hence the Open Feast – a friend of Bertrand's swore it was a cheap holiday. The organisers were a group called The Bastion: they had an Insta, a sparsely populated Mastodon account, and a lean website (when I say *lean*, I don't mean it was elegant and minimalist, I mean that it looked like it had been cobbled together in a couple of hours, as an afterthought). Hard as we looked, we could not find any mention of prices.

ZOEY

'You call *me* a monster?' I said to Janis. 'Look at the next question: *Tell us about something you always desired and never quite achieved.* Blah blah blah. See what they're doing?'

'Gathering data.'

'To mindfuck their clients.'

'You don't have to go.'

'*You* were supposed to go,' I said, pretending to be annoyed, while actually being annoyed. 'But you had to get knocked up.' I rested my open palm on the bump of her belly, not because I particularly wanted to, but because I knew Janis liked it. She was stubbornly deluded I was happy about her pregnancy.

'It was a miracle.'

After three years of attempts, nobody believed a baby would happen. It was a miracle for sure, but I couldn't say of which kind. Janis had told me (even before telling her husband) and I had not taken it well. Until that moment I still fantasised I had a chance with her, and I still believe I did. I only had to find the guts to tell her how I felt, and she would have left that useless man she had fished on Tinder. She could have had a relationship with him and me both, for all I cared. I'd have been fine with that, as long as she kept the two of us on separate rails. But I hadn't found the guts, and my friend, my sister, the woman I loved, had a baby on the go with an hombre so shallow that even his dog couldn't remember his smell.

Ideally, it would have been Janis going to the Open Feast. She had something – an intuition, a sensibility – which I lacked. Janis was the one with the hunches about which performers to book and which stalls to approve. My talent was making hunches into spreadsheets.

Janis said, 'We can take a rain check and see what happens next year.'

'No,' I said. 'No, we need to go.'

There was an undeniable mystique about Becca and Ric, and in our industry mystique kept the till ringing. The Open Feast was an extra-niche event for now, one of those microscopic European productions all glam and no cash, an adorable kitten. But they do grow into tigers fast. Janis and I couldn't be the only big players pondering the Feast. Since the pandemic, everybody had been a bad choice away from sinking. Folks were on edge.

CHARLIE

Take it back, the website read. *Take it back. Your joy, your spark, your love, your lust, your rightful anger. It used to burn so bright, but then life happened. Time happened. You wanted to take the world by storm, until the storm took you, and left you shaken and broken. You were the tallest tree in the forest, the first to be hit by lightning. You learned to compromise. You learned to leave behind the fanciful ideas of your youth and be a functional adult. But something was lost in the process. You cannot name what it is, but you can feel that it's not yours anymore. We cannot give it back to you, but we can help you find it. Each of us is the hero in our own story. At the Bastion, each of us is also the sidekick in other people's. Together we are going to learn again the most important lesson there is: how to be fully alive.*

'Half inspiring, half scary,' I commented.

The site didn't say where the Open Feast was held, only when – every year, it kicked off on 22 June and closed on the 25th, the day after the Feast of San Giovanni, an important night in Italian folklore, as I would learn. Bertrand's friend refused to reveal the location. 'I just can't tell you.'

'Why?' Bertrand asked.

'I promise, it's great.'

'How so? What happens there?'

'What it says on the website – you come alive again.'

'What's that supposed to mean?'

'Go find out for yourself. What I can tell you is, these guys are a community, a small one. The Bastion, they call themselves. They throw this festival, the Open Feast, every summer. It's an underground thing, self-produced, all over the place but fun. Think early days Burning Man, that kind of vibe. Comfier, though. Not in the desert.'

'What kind of music is there?'

'It's not based around music. There's a lot of it, but it's more of a spiritual thing.'

'I don't get on well with preachy folks.'

'There's no preaching at the Open Feast, there's living.'

'You don't make it sound any less bonkers.'

'Kooks throw the best parties. God, I had a good time.'

'And you say it's cheap.'

'They've got a peculiar business model.'

'Peculiar how?'

'Can't tell you that either. Believe me, you'll be able to afford it, if you pass the application.'

And that, I think, caught our curiosity more than anything else Bertrand's friend said. What kind of festival asks for an application?

ZOEY

'Okay, this is downright creepy: they ask about my *sexual awakening.*' I read: '*It doesn't have to be the first time you had sex, although it might be.* What do you say? When did I awake to the joy of boning?'

'Hot cousin?'

'Yeah, hot cousin. Let's keep it simple.'

'Girl cousin, though.'

'Sex with a girl cousin it is,' I said, tapping away on my keyboard.

I answered the same questions as everybody else, about my fears, dreams, body, life. We all fibbed, but we were clearly visible behind the lies we told. As Becca and Ric taught, every lie grows out of a seed of truth.

A big deal has been made of those questions. The last one in particular has been bandied about as proof that we were (among other sins) a money-grabbing operation. The Bastion asked applicants for twelve months' worth of bank statements, and a ballpark figure of their net worth. It should be obvious, but I'm going to spell it out: the point was to charge the rich more and the poor less. If you find that awful, the problem is you.

I did what I needed to and sent the statement, blanking out my name. I wrote I was doing it for privacy reasons and hoped they would fall for it.

Thank you for being in touch, the confirmation email read. *You will be notified in due course regarding the status of your application. If we offer you a place, you will have two hours to secure it. A hundred and twenty minutes, which we start counting when we click on* send. *If you do not answer in time, the offer will expire, and you won't be able to apply for future events. No exceptions will be made.*

I set an alarm to go off every ninety minutes, day and night, to check my email. I never stopped giving the others a hard time for that. I hated it then, though I can see the wisdom of it now. Every year the Bastion had to insist to stragglers that nothing, absolutely nothing, would convince them to accept their delayed reply; not a work deadline, not a stomach bug, not a dead grandmother. Either you answered in time, or you were out, now and for ever. You see, this was not a rule, it was a tool.

The Bastion had to sift the wheat from the chaff.

CHARLIE

Bertrand and I slept in turns, which added to the hype. It was one of those silly things you do when you're twenty and that you remember for the rest of your life. We were already having fun.

One night he burst into the bedroom shouting, 'I'm in! I'm in!'

I stirred, yawned, dragged myself up. 'What time is it?'

'Two-thirty.'

'They're insane.'

'Insane is what we're looking for. Our last insane holiday before parenthood-induced sobriety.'

'Let's see if I'm in too.'

Bertrand jumped in bed. 'Either we both go or none of us does.'

'I won't drag you down into rejects hell.'

'Check your mail!'

He could barely keep himself from bouncing while I grabbed my phone, tapped on it, tapped again, swiped down.

'Well?' he said.

I raised my open hand. 'High-five, B.'

He high-fived me, hugged me, laughed. 'I knew it! I knew it! Hurry up, we've got,' he checked his watch, 'eighty-three minutes to secure a place.'

'How do we do that? We just say yes?'

'We need to pay.'

'Deposit?'

'The whole fee in one go. Fear not, my love, it's totally reasonable.'

I skimmed the email to get to the price, and yes, it was reasonable, for an all-inclusive holiday. Just within our means. It felt like a miracle. 'What's this about an NDA?'

'They're asking to sign and send the NDA they attached. Our place won't be confirmed until they receive it.'

'Did you read it through?'

'It's strict. We cannot talk about what happens at the festival, we cannot talk about the location, we cannot even talk about signing an NDA.'

'If we do, then what?'

'If we do and they catch us, we're in for more cash than our house is worth.'

That made me laugh. 'What happens in Vegas, eh?'

'Do you want to send the payment? I've got to pop to the loo one sec. I got too excited.'

I was already tapping on my phone. I transferred the money, signed and sent the NDA. One last wild hurrah before starting a family with the best man in the world, in the home we owned together. In the wilderness time of the pandemic, I'd forgotten how sweet life could be.

'Hurry up,' I called. 'You've got to sign your NDA too.'

Bertrand flushed. He returned to the bedroom with a hand on his temple. 'Do we have any paracetamol left?'

At those words, a stab of terror (pure, ancestral) hit me. I knew, beyond reason, beyond sense, I knew that this was not a headache. It was much more; it was an apocalypse, the end of our unfairly brief happiness, and of all possible futures. You know what I mean? I knew, the way I had known that catching the bug would have ruined my life. *Only it didn't,* I told myself. *This is your mind being mean to you.*

And while I told myself that, Bertrand was opening his eyes wide, in surprise or in pain, and his legs were giving way, and when I reached out to him, he was crashing to the floor, banging his head, his precious head full of thoughts, on the hard corner of the bed. Blood on the sheet, blood on the frame, but that didn't kill him.

It was a brain aneurysm. *Brain aneurysm*: those two words still fill me with a quiet rage. He was dead before he hit the ground.

THE BASTION

We all came to the Bastion through the same magic gate, which opened wherever we happened to be and took us to a secret spot in Southern Italy. Stepping through the gate was not really a choice, like it is not a choice for planets to orbit their star, or for birds to feed their chicks – it was our nature, unfolding.

We came by plane, by train, by car, by bike. We hitched. We were hungry to be there. We brought with us guitars, books, tambourines, condoms. We brought the two things we had been asked to bring – a gift for a stranger, and our most prized possession. We had been given a set of coordinates, a time, and a number to call if we were late or lost. We put the coordinates into our phones, and followed them to an abandoned car park not far from Brindisi Airport, a tiny international airport in Puglia, the heel of Italy. It was a famously beautiful corner of the world, but you wouldn't say that from the car park, a concrete wasteland behind an abandoned petrol station, the sign faded, the pump red with rust. It was indistinguishable from any other car park anywhere else. Ric said that all car parks are one and the same, and with the right magic you could enter from Italy and exit into Norway.

We were a splash of bright colour spilling over dull concrete, with our tattoos, our battered backpacks, our piercings, torn jeans, Glastonbury t-shirts, dreadlocks and drums. We all spoke English, more or less.

We tried talking to Charlotte, but she barely answered, and slipped out of the conversation at the first chance.

CHARLIE

I didn't want to be there, I wanted to be with Bertrand. What the hell was I doing in sunshine while he rotted in darkness? I wished I could lie with him wherever he was now, wrap my arms around him, close my eyes, and rest.

Seven months had passed since he'd died, and I was not one step closer to accepting it. It's not that I wished to die too, not exactly. But I did not care to live, and I'd seen enough pain in my line of work to know that one thing easily tips into the other. I went to the Open Feast because I knew that I needed to get out of the flat for which Bertrand and I had had so many plans. I needed to get out of Saint-Malo, of France. Of myself. I needed enough noise around me to bury the screams in my head.

But what's a good idea on paper isn't always such in the real world, and I was not coping with being in that parking lot with hyped-up strangers. At some point a guy approached me, with a drunk cheer and a beer can, and I snapped. The thought of spending four days at a party was too much. I just wanted to call a cab and leave before it was too awkward to explain. I ignored the drunk and headed to the lot's exit, rummaging in my bag for my phone, but when I looked up again, the vans were coming.

ZOEY

It was the usual crowd. A wide range of ages, but mostly from their mid-twenties to their mid-forties. A lot of body art, a lot of drums, some guitars, yoga mats and a pervasive scent of marijuana. It felt like home, really.

CHARLIE

The vans were old and dusty and sturdy. Everybody stopped in their tracks and dropped their conversations while the vans entered the car park and pulled over. The drivers opened their doors: that was my first sight of Lila. And God, did I hate her on the spot. This young woman came out of one of the vans, in dungarees and a white t-shirt, with a shaved head and big eyes. She reminded me of Bertrand. She had the same expression he had half of the time, mindlessly happy, as if good news was just around the corner. Life had not come at her yet. She was like fresh milk, and what happens to fresh milk in the sun?

She brought her hands to the sides of her mouth to make a megaphone, and shouted, 'Ladies and gents, your ride is here. My name's Lila.'

This cunt, I thought. *Doesn't she know that good luck never lasts? That the world is red in tooth and claw?* I thought (I'm not proud of it) that the sooner she learnt, the better. This thought went as abruptly as it came and left me reeling with guilt. So now I wasn't only feeling out of place, I was also feeling bad about myself. While Bertrand rotted in darkness.

'Before we go,' Lila said, 'I've got to ask you something.' She left an ominous pause. 'I'll need your phones. Tablets too, smartwatches if you've got those. Basically, anything you may use to communicate with the big blue world while you're with us.'

I looked from the phone in my hand to the young woman in front of a van.

'We've got the privilege of your presence for such a short time,' Lila said with that smile of hers that you couldn't help but trust. 'We're not going to share you while you're with us.'

A woman asked, in an American accent, 'What if I need to make an emergency call?' (Yes, it was Zoey.)

'What do you think? You come and collect your phone. Obviously, something so important means that you must go. No stress, we're going to immediately take you to the airport or wherever you need to be.'

ZOEY

Basically, no phones allowed, and the only way to get them back was to leave the Open Feast.

CHARLIE

Lila went on, 'Also, your families can make *their* emergency calls to the number we gave you. An emergency call means, obviously, *emergency,* and once again, we're going to take you where you need to be. Any questions?'

There wasn't a peep.

'Okay then. This is your last chance to call your mates and tell them the crazy hippies are kidnapping you.'

A few laughs, some uneasy. Some people were tapping on their phones. I weighed mine in my hand: four days and change without a phone, four days and change cut off from the debris of the life I'd lost. I couldn't think of anything better. What would Bertrand say? *Go. Live a little.*

I dropped the phone in Lila's burlap sack.

'By the way,' Lila said, when we were done. 'Just in case you happen to have a spare stashed in your fleshy cavities, there's nothing I can do other than beg you, please, please, leave it there! Don't check your email, don't text, just... don't. You'll thank me later. Four days off TikTok won't kill you. Okay? Okay. Come on now, let's have some fun.'

Giving up my phone made me feel untethered, which was not a bad thing, because the stuff I had been tethered to was dragging me down. I was not counting on having fun at the Open Feast. But finding respite, maybe.

LILA

Charlie gave off pain like a radio frequency. People who hurt so much are easy targets for all sorts of bastards; she was lucky she was with us. I wish I could have hugged her, but we had procedures in place.

I didn't have a doubt she was one of us.

THE BASTION

Oh, what a glorious ride that was! The road left ugliness behind, winding between unkept fields overflowing with flowers and birds, then shaded olive groves and a maze of vineyards. We embraced our guitars, we sang David Bowie, joints made the rounds. 'This is the typical landscape of Salento,' someone commented, an exquisitely useless thing to say, considering that we all had googled it beforehand.

Another one cried, 'The sea!' It was ahead of us, in the distance, a shade of blue barely darker than the sky. We reached the Litoranea Salentina, a coastal road winding past dunes, between the beach on one side and open fields on the other. We passed by ancient towers facing the sea. We saw a sign, *Portodimare,* and drove through a village of people in flip-flops and trunks; we kept going, out of the village, into wilderness again.

The vans turned left, off the tarmac and onto a dust track, then turned again between brambles and flowers. Kestrels chased us, flying over plains which stretched farther than our imagination.

We started a call-and-response. *Deep into the country,* it went. *Deep into the country we go. Away from it all, away from it all we go.*

Away with hidden things we go. The sunlight was unapologetic like a good tongue kiss.

We got to a tall wall enclosing a pinewood. We entered through a wrought-iron gate, and drove under the fresh shade of the pines. We noticed the hammocks hung between trees, and the white canvas shelters, and then, out of the pines, out of the heat shimmer, Villa Abbracciavento appeared.

The vans pulled over, and a quiet sank in. It was like plunging underwater after jumping from a rock on a hot day – that sudden silence, and coolness. We needed a moment to recoup. We listened to the rattle of crickets and the intense chattering of birds we would come to know like family. The breeze on our face reminded us what was so great about being alive. We inhaled wild chamomile, rosemary, seawater, and something else, something animal, not unpleasant but unfamiliar.

Villa Abbracciavento was a diva of a bygone era who had been living high and was spending her sunset years the same way as she had spent the others: on her own terms. It was graceful and indolent, all white archways, rounded angles and honey-coloured tuff. The paint was peeling, the tuff worn away, weeds creeping in the space between the patio's terracotta tiles, bright flowers growing in the cracks in columns and walls, and Villa Abbracciavento, magnificently, didn't give a damn.

ZOEY

I was famished. I threw myself on the refreshments set on the porch: cool white wine, meaty green olives, and *taralli*, crunchy rings of oven-baked dough with fennel seeds, which left a liquorice aftertaste in my mouth.

A massive pig with a friendly muzzle made its way on the porch. Some jumped. 'Don't worry, he's harmless,' the shaved woman with crazy eyes said. 'Cleaner than most people too. He's called Napoleon. Feed him and he'll be your friend for life, as in he'll follow you everywhere begging for more. Don't say we didn't warn you.'

A guy wisely noticed, 'Napoleon, like the pig in *Animal Farm*,' to show off that he could read.

The girl showed us the compost toilets and the showers – wooden buckets hanging from a hook, with a shower head stuck in their bottom. Bamboo screens lent some privacy. The water came from artesian wells, heating was solar-powered. We had to raise our heads and squint to discern the solar panels, hooked on the top of trees.

The girl told us to leave our luggage under one of the canvas shelters, or inside the Villa if we preferred. Nobody would touch our stuff, not even Napoleon.

'And you're sure of that,' I said.

'If you aren't, how're you going to survive the next four days?' was the answer.

We could crash for the night wherever we wanted: on one of the cots under the shelters, on one of the hammocks, on the beach. Inside the villa too, on the ground floor. The one area off-limits was the upper floor. That was staff only.

At the back of the property, a flimsy wire fence with a little gate marked the boundary. Beyond the fence was the beach. Pinewood gave onto sand dunes thick with juniper, which gradually became fine sand, and then the ocean. We were given a key to the gate, but frankly we could get out from one of the many gaps in the fence.

'The beach alone is worth the price,' someone said.

Depending on what you paid, I thought.

We were told to take it easy until dinner and the opening ritual. A few were expecting a goat slain upon an altar or something. Me, I'd have put my money on folk music.

LILA

That was our last Open Feast. When Charlie and Zoey joined us, we became complete, and we could finally get to work.

There were six Opens in total. Only six! It feels like there were six hundred. If I woke up tomorrow to Becca asking me this or that question about the organisation of the next Open, I would shrug and answer. But no – there were only six and there won't be another. I was there for all of them – ever since the first one.

Each of us came to the Bastion for our own reasons, personal reasons. Zoey came for business (and to show her friend Janis that she, too, could have a life); Charlie was desperate to keep her head above water; Mikka was a curious drifter; the Nameless was stuck; Sam had been dumped by his girlfriend of nine years; Imogen came, like me, from an abusive family (only rich); so on and so forth. None of us could imagine what was in store – the magic, the friendship, the glory. None of us could imagine what the Bastion was *for*.

When I found them, I was nineteen and already out of options. I'd never moved from my dive of an industrial town in the Po Valley, in Northern Italy. The best I can describe it is a growth of blocks of flats like pimples around the cancer of factories. The townsfolk stooped in the damp shadow of the lights of Milan, always grasping for those lights, rarely reaching them. My life had been smouldering in the tiny gap left between the cement and heavy skies. I didn't know what I wanted, but you must be mad to want *that.*

On its first year, the Open Feast was smaller and scruffier than it would become. Becca, Ric, Mikka, the Nameless and the others were still working out the kinks. The hot water didn't work half of the time, meals were always late, that sort of thing. None of that mattered in the least. For me, that year was all about Galen.

My poor Galen! We met as soon as we arrived. We dropped our backpacks under the same shelter, and he introduced himself in that creamy Greek accent of his. 'I'm Galen.'

I mumbled, 'Lila,' and scuttled off before he had time to put in another word. He was so handsome that just looking at him was inappropriate. He had long dark curls, a strong nose, full lips, muscles that moved like a dance team. Way out of my league.

Most people were heading to the beach, so I went for a walk in the pinewood. I was getting anxious; everyone was cooler, brighter, more awesome than me. Look at that girl's pink hair! Look at those two, already flirting! Look at that man, bare-chested with those dragon-shaped nipple rings! Look at the tats, look at the shirts! Look at that one, playing with Napoleon! I approached groups and then walked past, opened my mouth and then closed it again. I had found my crowd, but even there I didn't fit, so I sat under a pine, my back against the trunk, and lit a roll-up. I was aiming for the indolent pose of someone taking a breather between one spot of good time and the next.

'Lila, right?' It was the man who had been driving the van I arrived in.

'That's me.' I straightened up. 'And you are...?'

'Ric.'

'*The* Ric.'

'*The* Ric,' he agreed, almost laughing, as if his name were a private joke we shared. He switched to Italian. 'Good times?'

'Plenty.'

'That's good to hear. Me, I take a while to be comfortable around new people.'

'Yeah, it's like that for some,' I said, with the implication that it was not so for me, never for me.

'Then again, new people are the raw material of old friends.' Ric took a hand to his head. 'Love the hair.'

'Oh, I've kept it shaved since I was little.'

But really I had shaved it halfway through my long journey there.

Why did you lie? the others asked me later.

I pretended I already was the person I wanted to become, I answered.

'Good stuff,' Ric said. 'Listen, on our way here, I noticed you've got a drum with you. I busted mine this morning – stepped on it. I know, I know. I get clumsy when I'm nervous, and this is the first time we're doing this.'

'You mean the Feast?'

'Our gang has organised smaller events before, but nothing bigger than a weekend workshop with a bunch of people. Nothing on this scale. Butterflies in the stomach and all that. Anyway. We were supposed to get some drumming tonight, which is not going to happen without, well, without a drum.'

'You can borrow mine.'

'No, I was going to ask – would you drum for us?'

'I'm not very good.'

'You can't be worse than me. We don't need anything fancy, just a beat around the fire.'

I didn't want to say yes – the thought of drumming in front

of all those people was terrifying – but, like always, I was unable to say no.

THE BASTION

We should have gotten rid of the Nameless earlier, before the first Open Feast started. He was always riling us up, the shit-eating fly in the ointment. He was our biggest mistake – not only Becca's, though as usual she blamed herself, but of all those who had already found their way to the Bastion by then. We'd rather not think about him at all.

Though Lila said it didn't show on the side of our guests, the first Open felt like a disaster on the production side. It was four days of back-to-back emergencies. We had accounting troubles, solar panels malfunctioning, too little food on the second day and too much on the third. None of us had any experience in producing large-scale events (though the scale was not that large – we had around fifty guests that year). The only one who had some skill was Mikka, with his experience as a roadie, and the only one who kept a cool head all the time was Napoleon – he was just content to grub around and make new friends, a life teacher for us all. Even Becca raised her voice once or twice.

Mikka had a specific anxiety, that somebody would go for a night swim while drunk or high, and drown. He couldn't shake off the certainty that it would happen, and would destroy us even before we got started. The media would make mincemeat of us, plus, we hadn't taken any insurance (couldn't afford it), and we would be financially ruined. Not to mention that a person would be dead.

But nobody died and nothing terrible happened. In hindsight, the festival was far more successful than it had any right to be, with an inexperienced crew gathering more than fifty strangers in a pinewood by the beach for four days of self-discovery, drugs, sex and magic. Fate was unfolding, and without the Nameless, we would have enjoyed ourselves more.

But the Nameless was with us. When we weren't dousing a fire, we were arguing with him. It started on the afternoon of the first day. The Nameless was in our private kitchen, on the upper floor of Villa Abbracciavento, for a quick coffee break with Ric and Sam. Ric was excited. 'At least two potentials,' he said. 'Lila, the Northern girl, and that Greek, Galen.'

Sam whistled. 'That bloke is like honey on toast.'

'We like them young, don't we?' the Nameless said.

Ric gulped his coffee. 'What's that supposed to mean?'

'I can see Lila, but Galen? Are we sure?'

'Not yet, but it's for Becca to say.'

'That guy rubs me the wrong way.'

'Did you even talk to him?'

'I don't know, it's the way he walks around, as if he's expecting people to throw themselves at his feet.'

Sam said, 'I'm guessing that's what he's used to.'

'You can't wait to do him.'

Ric sighed. 'What's your problem? Still sour for the website?'

We'd had a major row over the Open Feast website. The Nameless wanted to make it look *sleek*, while everybody else preferred to keep it simple. He said that a clumsy site wouldn't attract *the right kind of people*. Becca and Ric had to gently remind him that we did not need to attract *any* kind of people, we only had to keep the door open and see who came through.

The Nameless shrugged. 'Nobody listened to me then, and nobody is listening to me now.'

'For fuck's sake, mate, we have a bunch of strangers to take care of, two potential new members of the family, and you're whining you don't get enough attention?'

'That's not what I'm saying.'

Ric rinsed his cup. 'We don't have time for this. I need to get work done, and you too if I'm right.'

Sam wrapped an arm around the Nameless. 'Stop giving yourself a hard time,' he said, in his most companiable tone, 'and let's go have some fun.'

Ric was fond of quoting a verse of T. S. Eliot: 'In my beginning is my end.' He said it had stayed with him since he found it as a boy, while he was looking for words to impress a girl. His attachment to that line was a prophecy.

CHARLIE

The day was tough. I resented the buzz of activity, the *aliveness* of everybody there. I would hear a new accent or notice a tattoo and I'd formulate in my head a comment to share with Bertrand, and once I got as far as opening my mouth before remembering that Bertrand was not there. I managed to avoid talking to people, mostly, but it required a huge effort.

ZOEY

We sat down for dinner. Sturdy tables were set under pines strung with warm fairy lights. Storm lanterns, giving off the scent of good-quality oil, hung from ropes and low branches, making humans, trees and owls into a thousand shadows. The wine? Better than what you'd normally get in NY. The eggplant and tomato pasta? Best I ever had. Nothing was lavish, but the Bastion hadn't skimped on anything. This is what troubled me: if these guys turned a profit, it must be slim, so the business had to be elsewhere. But where? The Bastion had a plan, and competitors with a plan were my least favourite thing. More than once my hand went to my bag, instinctively, to grab my phone and text Janis, but I didn't have it. I wished she was there with me, and not home with a baby screaming in her ears.

After the *affogato*, a dessert of gelato drowned in coffee, a man rung a bell and stood up. Even Napoleon, who had been shamelessly begging for food scraps from the tables, turned to him. I scratched the pig's head. He was my favourite fellow, so far.

'Let me start with a thank-you,' he said. 'You came all the way here, trusting us with your time and money. We're going to do our best not to disappoint. I'm Ric.'

This unassuming man here, in denim and khaki shirt, was the famous Ric.

'We are a beautiful bunch, here at the Bastion. When you put beautiful people in a beautiful setting, lots of things can happen, and I'm telling you, most of those *will* happen.' He smiled at our hoots and whistles. He carried himself with easy-going authority. He was one of those men with a large smile and strong hands: he didn't look like one who enjoyed violence, but neither did he look like one who would squirm from it. His nose was crooked in the way that noses get crooked in fights. All in all, not someone you wanted to mess with.

'Good things, I mean. As for the bad ones, we only have one rule, but on that rule we are dead serious. The Golden Rule, have you heard of it? We didn't make it up and we didn't name it. No, in one version or another, it's there in every spiritual tradition ever known to humankind. In the Bible you'll find it worded this way: *Do unto others as you would have them do unto you.* In other words – don't be a dick. Be respectful of other people, treat them as you want to be treated. I see a lot of nodding heads, but let me stress, the rule means that we shall endeavour not to offend *and also* not to be easily offended. You might not like everything you see, and I promise, you won't like everyone you meet. I'll go further and say that you might find some of the goings-on *actively distasteful.* Such is life – deal with it. If anything makes you uncomfortable, it means, by definition, that it's taking you out of your comfort zone – which is good. You came here to be *alive,* right? It's hard work, being alive.'

Ric didn't leave space for questions. 'At early stages,' he explained to us later, 'so-called questions are underhand bickering.'

What he did was flash his reassuring smile and say, 'I'll leave you to coffee now. Ritual team, with me please. Everybody else, when you hear the drum, chase it.'

The beat grabbed us by our happy full bellies and dragged us through trees and bushes, between two lines of garden torches, to a starlit glade. I felt the bonfire on my skin even before seeing it. It was taller than all of us. To get to it, we had to pass between two fire jugglers, both bare-chested. The woman on the right was drawing spirals of fire with her poi chains. She slithered in the air, snapping up, sliding down, like a serpent. The man on the left jumped and twirled, making interlocking circles by spinning his staff.

The drummer was Lila, the young woman with the shaved head and big eyes. Someone pronounced her name in the voice of one who's bragging they know a celeb. I thought she looked cool, self-assured. She looked like someone who takes no shit. She reminded me of Janis, in many ways.

The drumming faded, the fire jugglers slowed to a halt. We shut up and listened to the cracking of the fire, the chirping of crickets, the waves coming ashore, and a breeze blowing through twigs and leaves.

With the breeze came a woman.

LILA

I was excited to be in with the in crowd. Never happened to me before, and it went a long way towards soothing my social anxiety. As long as I was drumming, I had something to do, something to *be*, and I didn't have to feel like a failure for being unable to start a conversation. I sat by the fire and drummed with nineteen years of repressed energy until Ric gestured me to stop.

Becca appeared out of the trees from the direction of the beach, advancing with the gait of a queen or a cat or a priestess. She was simply dressed (a skirt down to her feet, a denim top, bangles). Her chestnut hair was long, left untied, which lent her a wild edge. She was enchanting. She stopped by Ric's side.

A guy coughed – I later learned he was the Nameless. He had a knack for doing the wrong thing at the wrong time.

Ric shot at him a brief, cold look, then said, 'Ladies and gents, give it up for Becca!'

We clapped hands and shouted, and when our voices died out, she asked, 'How was dinner?' in the Italian accent that would be such a large part of the way media depicted her worldwide.

I was beside myself and I could have answered, but Galen beat me to it. 'Great!' he shouted.

'Good. That's good. I'm not going to ask if you liked the wine, 'cause you drank all of it.'

I laughed along with everybody else.

'Don't worry, I was kidding; even you didn't manage to dry up our reserves. Anyway. It's been a long day, so I'll keep it short. I just wanted to say hi, really. We are going to do a lot of partying together in the coming days, and a lot of work. We'll get to know each other. If you've ever felt you want to hit the reset button on your life – to have a chance to start over and do things better – this is the chance. Here at the Bastion we wipe the slate clean. It's going to be fun. Make no mistake, though.' She turned her eyes on us, and each of us felt *seen*. 'You will get out of your time here only as much as you put in.'

'We put in quite a lot of dough!' someone said, guffawing.

'And if dough could buy wisdom, darling, you'd be a sage,' Becca answered, and we all laughed, the joker included. 'But no,' she went on, 'money is not the tool to seek for what you're after. The spark you've lost – you cannot just buy it back. You will have to renounce all that you are in order to become all that you can be.'

What does it mean? I thought. *Is this when they take a virgin to the altar? Is this when they ask me to sign a pact in blood, or...*

'But before that, you need to *find out* who you are, and who you can be. Starting now. Don't make those faces,' she laughed. 'The first step is easy and all of them are fun. I want you to think about why you're here. What do you want from your stay with us? Step to the bonfire, and say aloud what it is that you expect from the Feast – what it is that you desire. Be real. Nothing is too small, nothing is too big. Nothing is off-limits.' Becca turned to me and said, 'Lila, will you go first?'

I was amazed that Ric had taken the time to tell Becca my name, and that Becca had remembered it. I panicked. I didn't know what I was going to say. But once again, I could not refuse, so I walked to the fire, very conscious of the many eyes weighing me down like a backpack full of bricks. I came too close and the flames burnt the tip of my eyelashes. I stepped back. A word came to me, as if written in fire against a dark sky.

'Louder,' Ric said, in good spirit. 'We can't hear you!'

'Purpose,' I said. 'I wish to find some purpose.'

Everybody cheered and clapped. Later someone told me they were in awe of me. I lacked purpose! The badass drummer was as troubled as everybody else; that gave others the courage to speak up. *Me,* inspiring somebody else? Most definitely a miracle.

I returned to my place, took my drum in one hand and the stick in the other, and started back up, with more energy than before. The world felt electric.

One by one, I saw the others walk down to the fire. *I want new friends!* they said. *I want to be inspired! I want a kiss, a hug, some sex, a miracle, a wonder.* 'Clarity,' Galen said.

Then we toasted with a herbal liquor, shouting '*hurrah!*' in one voice.

Ric said, 'This is all for now. Stay at the fire if you want, or go to bed. Tomorrow, we start in earnest.'

We went to bed early, after one last drink, joke or smoke. Usually nothing much happened on the first night, except for six years later, when Charlie caught a glimpse of magic.

CHARLIE

My plan was to stay up until everybody had found a place to sleep and then go find mine, where I was sure I would be left alone. Even on better days, I always liked to linger by myself in places that normally I'd share with others – cafés after closing time, empty churches. Where nothing much is happening, everything can.

The pinewood was warm, and pleasant, and sweet. A mouse was scratching the bark up above, with a lullaby sound. I thought I might grab a blanket and sleep on a hammock, as others were doing. Spending a night under the stars; Bertrand would have loved that. Wasn't it on our pre-natal bucket list? The list of things we wanted to do before the baby would take over our life. I wasn't too sure what was on that list. After Bertrand died, sinkholes opened in my mind; there were many things I should remember and didn't. When was our first trip to London? What was Bertrand's favourite restaurant? What was his cousin called? My mind was protecting me by erasing my dead husband as much as it could. It was an impossible task – the only way to erase Bertrand was to erase the whole of me.

I heard music.

Or I imagined it – it was too faint to tell. I stretched my ears; yes, there were notes in the air. What melody was that? It was just out of my memory's reach, but so, so close. The music came from a point far into the trees, from the direction of the sea. A saxophone. Not any saxophone, but *the* saxophone, the one Bertrand played.

I recognised the tune and it was like a slap in the face. 'Stairway to the Stars', a standard, Bertrand's favourite, his *pièce de résistance.* I brought a hand to my mouth. This had happened before. I would hear Bertrand's music, smell his cologne, see his broad shoulders carve a path in the crowd. When that happened, I'd prick or bite myself, and that was enough to make it stop. I bit my fingers now.

The music continued, played with Bertrand's timbre, in Bertrand's voice.

I was possessed by a burning desire to be with the music, which left no space for amazement, fear, or any other emotion.

The saxophone was calling to me, and I followed, by what little moonlight there was. The music became louder. I picked up my pace. I broke into a run, leaping over roots and rocks, sidestepping spiky bushes and lowering my head to dodge low-hanging branches. The music got louder and louder, as loud as it was when Bertrand played at the park for me as I sat on a bench, his audience of one. I felt his presence. The source of the music had to be close now, just behind the next pine, and I ran to the tree, and past it.

I found myself by the fence giving onto the beach. A sharp crescent hung in the sky, lending a silver hue to the dark water. 'Bertrand!' I cried. There was no one but me, and still the music was perfectly clear; it was Bertrand's breath coming through Bertrand's saxophone. I whipped my head back and forth. I couldn't see him anywhere. The tune was almost over and I was turning on myself frantically, until my head spun. I prayed to God (though I didn't believe in God) that I could catch a glimpse of my husband, the wonderful man playing for me, but the tune came to an end, and the trees were silent now, and I had no proof that anything had ever happened.

I fell on my knees. I did not have enough strength left to stand.

The back of my hand brushed against an object half-buried in the sand. I wiped my tears and dug it up. I held it high, to catch every last drop of moonlight. It was a blackened, rotten saxophone reed – a Vandoren, the brand Bertrand used.

ZOEY

'What do we live for?' said Becca. 'This is the most fundamental question we can ask.'

Becca sat under an extraordinary fig tree with one leg extended, the other bent above it, her hands leaning on her knee. I hadn't noticed the tree before that moment (Becca said the tree was a *her*). It was strange that I'd missed her. It would take two people to hug her trunk. Her skin was silver-lucent, and smooth, like moonlight made wood. Her many branches were strong, fit to carry fat flowers we would feast on. Later I was told that some forgotten master had grafted on the trunk as many as six varieties of fig, in a circle. Different parts of the tree would flower at different times of the year, from spring to winter, with figs of different colours, shape and flavour, repeating around that trunk the cosmic wheel of the seasons. That tree was a monument. The shade of her canopy was sweetly scented.

Under that tree, Becca and (more occasionally) Ric taught.

'Our whole life – what we believe, what we do – hinges on whatever answer we give. What do we live for? Since before we are born, there is a whole world deciding for us: our family, society at large, seven billion strangers screaming in our mind what we should do, how we should behave. Making laws for us to follow, and inflicting punishments if we dare to differ. When you become aware, deeply and truly aware, that all rules are made up, that your very desires and fears were decided by others – what is left, at that point? Too many people sleepwalk through life never wondering. They get by jumping when they're told to jump, bowing their head to necessity, obeying, always obeying, their betters. Theirs is plain, brutal survival, with no beauty, no grace. If all you do with your time is bide it until you die, you spend your life lying on your deathbed. How can we stand up, then? What is worth living for? What is ultimately *real*? Ric and I don't have an answer for you, nobody does. What we *can* do is show you how to go and find your own. Last night, one of you used the word *connection*.'

I struggled not to laugh. That was me: rubbish about connection never fails to hit the spot with a certain type.

'That word is a double-edged sword. Connection can be as much a tool for liberation as the sharpest tool for oppression. We are connected to family, friends, colleagues, society at large, and they all have very specific ideas on how we should look, act, think. We sheepishly follow. They tell us we are awkward and we believe them, so we stop dancing. They tell us we are strong and we don't allow ourselves to be afraid. Or we go the opposite route, we play the rebel, the antagonist, and we delude ourselves that by doing the opposite of what we are told we shall be free – even then, *even then*, we are playing by other people's rules. However we move, the people around us set the limits of our freedom. And yet, we can only be free within a community, for we are a social animal, and when we give up on our fellow humans, we give up on life. A craving for friendship is part of our human nature. Hell is other people, Sartre said; but so is Heaven.'

I mean, she wasn't saying anything new.

She also wasn't saying anything I disagreed with, in principle.

CHARLIE

I listened to Becca's grandiose bollocks from the edge of the crowd, and it was all I could do not to grab that cunt by the throat and pin her against that massive fig.

'We asked you to come here with a gift for a stranger,' Becca said. 'Now it's the time we use it. Go get it, and give it to somebody. Spend some time with them. Have a conversation, but here's the thing – I want you guys to be physically close, closer than you'd normally be. Look each other in the eye. There is no need to turn this into a pantomime – you don't have to stand like mannequins – but whatever happens, do not break eye contact. It will be uncomfortable; go with it. When you both decide it's time to wrap it up, the person who received the gift can either reciprocate or go and give theirs to somebody else. Don't take it personally if they don't reciprocate – a gift should never be an obligation imposed. Makes sense?'

I watched Becca stand up as the others dispersed to fetch their gifts. I approached her and said, 'A word, please.'

'Charlotte, hi. What can I do for you?'

'What game are you playing?'

Becca tilted her head, puzzled. 'Excuse me?'

'Come off it, cunt.' (I was mad.)

'Charlotte, what happened?'

I made a scoff which was more like a snarl.

'I cannot apologise without knowing what I did wrong.'

'Last night. My husband's music.'

'I don't follow.'

'My *dead* husband.'

Becca seemed genuinely taken aback. 'So this is why Bertrand didn't come,' she said. 'I'm so sorry, Charlotte. We didn't know.'

'Was it a demo session, a bootleg?' I hated the tears coming to my eyes. 'I don't have any recording of Bertrand playing "Stairway to the Stars", his favourite song, *our* song, I don't have any recording and *you* do? That's... that's unfair. I don't care how you got it, I don't care what sick mind games you're playing here, I don't care, you can have your fun with the others. I'll be out of your way without any fuss, but I have a right to that recording, do you understand? I have a fucking *right*!'

Becca said, 'Did it sound like recorded music?'

'What else?'

'Please, Charlie, I'm really asking. Did it sound like recorded music to you?'

'It was my husband's playing style. I could recognise it anywhere.'

'I believe that. But did it sound like recorded music?'

I took the reed from my pocket and shoved it in her face. 'How about this?'

'I don't know what *this* is.'

'Yes, you do.'

Becca didn't answer.

'It's called a *reed*, a disposable piece of wood that goes into a sax's mouthpiece. Coincidence, huh? And it's not any reed either, no, it's the specific brand Bertrand used.'

'Where did you find it?'

'Oh, spare me.'

'You think we planted it.'

'His music, his reed – for fuck's sake, Becca, what else?'

Becca reached out a hand to me, and I recoiled. She let her arm fall. 'Stay and find out,' she said.

'I have a *right*.'

'If you feel you have to go, we will drive you to the airport, the train station, a hotel, you name the destination.'

'But you won't give me the recording.'

'I can't give you what I don't own.'

'I'm not going to leave without it, and I'm telling you, *Rebecca*, until then, I will be a pain in the arse. Your arse.'

And Becca, to her credit, answered: 'You'll do what you think is best. I appreciate that.'

Scouting for strangers was fifty percent exciting, fifty percent nerve-wracking. The most outgoing looked for someone cute, the others for someone safe. I was at a loss. What was I supposed to do? I almost approached this or that person, without ever making it, so what happened is that I watched people pairing up quickly while I was being left behind. Story of my life. I strode towards a pink-haired woman, but someone got there first. I fretted on, pretending it was never my intention to talk to her. I was considering approaching Napoleon and pretending I was giving him the gift as a joke, so as to have a reasonable excuse for not having met anybody without losing face, when a voice called, 'Hey.'

I didn't think the voice was calling to *me*, so I kept walking.

'Lila, is that right?'

It was Galen, striding as if the world was his family estate. He had a box wrapped in red paper.

I was vastly unused to cool people noticing my existence. 'Think so,' I said, and stood there. 'I mean, yes, it's me. Lila.'

'Is it okay if I...?'

'Yes, sure, of course.'

'Great. Let's go sit somewhere.'

'The beach maybe?'

'It'll be scorching, this time of day.'

'Okay.'

'Follow me, I've found this nice little spot.'

I could scarcely believe this was happening to me. We walked away from the main action, to a ruined hut covered in twisty shrubs, the whitewash half-gone. Attached to the hut was a narrow brickwork seat, barely higher than ground level. 'Isn't it nice?' Galen said.

The wind brought voices in snatches from afar.

'Awesome.'

Galen eased himself into the seat, and I briefly pondered whether to sit too, but there wasn't enough space, so I let myself slope to the ground. A part of me resented him. I didn't need his charity.

'Becca said we should stay close,' he reminded me, patting what little space was left beside him. I moved there. My leg was flush against his, no matter how I tried to shift it away.

Galen chuckled. 'I'm weirded out too.' I made to stand up, and he touched my arm – gently – to stop me. 'Doesn't matter.' He held out the parcel. 'Here, this is for you.'

The parcel was meticulously wrapped in crepe paper, tied with string. Beneath the paper was a cardboard box, and within the box, a white cloud of cotton wool. I parted the cotton wool and saw the pink and brown tip of a mouse's snout. That was his present – a mouse?

I raised my eyes to Galen's expectant expression. I looked in the box again. The mouse hadn't moved. Only then I realised it was not alive. Duh. I pushed aside more of the padding to reveal the whole thing.

It was not a mouse.

The thing in the box was... it was nothing I'd ever seen. The snout was a mouse's alright, but the body was swollen and covered in feathers. It had three pairs of thin legs ending in a bird's claws, with sharp talons. Rather than one tail, the thing had – I counted – five, of different colours, lengths and textures.

'Be careful,' Galen said. 'It's more fragile than it looks.'

I set the doll on the palm of my hand. 'Looks real.'

'It is.'

I didn't want to contradict him, but...

'It's an Oddball,' he explained. 'Ever heard of Charles Waterton?'

'Guitarist?' I shot in the dark. I had no idea who Charles Waterton was.

'Is there a guitarist called Charles Waterton?'

'I... guess so?'

'I'll have to look him up,' Galen said. 'It's not him though. *My* Waterton was this Victorian naturalist, a weirdo through and through. He took up taxidermy as a hobby, but he wasn't content with stuffing dead animals. No, he made up new ones. He would smash together this beast and that beast to form a one-of-a-kind creature, a dead chimaera, if you want. He inspired my work.'

I turned the beast in my hand. I couldn't spot any juncture; the parts blended seamlessly into one another. 'Do you kill the animals yourself?'

'We're supposed to look each other in the eyes.'

'Sorry.'

'Is it as strange for you as it is for me?'

'It's very strange.'

'Glad to see I'm not alone.' Galen smiled. 'No, I don't kill animals.'

'I'm vegetarian,' I volunteered.

'You don't have to worry. I gather roadkill, bodies from pet shops. It's an art project I'm doing. I make the Oddballs and hide them in libraries, bars, all sorts of public spaces, for strangers to find.'

'To freak them out.'

'To jolt their reality.'

'So that's what you're doing? Jolting my reality?'

'I just thought you might like it.'

'I do. It is... it's probably the best gift I ever got. Thank you.'

'Listen, may I ask you something?'

I put the Oddball back in the box. 'Sure.'

'What's the deal with Becca and Ric? This community you guys have, the Bastion – I'm picking up good vibes. It's making me curious. What can you tell me?'

That explained a lot. Galen was bothering with me because he thought I was an insider. I was tempted to lie, but it was beyond me. I admitted I was not part of the community.

'You were in the ritual team.'

'Ric's drum was busted, I stepped in. I just got here yesterday, like you.'

'Yeah, I saw you, but I thought you were coming back from a trip or something.'

'Sorry,' I said. I wished I could cease to exist. I quickly took from my pocket the gift I had brought and pushed it into Galen's hands.

'A Zippo lighter,' Galen said. 'Cute. What does it mean?'

I'd bought it at a petrol station on the way.

ZOEY

By the second night affairs were blossoming, mortal enmities had started, and the outside world had lost its weight. Napoleon the pig was more than a mascot, he was one of us, and we found it inordinately fun that a pig was one of us. The spectacular fig tree under which Becca taught her lessons was like home. Our lives (mine too) before the Feast were fading to a dim memory. Everything that mattered was inside the pinewood. It was like regaining the intensity of being thirteen, when every summer was a complete lifetime, from birth in June to death in September.

Janis and I called it the Festival Time Warp. It happened at every festival I'd been to, but here it was magnified tenfold. Janis. I couldn't wait to debrief with her.

Taking our phones forced us to focus on the people physically with us. The gift exchange had been an even smarter move, a bonding activity dolled up in spiritual garments. I'd spent a pleasant couple of hours with a man ten years younger (he gave me an amethyst, I gave him a brass compass), good-looking in a nerdish way. At the evening bonfire I was searching the crowd for him. Janis and I should implement a similar activity for the next SoulJo. Could it work for a larger crowd? We could make it work.

'Looking for someone?' a man asked.

I had noticed him earlier, a straight-backed, leathery dude in his seventies. He was dressed in dark green linen trousers, a linen shirt, a few rings (skulls and black onyx, the usual rock'n'roll fare) and a necklace shaped like a chain of interlocking bones.

Older Festival Guy was a staple of the scene. As a rule, OFGs were either stoners who've been high 24/7 for the length of their adult life, or folks desperate to gain back a coolness they never had in the first place. I answered, 'Just soaking in the atmosphere.'

A party had started. The drummer, that shaven-headed young woman called Lila, was beating with the passion of a newlywed, and others had joined in, with any drums they had with them. A red-haired man danced in a forcedly clumsy way, like a drunk marionette, attracting laughter and cheers. The scent of marijuana was thick and strong.

'I'm Mikka.'

'Zoey.'

'I know.'

'Creepy.'

Mikka answered with laughter. 'I read your application.'

Older man leering after younger flesh, I thought. *How cliché.* Then again, what had I been doing with the hip nerdish bloke? 'So, it's you I've got to thank for being here.'

'No, I just offered my opinion. Ultimately, who's in and who's out is in Becca's hands.'

'She's the boss.'

'Not a word she'd use.'

Napoleon's muzzle tugged at my hand. I scratched his head. My first instinct had been right: he was a good fellow. 'If she calls the shots, no matter the words she uses, *boss* is what she is.'

'Spoken as a matter-of-fact landlady.'

'I can't quite place your accent.'

Mikka fished a roll-up from a chest pocket and lit it with a battered Zippo. He took a drag and passed it to me. 'Helsinki.'

'It's cold up there.'

'One of the things that brought me down here.'

Some people were singing Ed Sheeran now, 'Castle on the Hill'. Not a fan. 'And how long have you been down here? With the Bastion.'

'I'll pass on that question for now.'

'Why?' I said, teasing, kind of.

'It's one of those situations – I'd tell you, but then I'd have to kill you.'

'Tired jokes are bad for business.'

'This is what you think we're doing here, Zoey *Pagano*? Business?'

I did not like the emphasis on my made-up surname. I handed back the joint. 'It's a festival. People pay to attend. This young man I was talking to earlier on, you charged him a fortune.'

'He's got money. He works in an investment bank in London.'

'If he couldn't afford the fee, he wouldn't have paid, and you wouldn't have a business.'

'You're not one for nuance.'

'Twitter murdered nuance. I make do with what's left.' I looked at two people smooching by the fire. They were going at it with all they had; their hands were in each other's trousers, and I suspected they would end up fucking right there, if no one stopped them (no one stopped them). 'Don't get me wrong, I'm not judging. Spirituality, art, science, they're all industries at the core, with a product to sell. Always have been and always will be. As long as your product is good, I don't have a problem with that.'

'And what do you make of our product?'

'The weed is first-rate.'

'This is good land for it.'

'And Becca is whip smart.'

'You like her.'

'Let's say I get her.'

'We all believed that at first.' With the two fingers holding the joint, Mikka pointed at the bonfire. 'Here she comes.'

The fairy ring of her bangles replaced the music.

LILA

Becca came to the fire and asked, 'Are you having a good time?' She'd changed into another long skirt and denim top.

We were clapping our hands, hooting, cheering.

'We have been exchanging gifts. Sometimes more. Yeah, some of you guys were pretty noisy.' We laughed. 'It's been easy so far, but now, now we're done with easy. Are we ready to get real?'

The only answer possible was, 'Yes!'

'We're going to need a lot of trust in each other for our work to come. Tonight, we move the signpost forward. We are going to walk to the fire, one by one, while Lila gives us a soft drumming.' She turned to me, 'Can you do that? Yes? Thank you! So, we are walking to the fire, and there, we are revealing to our community a secret we have. Loud enough for everybody to hear. Mind: it needs to be a *real* secret, painful, shameful, or it could even be happy – but it must be something of consequence. If all you give us is a sound bite, we won't buy it,' she said, in the tone of one who is joking, but also not. 'And we will ask you to try again. Won't we?' she asked, raising her voice.

And we answered, 'We will!'

'Push through your fear. We are grabbing the monsters which lurk in the darkness of our soul and we're throwing them to our friends, so that we can rip them apart together, and feast on their flesh. Who's in for some ripping and feasting?'

'We are!'

Becca smiled, and I felt we had done good, pleasing her. 'Who's going first?'

I was shocked to hear Galen call out, 'You start, Becca!' He was shoulder to shoulder with an elderly gentleman dressed in linen, who laughed at his suggestion. For the whole evening Galen had been surrounded by an endless stream of women and men in equal measure, and I had watched from afar, too busy drumming to approach him. A ripple of unease traversed the group. The Nameless made a face.

'Sounds about right,' Becca said. She walked to the fire, as if dancing to the music of her bangles. We held our breath; a hoopoe called.

Becca said, 'I'm on a mission.'

Her face was serious, her voice was grave. In the suspended

time in which I didn't know what to make of her words – whether to take them literally, or metaphorically, or as a joke or a cypher – she asked me, 'You want to be next?'

I left my drum and took small, uncertain steps towards the flames. When I made it there, Becca took my hand. I was stuck for words.

'Let it go,' Becca whispered, only for me.

I looked into the fire. I looked at Ric, at the others. I didn't dare look at Becca. 'I'm stupid,' I blurted out. 'This is it, I'm stupid. And pathetic, and... I don't like myself, is what I'm saying. I'm sorry that I don't have anything, I don't know, deeper, but I swear, this is important to me, it really is. I don't like myself very much.' I hated my quivering voice, like a duckling's; I hated my puny words, coming straight after Becca's revelation. I was afraid she would ask me to try again and give the good stuff this time, but that was the good stuff, the most painful secret I had, although I was not smart enough to give it justice. 'I don't like myself at all.'

Becca leaned forward and kissed my cheek. 'I do.'

I'd never felt such love before, not from my mum and dad (certainly not from my mum and dad), not from the only loser boyfriend I'd had, not from anybody.

The others exploded in cheers.

THE BASTION

On the Night of the Secrets we heard the wildest stories. There was this one man who had been working in a charity for children in need, stealing from it, and had never been caught; he felt bad and wished to repay, but he had three children of his own and zero cash to spare at the end of the month. And there was a woman, a tall Valkyrie, who, when she was eleven, had killed a penguin at the zoo. She'd noticed a rock by the enclosure and decided to throw it at one of the penguins, for no reason she could tell to this day, and the penguin had fallen dead. Rotten luck. This other guy, three times in his life he had seen his reflection in the mirror move out of synch, like a mime; the third time, the mime had grinned (the guy was not smiling at all) and mouthed the words, 'The fourth will be it.' That was twenty-nine months, three weeks and one day earlier. The guy had been scrupulously avoiding mirrors since, but it was only a matter of time before he slipped and looked into one, and then what? There was a girl, less than twenty years old, who'd killed a man, and she said she'd grab a sushi knife again, and again slice his neck, a thousand times, if given the chance. We told our secrets, we listened, we drank and smoked, and when the stories were over, we made music and danced until late.

ZOEY

I woke up hungover and naked in the nerdish guy's arms. Nice chap. Good arms. He was being all considerate and New-Man-like. He apologised for the wine breath, think about that. Mine couldn't be any better. I bolted out to get a shower before the queue formed. Hell if I remember his name.

LILA

Everybody woke up hungover and naked in somebody's arms, with Napoleon sniffing his way among our bodies. Everybody but me, that is. I woke alone.

After Becca's mark of approval, people wanted to talk to me, be with me. Galen had been winking at me every time he took out the Zippo. It was too much fuss. I had to scramble off and hide in a hammock, where I pretended to sleep until I slept for real.

That day Ric took charge of teaching. Like Becca, he held court by the fig tree, where he had set some Indian trunks, orange and green and yellow. Ric's style was different from Becca's; a little harsher, a little earthier. Becca was forever gazing at things only she could see, while Ric's eyes never strayed from you. The way he would make you feel seen, nobody else could.

'You know those films,' he started, 'where there is a ticking bomb, and the hero cuts the right wire in the nick of time?' He slapped his open hand on his chest. 'We've got a ticking bomb right here, where our heart is, and no hero is going to cut the wire. Cheesy endings are not in the cards. A bittersweet one, if you're lucky; a memorable one, even. But this bomb? It *will* go off.'

Galen said, 'Not for a while.'

'Hopefully,' Ric laughed. 'And it's going to be too soon anyway. But listen to me: in olden times, snakes were considered immortal. You guys might have seen the ouroboros, a drawing of a snake eating its own tail, forming a circle. Have you seen it? Yeah, okay, nothing to call home about, it's everywhere – TV series, comic books, everywhere. It's a symbol of eternity. The bottom line is, snakes are for ever. The reason is simple: they shed their skin. They renounce what they were and they become something else, and thus they go on living. We associate eternity with the unchanging, but the opposite is true – only what's always changing never stops living. Last night we started shedding our skin, by letting go of our secrets.' He brushed his hands. 'Now let's finish what we started.'

He opened the trunks. They contained masks of countless different colours, shapes and makes. There were leather plague-doctor masks, cheap black plastic masks, hand-sewn lace masks, horned masks, masks which covered the entire face, or half of it, or the eyes only. There were devil masks and fox masks and lucha libre masks; there were super-hero masks and skull masks, and those paper masks they sell at newsagents, with empty eyes and the face of famous characters (the late Queen of England, a disgraced actor). And there were other masks, more disturbing, which almost reminded us of creatures we should remember but didn't. Ric invited us to pick a mask at random, without thinking, and spend some time with it. We were to listen to the mask. I saw some people roll their eyes at that New Age nonsense – masks don't talk. But they played along.

'Put on your mask now,' Ric instructed us after a while. 'Stop your inner chattering, and let the mask talk through you. Life's too precious to waste it trapped within the limits of what you think you are. Let's explore other avenues.'

I picked a beautiful kestrel mask cut in leather, which fit my face as if tailored to it. The instant I put it on, I saw a kestrel silhouetted against the stark blue sky above us. I took that as a sign, the external world rhyming with my inner one.

The beginning was faltering, untidy. We wore the masks and goofed around. Gradually Ric's voice, which didn't take itself too seriously and so allowed us to humour him, eased us into a different state of mind. 'Stop playing the character of yourself. In your daily life you wear a mask too. Your identity, your precious identity – it's only another mask in the end. Get rid of it, and give space to this other one.'

We talked to each other as if we were our mask. I started understanding what Ric meant. The mask I wore normally was no more real, and no less random, than this one. I had been prey all my life, and that had been my choice. I could change and be a predator if I decided. It was as simple as switching mask.

'Act like your mask,' Ric said. 'Be your mask! Let go.'

Some kind souls brought shots of strong grappa. It tasted of grapes in the sunshine and lit a fire in our belly. The shots kept coming.

Gradually, we changed. Those with a bird mask sang and flew, the strange creatures slithered and swayed, those in mysterious lace masks stood tall and sexy, the foxes played tricks, and Napoleon was one of us more than ever. The air filled with our shrieks and cries and uncanny noises. We crowed and croaked and squawked, we sung and we barked. Yet more grappa made the rounds. We licked the fig tree's smooth trunk.

I addressed the others imperiously, the way a predator does; I hovered and searched for my prey and finally swooped on it, running to Galen, jumping on him – literally jumping – and planting my tongue in his mouth.

CHARLIE

The carnival gave me the occasion I was looking for. I slipped away. I didn't want to renounce myself, and I certainly wasn't going to get wasted on whatever shit the Bastion put in their spirits (I can say now they didn't put in the spirits anything that shouldn't be there). With almost everyone joining in the shrieking mob, it was as good a time as any to search the villa. I wasn't expecting to find a physical recording of Bertrand. I was after bartering chips, stuff with monetary or sentimental value, or dodgy stuff – anything I could use to force Becca and Ric to hand me Bertrand's song.

That was my thinking, but I wasn't thinking straight. No one does when they're grieving.

Truth was, I felt that they'd violated my intimacy, and I wanted to violate theirs in turn. It was retaliation, pure and simple. When I explained that to the guys, later, they got it. We all understand retaliation.

The pinewood was quiet. I could hear their cries and, from the beach, an echo of the first tourists in the season (children playing, fathers calling). I had to make a conscious effort to remember how much time I'd spent there: less than two days, was that possible?

I entered Villa Abbracciavento. The front door gave onto a large living room, with a tall star-vaulted ceiling, and a floor paved in blue and green *cementine,* vintage tiles in coloured concrete. The walls and ceiling were the dazzling hue of whitewash, except for the vault's eight arms, which were antique rose. On the floor were yoga mats and inflatable beds, neatly laid. There were other rooms on the ground floor, used by those couples, throuples and groups who preferred some privacy. I took the stairs to the first floor. Hanging in Bertrand's circles I'd learned that the best secrets are kept behind *staff-only* signs.

I was shaking, afraid of what the Bastion might do if they caught me. I was far from a rule-breaker by nature. Bertrand had to make Herculean efforts to convince me that paying road tax a week late wouldn't make the gendarmerie swarm our place. *So what if the Bastion people catch you?* he would have said. *They'll only shoo you away.*

Bertrand was arrested once. He was not always right.

The staircase gave onto a room lined with wooden doors. I paused, listened. Was there a sound coming from one of the rooms? A person breathing? No – it was only in my mind.

Some doors were closed, others ajar. I headed to a closed one and tried the handle, which turned. It was a bedroom: a bed, a bookshelf, a lamp made of driftwood, a chest of drawers, a lingering male scent. I pulled one drawer open – it contained a bundle of boxers and socks. I reluctantly rummaged through it, finding nothing.

It was uncomfortable to sift through a stranger's underwear; I started feeling like a creep, and a silly one at that. I left the room and tried another door, which was also unlocked – round table, chairs, table football. I did not go in. I tried all the doors, and they were all unlocked. I felt bad now – the Bastion left their doors open, and trusted us not to pry. I was prying. Who was the villain here?

'Okay, just to cut it short.'

I whipped my head towards the staircase and there she was: Lila.

LILA

Charlie looked positively embarrassed.

CHARLIE

'Go on, poke around to your heart's content,' she said, climbing the last steps. 'As long as you don't expect any drama. No rotting corpses, no blood on the walls – we're not that kind of cool. Full disclosure, I do have a skull in my room, a real one, but I don't drink from it or anything.'

'I wasn't... uh...'

'You were too.' Lila was like that: disarming.

'Were you following me?'

'Becca asked me to keep an eye.'

'She thinks I'm trouble.'

'She sees you're lonely. You were in Mikka's room. Do you want to search mine next? Told ya, skull! It's the best.'

'No need,' I said, bowing my head, humiliated.

'Are you sure? I'm not being funny; if poking around would put your mind at ease, be our guest. Get it out of your system.'

I didn't want to. Or – better – I was too embarrassed to accept.

'Cup of coffee then?'

'I've got to go.'

'Yeah, because you're so very busy. Come on.'

I couldn't help but follow Lila to a small kitchen, a rustic affair with just enough space for a chunky table, three straw chairs, a fridge and an induction cooker.

'The kitchen downstairs is always busy with folks taking turns to make the meals,' Lila explained. 'This one's for our little comforts.' She took a moka pot and opened a glass jar of coffee. The scent made me want to cry.

'What's up?' Lila asked.

'Nothing.' I pressed the bridge of my nose.

Lila filled the pot, put it on the stove.

'My husband was a coffee aficionado,' I said.

'Yeah, I was going to mention – I'm sorry. We thought you and him had broken up.'

'Brain aneurysm: it killed him in front of me, just like that.' I snapped my fingers.

'Shit.'

'Shit indeed.'

Lila watched the pot, while I watched nothing in particular. 'We were going to have a baby next autumn,' I said. 'We wrote down this list of names for girls and boys. My favourite was Desanges, for a girl, after my mum.'

'A lovely name.'

'It's what tortures you, the projects that remain on paper. The things Bertrand and I did, no one can take them from me, but the ones we never got to do, they're gone. A baby! Visiting Australia! A second house, if things turned out well; a little hut on the beach or deep in a forest. Getting old together. It's not the memories I have which hurt the most, but the ones I will never have. Like – we'd bought this sofa from Italy, some days before he died, and Bertrand was psyched up, the way he got sometimes, like a child. He said the colour was awesome, the best he'd ever seen. He was practically jumping up and down. We had this game: I'd say, *Sofa*! and he'd say, *Yeah, baby*. They delivered the fucking thing a week after the funeral. He never got to sit in it.' I swallowed. 'God, I'm so angry at him.'

Lila poured the coffee into two cups. 'Milk, sugar...?'

'Just sugar, thanks.'

Lila pushed a sugar jar towards me, and gave me one chipped cup and one spoon. She went to the fridge to get milk for herself.

I said, 'Sorry.'

'What for?'

'The word salad. I'm trying to do better, but when I think of Bertrand, I just lose my mind.'

'You can talk to me as much as you need.'

'May I ask you something?'

'Sure.'

'You seem like a decent person.'

'High praise.'

'Why do you run with this crowd?'

'They're decent. Better than.'

I scoffed.

Lila sat down in front of me; the table was small, and we sat very close. 'Let me share something with you. I had a boyfriend who passed, like your husband. I'm not putting my loss on a level with yours – we were together for seven months, and Galen was a difficult man, with enormous issues. All the same, when it happened, it struck me real hard.'

I stared into my cup. 'Of course.'

'Becca and Ric and Mikka and the others – they were there for me, and I don't know where I'd be without them.'

'How about your family?'

'This is my family now, and I'm so much better for that. We're not perfect, Charlie, and any of us can be as big an asshole as anybody out there. Becca? I'd carve her eyes out when she goes full princess. Mikka – all worldly and wise, always an opinion on goddam *everything*. But we *try*. We believe in what we're doing here. We do our thing, and helping people is a big part of our thing, you know? I swear, Charlie, I swear, we aren't hogging any secret tapes of your husband.'

'I'll go as far as to accept that's what you believe.'

'What sinister plan could we possibly have?'

'I *know* my husband's sound.'

'And I don't doubt that.'

'What are you saying, then? That I was imagining it?'

'Not at all.'

'What else? A *ghost*? Please.'

'How did you feel when you heard the music?

'Angry.'

'No, I bet the anger kicked in when the music stopped, and

you decided that we were having you on. I mean before that, before you asked questions and instantly gave yourself answers. While the music played – how did *that* make you feel?'

I had to think before giving an answer. I said, 'Hopeful.'

'Then why question it? The music was like a rainbow, one of those random gifts which remind you the world is large, and contains so much good.'

'A gift from whom?'

'Us.'

'So you did what, you conjured Bertrand's music and his reed?'

'It's more like, you wouldn't say that droplets in the air *conjure* a rainbow, but the rainbow comes because the droplets are there. We are the droplets.'

I examined Lila for the tiniest hint of sarcasm, or doubt, at least. I found nothing. 'You believe that,' I whispered. 'You truly believe that.'

'Droplets don't believe in rainbows – they know.'

THE BASTION

The second night, Becca said, 'We asked you to bring with you your most treasured possession. An heirloom, a childhood toy, a memento from a lover lost for ever. An object dear to your heart, irreplaceable. Do you have it with you?'

We answered, *yes*, keeping the unease from our voices. The flames were very tall.

'Tonight, we let the past go. The good *and* the bad. We need to get rid of every last bit of our old skin, so that tomorrow we may be reborn. Make the past burn!'

We looked at each other – nobody was stepping back, so we all walked to the fire, one by one. Everybody was game because everybody else was game. We burned the polaroid of Dad when he was seventeen and eager for his life to begin (before the bottle), we burned a lock of hair from the girl we kissed in our first car, we burned the first edition we read of *The Lord of the Rings* (a Spanish one, tattered and mended with brown tape), we burned a crucifix, a pair of gloves, a plastic watch, a Smurfs lunch box, ballet shoes, a medal, a personal letter from Bob Dylan, a kippah, a grinder, a purple scarf with a hole, a Cypriot folding fan, a collar, a diary. We were upset at watching them burn. Our upset mounted and mounted, until it peaked – and then blew. Lila was drumming the kind of beat that makes your whole body throb. Everybody else was cheering and swaying, and what was left for us but to join in? A little of the mad energy of the day was coming back. We felt powerful. It was profound, what we were doing. It took courage. We were being real; we had every reason to be proud. We laughed and shouted encouragement at those who hesitated, we kissed more people than ever before; men and women, we didn't really care, we were all in it together.

Charlie held in her fist the saxophone reed she had found on the beach. We knew that something momentous was going on. We watched her get so close to the fire that we thought she would burn; we watched her show the reed to Lila, who was drumming on the other side of the fire, and we watched Lila smile and nod, without missing a beat, and we watched Charlie let go of the reed in the flames.

Before morning she left us.

CHARLIE

I was made of anger. Lila was sincere, but the music and the reed were obviously impossible. I was an atheist; I didn't believe in any god, ghost, soul, magic or voodoo – I believed in a muscle pumping blood through my body, synapses misfiring; I believed in what I could touch, cut and sew. Lila being a true believer only made her another victim. I wasn't planning on joining her.

I didn't need any more confusion in my life.

When Becca asked us, at the bonfire, to burn something, my thought was, *I'm burning you all, cunt.* So, I threw the reed in the fire; to me, it symbolised the Bastion. I was renouncing *them.* Silly, I know. I asked Lila to call me a cab for the morning, and I was expecting resistance, but she just said, 'Done.'

Napoleon the pig came by my hammock that night. He licked my hand before leaving.

ZOEY

I took to the fire a black-and-white photo of a soldier on a bike, with a balloon tied to the handlebars. 'Grandpa,' I said, 'was the only man in my family who ever had my back. I have this one photograph of him, and it's been with me since I was a little girl. But I'm not a little girl anymore. He, of all people, would understand.' I threw the photo and brought a hand to my forehead in a military salute. It was a decent scene, all in all.

Mikka was waiting for me in the circle. 'God,' he murmured in my ear, 'what a load of bollocks.'

I ignored the goings-on at the fire and turned to him. 'Hey!'

'Where did you get the photo?'

'Mum gave it to me.'

Mikka laughed.

'Why are you laughing?'

'I've been hanging with spiritual folks since I was sixteen and I've seen some top-notch liars in my time. You're not top-notch.'

'Okay, fine, I got it from a stall. Fifty pence; a rip-off, if you ask me.'

'That's more like it, Zoey *Lee*.' He was still murmuring.

I looked at the others: nobody was minding our conversation. 'Should I throw my hands in the air and act surprised? Because it was absolutely obvious you knew who I am.'

'Aren't you going to ask how?'

'Do I care? Okay, I'll guess. You came to the early Soul Journey festivals, when Janis and I were hands-on, always around.'

'Only one, the very first one.'

'That was dreadful.'

'I know! Soggy weather, soggy land, and what the hell happened with the catering?'

'We were young and inexperienced, and a son of a bitch took advantage of that, is what happened.'

'I remember you girls very clearly, though. You had so much raw enthusiasm, it was great. I'd have bet on your success.'

'Not enough to come back the next year.'

'I was planning to return. SoulJo went mainstream before I had a chance.'

'And you're too good for mainstream.'

'How's your girlfriend doing, by the way? Or is it *wife* now?'

That stung, and I couldn't tell whether Mikka had said it on purpose or not. 'We're not together. Never were.'

'Oh. Apologies. It seemed like that.'

'Listen, this is cute, but if you're going to send me packing, I'd rather save time and go now.'

'No one is sending you away.'

That was hard to believe. I pointed my index finger upwards and made a circular motion. 'This smells like a beta run, and I am competition.'

'You're *wildly* off-target.'

'Enlighten me, then.'

'Let's go find somewhere quiet.'

'I'm not going to fuck you.'

'Darling, you grow a cock first, then we'll see about that.'

We left the fire and headed to the sea.

The beach by night is a different creature, more aloof and mysterious than its daytime sibling. The night when Mikka drew back a small corner of the curtain for me, the sky and the water were black on black, the stars shining like bad ideas. Moonlight traced a path on the sea, on which I thought it would be easy to walk, reaching the moon above from this land below.

Mikka squatted, found a flat rock, and threw it on the moonlight. The rock skipped three, four, five times, before sinking in the black water.

'You've got your life skill sorted,' I joked.

'You should see me juggle.'

I inhaled the scent. It felt like adventure, but the kind of adventure you imagine when you're young, where you inevitably end up on top. The kind of adventure you stop believing in after you've seen the first friends fall, and after you've faced ruin once or twice. 'I can't believe I hadn't come to the beach until now.'

'The Open Feast is full-on. People tend to get carried away and forget the beach is right here. The Feast proper, with teachings and stuff, ends tomorrow night. The next day is for winding down. Swim, check out the bars in town, buy crap to take back home.'

'You've got a clever set-up.'

'I won't argue with that.'

'How long have you been going, again?'

'This is the sixth year.'

'You started a little before the pandemic.'

'They never really closed Puglia for summer.'

'Events were banned in the whole of Europe.'

'Mainstream events were banned, but, you know.'

'You're not mainstream.'

Mikka threw another rock – six bounces.

I squatted, fished for a rock. 'The question being, what *are* you?'

'You mean metaphysically or...'

'Shut up,' I chuckled. I found my rock and threw it the way Mikka had done. The rock sank.

'Arm and wrist. The movement should pass from arm to wrist to rock, like a wave.'

'Spare me the lesson on How To Mindfully Bounce Rocks. This is the bull I sell for a living.'

'And yet you can't bounce rocks,' Mikka said, picking another.

'Tell me, Gandalf, are you going to answer my question, or is your plan to leave a trail of breadcrumbs which will lead me to a mind-blowing reveal, in due time? Because if that's the case, I'm going back for another round with whatshisname, that young man with tortoiseshell glasses. What is this festival *for*? You say it's not a beta run, fine, but the business can't be here, 'cause from what I've seen, it's lucky if you break even.'

'We're not in it for the money.'

'Then you're the truly dangerous ones.'

Mikka was having the time of his life. 'I understand why some people might feel like that. It's simple: the Bastion is a community of spiritual seekers. The Open Feast is how we give new people a hint of what we do, and see whether we recognise any of them as one of us. This one,' he changed topic, his eyes on the sea, 'gave me a paltry three bounces.'

'So you're a cult and the Feast is your recruitment drive.'

'We're not a cult.'

'Said every cult member ever.'

'You make a lot of adulting noises, as if you need to hear them yourself.'

'The pop psychology bit!' I laughed. 'It's a veritable New Age smorgasbord you guys have got here.'

Mikka made another rock bounce on moonlight. 'I remember you, at that first SoulJo. You were enthusiastic. Eager.'

'One is wrong a lot, when one is young.'

'How did you come to be so wrong, then? What brought you to fall in with us weirdos?'

'Not everybody has an origin story.'

'Okay, but do you?'

I weighed him up. *Why not,* I thought. My story was not a secret, only something I was not fond of sharing. 'Ever heard of *aphantasia*?'

'I hate to admit I haven't.'

'Means I have no visual imagination, none whatsoever. I can't visualise anything. *I can't,* no more than you can piss fire.'

'Why, can you? Piss fire, I mean.'

I made a grimace. 'My mind's eye is blind.'

'If you close your eyes and think about my face...?'

'I can only see your face with my eyes open. There is no figuring it. I've got zero images in my head.'

'And that's a real thing.'

'Yup.'

'Were you always like that?'

'I only found out at college.'

'How could you *not know*?'

'Because I didn't even think the opposite was possible, up to that moment! My girlfriend at the time, a psych student, was going through a Jungian phase, and asked me to help her develop her skills of active imagination. The basic idea was that I would visualise stuff with my inner eye, and she would guide me. It dawned on me that when she used the word *imagination* she meant something wildly different from what I knew. I asked her, *What do you mean, you see things in your mind?*, and she answered, *you just do*.'

'She was not a great psychologist,' Mikka joked.

'That she was not. I'd heard the expression *mind's eye*, and I'd heard people talk of things they imagined, but it'd never occurred to me that those were actual images coming to their mind. It'd never occurred to me that such a thing was even possible. I shut my eyes, all was black, and I'd just took for granted that was how everybody lived.'

'How did you feel about finding that wasn't the case?'

'Excited. Curious. I signed up for a pathworking weekend guided by a Scottish Kabbalah teacher. It was crap, but did jolt something inside, and the next step was a Zen meditation retreat. The snowball became an avalanche.'

'And now the avalanche is tired. It lost momentum.'

'Can I be honest with you?'

'I'm a big boy.'

'Okay then. See, I've been around priestesses, monks, witches, gurus, magi, tarot readers and spiritual influencers. I've done mushrooms, hugged trees, danced with my belly, read Sheldrake and slept with a High Priestess of Aphrodite. And all that I've found in the end – *all that I've found* – is a terrible emptiness, a desperate void, a pitch-black pit full of nothing at the centre of the world. Those myriad wonderful things poets tell us are in heaven and earth? Different configurations of dust, all of them. We're that too, another configuration of dust, with nothing to mark us out except for our delusions of grandeur. A handful of dust briefly dreaming of being divine.'

'Dreaming dust sounds awesome to me.'

'It's still dust. Gonna be wiped out.'

'At the Bastion, we stumbled upon a different sort of truth.'

'I'm sure you did. That truth being...?'

Mikka brushed his white moustache, satisfied. 'This was me, baiting you. After the Open Feast, why don't you stay a little longer? So you'll see for yourself.'

'I've got a life to go back to.'

'Just a few days.'

'I couldn't stand one more second of'—I air-quoted—'teaching.'

'You won't have to. You can go to the beach, take walks in the countryside, have a chill time. Oh, it goes without saying, with the Feast over you'll get your phone back. We also have Wi-Fi, so you can work from here.'

'All this, for a small charge of...?'

'That's an obsession you have! Free of charge, Zoey, can you believe that?'

'No.'

'There's eighteen of us, in the Bastion. One more mouth to feed for a short while won't make a lick of difference.'

'How the hell do you fund this operation, Mikka?'

'Isn't she trusting.'

'No, she isn't.'

Mikka laughed. 'I've got nothing exciting for you, sorry. We own some land, a farming micro-business. Defining it as *boutique* would be overselling it. We produce a little meat, a little cheese, some wine, some figs we make jam with. We sell to local shops and make enough to get by, mostly because we need little.'

'And you need little because you're so spiritually advanced.'

'Is it such a bad thing, needing little?'

I was intrigued. The Bastion had underground clout; sometimes these things fizzled out, sometimes they didn't. If these folks ever made it big, if Becca was a female Osho for the vibrantly diverse twenty-first century, I wanted to be there from the get-go. There was a chance that rather than being a competitor, these folks might be our next contractor. I wished Janis was here, with her hunches.

'You've got this *different sort of truth* of your own, big woo-hoo – who hasn't? There're a million new truths on Reddit every month. If you want me to change my flight, which is expensive, and give the Bastion more days of my precious time, which is *far* more expensive, you'll have to flesh out your offer.'

'You're talking as if you were the one doing us a favour.'

'That's the way I see it.'

'The way *I* see it, we're giving you a free holiday.'

'What's in it for you?'

'You know the answer. You think it's rubbish, but you know it.'

'And do you have the guts to say it aloud?'

'Okay, fine,' Mikka sighed. 'We recognised you. You're one of us, Zoey Lee.'

Okay, so that was the pitch. *You're one of us.* I'd heard it before. There was nothing in the Bastion which I'd not seen before, except for Napoleon. So why did they make me curious? Perhaps I was having one of Janis's hunches. This was easier to believe than the other possibility – that they might actually have something I needed.

LILA

By the third day we were under-slept and happy. The world beyond the trees had disappeared. It was a vague memory, if that. All that we needed was with us.

Becca and Ric taught together that day. When we sat by the fig tree, they told us that last night we had completed the shedding of old skin, and it was now time to come to new life. We would start with undressing. Every creature, they said, comes into the world with no frills.

I was astonished when Ric unzipped his trousers, and Becca slipped out of her long skirt. No one sniggered, no one cracked jokes; we were long past that. The shadows of pine needles tattooed their bodies. They were the most beautiful things I had ever seen.

Some of us jumped at the opportunity and started taking off our clothes. Galen was already shirtless, beaming at me. Blood was pulsing in my temples. I was not sure I could do it; then I saw a girl with slanted blue eyes kiss Galen on a cheek, her naked breasts pressing on his shoulder, and I took my hands to the hem of my t-shirt.

We all got bare-arsed in the end. The warm summer air tickled my skin. We were laughing, messing around. It was very strange for the first ten minutes, and then, not at all.

Becca and Ric told us that the coming night was a night of magic in Italian lore. Two witches from the Bible, Herodias and her daughter Salome (the one who with her dance, irresistible, convinced King Herod to cut off San Giovanni's head), would lead a horde of witches across the black skies. Fires would burn all over the countryside in celebration of the longest day, which marked the arrival of summer, but also the start of the lengthening of night.

Becca instructed us to give a massage to the person sitting to our right, while the one on our left massaged us. We made a chain of hands and shoulders, and tired as I was, naked as I was, I forgot to be self-conscious. Giving a massage while being massaged was hypnotic – you could feel on your shoulders the same movements your hands were making on somebody else's. The boundaries between our bodies became fuzzy, and I felt the skin I was massaging as my own.

We anointed one another with thick green olive oil.

Lunch was fresh fruit and white wine. After, we danced to an upbeat tune played on drum and a theremin connected to a portable power station. We gathered the wood we needed for the fires, and we piled them up on top of pinecones and the needles we used as tinder. We built two fires, a tall one and a smaller one. I had a lot of fun messing around stark naked in that delightful midsummer haze. Seeing each other's bums had already become the norm, just another thing we had been doing for ever. Napoleon weaved among us, and we pretended he walked on two legs, just like us. Galen would make Napoleon's voice.

Late in the afternoon, before lighting the fires, we played with body paint. There were jars of colours laid by the fig tree, which we used to draw figures on each other. I took my sweet time with fingers on skin, and the girl who was painting me did the same. She circled my breasts, my clavicles, my shoulders, making dragons and geometrical patterns. Then she drew two flames on the inside of my legs. She had a light touch.

The boundaries keeping us apart crashed down once and for all. We finished in the uncertain red of sunset, and then we lit the fires. The big one was a tower, a castle. We threw in it heads of corn, heads of garlic, for good luck. After that, in groups of two or three or four, we held hands and leaped over the small one, screaming a dream, a dare, an oath, or just screaming with happiness.

Galen and I leaped together, and after the leap we kissed. Ric had taken on drumming, and Sam was on the theremin. We kept the kiss going. A voice inside me shouted to stop now, before it was too late – but I listened to the drums and the theremin and not to the voice, which sounded like my dad's. *Too late?* It would never be early enough. The music was unpicking what was left of my old self, of that fucked-up sack of worries that I had been in the world I'd left behind.

Galen and I kissed by the heat of the fires, and we caressed, and kissed some more. His kisses moved from my lips to my neck. He nibbled my earlobes before going down on his knees. He grabbed my thighs and sank his head between my legs.

And while Galen's tongue tasted me, a new pair of lips was on mine. They were Becca's. I kissed her back. Her skin smelled of woodsmoke and sage, and there was an aftertaste of good strong wine on her tongue. Another man joined us, and now three sets of lips were kissing, three tongues. I leaned against the fig tree. It was beautiful. Yet another mouth came to my breast, biting my nipple lightly. I laughed. I reached out with my hand and touched smooth hair. I heard moans and I didn't know if it was me. Herodias and Salome gave us their blessings from the black sky prickled with starlight.

We went on all night.

THE BASTION

Too much has been said about us. We have been tasty fodder for journalists, influencers, podcasters, every parasite out there with an opinion and a data plan. They called us monsters, they called us maniacs, and we were never given a right to our own voice; not in the news, not in the sham processes we were subjected to.

Our orgies took front and centre. Few people openly attacked us for them. Everybody was okay with consenting adults doing what they like, *but*. There was always a *but*.

This is their shame, not ours.

LILA

A gentle touch startled me awake. I came to my senses to see Ric, his clothes back on, bent over me. He brought a finger to his lips. He shook Galen awake next. Galen's limbs were entangled with mine and another person's, but Ric let that one sleep. He stood up and walked away. Galen and I could only follow, naked as we were.

'What's this?' Galen whispered.

I had a splitting headache, my vision was blurry, and my legs had barely enough strength to carry me, after all I had drunk, smoked, done. The pinewood was like a smudged watercolour. I heard a humming and a faint theremin.

I saw them by the ruined peasant hut.

They had their arms wrapped around each other's shoulders, all except for Sam, who was waving his hand around the theremin, conjuring sounds out of thin air. They were swaying left and right, humming the tune Becca had been taught, and had taught them in turn; Sam was humming with the others. It was unlike any sound I knew. It was the sound the wind could make if the wind had a throat. Ric swung one arm around Becca's shoulders, one around the Nameless's, and joined the hum.

Galen and I, naked, amazed, searched for one another's hand.

'Look,' Galen said. I raised my head.

The stars were changing.

There were more of them, far more than I'd ever seen, at Villa Abbracciavento or anywhere else. It was a prehistoric sky, from a time before the first human lifted their eyes to the universe, and earlier still, a time before the first creature evolved eyes to see. A moonless sky. There were only stars, too many stars, crowded, crammed, too close together. A sky so rich it was obscene. Impossible.

The hum dropped in volume.

Becca's voice rose just above it. 'Do you remember I said I am on a mission?'

I nodded.

'I need you for that.'

2

OUR REVELATIONS

LILA

I laughed. I was given an earth-shattering revelation and my immediate reaction was to laugh. It was just too beautiful! A week earlier, I was living with my mum and dad in this dull grey town, all factories and dim streetlamps. Now I found myself in a pinewood by the beach, reeling from the best sex I'd ever had, holding hands with a hot guy, under a sky... no, I can't describe that sky with simple words, the way you do a car or a piece of furniture. Could you describe love that way? Could you describe death? Sam wrote a melody to give a sense of it, and Imogen a prose poem.

A lot of folks made fun of us, saying that we could not give an account of so many of our experiences. We insisted that we could, and we had, if only they bothered to look at our art with an open mind. But they wrote it off as sentimental garbage, and asked to see hard proof, which we obviously could not produce. They said we were drunk, high, sexed-out, carried away, all of which was true, but it was like saying that a nail cannot possibly be in the wall because it took a hammer to drive it there. The kinder ones called us brainwashed, the others, the vast majority of them, said we were quacks. Not that we cared. Becca and Ric had got us ready for that moment. They taught us that people will want to destroy what they don't get. It was just too beautiful. All of it.

Galen squeezed my hand before asking Becca, 'What do you mean?'

'What I said.'

The hum continued.

'You said you need us for your mission.'

'Yes.'

'Which is...?' Galen asked with the devil-may-care attitude we loved.

I wished I could be more like him; so cool, so carefree. I looked at the sky, and it was an earthly sky again; a good one, fat with stars and dripping with the white of the Milky Way, but earthly.

Becca said, 'You have questions – rightly so. I promise we'll explain everything, starting tomorrow, but you're going to have to stay with us for a little longer after the others leave. Can you do that for me?'

'Sure,' said Galen, without a moment's doubt.

Only then it occurred to me that I was naked, and Galen wasn't holding my hand anymore. I think I had the smallest voice in the world when I said, 'I can't.'

'Why?' Becca asked.

'I'm skint. I can't afford...'

Becca took my hand and kissed it. 'Oh, Lila. You don't have to pay a thing.'

'I don't want to be a bother.'

'You could never be a bother.'

It was an immense relief to hear Becca say that. I wanted nothing more than to stay. It wasn't that I'd never been so happy in my life; it was that I had discovered I'd never been happy, at all. Not before finding this. I briefly thought of calling Mum, and discarded the idea.

THE BASTION

We sensed Lila and Galen's excitement. Ours was twice theirs. The Open Feast had been hard work, and we could not be sure it would pay off. It had, in spades. After stagnating for too long, we were on the move again. We couldn't wait to see where the road would lead us.

LILA

I found a string of texts and voicemails on my phone. *Where are you?* they said. *Sweetheart, we love you. We are so worried for you. I can't sleep for how worried I am. Why are you doing this to me?* And as was to be expected: *Dad is beside himself.* As if that was rare. Also: *It's not too late to say you're sorry.* The messages swung between the guilt-inducing to the threatening. Mum's voice was on the verge of breaking down in one, and firm in the next one, when she ordered, *this has gone on long enough. Call me, Daniela.*

I told Galen, and his comment was: 'So you still live with your family.'

We were by the peasant hut. I was sitting on the masonry seat, Galen was splayed out on the ground, intent on turning a robin's body into one of his Oddballs. It took me a while to get a sense of what he was doing; a jeweller's lens on his right eye, he was attaching a pig's tooth to the bird's red breast, making it as if the tooth was bursting out of it. I was not sure how much I liked it, but it was impressive.

Against my will, I admitted that yes, I lived with my family. Saying to world-trotting Galen that I slept in the same bed which I did as a little girl was not great.

'And why didn't you just say that you were going somewhere?'

'I left a note.'

'Yeah, but why didn't you tell them?'

'They wouldn't have let me go.'

'Aren't you nineteen?'

'Yeah.'

'So what could they do?'

I shrugged, hoping to mirror Galen's attitude.

'They're bad then,' he said.

'Not very,' I answered. I felt as if I were betraying Mum – maybe Dad too – by complaining. 'Just... a bit much.'

'I left home at fourteen and never looked back.'

'How come?'

'Mum was on crack and Dad pimped her out.' He paused, looked at his work in progress, took some more stuffing from a pouch. 'So.'

I felt terrible. Here I was, complaining about two perfectly sane parents to someone who'd been raised in hell. 'I'm so sorry, Galen.'

'Water and bridges. I barely remember their faces.'

My answer was killed in my throat by Becca's voice. 'Am I interrupting?'

'Not at all,' said Galen.

Becca sat down with her distinctive grace, swaying like a ribbon in a breeze. 'I'm sorry we've been ignoring you two. With all the people leaving – it's mental.'

'We're having a good time.'

'I promised we would talk.'

Galen put away the half-formed Oddball. 'That you did.'

'Let me tell you straight away, I can't answer many of your questions.'

'Can't or won't?'

'A bit of both.'

'Fair enough.' Galen pointed his smile at me. 'You first?'

'Sure. I...' I paused. 'That sky. Did I see it?'

Becca said, 'Did you?'

'Yes...?'

'Good.'

Galen asked, 'And what was it?'

'A French scholar, Claude Lecouteux, wrote that *the light of the Otherworld is different from that of ours*. Almost all religions postulate an Otherworld of sorts, a place for spirits, gods and lost souls – and it shines with its own light. The sky you have seen, that too shines with its own light.'

I opened my eyes wide. 'You took us to Heaven.'

Becca shook her head. 'We already *are* in Heaven. And Hell. The Otherworld is around us and within us, like air, like thoughts, like a colour we can't quite see, not without some training.'

'Training you can give us?' Galen asked.

'We are going to teach you how to shift consciousness. Everything is conscious, and even more, everything *is consciousness*. Every person, every tree, every rock is ultimately made not of atoms, not of quarks, but of consciousness. Matter is nothing but one of the shapes that consciousness – or *soul*, if you want to use a more poetic language – can take. When one shape comes undone, in death, the soul goes on and forms another. Everything is forever becoming something else.' Becca touched the pine needles and dead leaves covering the ground. '*This* is the Otherworld.' She brought the hand to my heart. 'This is Heaven, this is Hell, this is Faerie, this is the place where spirits and monsters and demons and angels live. *This*. The dullness and predictability of the everyday world is an illusion. We gave you a peek at the beautiful truth hidden behind it.'

'How do you know all that?' I asked, and I wanted to slap myself for how challenging I sounded.

Becca smiled at me. 'I had an experience, a revelation. And so will you, if you stay. We will guide you through a specific set of exercises which will break open the gates of Heaven and Hell for you.'

Galen smirked. 'Not afraid of overselling?'

'Not a bit.'

'You really, really want us to stay.'

'I'm not being shy about it.'

'Because you need our help with your mission.'

'*Our* mission. We are in it together.'

'And the mission is?'

'Not yet. It would be like wanting to run before learning to walk.'

'I can run.'

'Oh, Galen. We all believed that, when we started, and we were wrong.' Becca put a hand on his cheek. I was surprised to find I was only a little jealous, not much. 'But trust me – trust *us* – and you will learn to walk, and run, and fly.' Galen put his hand on Becca's, looked at her. After a moment, Becca drew her hand back. 'If I told you now what it is that we're going to do, you'd probably leave. Stay. Go through our training. We're going to start with some simple breathing routines. See if they do something for you.'

'What if I told you I'm leaving if you *don't* tell me?' Galen said, in that charming tone of his that was impossible to determine as serious or light-hearted.

'You're too curious to do that.'

'You sure?'

'Go on,' Becca said. 'Nobody's stopping you.'

Galen shook his head and laughed.

I had to ask, 'Sorry, but how long are we talking about?'

'I couldn't say.' Becca sighed. 'Look, we're a community here. Ric and I may be the figureheads, but we make things happen all together, as a family. Ric and I don't control everything. In fact, we don't control *anything*.'

Becca looked at me in a way that almost overwhelmed me. I was not used to being looked at as if I mattered.

'It is far too early to talk about the things you want to talk about,' Becca went on. 'You will need to go through some experiences first. Stick with us and it will make sense. I promise, I *swear*, you're going to get to a point where our truth will be so easy to grasp, so obvious, that you will laugh at yourself for not having gotten there earlier. But you can't do that alone. You'll have to attune yourself to us, and we to you, and then – then you will see. Trust us, and *you will see*.'

'Broadly, how long will it take?'

'What are you so worried about?'

'My family, back home.'

'Call them if you need. Reassure them. Only, please, don't disclose our location, and if you could avoid referring to what we told you last night, we'd be grateful. Apart from this, stop worrying, Lila, and have fun. You're lovely. You can stay for as long as you need.' She paused. 'I almost forgot. While you are here, would you suspend your social media accounts? All of them. It's okay to use email, your phone, but social media is too distracting. We need a certain intensity, to get where we need to get. Do you have a problem with that?'

We didn't. No Swallow ever did.

THE BASTION

Our guests left like an August storm – it was all sound and fury for a few hours, then no more. Some spent the last day on the beach, others checked out the village, some couldn't believe what they had been up to the night before, others fucked against trees. Some wrote in their journals, some cried quietly in a corner; some asked, no, *begged* us, to sell them the stuff we used, as if it were something that could be bought and sold. We were glad nobody was hurt, nobody made too much of a fuss. We had the occasional jerk who knew their rights and wanted us to do this or that for them, but nothing we couldn't handle. No serious incident ever happened during an Open. Make what you want of it.

We organised transfers, hotels, we found lost items, we wrestled the logistics of shepherding a hundred or so people back to their tragically nondescript lives. Then, with the last health panic sorted, the last goodbye exchanged, the last flight departed, quiet descended on our little pinewood. Napoleon was disappointed; he felt lonely.

We were too knackered to do more than have dinner and go to bed. Swallows (that's what we called newcomers) would be ravenous to throw themselves on their phones – as if their lives could ever go back to what they were.

ZOEY

First thing I did was call Janis. I was dying to hear her voice – maybe boast a bit about the orgy. Not my first group sex experience, but the best by a mile.

'Turn on the camera!' Janis demanded, as soon as she answered. 'Ellie wants to say hi!'

I was pretty sure that a four-month girl did not want to say hi. Before Ellie was born, I'd expected to feel flutters of love for a baby who was my niece in all but blood, but all I felt was a mild annoyance. Ellie was noisy, smelly, red and wrinkled like a drunkard. 'I promised I wouldn't.'

'You promised to whom?'

There was a gurgle, like a blocked sink – *here we go, the bloody baby again*. Since Ellie was born, having a conversation with Janis had become impossible.

'The Bastion. They asked me not to use the camera on-site.'

'Aren't you at the airport?'

'Actually, no. I'm staying for another week. Something like.'

Ellie started crying. Janis hushed her, then raised her voice above the crying.

'Zoey, what's going on?'

'One of their old-timers recognised me from SoulJo. He got the picture of why I'm here, and was nonplussed.'

'Plucky.'

'They say they're not the competition. They say – they say the Open Feast is not a business.'

'And you believe that.'

'It might just be true.'

'Which is a good reason to get the hell out of there ASAP.'

'He treated me to the usual story. You're one of us, we recognised you, et cetera.'

'Are we talking nuts, perv, or a bit of both?'

'Neither, that's the thing. They're harmless,' I lied. By then, it was very clear to me that the guys were not harmless. Still, I was not worried, not yet. I was figuring them out. Once I'd have been able to think out loud with Janis, but then the baby had come, requiring her attention 24/7. 'They're more Merry Pranksters than Heaven's Gate. Their leaders, these Becca and Ric guys – they've got a *je ne sais quoi*.'

'You're thinking partnership.'

'You know spiritual types, it's never about money until it is.'

'Just stay away from the Kool-Aid, okay?'

'Drank that already,' I joked.

CHARLIE

I couldn't step inside my flat.

It had been raining all day. I hated every drop of water falling from the grey sky, every shiny wet cobble paving the street, every brick of every house. I hated the cab which had brought me from the airport to my building, I hated the dark oak door and I hated the cavernous corridor which opened behind, I hated every step of the staircase leading up to the third floor, I hated the smooth iron banister and I hated the door to my flat. I hated the keys I put in the keyhole. I hated the grating noise the door made when I pushed it open.

From the threshold, I could make out the living room in semi-darkness. It had changed little since Bertrand and I had bought it. I hadn't found it in me to paint it the colour we had agreed upon (a light blue), to buy the furniture on the list we'd drawn up, fix the electrics and the plumbing. The only new thing in that room was the sofa Bertrand had never seen, and it struck me what an evil thing it was. It stared at me with idiot eyes, and the space between the seat and the back was a hungry mouth which would swallow me whole if I dared sit. I did not hate the sofa, I was afraid of it.

It was physically impossible for me to enter the flat and find myself between walls that resonated with the echo of Bertrand's booming laughter. I remember thinking that a better version of this world must exist, where he was alive, and we were coming back together after a great time in Italy with the mad hippies. In that version the rain was a romantic companion which played a lulling patter on the new windows, and we were going to order pizza and curl up on the sofa. In that other version, I had a life to love.

Whereas in this real world of ours the grey was relentless, raindrops rapped on the old window like a vampire's knuckles, and the sofa stared at me with its idiot gaze. I couldn't breathe. My throat was blocked; my lungs had forgotten how to do their job. I had to close my eyes, lean against the wall, count to ten. I managed to suck some air in. I turned back and headed to the staircase, forgetting the open door. I went down the steps, through the cavernous corridor, out the front door, into the rain, and called another cab.

ZOEY

After saying goodbye to Janis, the red dots on my phone urged me to check my socials, check the news, and I obeyed. Shockingly, the world had not changed while I was away. An acquaintance was pretending to be well-read, posting Instagram quotes lifted off Goodreads; a yoga influencer for whom I'd once had to source a substantial amount of MDMA was preaching against Big Pharma on Facebook; a storm had exploded on X over a rapper who'd said something or slept with somebody or done a bit of both.

I had this thought, that life was dull when you looked at it from a distance, a sequence of a small number of patterns repeating endlessly. Humans fucked up in the caves in the exact same way they fuck up in skyscrapers and they will fuck up on spaceships. I could become a millionaire, and nothing would change; I could die, and nothing would change.

I quickly put my accounts on hold, with a sense which was half guilt and half relief, and put away my phone. That was what had pushed me on my own journey when I was younger: fear of a life off the shelf. My journey had ended in nothing much. It had ended with me having to accept the terrible emptiness at the core of existence, the desperate void, the pitch-black pit. Off-the-shelf was all there was. What some called mystery was ignorance glorified.

I was jealous of Ellie, who hadn't seen the pit yet. I was jealous of the Bastion, of these bonkers hippies, of Mikka's *different sort of truth*, of their sweet bollocks. If only I could buy that. If only I could fall asleep in the midst of this real wasteland and dream it into a fairytale forest. It would be so comforting.

I liked Mikka, as a person. I liked Becca, and I liked Ric, rough around the edges as he was. I liked that young drummer with crazy eyes, Lila. I liked all the Bastion people I'd met. If only I could turn off my brain like them, I might be happier. Or maybe not. When I had tried that in the past, it had never worked out. I had a string of abysmal relationships, a few tattoos and one scar to show for that.

The pinewood had a different vibe that night, with no drums, no moans or young nerds in the woods. It was difficult to believe that only yesterday I was in a massive orgy among these trees. Memories came back to me. I did not know the names of all the people I'd kissed and fucked the night before, and my condition made it impossible to visualise their faces, but my body remembered every single touch and every single stroke. All that chaos, that wild abandon, and now – this quiet. My only company were the crickets, a critter munching the bark of a tree, and sea waves coming ashore. I climbed into a hammock. Mikka had offered me a room, but I preferred to stay under that starry sky. It was the one thing bigger here than in New York. It was not bad to rock to and fro, like a baby in a cradle, with the woods and the sea lulling me to sleep.

THE BASTION

'So – we're positive,' Ric said.

We had waited for Zoey to fall asleep (Imogen, who had gone hunting since she was little and could be as silent as an imaginary friend, kept an eye on her) and then we had gathered in the kitchen. Sam was now pouring sweet-smelling shots of limoncello (the smell was the only thing going for Mikka's limoncello) and passing around the glasses, with shaking hands. Imogen was in the window smoking one of her rare cigarettes, Ric was drumming his fingers on the table, Mikka was playing with one of his rings. Others were pacing up and down the room, fiddling with a beer bottle's label, searching for something in the cupboards for no reason at all, so on and so forth. We were like a bowstring being pulled.

Becca gave one nod. 'Zoey and Charlotte were the last Swallows.'

Each new Swallow brought us closer to a change of season. Now all of them had come home.

Imogen spoke in the husky voice that was to become world-famous. 'Charlotte left.'

'I'm on it,' Lila said. She took a glass of yellow liquor. 'She'll be back tomorrow night, the next day at most.'

'You're the only one of us the French one doesn't hate from the bottom of her heart.'

Becca said, 'Love and hatred speak the same language, with a different accent.' She turned to Lila. 'Are you still happy being on Charlotte's case?'

'Very! I like her.'

'How about you with Zoey, Mikka?'

'A bit of a challenge,' he said. 'A lot of fun.'

Imogen pointed out: 'Zoey thinks we're weird.'

'She moved on from thinking we're grifters; it's a step up.'

We were venturing into new territory. Think about how it feels, after years of attempts, to be pregnant and close to giving birth. You've built a new room for the baby, you've bought new clothes, security systems and toys; you know your life is going to change radically, and you cannot wait for it to happen, although you don't have a clue what'll happen next. Longing, fear, hope, bafflement, and a subtle sense of having lost your way in the woods, all come together. Think about that, and you will feel a pale shade of what we felt that night.

Sam admitted, 'I'm a wee bit nervous.'

'What for?' Lila asked, opening her eyes wide. 'This is *epic*.'

'Shall we put the Slaughter in the diary?' Imogen said.

'Yeah,' Sam said, 'let's get the ball rolling.'

Becca took a glass. 'Five days?'

'I'd say three,' said Imogen. 'The sooner the better.'

'Five. It leaves us more breathing space. Ric?'

He nodded.

We agreed five days was better, and Imogen shrugged and said it wasn't her hill, though every opinion Imogen held was her hill. We toasted and then we hung a little longer, chatting, laughing, boasting about how great our last Open Feast had been. We had gone out with a bang. We praised Imogen for how she had organised the transfers, Sam for how he'd run the kitchen; we made fun of Mikka's many conquests (he was a champion), and before going to bed, we raised a toast to poor Galen, as was traditional. Becca and Ric used to say that to walk into the future, we must never forget the past. You cultivate hope by admitting regret.

ZOEY

I was not an early riser as a rule, but I woke up just past dawn. The sky was apocalyptic blue. A scent of baking bread and pine sap: this is the first thing I remember of the next morning. I yawned and dismounted from my hammock. I followed the scent to the tables, where I found Mikka and Sam (I'd barely spoken to Sam by that time) setting down jars of jam and jugs of milk.

'Morning,' Mikka said.

'You don't want to talk to me before coffee.'

'In the kitchen,' said Sam. 'The pot's on the stove.'

'You want some?'

They did. I shuffled my feet to the kitchen, where the scent of bread ruled and a giant moka pot sat on an induction cooker. I turned the cooker on and waited, enjoying the sight of loaves of bread and heaps of croissants on the kitchen counter. When the coffee was ready, adding its own scent to the mix, I poured three cups and came out again in a delicious cloud.

'Thank you,' said Sam.

I considered him properly for the first time, this lanky man with curly hair who dressed in Indian shirts and leather vests, and spoke English as if every sentence was the verse of a song. 'Irish?' I asked.

'County Clare.'

'I had a girlfriend from Kilkenny, back at uni.'

'Did you ever visit?'

'Never had a chance.'

'It's beautiful. Very different from here. A deeper green, a pastel blue.'

'How did an Irishman end up in Southern Italy?'

'How did a New Yorker?'

I pointed at Mikka. 'This one here offered me a free holiday.'

'You bought that bullshit?' Sam said, with a laugh. 'Well, too late now, I may as well cough it out – we're fattening you up for the sacrifice.'

'When would that be?'

Sam lightly pinched my arm. 'It's going to take a while, I'm afraid. We'll have to rid your system of all that avocado and quinoa first.'

'Shut up,' I laughed. 'Actually, could we get on with the fattening? Where are the others?'

Mikka said, 'With Becca, for the Breathing Spell. We were setting the table before joining them.'

'The what spell?'

'Come and see.'

'You said I didn't have to sit through any more lessons!'

'You don't. You've seen where the breakfast is. Go on, help yourself.'

'Thank you.'

I made a show of going back inside to get food. It was lame. Scoffing bread and jam on my own was not how I'd get insider knowledge of the Bastion.

I circled back to go with Mikka and Sam.

THE BASTION

Every day before breakfast we would take ten minutes to sit in the shadow of the fig tree, or indoors in bad weather, and breathe together. 'Breathe in at my count of six,' Becca said, and counted to six. She made us hold our breath for a while. 'Now breathe out at my count of six. Just drop your breath, as if you were releasing a weight.' And out we went.

Swallows invariably stumbled, inhaling too quickly or slowly, exhaling too early or too late, until they realised that breathing with the rest of us required them to listen as much as to act. Becca would gently correct each of us individually, inviting them to slow down or pick up their pace. We practised until we could do it with little thought and then we kept practising until we did it without any thought at all. By that point we were inhaling and exhaling like one person, with one nose, one throat, one set of lungs.

It is written in the Bible that the Lord breathed life into the first man's nostrils. Becca and Ric did so much more than that! They showed us how to breathe life into one another.

ZOEY

They produced a beautiful sound. I had been around countless self-styled gurus who made ridiculous money by telling their disciples to do what every goddam human does anyway – breathe – but this was different. I had never been with a group of people who inhaled and exhaled as one, eighteen sets of lungs expanding and contracting in unison. It was like sitting in the lap of a purring giant. I couldn't admit it to myself yet, but I wanted in.

I felt bad when Becca asked me to slow down my exhale, and the others to make it a tad quicker. I felt I was ruining a great thing. Like spitting in Mona Lisa's face.

THE BASTION

Of course, it was not her fault. We would never impose our pace upon the Swallows. They attuned to us while we attuned to them, changing us while they allowed us to change them. It was a ballet where everybody led, and nobody followed. We are all equal in the Bastion – this is what people, to this day, refuse to understand.

Either we are together, or we aren't anything at all.

CHARLIE

I checked in at a business hotel, a place so generic it was no place at all; just a roof, a mattress, a radiator. I ran a shower and stood there until the water was cold and there were hags' faces on each of my fingertips. Then I wrapped myself in a thin bathrobe the consistency of sandpaper and sat at the squared desk. I took my phone to check the news, and I swear, the moment my fingers closed around it, the phone pinged with a message from an Italian number.

It's Lila here. Just checking, are you home ok?

The drab rain against the window made me think of the soft southern night, with its scent of pines and sea. Now that the visitors had left, Villa Abbracciavento had to be beautiful. *Yes, ty,* I answered.

I stood there, watching the three dots that meant Lila was writing. Her new message read, *Sorry! Didn't realise it was this late. Hope I didn't wake you up.*

I wasn't sleeping.

I thought of the crackling of the bonfire. I watched the three dots again, and was disappointed when all that came through was a kissing emoji.

It was not only our flat that still resonated with Bertrand's voice; it was every raindrop, every brick in Saint-Malo. After putting the past on hold, returning to it was impossible.

I had heard Bertrand's music, back in the pinewood on the beach.

The sax was not the dismal echo haunting me here, but his real voice, his real breath coming through his instrument. That night, before the disappointment, before the rage, I had been, for a fleeting moment, happy. It had been a basic joy, like a girl getting her favourite ice-cream flavour after a long winter.

I saw the immense fig tree under which the Bastion gathered, every lobed leaf like a hand. I heard the buzz of the bees attracted to the scent of figs.

I grabbed the phone and tapped Lila's number.

'Hey, Charlie!' The crickets came through from her side. 'What's up?'

'I was wondering if your offer was still valid? Could I come and stay?'

'I'll have to check with the others, but I don't see why not.'

'A week or so. How much will that be?'

'You'll be our guest.'

'I don't want that.'

'Okay then, a million euros. Per day! I don't know, Charlie, we'll ask you to chip in for groceries if you insist.'

'What else will I be asked to do?'

'You're an adult and you'll do what the heck you want to.'

'Thank you,' I said, after a beat. 'I appreciate it.'

'I'll check with the others and I'll get back to confirm, okay?'

My hand was unsteady when I put the phone back. I needed this.

THE BASTION

We let Charlie wait, or she might have changed her mind again. *With all things in life,* Becca said, *there is a time to push, a time to pull, and a time to sit and wait.* The next morning Lila texted, *All sorted. I found a flight for tonight with one change! Details in your mailbox. Hop on the plane and we'll meet at the airport.*

That night Charlie was with us.

CHARLIE

They welcomed me with a light snack of bread, mozzarella and prosciutto. They had to shuffle sleeping arrangements around, so that first night I crashed in Lila's room. I slept late into the next day, skipping breakfast, skipping lunch. I woke up sweaty and dazzled in the suffocating heat of early afternoon.

It took me a few moments to remember where I was. I felt a rush of tenderness when I came back to my senses and noticed Lila's meagre possessions. A cheap journal and pen on her bedside table, next to the skull she had mentioned; a Polaroid photo of an extraordinarily beautiful man attached with Blu Tack to the wall above the bed; a colourful drum leaning against another wall;

Lila's clothes, scattered around. This young woman was trusting me, a virtual stranger, with her personal space, the same space I had planned to invade. Who was the good guy here? I touched the skull, and yes, it was real. I wondered if it was okay to ask where it came from. There was something else I needed to do first though.

Villa Abbracciavento was quiet, and so were the woods. It was the suspended time of *controra,* when it is too hot to work or think. Everybody was napping in the shade of trees, to the chirrup of crickets and the echo of sea waves. I headed to the kitchen, where I found a cafetière already set with ground coffee. A note said, *Charlie! Just add water. xx Lila.* I made coffee and headed outside with a cup. At other times in my life I would have found the day unbearably hot, but the sunshine was drying me up, burning toxins away. I felt good. Alive. As if my blood was running again after stagnating for months in a metallic bog.

Becca was sitting in a round wicker chair which hung from a thickly foliaged carob tree, with a glass of iced tea and a book. I waved at her and got closer. 'Good afternoon.'

'Hi there.'

'What are you reading?'

Becca handed me the book, a graphic novel with a grinning sailor on the cover. It was a Corto Maltese book. I said, 'I didn't take you for a *bande dessinée* person.'

'Why not?'

'I didn't think you'd read fiction at all.'

'Fiction is reality waiting to hatch.'

'Is everybody asleep?'

'Give it a couple of hours and they'll be hopping all over the place.'

'Listen... I was looking for you, to say thank you.'

'What for?' Becca stood up. 'Come, let's stretch our legs.'

I followed her. 'For having me here.'

'We are not exactly short on space.'

'Still.' I mustered the courage I needed for what came next. When I'd had fights with Bertrand, he had been the first to smooth things over – I'd never learnt how to say sorry. 'I owe you an apology, I suppose. At the Open Feast – I came at you hard.'

'I'd do the same if I thought someone was playing with my head.'

'It's fading, you know. The memory of that night. When I think back, I…' Finding the words was painful. 'I remember it the way I remember dreams and fantasies. There have been so many times when I thought I could smell Bertrand's cologne, or when I stretched my hand for him in bed, first thing in the morning, and could almost find him. The memory of the music feels every day more like the memory of one of those times.'

'The music was real though.'

'I think so, for now, but next week? Next week I'll believe it wasn't.' I was struggling to keep my voice steady. 'Burning the reed was stupid. I wish I still had it. I have nothing to pin that memory to, you know what I mean? I'm begging you, give me something. Anything. I don't want to forget.'

We were walking through a patch where pines and eucalyptus trees opened up in a circular glade, and flat white rocks jutted out from the earth. We kept walking. 'Why?' Becca asked. 'Why is this memory so important to you?'

I let out a sigh, brought a hand to my mouth. I closed my eyes, took a long slow breath to keep my tears at bay. 'I'm a doctor. I've seen hundreds of people die, and nobody ever come back. That night – it was the first time I hoped Bertrand might still be *somewhere*.'

We had come to the fig tree. Becca spread her arms, and I accepted her hug. She kissed my head, my cheek, and whispered in my ear, 'I have something to tell you. Do you promise to give me a fair chance?'

'Yes,' I said. 'Yes.'

Becca gave me a last squeeze, a last kiss, and let me go. 'I believe your husband was telling you to stay.'

I wiped my tears.

She asked, 'Have you ever heard of the notion of the Mother Tree?'

'The oldest tree in a forest, sort of a hub, connected to the rest of the forest.'

Becca turned to the fig tree and kissed the bark lightly. 'This is our Mother Tree, and we of the Bastion, we are the forest. We create our own ecosystem, where things grow that couldn't otherwise. When we are together, at our best, extraordinary things grow. It was us, the Bastion, who made reality thin enough for Bertrand's music to pass through.'

I looked at the branches, motionless in the afternoon heat.

'I don't think Bertrand was playing for you,' Becca went on. 'I think he *was* the music. The energy, the consciousness that used to be Bertrand is now music. And the music was telling you, *what we have lost together, you will find here*. Home, family, yourself. Bertrand was giving you a thread you would follow back to us, so that we could talk, you and I, right at this moment, the way we are talking, you and I, right at this moment. He wanted you to hear some words from me.'

'Which words would those be?'

'I need you, Charlie. *We* do.'

I waited for Becca to say more, and when it didn't happen, I asked, 'What for?'

'Stay, and find out.'

'No offence, Becca, but I don't know if I can trust you.'

Becca brought a hand to my face. 'Then don't. As long as you stay.'

THE BASTION

We had two get-togethers every day: the morning call over breakfast, and another before bed, which Sam had named the all-in-all. It was how we tracked our progress as a community, to see what we could do better, what we could stop doing entirely.

In the immediate aftermath of an Open, our concerns were practical: we had to tidy up our place, return the gear we had rented, triple-check the accounts, answer the messages asking for lost goods, and decline the requests of those who wanted to secure a place for next year. What they'd had, we reminded them, was a once-in-a-lifetime experience, and now it was up to them to make something of it. One of us (Sam, usually) scoured the Internet to make sure everybody was respecting their NDA. An early incident with a Chilean throuple had taught us that the temptation to break it was stronger in the immediate aftermath of the festival.

Zoey was born for backstage. Nobody worked harder – or better – than her at untying hammocks and packing shelters. We were having trouble with a Canadian who claimed she had lost a ring or a brooch or a diamond at the camp and was threatening to sue if we didn't give it back; Zoey asked the one who was talking to them to hand her the phone, and settled the matter with a small amount of rightly placed words.

'You did the work of five people today,' Mikka commented.

'No, *you* did the work of one-fifth of a decent stagehand,' she answered, in a teasing voice.

The legend of Zoey's uncanny stamina started then. After doing the work of five people during the day, she could drink anyone under the table, even Ric, at night. We saw her guzzle a bottle of wine and uncountable shots of liquor and still walk to her hammock on steady legs. 'It's work,' she explained. 'Keeps me strong.'

CHARLIE

I did not really engage until the night of the Slaughter. I went along with the breathing exercises because I had nothing better to do. I was reasonably polite, I hope. I would only talk to Lila though. I was not interested in anybody else. I kept myself to myself. I had come back to be better alone, if that makes sense.

ZOEY

I thought of Janis all the time. She would have loved this, absolutely loved it. It was like being young again, working on SoulJo hands-on, rather than hiring people to do the fun part. She could have been with me, and instead, she was stuck at home with a baby who couldn't talk and a husband who had nothing to say.

Against all my expectations, Becca and Ric chipped in as much as anybody else. I had to admit that Becca shovelling quicklime on a hole filled with strangers' shit was unusual for a guru. As for Ric, he did *not* make a pass at me, which again, was refreshing. There was an inner circle – Mikka and Lila were closer to Becca and Ric than anybody else – but it was played lightly, and it did not have an impact on the others' morale. I didn't get the sense that folks were vying for the Beloved Leaders' attention, none of that crap. And that was refreshing too.

The only other new face was Charlie. You would expect we would hang a lot, but no. One night I asked Mikka over a drink, 'What's her story?'

'Her husband died some months ago.'

'She's grieving then. Must be prime material for you.'

'That was uncalled for.'

'Was it now?'

'Every spiritual seeker is a little broken.'

'Are you?'

'I was.'

'But the Bastion made you whole.'

'The Bastion is where I was meant to be.'

'Meant by whom?'

Mikka made a sweeping gesture, embracing the dark trees, the sky and the stars.

'And Charlotte and I are meant to be with the Bastion too.'

'You're here, aren't you?'

I raised my bottle in a mock toast.

'What do you make of her?' Mikka asked.

'She's okay I suppose.'

'But?'

'A little stuck-up. I don't want to be horrible.'

One morning I woke up full of energy and with nothing to do: the last shelter had been put away, the last email answered. I caught a whiff something else was on.

'Nope,' Mikka said. 'You can't help with this.'

After all the work I'd done, I didn't like to be left out. 'Inner circle only?'

'I'll see you at the bonfire tonight.'

'There's a bonfire tonight?'

'As I just said.'

I'd barely looked at my phone lately, just enough to see the numbers on the notifications become bigger. There were probably some emails I should answer, but the idea of going through hundreds of pointless messages made me feel weary to the bone. Plus, there was dazzling sunshine and a delicious scent of rosemary and juniper in the air.

I went to the beach.

The warm sand under my toes was a massage. After a moment's thought, I slipped out of my bathing suit and ran towards the seashore. I had skinny-dipped before, in rivers and ponds, never in the sea. When I sunk into the water, a powerful sense of freedom seeped through me. The water caressed every inch of my skin, enveloped me, until my skin became water, became the endless sea. I was as big as the planet, touching the shores of America, Antarctica and Africa. I floated on my back; the sea held me. I wished I could stay like that for ever, never returning to that jagged-edged disappointment called the real world. It was a thousand years before I swam to shore and wrapped myself in a soft towel.

THE BASTION

We made a tall fire for the Slaughter. Lila drummed in the smoke and shadows, drinks and spliffs made the rounds, and we undressed. There is no dancing like dancing naked.

We were a smaller group than during the Open Feast, so the energy was softer, but we were family, so it was more intimate. Charlie stood by Lila, at the edges of our circle. She kept her shirt and jeans on, but when Sam came to her and took her by the hand, she let him drag her towards the fire, and when he made one of his funny moves, pretending to be John Travolta in *Pulp Fiction*, she laughed. She accepted a drink, she accepted a smoke.

A sturdy bench was by the fire, and a brown wooden bucket.

We heard the shrieks before seeing Napoleon. He started up the moment Becca and Ric began leading him towards the bonfire. They had to push and pull. When he let out the first cry, those at the fire stopped what they were doing, and let silence take hold. Napoleon's call was human, almost. It was a surprise for the Swallows to see him come out of the dark tied to a rope.

'What did you expect,' Sam joked, 'a child?'

Zoey whispered, 'What the fuck?'

ZOEY

I mean, *what the fuck*?

THE BASTION

Ric tied a noose around Napoleon's muzzle, muffling the shrieks. It was hard work to keep him from running away. Somehow Napoleon (the pig was called Napoleon every year) knew his time had come.

Becca brought a loving hand to the pig's face. 'We do not have the luxury of turning our back on our responsibilities,' she said. 'Not us. And this is what taking responsibility is like: ugly, unpleasant, ultimately necessary.' She unsheathed her knife. 'Tough calls are part of life. We do not squirm away from them, nor do we treat them lightly. Here we only eat the meat of animals we kill ourselves. Tonight, we undo Napoleon's shape to strengthen ours, and we are aware of the good and bad that this entails, and we take responsibility for both.'

She stopped talking and Ric spoke. 'Where violence is a fact of life, cruelty is a choice. We accept the fact and refuse the choice. Napoleon has been bred outdoors, roaming free, among friends, and will be slaughtered the way pigs have been slaughtered for millennia, with little pain, by human hands using simple tools. He led a good life, his death won't be mechanised butchery, no part of his body will go to waste. We do nothing more than what is necessary.' He unsheathed his knife too. 'But we do what is necessary.'

'Charlie, Zoey,' Becca called. 'If you please.'

CHARLIE

Becca's words resonated with me. I could understand a vegetarian having problems with what she was asking us to do – but a meat-eater? With what right?

I'd cut too many patients to be squeamish.

I turned to the other new person, Zoey. It was, I think, the first moment of connection we had. She looked unsure. I gave a brief nod and made a move towards Napoleon. I was the only one with my clothes on.

ZOEY

Honestly? I'm not sure I'd have gone forward without Charlie. When she nodded at me and moved, I had to follow. Wussing out was not an option. I was thinking it might be a prank. That they would stop us just in time, like Yahweh did Abraham with his son Isaac. Yahweh, that old rascal. Yes, it had to be just like that.

CHARLIE

'You have been partaking of our food,' Ric said. 'Now partake of our responsibilities.' He handed Zoey his knife. I took Becca's.

Becca and Ric pushed Napoleon onto the bench, turning him on one side. They kept it still while Mikka slipped the bucket under Napoleon's throat. Ric grabbed the pig's head. He and Mikka struggled to keep him still while Becca took my hand with the knife in her own hand, and Zoey's in the other, and brought them to Napoleon's throat. She gently guided our hands along the hide, to the right spot. 'Lift your knife,' she said, in a voice full of love, 'and bring it down here, at this angle. Sink it in. Don't hesitate and don't aim for the hide, or you'll make a mess. Aim for what lies beneath. If you falter, Napoleon will suffer needlessly.'

Zoey and I exchanged one last look above the pig's muffled shrieks.

'Okay,' Zoey said.

Our knives went up and then down together, and thick blood poured into the bucket. A drop or two landed on our faces. Becca extended a hand towards the cascade of blood pouring out of Napoleon's throat. She licked her fingers. She nodded: it was good, healthy blood.

Soon, Napoleon stopped shrieking.

I remember the cracking of fire and the dripping of blood.

THE BASTION

Later that night, we heard Zoey scream.

We heard her from our beds and our hammocks, we heard her from the kitchen and the embers of the bonfire. Her scream filled the pinewood, and we rose from our places and followed it to the shower, where Ric banged on the door, calling, 'Zoey! What's happened?'

ZOEY

There was a place in Queens, one of the rare surviving shacks from a different age in the history of NY, whose pork ribs were better than a Michelin-starred meal. I'd eat there whenever I was in the 'hood. Janis had flirted with a plant-based diet for two years, but in a scene where vegetarians and vegans are a dime a dozen, I'd stuck to my steaks and burgers and bacon. The Bastion's rule made perfect sense: as far as meat-eating goes, I'd just done the most ethical deed of my life.

It did not feel like that though. I had never killed anything bigger than a mosquito, and certainly nothing that cried. Napoleon's cries sounded so much like a human's. *Napoleon*. As I said, I liked that fellow. Why did they have to give the pig a name? Everybody knows you don't name animals you're going to kill.

But then, I supposed that must be the point of it. The Bastion named the pig so as to take fully on board the reality of what we were going to do to it. These guys did not fuck around. My interest in them had gone up a hundred notches.

I was in the shower, and I was barely noticing the chill of the water on my skin. I was taking a shower outside rather than in Villa Abbracciavento because the thought of entering an enclosed space with the death smell on me made me reek. I wished I could scrub my body from within.

I was struck by how simple the killing had been. I'd not felt bad, or good for that matter. I'd not felt anything much, except for a slight physical revulsion when Napoleon's thick hide had offered some resistance to the knife. I had done what Becca said, aiming for what lay beneath the skin, and Napoleon had stopped shrieking. There was nothing to it. My knife had touched Charlotte's, beneath the hide, with a faint *cling* I'd heard or perhaps imagined.

I was glad, for a change, that Janis wasn't with me. I could hear her voice in my head saying, *why did you go on with that?* and the obvious answer was, *why not?* Napoleon was organic, free range. Ethical meat.

After the kill came the butchery. Ric and the English woman, Imogen, had taken care of the bulk of it, with me and Charlie helping. We gathered the blood, sliced the body open, took out the entrails, squeezed the intestine clean, hung it from the low branches of the fig tree, removed the organs. Now the enormous fig tree was garlanded with Napoleon. The sight of the entrails swaying by the orange light of the fire made my head spin. I could still see Ric slicing Napoleon's belly. I could still see my own hand...

I leaned with my forearm on the wooden pillar holding the shower's bamboo screen, and rested my forehead on my arm. What was happening? I closed my eyes; the images were coming, vivid, lurid. The pig being pushed onto the bench. The knife. Blood on Becca's lips. A bucket full of steaming blood. Imogen's hands sinking in the cut in Napoleon's belly, prying the flesh open. The fig tree festooned with bloody interiors. The tree becoming bigger than ever, the size of a hill, a mountain. Charlie, the one clothed woman in the midst of naked people. The fire. I was seeing it all, with my eyes closed.

I screamed and kept screaming.

I had just got a grip of myself when I heard a banging on the door. Ric shouted, 'Zoey! What's happened?'

I turned off the water, and pushed the door open a little, enough to reach and grab the towel hanging from the screen. I came out wrapped in the towel, my skin rough with goosebumps, my hair wet, my head on fire. 'What did you do to me?'

The whole Bastion was there, a small crowd staring at me. They opened their ranks to let Becca come through. She said, 'Why do you ask?'

'With my eyes shut – I can see the butchery. But not only that. I can see the lake house we would go to when I was a little girl. I can see my friend Janis's face. I can imagine the fig tree grown to a gigantic size. I shouldn't be doing any of that! I can't. My condition, *aphantasia*. I was never able to actually *imagine* anything.' I closed my eyes. 'Now I can. I shut my eyes now, I see all of you standing.' I opened them again. 'What did you do to me?'

'We brought you home,' said Ric.

THE BASTION

Bringing Zoey home was hard work. You could almost say that she was balancing out Lila, for how easy it was with her. Lila was born to make people love her. She had a childish sense of wonder, but she was a clear-thinking adult when it mattered.

One morning, on her first summer with us, she strung a loop of fabric to two sticks, filled a bucket with water and eco soap, and started making giant bubbles. They floated lazily among us like enormous amoebas, refracting sunlight into rainbows.

LILA

We all have one special season, or one special day, whose memory we store in a safe place to take out when we have been knocking against the hard corners of life. A Christmas morning, at nine, in which you miraculously got what you wanted, rather than a jumper, socks and pyjamas as per usual; at fifteen, the autumn you spent with the dreamy stranger from a town next to yours, your first lover; your university years, fruitful and filled with parties, culminating on the night of your graduation, when, a grin on your lips and a Spritz in your hand, you were looking forward to the string of successes that adult life was going to be. There is an element of self-deception in the way we look back on those times; we were only happy because we didn't have the full story yet. But we *were* happy.

That summer I was happy. Everybody was. The first Open Feast had been a success, the locals were leaving us to ourselves, and everybody was fond of me and Galen. They called us *Swallows,* in a way that made me feel not as a newcomer who still didn't know her way around, but as a member of the family.

In darker times, Sam said aloud what we all thought without having the courage to say: that he would give everything to go back to that summer, to live there in a loop and never leave. I think we could have done that, if our responsibilities hadn't forced us in another direction.

THE BASTION

We watched Lila's progress with a tremendous sense of accomplishment. It was such a privilege to see her shyness give way to enthusiasm. Galen's attunement was slower, but Lila got there in no time. She was breathing in synch with us before the first week was over.

LILA

Towards the end of July, we moved on to pathworkings. I was excited to get to a new stage. I'd not forgotten Becca's promise, that she'd break open the gates of Heaven and Hell for me.

'A pathworking,' Becca explained, 'is a guided meditation – a path in our mind which we explore together. Specifically, we are going to explore our very pinewood, the place in which we live, seen through the lenses of our inner eyes. What is going to happen, what you are going to see, is in your mind, but not only in your mind.'

Ric said, 'We are told that we live in two worlds. We have a body and we have a soul, a ghost and a machine. Some believe the soul is immortal and will live on after our body breaks down, others think that *soul* is another name for neurochemistry, and as such, it will die with us. Either way they agree there is this physical reality here,' and he touched his breast, 'and another reality inside,' and he brought a hand to his head. 'This is common knowledge. This is also a bag of bollocks.'

'It is a simplistic duality,' Becca said. 'One we will transcend. We will get to a point where the world of matter and the world of soul will be seen for what they are: two different ways of looking at the same thing. If we are ready, please, close your eyes and follow me.'

We took twelve breaths, following her lead, each slower than the one before.

'Keep your eyes closed,' Becca said, 'and open the other eyes you have, the inner eyes. You are in the pinewood. It is the same as ours, but not *exactly* the same. The place where you are now is lying just below the surface of the one you know. Pine needles are greener, and sharper. Trees are taller, rocks sparkle with salts, and the blue in the sky, it's a blue unlike any you've ever seen. Spend some time in this Inner Pinewood. Explore. See what you find.'

I imagined the inner pinewood vividly. Giant soap bubbles were floating all around. I touched one, which gave way under my hand without bursting. *It's my world,* I realised, elated, *I'm a goddess here*. I climbed on the bubble and lay down, with my hands crossed under my head, looking at the sky. The bubble carried me through trees, floating gently, and I felt like dozing. I wondered whether I was falling asleep only in my imagination, or in reality too.

'In your own time,' Becca said, 'find a path through this Inner Pinewood.' Her voice came from the trees, the earth and the sky.

I jumped down from the bubble and saw the path, a dirt track starting between two eucalyptus trees, poised like columns on the forefront of a stage. 'The path goes downhill. Walk it, and keep walking it, and walk. Down, down and down,' Becca's voice invited.

I walked down the path, under a blue sky turning orange.

'Now you've arrived at another place. It is a place you love and cherish. What place is it?'

It was the peasant hut. Of course. It was where I had talked to Galen for the first time, where I had seen the strange sky, where Becca had promised me magic.

The bubbles were gone.

There was a chill in the air. I could make out – something. A sound, maybe a voice. I took one step towards the hut, then another. What was different? The hut was freshly painted. I took another step.

The hut's door banged.

I jumped and stopped in my tracks. The bang had been only in my mind – right? I could tell the difference between this make-believe world and the real sounds (birdsong, breath) coming at me through my ears. Of course I could.

Silence, then – the door banged again. The whole hut was now banging, as if immense fists were punching the walls and the roof from within. Transfixed, I saw the hut bulge. I saw it heave, I saw it swell. The banging grew louder. The door's hinges stretched, but they didn't give. *Thankfully.* The banging grew louder still. A wall cracked.

Becca's voice said, 'Go inside.'

As if.

But then I reminded myself that this was my own imagination, and who's afraid of their own imagination? I just had to open my eyes to go back to the real world. That reasoning made me lose focus. I couldn't see the hut or the pinewood anymore, just a jumble of images (Galen's head sinking between my legs, my hand slashing Napoleon's throat, the other girls at school throwing a volleyball at me pretending it was a mistake).

I wasn't doing the meditation right. I could never do anything right. I furiously tried to pick up the thread. *The lovely place,* I thought, *the lovely place.* The harder I tried, the less it worked. *Focus!* I ordered myself. My mind answered, *fuck you.* I was panicking.

'What do you see?' Becca asked. 'What do you feel?'

I opened my eyes. Becca was looking at me. She smiled, mouthed, *it's okay.*

I shut my eyes again, and now, in my imagination, I was safe in Becca's arms.

Mum and Dad came at dusk.

THE BASTION

They came in a black BMW. Our gate had a bell they did not bother to use. They just pushed the gate open (we never kept it locked at that stage) and drove down our little path among the pines and the eucalyptus trees. They pulled over, blew the horn twice, and got out. Lila's father was dressed in loafers, jeans, a light green polo shirt, Ray-bans, a ruby ring. Her mother wore a yellow dress, pearls, and a dark expression on her face.

Sam was cleaning the porch when they came. He leaned on his mop and said, 'Yes?'

The man marched up to him. 'I want my daughter.'

'That's dicey, man.'

Lila's dad started as if to hit Sam – and Sam recoiled. Poor Sam, he was a gentle soul, better at talking than thinking things through. 'Jesus. Calm down.'

The man shoved Sam. 'Don't tell me to calm down!' He shoved Sam again.

We were coming, attracted by the commotion. Ric came out of Villa Abbracciavento and saw this stranger manhandling one of us. 'Please, stop,' he said.

The man's head whipped to him. 'Or what?'

Ric offered him a hand. 'I'm Ric.'

The man stared at Ric, stared at his outstretched hand. 'Dr Vincenzo Brasca,' he said, refusing to shake it.

Ric let it fall and asked the woman, 'And the lady is...'

'Daniela's mother,' she answered.

'So you don't have a name then.'

'I'm a judge,' Dr Brasca huffed and puffed. 'Get it? A judge. I could call the police and have you arrested. They work for me, *capito*?' He took out his expensive phone and shook it in front of Ric's nose to make his point. 'I want my daughter. *Right now.*'

We saw Ric clench and unclench his fist. We saw him look up at the sky, the way he did when he was struggling to keep control. We half-hoped Dr Brasca would try and shove him too. 'Come with me. I'll get you guys a drink, something to eat. Must have been a long drive.'

'I'm taking my daughter and leaving.'

'While we wait.'

LILA

I was on the beach with Galen and the Nameless. We chatted away and drank cold beer in the water, at its warmest at sunset, until the early stars came out and we made our way back in that in-between light which is not day anymore and not night yet. I was laughing and seriously considering an idea Galen had proposed and the Nameless had endorsed (it involved ropes: Mikka apparently knew the rudiments of Shibari and was happy to give lessons), when I saw Mum and Dad sitting at the dinner table as if at a funeral reception, with wine and taralli, in the light given off by the oil lamp hanging from a rope above them. Dad was shooing away a mosquito. It took me a few breaths to register what I was seeing – two worlds colliding.

I felt this terrible loss inside me. What I had with Galen, with the Bastion – it was over. I was expecting Dad to shout at me, but it was worse. Mum jumped to her feet and said, *thank God you're safe!* and she started crying, and she made me feel the way only she could make me feel: like I was the lowest human being on Earth.

Galen and the Nameless receded into the trees, leaving me alone with my family. Mum hugged me – not in the soothing way Becca did, but with a proprietary hug, one which didn't say *I'm yours*, but rather, *you're mine*. Mum sobbed on my shoulder, then suddenly grabbed me by the arms and shook me. 'Why did you do this to us?' she asked. 'Why?'

'Mum...'

'Sit,' Dad's icy voice came.

I was a well-trained dog: I bowed my head and obeyed. I sat down quietly in front of him, at the same table where I had joked and flirted with my other family. It was like the pinewood disappeared. The trees faded, the sound of sea waves stopped, and the lantern was this theatrical spotlight pointed on us: Dad, Mum and me. We were alone on stage and everywhere else was black.

'Before we leave,' Dad ordered, 'you are going to tell me who these people are and what you are doing with them.'

'How did you find me?'

'Answer me!' he shouted, slamming a hand on the table.

I jumped.

THE BASTION

We were watching.

It was painful to see our beautiful Lila with her head down, her shoulders bent, her hands folded in her lap. Ric's expression was like bark, rough and still. Lila's father could not see him, and never understood how close he was to getting hurt that night.

'Sorry,' Lila said, after her father shouted in her face.

Ric clenched his fist.

'Don't be an idiot,' Becca whispered.

LILA

Dad asked me if this was some kind of squat, and I answered that they owned the land.

'Who's they?'

'My friends. Becca and Ric.'

'Some friends! Stealing children from their family.'

'I'm not a child and I came here of my own will.'

'I've never heard of these *friends* before.'

'Because you know everything about my life.'

'I should.'

I turned to Mum. 'Say something.'

'Daniela, what did you do to your hair?'

'It's just a haircut.'

'Your beautiful hair.' Mum shook her head slowly. 'We're worried for you.'

'I'm fine! I needed some time. To clear my mind.'

'You could do that at home.'

'Some time on my own.'

'*Time on my own!*' My father mocked my voice. 'Can you even hear yourself? You say you're not a kid? Then stop whining like one!'

'We are your family,' Mum said. 'We want what's best for you. Put yourself in our shoes. When you called me, you said you were staying with friends, but we find you here, in this remote place, with people we don't know. Dad and I are just trying to understand.'

'I met them online.'

'My poor little girl, they groomed you!'

'I'll have someone look into it,' said Dad.

'It's nothing like that! They threw a party, that's why I came here. Then I decided to stay a little longer.'

'With what money?'

'They're just letting me stay.'

'Of course, because a bunch of perfect strangers would just *let you stay*!' He was raising his voice again.

'They did nothing wrong. I did. I shouldn't have run from home, you're right. But it's not their fault.'

'You couldn't even finish school,' he said, hitting me with a disappointment more brutal than a slap. 'What do you know.'

The ring of bangles came to me like the bell of a ship in the fog to a castaway. Three heads turned towards Becca, who said, 'Apologies.'

Whatever remark Dad had, he kept to himself.

'I'm Becca, the owner of this house. We're about to serve dinner.'

He said, 'We'll be on our way. Lila, go pack.'

I stood up, defeated.

'Stay,' Becca said. 'For dinner.'

'It's a long drive home,' Mum said.

'Indeed. You can stay the night and leave first thing tomorrow.'

'No, thanks.'

'I'm asking as a personal favour. It seems we started on the wrong foot and I'd love to have a chance to rewind and start again. Please?' She winked. 'Besides, you've been driving all day, and you've had wine. It'd be ill-advised to jump in the car now. You know what would be perfectly advised though?

'What?' Dad asked.

'More wine.'

THE BASTION

We had more wine. That, and *tubettini* pasta with a broth of mussels and fresh tomatoes, sea urchins we had fished that afternoon, our own prosciutto, watermelon from our field and peaches from our tree. We managed to surround those morons in a cloud of love. We taught them to open the sea urchins and scoop the contents with a spoon. We never let their glasses go empty.

Lila's father looked at Becca the way a greedy kid looks at a fat cake overflowing with cream. He kept licking his lips when he thought nobody would notice. It was disgusting, and each of us – each of us, even Sam, the most peaceful man you will ever meet – dearly wished to head-butt him. But we pretended to laugh at his jokes, for love of Lila. We pretended to admire the quick-fire career he told us everything about, and to humble ourselves before his status, as a judge in the North, where money was. Each sip of wine made his sexual innuendos more explicit. Our laughs became more strained, and he did not notice, or did not care. Halfway through the dinner he felt in control of the situation enough to boast about how he had found us – by asking 'his guys' to trace Lila's phone.

'Is that legal?' Galen asked. 'Lila isn't underage.'

The man grinned at him. 'I'm still her father.'

A glance from Becca killed Galen's response. He just nodded and asked us to pass him the wine.

Dr Brasca's wife was no better than him. She was one of those people who make a faux meekness their shield and sword. She used love as a currency with Lila. She would say, 'Daniela is my whole world. She always came first for me! I could have had a great career – I was a teacher, and I was going to become head teacher when Daniela was born, a prestigious school, but I left my job to be a full-time mum. Didn't I, Daniela?' And Lila's only choices were to answer *yes* or throw a tantrum like a child. When she answered *yes*, her mother would go on, 'So what did I do wrong, that you hate me so much?' and Lila had to debase herself and say she didn't hate her at all, she loved her, in fact. And on and on it went.

It was a ghastly dinner, and one we think back to with pride. We kept our cool. We were nothing but amiable. Sam didn't suddenly let out a howl, as he would do on other nights for a laugh, Mikka didn't tell any prison stories, and when Dr Brasca complimented the prosciutto we did not tell him we had slaughtered the pig with our bare hands. There were a couple of us who would often sing sea shanties at dinner, and they refrained. Another who usually refused to use cutlery (for his own political reasons), but that night he did. And Ric – Ric was the best of us, for how he kept his temper under control.

'We are a group of friends,' Becca explained. 'Sharing the chores.'

'A commune,' Lila's father said.

'That's a loaded word. Let's say we are a home for those who don't have a home elsewhere.'

'Commendable. But Daniela has a home, whatever she might have led you to believe. A good one at that. A luxurious one. She doesn't know how lucky she is.'

'I see.'

'You're a smart woman, you know the type of my daughter. She had everything growing up, *every-fucking-thing*. It is our fault for spoiling her! Her mother doted on her too much. Me, all I have – my career, my house – I worked hard to get.' He shook his well-groomed fist, as if he'd climbed mountains and fought wolves bare-handed before heading for a manicure. 'Daniela has no idea. She doesn't appreciate how good she has it.'

'Arrogance is such a problem.'

'Exactly! A problem I never had. Always worked hard. Very hard. I still do. *I work hard*. At everything,' he added for good measure, raising his eyebrows.

And Becca pretended not to understand, and smiled, and kept her conversation polite, while Ric imagined what fun it would be to stick two sea urchins into that man's eyes, and a third one down his throat.

LILA

That was the worst dinner of my life. When it was over, I pretended I'd always slept on a hammock (it was out of the question that I could spend the night in my room with Galen) and headed into the pines, for what I was expecting to be my last night with the Bastion. My parents were sleeping in the room I shared with Galen.

I'd been cast out of a dream. Kicked back to grim reality. And perhaps for that reason I felt the aliveness in our land stir. I felt that the strange sky was just out of reach, and if I looked at the right angle, I would *see*. A thin line of smoke came from a spiral-shaped mosquito fumigator on the ground. Even that smelled better here than it did back home.

I was sobbing silently in my hammock when Galen arrived, with a throw folded under his arm. He brought a finger to his lips to gesture me to be silent, and leaned over to kiss me. His tongue touched my teeth and I shivered. He caressed my cheek, then peeled away from me and unfolded the throw on the ground. The throw had a Cheshire Cat on it. Galen took off his t-shirt. I pointed my toes to the ground and, with my bum still in the hammock, took off mine.

Soon we were naked, skin on skin, rolling on the throw. My kisses had the desperate quality of last times, but then I let Galen draw me out of myself. I loved the face he made when he came, biting his own lips not to cry out. I had to bite his hand, and shook violently.

Afterwards, Galen whispered in my ear, 'Ric said to meet him on the beach.'

'What? Why?'

He didn't answer. He gave me one last kiss and gathered his clothes. I watched him leave, and after a while, I put my clothes back on and headed to the beach.

Ric was sitting on a rock with his feet in the almost perfectly still water, smoking a joint. When I sat down with him, he handed me the joint. I took a long drag. No weed tasted as good as the one we grew. 'I'll miss this,' I said. 'Among other things.'

'You don't have to leave, if you don't want to.'

'I have to, though.'

'Why?'

'They're my family.'

'That doesn't give them power of life and death over you.'

'You don't know them. They'd never forgive me, they'd...' I trailed off. I raised a hand. 'Only daughter here. Mum would be heartbroken.'

'When love is a leash, it's no love at all.'

I handed him the joint. 'You think my parents don't love me?'

'Say you love your cat. You want what's best for him, because, yeah, you love him. You want him to be safe! And he's not very safe wandering around, picking up slutty lady cats, getting into fights with streetwise tomcats. So you cut his balls off. We may discuss the nature of your love for your cat until the world's end, but the inescapable reality, the one bare fact, is that your cat does not have any balls anymore.'

'But he's safe.'

'Tell that to the cat. What do you think he'd answer, being a cat? He'll say, *better safe than sorry is no life. Better sorry than safe, by a mile.*'

I chuckled.

Ric asked, 'What's waiting for you back home?'

'Dad wants me to go back to school, but I'm not doing that. I've been working temp jobs this past year, shops, call centres. I'm going to find something.'

'Call centres! Fucking hell. There's plenty to do on our farm. You don't have to work, but if you want to, you can.'

'And what happens when you get tired of me?'

Ric took one last drag. He snuffed the butt on the rock and pocketed it. 'Do you *get tired* of your friends? Is that the kind of person you are?'

'No!'

'Us neither.'

The weed gave me the courage to say, 'You don't get the full picture.'

'Help me out.'

'Dad and Mum *will never allow me to stay*. If I don't go, Dad will call the guards on you guys. He's top brass, that part is true. They'll find your weed, the other stuff, they'll make your life hell. I've got to go for sake of you guys, if nothing else.'

Ric was rolling another joint. I took in the subtle music of backwash, and the immense expanse of the dark sea. I wished I was a pirate queen, sailing and pillaging, with Galen by my side, and lovers on every island, treasure on every far-flung beach. There was so much to explore, to enjoy, so many colours beyond the astroturf of my town, so much chaos beyond Mum's tidy kitchen.

'He does that a lot, your old man?' Ric said.

'Does what?'

'Uses his taxpayer-funded privilege to get what he wants for himself.'

'You have no idea.'

'How interesting,' Ric said, and licked the edge of the fresh joint. 'He must have broken the law many times.'

I turned my head to look at him.

'You don't have to do anything you don't want to,' Ric said. 'You don't have to go, you don't have to stay. You're free to make your own choices. It's only a matter of finding the balls to do what it takes. It's scary, I know, but do you remember Napoleon?' Ric lit the joint, the little flame of his Zippo blazing on his face. 'Choices. Responsibility.'

'You guys do want me to stay.'

'We're not going to pressure you, or we wouldn't be any

different from your mum and dad, but let me be clear – yes, we want you to stay. So. Fucking. Much.'

'Why?'

'We need a drummer.'

I took the joint from Ric's fingers. 'You must need one really badly.'

'Yeah, we drum a lot round here.'

'What else?'

'Galen's hot and if you go we're afraid we may lose him too.'

'Hey! I'm hot too.'

'Smoking, but it didn't feel appropriate to say that.'

I laughed. 'And that is all.'

'All I'm going to say for now, yes.' Ric took his feet out of the water, and stood up. 'You can finish off the spliff. Good night, Lila.'

'Good night, Ric.'

He left me alone on the beach. The lights of Portodimare twinkled in the distance. A hoopoe called from the pinewood. The sea was quiet, the sky full of stars, and it was all good.

THE BASTION

Lila came to breakfast with her backpack ready. We were crestfallen, most of us, but then we noticed she didn't have her drum, and Galen smiled and winked. After a quick coffee, Lila jumped in the car with her family and left.

'I was terrified,' she would say later.

Of what? we would ask.

'Of never making it back.'

Passing through the pinewood's gate made me sick. I struggled to keep the coffee down. We weren't out of Portodimare before Mum and Dad were lecturing me about my future. Dad had arranged for a private school in Biella to take me. I'd get a diploma by next summer, and after that, I would start law school. If that was not good enough for me, I could suck it up and do it anyway, one day I'd be grateful, et cetera et cetera.

I realised I was furious.

Ric, Becca and the others had treated me like an adult. A *badass* adult. They wanted me around for no other reason than they liked me. They trusted me; they were teaching me their secrets. Mum and Dad had taken a lot from me. I wouldn't allow them to take this too.

It was a long, joyless journey, in a car which clocked up miles like a chore and pressed on me with the brutality of a prison. We stopped for lunch at a station, where they had mass-produced pizza which, after weeks of real food, had all the flavour and taste of an ashtray bottom. I barely spoke, which infuriated Mum and Dad. 'You could learn something from your friends back there,' Mum said. 'They were a lot more polite than you.'

I have learnt, I thought, but I kept my thoughts to myself.

We made it to our town by early evening. I was surprised – pleasantly so – to look at the condo where I grew up and feel absolutely nothing. No longing, no hatred. That place was not home anymore, it was the context of a life which was not mine. I was there out of necessity. I would do what must be done and get out.

And so that night, when my parents slept the sleep of the just after the long drive and the disruption of the last couple of days,

I slipped inside my father's office, fired up his computer, typed in the password (the same since time immemorial: Mum's name and her date of birth), and backed up the computer's disk on a cloud service. While the backup went on, I took Dad's phone and my own laptop, and backed up the first on the second, then on the same cloud service too, for good measure.

It took me a couple of hours, which I spent reading through my father's chats. Then I went to my old room for a farewell. The girl who had been sleeping in there was dead. Nobody would miss her, certainly not the new Lila. I took my backpack, called a cab, and before leaving, I knocked on my parents' door.

'Lila?' Mum called from the room.

I went in and turned on the light.

They squinted, drew themselves up. 'What's going on?' Dad said.

'I'm leaving.'

'No, you're not.'

'Shut up and listen.'

'I won't…'

I wanted to scream at the top of my voice. It wouldn't be the first time I'd screamed at them, and like every single time in the past, it would be useless.

What would Ric do? He would do what must be done, with an economy of words and movements.

'I backed up your computer,' I said. 'And your messages. An obsession for Asian girls, Dad? Could you get more of a racist cliche than that?'

'What are you talking about?' Mum said.

'Oh, Mum, come off it. You know what I'm talking about, you always did. But anyway, porn and prostitutes are the least of it. The deals – now, *they* are the good stuff. The strings you pulled.

The favours you asked and conceded. Starting with the most recent, your tracing a private citizen's phone – mine. Creepy as fuck, and also, illegal. No, Dad, I said shut up.'

He obeyed.

'I'm leaving now. Where I'm heading is none of your business. You're not only going to leave me be, you're also going to leave my friends be. You as much as look at us the wrong way, this goes public. *Capito*?'

'Daniela...'

I took out my phone. 'You say, *yes, madam*, or it goes public now. I'm dead serious.'

Dad leaped out of bed with the grunt of a boar. I stepped back, but I was weighted by my backpack, and Dad was on me, slapping my face so hard to make my head snap to the side. He grabbed my wrist, while Mum shouted; for him or against him, I couldn't tell. He had never beaten me, not really *beaten*, but he had slapped me, and he had only stopped spanking me at around the age of ten. When you've been programmed to be afraid, it's hard to snap out of it. I was on the verge of letting him take the phone, and the next steps would be deleting the backups, and apologising, and going back to being a good daughter, this awful idiot's good daughter.

But the Lila who would have acted this way was dead, and reborn as a new woman. I was not the one who got dumped by a loser boyfriend via DM; I was the one whose drumming was the backbone of glorious parties, I was the one who'd landed the hottest boyfriend on planet Earth, I was the one who had seen the light of impossible stars. I worked magic. I was on a sacred mission with my secret family. I was with the Bastion.

And they were with me as I fought back. They lent me their strength when I shoved my father. We rested a hand on his head, we stuck a thumb in his eye, and pushed. He screamed like Napoleon, and it pleased us. We hit him in the belly, in the balls, we made him double down and crash to the floor, and we kicked him in the back. Only once, no more, for violence is a fact of life, but cruelty is a choice.

'You guys come close to us,' I panted, 'you're finished.'

The cab was waiting for me downstairs. The flight Galen had booked for me was on time, my journey back unadventurous. The guys made me linguine and we celebrated my freedom with our best white wine, a bonfire and music. The orgy that night was delicious.

ZOEY

When I tried to explain to Janis that I was going to spend the rest of summer with the Bastion, I found myself hitting a wall.

'First you fall off the face of the Earth,' Janis said, and her voice was angry over the phone. 'You don't answer my calls, you don't read my texts, you make me worry sick. Now you call me to say you're going to stay there *for the entire summer*?'

The baby cried in the background.

'You're not listening,' I said. Janis's lack of understanding was pissing me off. 'What happened yesterday is... I need to make sense of it.'

'It was literally – and I mean literally – all in your head!'

'Yes, it was!'

I felt the frustration common to all those whose experience of the world does not align with what an experience of the world is supposed to be. The best-meaning people will say they listen to you, and they'll think they're doing just that, but what they call *listening* is a translation of your stories into theirs. Rather than try and imagine what your life is like for you, they try and imagine what your life would be like *for them*, which is only apparently the same. With a condition as elusive as mine, this happened all the time. Most folks couldn't even understand what the condition, in practice, entailed.

'You know how many doctors I've seen,' I said. 'And hypnotherapists, and gurus. Nothing helped. There is no treatment! No one even knows what causes aphantasia in the first place.'

'Except for the hippies in the woods with their secret elixir.'

'I close my eyes now, I see Ellie in your lap.'

'Ellie would rather see you for real.'

'But she will! Come September, she will.'

'What did they do that's so special?' Janis insisted. 'How did they... heal you?'

'A mix of things. I don't know, I'm trying to figure it out.'

I didn't mention slaughtering Napoleon. It allowed for an all-too-easy pop-psychology explanation: I had gone through an edgy experience, my first kill, and that had opened a door in my mind. It did not hold water. I'd enjoyed my fair share of edginess before, and the door had remained solidly shut.

'I don't follow. Okay, let's say they found a new spiritual tech, some trick of the mind. You know what, great, our hunch was right, there's something to these folks. See if you can manage to sign them for SoulJo. If they're in, you can fuck off and come back home; if they're out, same.'

The other secret I kept from Janis was what Becca and Ric had told me the night before. *We are on a mission and we need you*. The kind of words which normally would send me packing – and yet. It was too awkward to explain over the phone. When I went back to NY, Janis and I would have a full debrief in person, hopefully without the baby crying between us.

I played the irony card. 'But it's so beautiful here. Best holiday of my life.'

'With a cult. In their secret lair.'

I laughed. 'Don't get too excited, it's more Club Med than Dennis Wheatley.'

'We've got lots to do though.'

'SoulJo is in May! I can easily work from here at this stage. I've got Wi-Fi, I've got a laptop, I've got a phone.'

'Well, please use them then. My hands are full enough with Ellie, I can't take care of the whole business on my own.'

'It was only a few days, okay? I got carried away. I will be more present from now on, I promise.'

The baby gurgled and murmured.

CHARLIE

The Bastion brought me back to life. I went from talking only to Lila to also talking to Becca, then Ric, then all of them. I was able to make Imogen laugh, which, I was told, was unheard of. 'Your accent,' Imogen said. 'I love it.' I'd mess around with Sam, and though it would be the end of summer before I slept with him (or anybody else), I allowed him to strip me of my clothes, innocently, at the fire. From then on, I'd dance naked like the rest of them. You never heal from the kind of loss I went through, but you can build a wall around the hole it left, and contain it.

The pathworkings were the highlight of my day. Becca and Ric would take turns guiding us, alternating their styles (Becca's richer, Ric's starker), and gradually adding elements to the Inner

Pinewood – Villa Abbracciavento inside and out, specific trees, large rocks – until one place became almost the exact double of the other, and the pinewood in our mind was like the real one, with the volume turned up high. When I closed my eyes and journeyed there, I was swept up by a sense of possibility. This place was real in a different way than the mundane pinewood, but no less so.

In this place Bertrand's music was always playing. His voice was unmistakable. No one else made the saxophone vibrate that way, no one else imbued 'Ruby, My Dear' with such vitality. Bertrand would play other songs too, and I would giggle and spin with my arms outstretched. On the best days I would see the music as a serpent of deep-blue light slithering through the trees.

It was more than the music; Bertrand's presence was everywhere. Now it was the scent of his skin in the sunshine; now it was the waves of worry he gave off before a concert; now it was the stuttering joy of our wedding day. It had to be more than just memories. Becca had said that the music was Bertrand, and maybe so were the scents and the emotions. My husband had come back in a way I could sense, if not see. It had to be true. An illusion would be too cruel.

'We're going to take a couple of days off,' Ric announced at morning call. 'Then we are ready for the Receding Wave. The grand finale.'

ZOEY

It was Mikka who proposed we go for drinks in the village. I'd all but forgotten a village existed, and I said yes mostly because he seemed so eager. Lila wanted to go too, and cajoled Charlie into going with us. As I passed through the gate, I realised I hadn't left since I came for the Open Feast.

We took a pavement sided with palm trees. We walked by couples, prams, whole families, elderly people, teenagers and cigarettes. Absurdly, cars would run on the road, noisy and foul-smelling. This was real and the pinewood was real too, and the two realities didn't gel. To start with, everybody had their clothes on.

Lila and Mikka were used to switching their mind-frame between our heightened world and this one, but I wasn't. Making our way to the village exhausted me. 'It's worrying,' I said. 'I'm not sure I can take people anymore.'

'What's worrying about it?' said Charlie.

The French woman is cracking jokes now, I thought. *It's progress, I suppose.*

The piazza was packed. There were people strolling, people sitting on plastic chairs spread in front of the bars, people lounging on short walls and benches, people everywhere. I said that it felt like a festival.

'It's like that every night, for the whole season,' said Lila.

'Do you Italians ever work?'

Lila made a so-so gesture.

The tables were all taken. We hovered above them and when a family left theirs, Lila swooped down on it before other groups did. So we secured a place in front of the Bar Aloha, a little kiosk blasting Italian pop music, with young people crowding to get drinks. 'No table service,' Mikka said. 'What are you having?' He took orders and bravely ventured into the crowd, coming back with a tray a little later. He gave Lila her beer, Charlie her mojito, me my whiskey on the rocks, and set the last glass, black liquor with ice, in front of himself.

'What's that?' Charlie asked.

'Try,' he said, pushing the glass to her.

She sipped the liquor, and gagged. 'Vile.'

'An old man's drink,' Mikka laughed.

'This guy could drink gasoline,' I said.

Mikka made a mock bow with his head. 'Thank you.'

I closed my eyes. 'I can visualise you quaffing that dreadful limoncello you make.'

'Our Zoey,' Mikka teased, 'who believes in miracles now.'

'I don't *believe*. I know. The miracle is in here, in my head, every time I shut my eyes.'

'I was weirded out for weeks after my first Napoleon,' Lila said.

'I've seen plenty of death in my job,' said Charlie. 'My husband passed right in front of me. Couldn't care less about a pig.'

Lila's voice went down a notch. 'Of course.'

'It was helpful though,' Charlie added, with a smile. 'It made me think that a life gone is not necessarily a life wasted. I feel good. Better than I have in a long time.'

Mikka lifted his glass. 'Cheers to that.'

'Cheers,' the others answered.

I told Lila, 'You're vegetarian.'

'That I am.'

'And you killed Napoleon all the same?'

'Everything is alive, Zoey. Every rock, every tree, every fruit, every leaf. The Cosmos and the dust on every planet, it's all living. Forests communicate, mushrooms grow networks. Who are we to think that only animals suffer? Why not the tomatoes we rip from the vines, why not the peaches we pull from their branches, why not the rocks on which we walk? I'm vegetarian, yep, but I know that if I asked a carrot, they'd beg me to go get a steak. At the end of the day we do need to eat, and we need to cut trees and rocks to make houses. For something to live something else must die; for one thing to continue, another must end. This is what we mean when we say that violence is a fact of life. The stuff that goes on in your body every time you put a morsel inside – it's brutal. Teeth slashing and pounding, acids boiling.' She touched her belly. 'Wars are being waged inside here as we talk. We make our choices as to which kind of violence we are or aren't comfortable with, like me refusing to eat meat, but doing away with violence altogether? That's not an option. I needed to understand that. I'd never have managed to escape those assholes from my birth family without that lesson. I'll be grateful to Becca and Ric for ever.'

I closed my eyes and Napoleon rushed back to me. 'I'm seeing Napoleon. It works every time.' I pointed my whiskey at Mikka, then Lila. 'Why's it called the Receding Wave? Anyone?'

'Because,' Lila said, 'what happens before a tsunami...?'

THE BASTION

'The Receding Wave starts at noon,' Ric explained at morning call. We were so excited! 'From today, no one is leaving the pinewood – not to go to the beach, not to go to the shops. Also, we're going to keep our phones, tablets and laptops off for the duration. We're going to have no contact with the outside, no contact whatsoever, like during the Open Feast. More so, in fact: there're no staff with their phones on, and also, we're putting away books, magazines, that sort of thing. Reading is a reaching out with our mind, and we're not going out, we're going *in*. What else? No alcohol, no drugs, and I'm including fags, coffee, chocolate and tea. If you use a wristwatch, put it away please. Same goes for paper calendars. We're taking all of them down. No artificial timekeeping of any sort. Does it make sense so far?'

We nodded.

'Also,' Ric went on, 'we're not going to speak. At all. We're not talking to each other, we're not singing in the shower, we're not muttering if that's what we do. No drumming, no music. No pathworkings either, no Breathing Spell, and obviously no morning call and no all-in-all. The one thing we *are* going to do, every night at the fire, is hum. The goal is to hum in unison, with the same timing, same pitch, same all. And before Zoey asks,' Ric said, turning to her, and we all laughed, Zoey included, 'this is going to last for as long as we need to reach a breakthrough, or otherwise until Becca puts a stop to it. One day? One month?' He shrugged.

Zoey said, 'I've got a question.'

'Course you do,' Ric laughed. 'Shoot.'

'What kind of breakthrough are we talking about?'

'No clue. We've never had one so far.'

'That's not encouraging.'

'Right?' Ric clapped his hands once. 'You've got the morning to say your farewells. We're meeting at Becca's tree at quarter to twelve.'

ZOEY

I had to see where this led, if anywhere, even though it meant taking another break from SoulJo. The overall usefulness for the festival was well worth it. The Bastion *worked*. I'd gained a power of visualisation I'd never had, Charlie was moving on from her loss with remarkable speed, and what did Lila say about escaping abuse? The next Osho, my ass. The Bastion had it in them to do some real good. The problem was telling Janis. Sometimes I felt that now Janis had moved on with her life, she didn't want me to do the same. She wished me to be a solid rock, a wet nurse.

Puglia was six hours ahead of New York and I was not going to freak her out with a call in the middle of the night. Even if I waited until the last moment it would still be early morning in NY, and Janis was one for slow awakenings. Talking to her before coffee was suicide. If the baby was keeping her awake, she'd be nervous. If the baby was letting her sleep and I was the one waking her up, she'd send me a telepathic death ray. I dropped her an email.

Hey Janis. DON'T GET MAD AT ME: I'm going incommunicado. I don't know for how long this time, a bunch of days I think, a week, tops. It's for a thing we're doing, I'll explain later. I'm answering all the emails I have and setting an out-of-office before shutting down, and I know, I know, it's going to be more work for you, but I PROMISE it's all freaky good for SoulJo. The Bastion are going to be a smash hit. I've got some crazy stories for you when we meet, like, properly bonkers. I'll do everything I can to apologise, okay? Everything. Still sisters? Love you lots, Zoey xxx

I hesitated before hitting *send*. With a freshly minted baby, the last thing Janis needed was an increased workload. But what was the alternative? Leaving now, after all the work I'd put into befriending the Bastion, would not be professional. My responsibilities towards SoulJo were more important than Janis's short-term worries. This *breakthrough* Ric had mentioned could be game-changing.

I left the email in my draft folder while I cleaned my inbox as much as I could and set the out-of-office. Then I went back to it, read it again, and hit *send* with a quick short tap, like a child touching a hairy spider. I immediately turned off the laptop, turned off my phone, undid my Apple Watch, took my Kindle, and put everything in my backpack.

Ready, steady, action.

THE BASTION

We flocked to the fig tree with our bags, our backpacks, our laptops and phones. Lila gathered our stuff in a pile at her feet. 'I'll lock this in one of the vans, as per usual,' she said. 'Is that all right?'

It was.

We were eager to start. We poured chilled shots of Mikka's limoncello (it was as bad as Zoey said, so bad that it had acquired a legendary status among us), with Becca watching over us, radiant with her smile, her long skirt, her bangles. She was beautiful. Her shot was the last we poured. She said, 'Are we excited?'

Very, we answered.

'Before we go, have your last words. Speak up, shout, make your voice heard.'

'Fuuuuck!' Sam said, and we laughed.

We howled, we sang, we shouted quotes of Maya Angelou and Bob Dylan, we exchanged declarations of love and lust. When the noise abated, Becca raised her glass, and we raised ours. 'And remember,' she said. 'This is the Inner Pinewood.'

She downed her glass, and we downed ours, and any questions Zoey or Charlie may have had about those words, it was too late to ask. We would have joked about how awful the limoncello was, but as we opened our mouths we remembered we couldn't.

The first afternoon was a farce. Sam would make exaggerated faces to convey his thoughts, Mikka would make obscene gestures, Imogen would roll her eyes and shake her head conspicuously. The novelty of not being allowed to use words made us hyper-communicate.

Those of us on kitchen duty made dinner in a ballet of arms stretched to point at this spice and that sauce, thank-you flourishes, friendly pushes and pulls. When we sat down to eat, the exaggerated gestures continued, to ask for the salt, cheese, a second serving. We were frustrated when another did not understand what we wanted. Our words were hitting the walls of our mouth to burst out, and we had to struggle to contain them. We reached out for a glass of wine and found only water.

The hum that night was a disaster. Getting the pitch right was hard at the best of times (it was necessary to find the right vibration, the right volume, the right tempo, synch the pauses for breathing), and Becca could only guide us through gestures. Imogen noticed Zoey's frustration, and shrugged at her. Zoey smiled a thank-you. She had never noticed before the way Imogen's hair fell on the right side of her face. She had found Imogen too stuck-up to be attractive, but that night she wondered how it would be to kiss her.

When we stopped humming, the silence around the bonfire had a strange pull. It was unusual to hear the sea waves so clearly, and the more-than-human voices in our pinewood. We stood there staring at the stars and the fire, on our own, or in groups of two or three, one's head lying on another's chest, and some of us saw shapes in the flames. For some, it was frustrating not being able to speak; others found it relaxing. You didn't have to come up with anything to say, so you could just sit back and chill. We dozed in the cozy warmth of the fire, or went to sleep.

The second day, boredom kicked in. There are only so many faces you can pull and so many times you can outstretch your arms. With nothing to do, nothing to read, no place to go, we had no clue what to make of ourselves, so we did nothing. The hours dragged on, limitless, for without clocks we couldn't tell when one ended and another began. By the end of the third or fourth day we were not sure whether it was the third or fourth day. Without a calendar, we couldn't say, and without the option of asking others, we were left to wonder by ourselves. Caffeine withdrawal gave us headaches. To entertain ourselves we paid attention to details, like the chirrup of crickets and the texture of sunlight dappling through the canopy of trees. *This is the Inner Pinewood,* Becca had said, and it almost felt like it.

More time passed. Boredom grew into anxiety. We itched to get out, have a swim, say something. The smallest mistakes would make us flare up. Imogen gave Sam a killer look when he dropped a plate he was washing and broke it, things like that. On such occasions our outrage boiled and bubbled inside us like a nauseating broth, until it consumed itself and disappeared. We wondered when we would finally get the hum right. We wondered what would happen then.

More time passed. Every night at the bonfire we kept humming and we kept failing. Yesterday's mistakes bled into tonight's. We couldn't tell whether Becca had just gestured us to drop our voice a little, or she had done that another night. The way we organised our days changed. With no notion of hours or minutes, we measured time by the natural rhythms of light, darkness and scents – and we noticed that the days were getting shorter. Our sleep patterns changed too: we snatched sleep here and there rather than getting a big chunk at night and a smaller one in the afternoon. Charlie missed the pathworkings, when she heard Bertrand's music, but she held to the memory of them. She would sit down for hours remembering them, and she could almost hear the music. *This is the Inner Pinewood.*

More time passed. We were having sex everywhere. You would take a walk and bump into a couple, turn a corner and be grabbed by a foursome looking for a fifth. At first we fucked out of boredom, then gradually sex became a part of our day and it was another thing we did, like eat and hum. Without words, our meetings were raw, stripped to the bare essentials. Zoey had a three-way with Sam and Mikka, which she had been angling for, although Mikka wanted to be involved only with Sam, to her disappointment. Sam and Charlie went for it (finally), and were they loud in the kitchen. Charlie's laughter, at the climax, filled us with hope – she was healing, at last. Our moans, our cries, came like voices from another reality. We fucked in any different number and combination, to exhaustion. Even Becca and Ric joined in, which they would rarely do.

Once, when she was with Zoey, Charlie heard Bertrand's music again.

She took her hand from Zoey's back to point a finger at her own ear. Zoey nodded, as surprised as Charlie – she heard it too. Charlie made a large smile and sunk on Zoey again, to the tune of Bertrand blessing her. *This is the Inner Pinewood.*

More time passed. We reached a new clarity of mind, in which we could appreciate the minute detail of the chirp of every bird, the fact that the bark of every tree was a miniature forest. We came to the end of summer, when days grow shorter, smells mellow, and the August heat evaporates. There was an easing in the air. We were wearing cotton jumpers at night now.

Summer's ending brought the first storm, with lightning and the thrilling scent of ozone. We repaired inside Villa Abbracciavento to watch the sky crack with blue light, and when the lightning subsided, we went out to dance naked in the rain. Every drop was a kiss on our skin. Reality was as vibrant as our imagination. *This is the Inner Pinewood.*

More time passed, and then one night we unlocked the hum, and broke through.

CHARLIE

My life was never the same again.

ZOEY

That night! Being there was – it was a privilege, that's what.

LILA

I was born for that night.

THE BASTION

Look: we do not believe in the supernatural. *Magic* is another word for nature. Humans evolved over hundreds of thousands of years knowing perfectly well that the world is deep. Only recently they decided that what they cannot measure must not exist, and how well did that serve them? They ended up collared and chained to monstrous machines which devour flesh to cough out fumes. Humans decided they were better than the rest of the world, and as a result, they were made insignificant. No, we of the Bastion know a bigger truth; we know that inside every tree is an abyss.

When, by a mixture of chance and exasperation, we touched the right pitch, a vibration went through our body, as if we had jacked our hearts to a giant sound system which blasted their beats back to us, times a million. The night sky blazed with an impossible number of stars, visible even as the full moon grew bigger. It was the first time Zoey and Charlie saw the other sky. They both dropped their hum, and made us stumble too. There was a silence; the sky dimmed. Then Becca started humming again, we followed, and a split second later, Zoey and Charlie joined in. Soon the sky bloomed once more.

You should have seen the colours! The black of the night was also purple, and the stars shone in icy blue, dazzling white, and the awe-inducing hue of sapphires. Silver moonlight took shades of mauve. Ric stood up, without a hitch in his hum, and went to fetch his and Lila's drums. They started drumming and we danced to their beat, without ever stopping the hum. We threw more wood into the fire and kept humming. We danced. Sam let out a long howl, then immediately his voice rejoined us. We clapped our hands on our bodies and stomped our feet.

Becca quickened the pace, and we followed suit. The dance around the fire became more and more frenzied, and when Becca started undressing, we undressed too. Our dance became more frenzied yet. We head-banged, we leapt, we slammed our chests into one another's, we shook.

And reality snapped.

Others were joining our dance. The shadow of a tree looked just like Bertrand, and his saxophone was playing to Lila and

Ric's tempo. A horse neighed: it was Imogen's. It had been buried under soft Hampshire grass for fifteen years. Out of the corner of our eyes we spotted them dancing with us, among us, people we knew and people we had never seen, and others yet, who were not quite *people*. They took our hand, kissed the back of our neck. We could never see any of them clearly. The moment we looked, they disappeared. But we knew they were there with us.

LILA

I felt two hands on my belly, and a body gently press against mine from behind. It was Galen, back from the dead. I swayed with him. I forced myself not to look at the hands and not to turn, so as not to make him go away. I saw strange birds fly out of the dark spaces among the trees. One had the body of a hedgehog, with a magpie's wing on one side and an owl's on the other. There was a serpent gliding on a bat's wings.

The Oddballs.

THE BASTION

We laughed and clapped our hands – Galen's Oddballs were coming back to us. They did not go away even when we looked. A badger danced awkwardly on skinny flamingo legs, and a cat with a fox terrier's face howled with Sam. Other Oddballs were nothing we remembered: an owl with the face of a wizened man, a kestrel with bone spikes all over its body.

From the tip of a flame a giant soap bubble was rising, like the ones Lila used to blow on her first summer, the happiest time we ever had. We elbowed each other, pointing at it. It made us go back to that time. Other bubbles came from the fire, and from the trees.

The fig tree, our Mother Tree, had grown immense. Each branch was large enough for two of us to sleep on, and some of the leaves could envelop a whole human being. She was brimming with Oddballs, slithering on her trunk, perching on her branches.

This is the Inner Pinewood. Lila touched one of the bubbles, and found it had the consistency of marshmallow. She heaved herself up. We tried to do the same, but the bubbles we touched burst in explosions of colour. Lila stood on her floating bubble, dancing above our heads, among the flying Oddballs. We whistled and immediately took on the hum again.

Then it came – a crash and a bang in the sky.

We jumped and looked up. The sky was bulging, as if brutally punched and kicked from the other side. Someone was trying to get in, and we knew it would be no good if they managed it. We stopped making any sound, except for the hum. A music was coming from the other side, an unpleasant melody of fiddles, almost human. It played revolting notes.

There was a scream from the dark side of the sky.

We recoiled, and dropped our hum.

'The fuck was that?' Zoey asked, the first words any of us pronounced in a long while.

The Oddballs were nowhere to be seen, and neither were the bubbles. Lila was standing on firm ground like the rest of us. The shadows we saw were ours, the sky had reverted to normal, and nothing was banging to beat it down.

The fire was still burning, the smoke rising.

CHARLIE

The next day we used words sparingly and clumsily. They boomed like gunshots in our ears. Besides, we did not have much to talk about. Mentioning the events of the night felt crass, and nothing else mattered enough to mention. None of us was looking forward to getting back to our phones and calendars. Clockwork time was a trap, and that night we had wiggled free of Time and Space themselves.

Hadn't we?

We had a big breakfast. We baked focaccia, sliced capocollo and mortadella, grilled aubergines, and brought to the table a whole prosciutto on a stand, which Sam sliced by hand with a long knife. We quaffed litres of strong coffee. Towards midday we headed to the beach. The summer crowds were gone; we had it all to ourselves. We swam, we threw a frisbee, we started ambling towards a normality of sorts.

When we returned to our pinewood, Becca and Ric announced they would take on kitchen duty for dinner, and asked me and Zoey to help. 'We're making pasta,' Becca said. 'By hand.'

'So we need hands,' Ric said.

We took a quick shower first. I was moving in a daze. Grief was not the first thing on my mind; it was a dull thump in the background. I was not used to that. I got to the kitchen with my hair still wet. The others were already there. Ric had arranged four mounds of thick dark flour on which he was sprinkling salt. 'Hey, Charlie,' Becca welcomed me.

Ric made a cavity on the top of each mound and poured water in it. 'Now we knead,' he said, starting on one of the mounds. We took one each.

Zoey sunk her hands in the flour. 'Ric, you making pasta is the single most incredible thing I've seen so far.'

'Not on-brand?'

'Less than it'd be for me, which is saying something.'

Ric chuckled. 'You'll have to put in a little more energy there. Dad didn't want Grandma to teach me; he said making pasta was for girls. Grandma answered that making pasta was for people who eat pasta.'

'She was a character,' Becca said.

I asked, 'Have you guys been together long?'

'Nobody gets it,' Ric said, in mock desperation. 'We're brother and sister.'

That made me stop in my tracks.

'Keep kneading,' Becca said, amused. 'Or you'll spoil the dough.'

'I thought…'

'Why?'

I didn't have an answer. Zoey did: 'You get on too well for siblings.'

'*You* say that!' Ric protested. He pointed a dough-covered finger at Becca. 'I bloody hate this woman! She ruined my life.'

'There wasn't much to ruin, sweetheart.'

I laughed. 'Okay, I'll need five or six months to reassess.'

'Speaking of reassessing,' Becca said. 'What do you make of last night?'

A silence fell over the room, filled with the zesty scent of coarse pasta dough.

I broke it, saying, 'It was real.'

'No less so than Bertrand's music.'

Zoey asked, 'Okay, but was it real the way a dream is real, or was it real the way we are real?'

'I don't know there's a difference.'

'When I think back to it, it does feel more like a dream than an actual memory. Okay, fine, we were awake, but not exactly sober either. A shared delusion? There are precedents in the history of psychic research.'

Ric said, 'When reality goes sideways we call it a delusion. Folks, let me see your dough… Yep, we're good to go.' We made four balls of dough, wrapped them in cling film. 'This needs to rest twenty minutes,' Ric said. 'Meanwhile – beer?'

'God, yes,' I said.

After so long without a drink, beer tasted like the first day of summer. 'It's time for you to know what we've been keeping from you,' said Becca. 'As far as we're concerned, you're ready. I've got to ask though – are you sure you want to go on? For people like you – good people, I mean – there's no turning back.'

'Be serious, Becca,' Zoey said. 'There's no turning back after yesterday.'

'Oh, but there is. You still have the option to set your life back on track. Go back home and in no time you'll be looking at everything you were up to here like a folly, a holiday fling.'

But my life went off track before I went to the Open Feast. Now it was back on again.

Zoey guzzled from her bottle. 'I'm not chickening out.'

Ric and Becca exchanged a look. 'You go,' she said.

Ric made a short nod. 'The lowdown is: you know all the weirdos saying that the end of the world is nigh?'

'Are they right?' Zoey asked.

'Not entirely. The end of the world is *not* nigh. Too late for that. The end of the world has come. Everything you know,' and he bent his thumb and index finger until they almost touched, 'is just this close to being done for. A lot has been lost already, and our family is the one thing standing between what's left of this,' and he knocked his knuckles on the table, 'and utter annihilation. We are humankind's last bastion.'

'And we are in damage-control mode,' Becca added.

For a while Zoey and I just let it sink in. We drank our beers, and when Ric announced that the dough was ready we followed his lead, taking a piece of it, rolling it into a cylinder, and then cutting the cylinder into smaller pieces using a flat-pointed knife. He showed us the thumb movement to shape each piece into an ear-shaped *orecchietta*.

'I'm gonna need some context,' I said, setting to work.

Zoey echoed, 'Yeah, me too.'

We were fussing with our first orecchiette; Becca had already made five. She said, 'Just to be level with you, we have little in terms of answers, and a lot of what we do have is educated guesswork.'

'Fair enough.'

'See what's going on all around us: glaciers are melting, fires larger than cities burn hectares of forest every day, hundreds of species go extinct every week. We breathe poisonous air, we drink poisonous water. The very stuff that should sustain life is smothering it. Covid-19 was bad and the next pandemic will be worse – it may be starting as we speak. Children starve in the richest countries of the world while their masters fly themselves to space on cock-shaped rockets. And while the world bends and falls, folk like you and me wake up in the morning and reach out for their phones to insult perfect strangers. Death, pestilence, famine, war – what did we expect, actual horsemen? An understated apocalypse is still an apocalypse. We are surrounded. *Things fall apart. The centre cannot hold.*'

'And we make the centre hold?' I said. I was not sceptical, only curious.

'Sometimes shit happens,' Ric said, 'and it's not the end of the world. You get your Ice Age, your pandemic, but you hang on. *Usually*. Lizards grow back their tail, humans learn to move around without sight. Shit happens, we survive, and if we're lucky, we may even thrive. That goes for animals and planets alike. Death, rebirth, such is the nature of growth. Not this time, though. This time the world has jammed badly, and it's our job to kick it back into gear.'

Becca's craftiness with the orecchiette looked preternatural to me. 'How so?' I asked.

Becca said, 'It may be a small action with far-reaching consequences, the tiny snowball starting an avalanche. We may just need to say one word to the right person at the right time. Or – or perhaps something more decisive.'

Zoey said, 'In other words, you have no clue.'

'We will,' said Ric.

'But you do know what happened last night,' I pointed out.

'We don't talk a lot about that. You overthink some things, you ruin them.'

'Let's talk only a little then,' said Zoey.

Ric turned to Becca: 'Do you want to take this one?'

She said, 'We have found a way to ... not *transcend* reality, but *be alive* to a wider one. We didn't go anywhere last night; no parallel dimensions, no astral planes. What we call the Inner Pinewood is always with us, always present, next to the Outer Pinewood, and inside it, and rolled around it. It is another way of looking at the same trees, the same sky, and the same land. The Inner Pinewood *is* the Outer Pinewood, experienced from a different perspective. The core of it is that we need to be together, and breathe with exactly the same rhythm, attuned to one another. That's what the hum is for. We'd used it before for short spells, but as soon as we moved even a little bit, the spell broke. Walking, dancing, was out of question. We've never experienced anything like last night. That was the breakthrough we have been chasing for years. We don't know what the next step is. We are in uncharted waters.'

'The banging in the sky,' Zoey said. 'Like someone trying to crash a party.'

Ric nodded. 'It was exactly that.'

'And who would that be?'

'No clue again.'

'No offence, mate, but you don't have all that many clues, for folks who are out to save the world.'

'Told ya.'

'You have a right to know our whole story,' Becca said.

ZOEY

No one sane would have bought that story, but then again, sanity is dolled-up dullness. Becca and Ric were earnest, which did not make them right, but could I take the chance? I'd spent my adult life enabling spiritual grifters to save the world one expensive workshop at a time. What if the Bastion was the real deal? What if *I* was the real deal? Could I in good conscience turn my back on that possibility, no matter how small? The world needed saving – this was the one thing no one could dispute.

And I needed some perspective; I needed Janis. Before dinner I turned on my phone and gasped. *4th October.* It was one and a half months since I'd sent my last email. I'd not realised. 'Call Janis,' I ordered the voice assistant.

'Zoey!' Janis's panicked voice came. 'Oh my God, are you all right?'

'I'm great.'

There was a sigh on the other end, and I thought it was the baby crying, but no, it was Janis.

'Hey,' I said. 'What's up? Why are you crying?'

'What's up? You're asking *what's up*?'

'I thought...'

'Zoey, you went off grid for *two months*!'

'It was less than that.'

A beat, then Janis asked, 'Are you serious?'

'Look, I'm sorry you had to take on my workload on top of yours, but I mailed you, didn't I? I told you I was going to disappear for a while.'

'*Fuck the workload!*' Janis shouted into the phone. 'I couldn't sleep at night!'

We hadn't talked in ages, and the first thing Janis did was scream at me? 'I see, we're doing the guilt trip now. I won't go down that road.'

'I called the police! They treated me like a drama queen. They said, *your friend is an adult, she wrote you she was going incommunicado, what's the problem?* They told me to get some sleeping pills. Sleeping pills, Zoey. And you are *great?*'

'You'd rather me be in a bad way?'

'FUCK YOU!'

'No, fuck *you*!' I shouted back. 'You have no idea the work I'm doing here, okay? No idea! You and your – your stupid baby, you think you're the centre of the world, that it's all about you, but hear me out: everybody can have a baby, it's not that hard, it's like, biology. There are people here, good people who're trying to *make a real difference.*'

A heavy breathing slowing down, then Janis said, in a voice that struggled to be level, 'You're not okay, Zoey.'

'Judgemental much?'

'I'm trying to help you.'

'You've got to understand, I found a good thing. You'd love it! Absolutely love it. You'd love the guys. They're our kind of people, Janis. You've been working a lot, too much, it's my fault, and you've got a baby, and... you're tired, stressed, you're not thinking right. I get it. We're good, no worries.'

'When are you coming home?'

That word sounded odd to me; I had a house in NY, but home? 'I need to sort out a few things here first.'

'You know what? Tell me where's *here* and I'm coming to you.'

'Why?'

'I miss you.'

'You want to check on me.'

'What's wrong with that?'

'You don't get it.'

'We'll find the money to pay for infringing the NDA if it comes to that.'

'It's not about money!' I said, my irritation melting into bone-deep sadness. 'Money doesn't matter. I'm with friends, Janis, what do you think?'

'Okay, fine, let me spell it out for you then – either you come home, or you let me come to you. There's no third option.'

'Really.'

'I can't stop you from doing what you want, but refuse me this and we're done, okay? I mean it. As friends, as partners. I'll pull out of SoulJo, I'll forget you exist. Done. It's going to break my heart, Zoey, but I swear, that's what I'm going to do.'

I said, 'Keep your fucking festival,' and hung up the phone.

THE BASTION

In retrospect, things did not start going wrong then; they started years before, with Galen's suicide. We learnt the details of his past when the rest of the world did. For the all-too-short time he was with us, Galen volunteered little and we asked nothing. He was Greek, this much we knew, from a city called Rethymno, on the island of Crete. He only had hateful words for it – he called it small-minded, conservative, stifling – although he pronounced them in a wistful voice. He boasted about his travels. He had been everywhere in the Mediterranean, taking odd jobs on ships and in seaside bars, doing stints of sex work every now and again. He'd spent two years in South America and hankered for going back to Peru. He hadn't talked to his family in years; he was better off for that, he said, considering that Mum was a junkie and Dad was her pimp. This is, pretty much, everything we knew. What else did we need? We knew what mattered, that he was one of us, and he was full of life. Nobody – nobody! – could have seen it coming. Nobody.

LILA

Galen was – well, as the saying goes, everybody wanted to be him or fuck him or both. It was not just his beauty, impressive as that was. That man was to sex what cake is to food: you don't have to be hungry to want a taste.

THE BASTION

Later Becca would remember a conversation she and Galen had

had, after sex, one night on the beach (back then, Becca and Ric would sleep with us more freely than they did after Galen's death). His head was on her chest, and she was lazily passing her fingers through his thick black curls.

'So we're going to save the world,' he said.

'We're going to try.'

'You promise you and Ric are not making this up.'

She laughed. 'Why would we?'

'To get in my bed?'

Becca kissed him. 'Do I need to lie for that?'

Though she and Ric bore no responsibility for Galen's death, thinking back to that night always made her sad. When the time came, we would have to take our final stand without Galen, and we would be weaker for that.

LILA

At first I had been jealous of Galen sleeping around. It was okay when we were together, but the thought of him going with someone else while I wasn't involved gave me the creeps. What if he liked them better than me? What if he dumped me? 'Love is not a zero-sum game,' Becca said. 'It is not a finite resource. It is a giving of freedom, rather than a taking of ownership.' At first I accepted her word on trust. I wanted to tie Galen to our room and never let him out, but I pushed myself to allow him to roam, and went roaming on my own.

It was amazing.

I slept with Becca as well, among others, but it was Ric I had the most fun with. Ric with his rough hands and his manners so decisive they were just shy of imposing; Ric who said what he wanted in not so many words. He had noticed me first, at the Open Feast. Saved me. I did not feel for him the kind of love I felt for Galen, which made the sex, to be honest, even better.

Galen was fine until the Receding Wave, when his behaviour shifted. He had arrived at the Open Feast with a tin can full of hash (the high-THC artificial crap that's all you find in the streets these days), a collection of pills, and a bag of what third-tier cheap coke he could afford. 'The worst thing I ever put through my nose,' Mikka commented. 'And you don't want to know what else I put there.' To his credit, Galen handed the drugs to Becca and Ric before we started the Receding Wave, knowing he would not resist them.

The following days were hard on him. The no-drug policy made him skittish. Some days he would be playful with everyone he bumped into, others he spent sitting for hours on end on the bench of the peasant hut, staring into nothing. Once Mikka was not in the mood for sex and had to push him away when he became too insistent. Stuff like that.

We did not have any breakthrough, of course (it would be six years before Zoey and Charlie came to complete us), and Becca put an end to the first Receding Wave on a desultory note. I didn't know what Becca was after. We had managed to hum as one person, and to reach the other sky, full of stars. What else could we achieve?

Weeks later – it might have been late October, early November – I found the shelf on which Galen kept his Oddballs empty. 'Where did you move them?' I asked.

'I tossed them away.'

My heart jumped. 'Why?'

He shrugged.

I ran to the bins. I could only find fragments – broken wings, cracked beaks, squashed bodies. When Galen reached me, I was sitting among the garbage, crying.

'It's no big deal,' he said.

'They were beautiful.'

'They were silly! Who spends their time making up things that don't exist?'

'Artists?'

'The world is ending, Lila, we don't need art. We need…' And there he stopped. He didn't know what was needed, only that it was nothing he could provide.

The world is ending. What Becca and Ric had meant as a stirring call to arms put an overwhelming pressure on my poor sweet Galen. *The world is ending.* He was not ready for the truth. But he had a radiant smile, straight shoulders and an indefatigable cock, so none of us, not even me, noticed. We believed that because he was beautiful he was also strong. If it was Becca and Ric's mistake, then it was ours too.

There were a million signs I ignored. Galen brought to our hum a doleful quality, but I found it romantic. He toned down his boastfulness, but I took it as a sign of maturity. His love-making became both mellower and more frequent, and I wrote that down to a change in taste.

He worked hard on the farm, all day, every day. He had a long experience of menial jobs, and what he didn't know how to do, he learned: he pruned plants, fixed tractors, carried rocks from one field to another, broke them with a pickaxe.

'There's no need for you to exhaust yourself like this,' Ric told him once.

'I know,' Galen answered.

Winter solstice came and passed, and we were gearing up for the next Open. I had picked a new Napoleon and was getting him used to hanging with people, the Nameless was updating our social media presence, and we were going through applications as they came, discussing what we should improve on. It was a good job we had our hands full, because a certain tiredness made headway. January is a mean time, February more so, with tempers getting shorter even as the days get longer. Fortunately, Galen's birthday was approaching – it was an excuse to plan a party. We made a walnut and coffee cake, his favourite, and bought candles. We bought a present too, a top-range whittling knife.

The night before his birthday (it was 23 February, how can we forget it?) I found Galen shivering in my arms. I thought he was coming down with a fever, but he said no. 'Shall we run?' he whispered, in the darkness.

'Come again?'

'Run away, only you and me. The world is ending but maybe we still have time to be happy before it's over.'

I squeezed him. 'We are happy here.'

'Very! But if we stay, we will have to… fight? I don't know. I don't want to be in the eye of the storm.'

'You don't mean that.'

'No, of course not.' Galen kissed me on my forehead. He asked, 'Are you afraid?' He kissed me again, on the nose.

'Not at all.'

He kissed me on my neck.

I said, 'I love you, Galen.'

'Back at you.'

We made love in silence. Later, in the course of the night, I woke up to see Galen getting out of bed. I groggily supposed he was going to the loo and dozed off again. In the morning he hadn't returned. I brushed my eyes, shuffled my feet to the kitchen and put on some coffee, yawning and stretching. No trace of Galen.

I glanced out of the window at an overcast day of sirocco, the south wind, muggy and nasty. I threw on a jacket and walked outside, calling his name.

THE BASTION

We found them by Becca's tree.

Lila was sitting on the ground, with her legs folded up in her arms and her chin on her knees. Her eyes were on Galen's body, which swung gently from a branch of the fig tree. It was a sturdy branch; the hanged man did not curve it at all.

Ric brought his hands to his head and said, 'Fuck.' Becca was breathing hard.

Lila turned to us, her eyes dry. 'Can we bring him back?' she asked.

3

OUR ROOTS

1

At two years old, Becca wasn't speaking yet. Mum and Dad were disappointed for the *brutta figura* she was causing them to make. Everybody praised their girl for her beauty, but then they asked, 'So, when are we going to hear her speak?' and you couldn't miss the sharp edge of judgement in their voice.

Her cognitive development was excellent, said the doctor. Well above her age, in fact.

(Listen to us, who know her well – nothing about Becca was ever average. She was *not* destined for greatness; she was great to begin with.)

She did have a tendency to get distracted more easily, perhaps, than was to be expected, but once she decided to turn her attention to the task at hand, she got it done briskly. 'Some children take longer to say their first words,' was the doctor's verdict. 'It doesn't make them any less smart.'

Which meant that Becca was lazy, Mum and Dad concluded. It was their fault, for making her life too easy. Now, regrettably, they had to change the tune. This is probably the main reason why they conceived the idea of having another baby, as a lesson for Becca. While they worked on that, they withdrew their attention from her. They would not compliment every cute face she made, they would not check what was wrong when she started crying, they cut down on playtime and stopped bringing her so many toys. They made her work harder for their love. It was for her own good, of course.

What they did not (*could not*) know was that the reason Becca did not speak was that she was busy listening. When she seemed distracted, she was in fact focused, though not on them.

She described it to us as a hum, a murmuring at the edge of her hearing, as if an indistinct crowd of people were talking sotto voce all the time, night and day, and the meaning of their words was beyond her grasp, but only just. She could almost get them but not quite, and she couldn't tell whether that was because the voices were too low, or because they spoke in a language slightly askew.

(We can easily visualise this clever little girl straining her ears to catch what the humming voices meant to say, at the expense of what the adults in the room did. We can visualise the adults resenting her for that.)

When Ric was born, a new mystery appeared in her life, this wrinkly creature so similar to her and yet so different. 'Your brother,' Dad explained in the hospital room, where Mum was in bed with Ric in her arms. Dad could have spared the effort. Becca knew all that was happening; she even knew the baby would be called Riccardo, already shortened to Ric.

'You're going to be jealous of him,' Dad went on, hopefully.

Becca reached out to the baby's chubby foot and said, 'Ric.'

She had found something worth saying.

(Oh, we wish we could have been flies on the wall, to see the first meeting of the two greatest minds of their generation! The seed that would grow into us.)

2

The voices went on whispering in Becca's ear, night and day, never pausing, never stopping. Becca did not find them disturbing.

They were a fact of nature. As the sky was blue and the sea was endless, so the air was thick with disembodied whispers. That was the only world she knew. She was six when she discovered that was not the world everybody else knew.

They had gone to Mass, like every Sunday. Becca had barely made it through one stuffy hour trapped in a pew, with a priest with pinprick eyes droning on about sin and redemption. The incense made her cough. The one thing she looked forward to, on a Sunday, was the time she was allowed to spend playing on her own in the pinewood (*our* pinewood) after the ordeal. Pines and eucalyptuses making shade with occasional carob and fig trees, the secret frame of this planet peeking out of the soil in white slabs of rock, and the beach waiting beyond the tree line. This was heaven, and she needed not to bow her head for her whole life and then die in order to go there. She simply needed not to be at Mass.

Dad spent all the walk from the church to the pinewood telling Becca off for her behaviour. He accused her of being distracted, disrespectful, a bunch of other things. Becca nodded and kept her mouth shut. Dad got nervous before lunch, when he was hungry. He was still venting as they entered the pinewood and headed towards Villa Abbracciavento.

(It was not a ruin, whatever most people thought. Their family lived there, using only three rooms, the kitchen and a bathroom, keeping all other rooms locked. Becca and Ric's ancestors were peasants who had managed to buy some land; not poor, but definitely not rich. Their paternal great-grandfather had decided to build his family a grandiose villa, '*comu li signuri*', 'like the gentlemen', which required far more money than he had. Spanish flu took him before he could finish the work and none of his descendants could put together either the cash or the motivation needed to finish it, so Villa Abbracciavento stood like that, the relic of a dream, waiting for Becca and Ric, the pinnacle of what's best about humanity, to make it real.)

The voices were louder inside the pinewood. Becca stepped through the gate and the volume turned up, like the chirping of cicadas rising suddenly on a summer afternoon. They did that sometimes. The voices would never rise enough to hide other sounds, human or otherwise, but they did rise enough to give her the sense she was on the brink of getting what they were saying; always on the brink, never quite there. It was infuriating.

Dad was ranting when they passed by one of the oldest trees, the fig that would become Becca's teaching place. She almost made out something the voices were saying, about a baton, or... but Dad drowned it out. She whipped her head to him and said, 'Shush!' and she hadn't closed her mouth before she knew she'd made a mistake.

He stood aghast for a split moment, then he clenched his teeth, tightened his lips and furrowed his brow in a hateful expression. He slapped her, and the smack smashed all other sounds. Ric started crying, Mum lifted him in her arms.

(If we could go back in time, we would make that awful man suffer.)

Becca sniffled, too angry to cry herself. She took a hand to her cheek. 'I was trying to *listen*!'

'You were not,' Dad said.

'Not to you, to the other voices.'

Mum was rocking Ric.

'There's no one else,' Dad said.

'You can't hear them?'

'We can hear your brother crying,' Mum said. 'And he's crying because of *you*.'

Becca bit back her reply. What was wrong with them? It would be a waste of time to enquire now, with Dad in a mood. She went back to her usual strategy of staying silent and nodding.

In the following weeks she tested the waters with her parents, her grandparents, the other children and the teachers at school, and came to the conclusion that no one but her heard the voices, not even Ric, though he was too little to say for sure. She was quick to adapt, the way children are. She heard voices and other people didn't, and there was nothing else to it.

3

Becca told Ric about the voices on the night of his fourteenth birthday. Dad had allowed Ric to have a small party, on condition that he prepared everything himself and tidied up afterwards, a lesson in the necessity of hard work. Becca was helping him out. 'Can you hear them, like, now?' Ric asked.

'Yes.'

'And you've got no clue at all what they say.'

'None whatsoever.'

'Psychos hear voices.'

'Says who?'

'Everybody...?'

'Tell it to Sigmund Freud. He heard voices too, more than once. No, I've looked it up, and, granted, some people who hear voices do hear horrible things, like, *kill your baby brother in his sleep! Smother him with a pillow!* But to other people, the voices just say stuff. Useful stuff too! A woman once heard a voice telling her to go get a check-up for brain cancer, and guess what, she had brain cancer. No symptoms, just the voice. The cancer was early stages, she got out lightly. Two more months and she'd have been fucked. Then there are the voices talking to mystics, prophets. Gandhi heard voices!' She paused. 'A whole lot of religions started with a random dude hearing voices.'

(She was young, and already knowledgeable.)

'But the voices in your head are just static.'

'There're two things I'm sure of, and the first is that they're *not* just static.'

'The other is that they're not in your head?'

'Exactly,' said Becca. 'My voices – they come from elsewhere.'

Ric didn't doubt his big sister's story, but he was not sure what to do with it. He just parked it there for the moment, another one of the mysteries, like girls, that were filling up his life.

(Isn't it mind-blowing that Becca and Ric were ever young? But then, Hypatia too had been a child, Plato a boy, and so the two key people in our generation have been green and raw.)

Time ticked on unassumingly for five years, until their dad died, and reality spun sideways.

4

The last years of Becca and Ric's dad were a time of cigarettes, a bad cough, and a refusal to see a doctor while there was still time. The funeral was busy – he was well-known in town. Notorious, some would say. When the proceedings were over and the house returned to silence, Mum sleeping with a little help from Ambien, Ric sleeping out of pure exhaustion, Becca found herself unable to go to bed.

The dinner table, set under a large print of the Virgin Mary, heaved under the weight of cold meat, pasta salad, focaccia, cheese, mashed broad-beans, bitter greens, sautéed mushrooms, oven-baked cod, and more. People had been bringing food to tide over the dead man's family. *Lu cunsulu,* they called this tradition. *The consolation.* Becca took some salami and focaccia and let herself fall on the floor, with her shoulders against the sofa in the living room. She did not need any consolation.

She had not been crying. Her father, the one and only, was dead, and she had not found one spare tear to shed. Even with all their fighting, she had thought she must feel some residual love for him, but now that he was gone, all she felt was relief; not as if she had lost something, but as if she had *gained* it.

(When they told us about him, Becca said their father was a man of his time, Ric called him a dick. The man thought himself smart, hard-working, perennially short-changed by life. He believed he knew better in every circumstance, which was seldom true. How could he not understand that his one role was to carry the semen that gave birth to Becca and Ric? And it was a role exalted enough.)

When Becca had got her nose pierced, Dad grounded her for a month. When she'd brought home her first boy, he didn't talk to her for a week, and when she brought home her first girl, he didn't understand what was going on, but he sniffed something was off and gave Becca hell for no reason he could tell. Dad had been a relentless force for destruction in Becca's life, and now he was nothing at all. She was free. With Dad rotting underground – *at last,* she thought with a shiver at the stark realism of the thought – there was a blissful peace in her head. A silence.

She jumped to her feet. Suddenly she felt this fear, this panic taking hold of her, and she didn't know why. She looked around, searching for clues, and after a few moments she got it – the voices were gone. Utterly, completely gone. It was disorienting, like suddenly missing a foot. She called to the dark house, *Hey! Are you there?* Nobody answered. She was sweating, her heart was pounding. Was it something wrong with her ears, with her brain?

Was she dying?

She said, *please! Talk to me.*

Nobody answered.

She grabbed a jacket and ran outside. She was walking on an alien planet. She couldn't trust her senses, which meant that she couldn't trust anything at all. She'd never heard such a silence before. She'd never been so lonely.

(We wish we could have been with her, comforted her. But we were yet to come.)

She went among the trees and – no voices. She walked on, deeper inside. There was just a slice of a moon in the sky, and the pinewood was so, so dark. She thought, *this is it, this is how I die*. Yet, she could not turn back. She was thinking, *if something has to happen to me, best for it to happen here*. And she had just formulated this thought when her mood shifted.

She was lusting to go deeper. She was lusting to be in the pinewood, to be *with* the pinewood, as if it were a person, a lover. She had always known that there was an aliveness in our land, but now that aliveness was reaching out to her. She felt that the world had become fully real at last, and she was breathing electricity, filling her body with power.

The shadows were shifting as she went deeper in. They reacted to her presence, changing the trees into starlight. She took a moment to make sense of what she saw. The trees were brown and green and solid, but at the same time they were made of cold starlight, and she was made of starlight too; her hands, her body.

She could see both realities at once, the dust of this world and the silver starlight.

Becca reached the fig tree. She rested her palm on its trunk. It was unyielding under her hand, and at the same time it was like a throbbing animal: warm, muscular, with a giant heart thumping inside, pumping blood, pumping starlight. Every leaf and every tiny bud were starlight, every rock, every mote of dust. She looked up at the sky. There were too many stars, far too many, and the blackness of the space between them was a billion times darker than any night she had known. That was her first sight of our beautiful eldritch sky. But now any difference between sky and earth, between Becca and the land, had gone. All was starlight.

Becca kissed the fig tree, and the fig tree kissed her back. The tree hugged her, and Becca hugged the tree back. She felt an urge to undress, and lean against the bark with her whole body. The tree grew starlight leaves, like large hands on her skin. She felt a warm rush of excitement when she let the tree enfold her.

The voices came back in a rolling billow, louder than ever before. Still bundled up with the fig, Becca shouted, 'What do you want from me?' Starlight flooded her and the fig, as if the fig was calling all the light to them, and then flared up in a last hurrah, along her skin, along the trunk, and upwards into the sky, before dying out entirely.

She was back to the woods she knew, under the same old sky. Her feet stood on solid ground, her hands were flesh and bones. She was reeling. The fig tree was smooth under her touch, and she was cold. All was normal, perfectly normal. The voices had returned, humming, whispering in her ears.

For the first time that day, Becca cried.

5

She only confessed her vision to her brother. 'I got a peek beneath the skin of the world, Ric,' she said. 'The stuff we want, the stuff we fret about, it's all rubbish. Status, career, money, nothing matters in the end. We're starlight and dust.'

(A deep thinker and a clear teacher, Becca truly was everything.)

Ric had been worried for her. Becca was funny, and she loved him, but she was also volatile, laughing with you one moment, shouting in your face the next. She drank more than Ric was comfortable with, and smoked marijuana with the same ease others went through fags.

'Had you done something?' he asked.

She looked hurt.

'I'm not, like, judging.'

'Ric, it was real. As real as you and me. As real as my voices!'

'Your voices,' Ric sighed. 'I don't know, Becca, maybe it's time you see someone.'

'Meaning?'

'I was reading that hearing voices can be a result of trauma, did you know that? What with Dad being Dad, I wouldn't be surprised if there was something he did when you were little that...'

'I thought I could trust you.'

'But you can!'

She shouted a 'fuck you!' and left.

They made it up, sort of, but it would be years before their relationship healed completely. The worst was yet to come.

Becca dropped out of university, where she had been studying Literature. After the vision in the pinewood, she didn't have it in her to bother jumping through the hoops of a degree to get a piece of paper which stated that she had been jumping through the hoops of a degree. It occurred to her that most humans give up their lives into willing slavery – to money, to an institution, to an unquenchable thirst for admiration or, barring that, at least a lack of contempt – and she could not take any of that seriously. How could that matter, when everything was starlight and dust in the end?

Her wilderness years began.

6

They were years of bad choices, odd jobs, and a ferocious loneliness that lodged the cold of January deep into her bones. There were brief days of joy, weeks in which she could almost believe she was back on track and the end of her struggles was in sight, but then something came up: she lost her job, her latest partner dumped her, she made yet another mistake. And she was lost again.

(We cry, when we think of those times. We wish we could take upon us Becca's sorrow, and let her free of it. She deserved happiness. But no – like every saint and every world-shaping mystic, she had to go through her trials, to come back stronger and sharper.)

Ric accused her of being full of herself, but the opposite was true: the vision in the pinewood had left her hollowed out. When she reached inside, she found nothing. Her voices were a fact and her vision too, but that was all she had to go with. She was at a loss as to what to do with those facts, or with herself, for that matter. So she experimented, and though in theory there are no failed experiments, in practice sometimes the test tube does explode in the scientist's hand.

Mum said that she would pay for Becca's studies but not Becca's parties. Her daughter was on her own. She found her first job in a bar in Rome, a faux-Western saloon owned by a freakishly tall man from Lecce who was either talking cars or snorting the cheapest coke on the market. It was a place of third-rate linoleum printed to vaguely resemble rustic wood, pixelated Sergio Leone movie stills, faux guns, with a core audience of package-holiday tourists drunk on minibar bottles, who couldn't tell the difference between Rome, Texas and Disneyland. The money was terrible, but it came in cash. It lasted until inevitably he made a pass, and when she refused, he liked that, because he liked wild horses in need of a firm hand. Becca was grateful to Ric for teaching her what he had learnt in his many scrapes – her boss had to call ER and have an eyeball squeezed back in place.

(Isn't it fun to think of that scumbag suffering?)

After that, it was out of the question that Becca could go back to work.

She kept drifting from job to job, and from town to town, serving tables, babysitting, making up CVs, spending three months as a shop assistant in a store owned by the cousin of a guy she knew from Portodimare, five as a cleaner in a fast-food joint on a motorway.

(What was that Allen Ginsberg said? 'I saw the best minds of my generation / destroyed by madness'. The best mind of every generation may be destroyed by sheer normality).

She stopped coming back home for Christmas and summer. Ric called her arrogant, irresponsible. 'You want to fuck up your life, fine,' he would say to her over the phone. 'I'm thinking of Mum. You should too.'

'Mum's fine since Dad died. Best thing that ever happened to her; now she can be the bitch.'

'Can you hear yourself?'

'Your horse is too high for you, brother. Come off it before you fall.'

'I'm trying to make something of myself, Becca.'

'What, do you want a prize for that?'

Their calls were like that, short and unpleasant. From talking three or four times a week and texting a lot, they went to talking once a week and texting little, then once a month with no texts at all.

Ric was too young, and too insecure himself, to understand that his sister was in pain. Becca's first boyfriend was getting married, her best friend from primary school had started a small law practice in town – cushy jobs, easy lives. It's not that she wanted any of that for herself, but they were getting on, and she was stuck. She told herself it is normal to struggle, if you are aiming for something more than an average job, an average family, a life off-the-shelf. You want to make your own rules? You cannot expect that to be easy. But after years of struggle, she started wondering whether she was fooling herself. She would say she was on this epic quest for *meaning, clarity,* that she was after *a life fully lived* – grand words, but here she was, scrubbing a stranger's shit from a bar toilet. The doubt started creeping in that she was sanctimonious about other people's lives because she couldn't get one.

And now she was in the second half of her twenties, and she felt it was too late to go back. She could only push further, and maybe, just maybe, a breakthrough would come. Just pushing a little further.

(Yes, Becca, hold on. We are waiting just around the corner.)

She was reading a lot: novels, short stories, spirituality books. She hoped to find some wisdom, something that resonated with her own experiences. She found tired stories reducing witches to a mere symbol of whatever cause *du jour* the author had taken to heart, New Age claptrap about the power of manifestation and how taking baths with aromatic salts was a strong act of magic. It was simplistic psychology in a psychic's caftan, as far from her lived visionary experience as accountancy handbooks.

She decided to have a go at writing; she could not do worse than what she had read. She wrote a short story about a girl who works out her grief over her parents' divorce through talking to her goldfish, another about a misunderstood god, a nice chap who can't find any followers because he's just too nice and people don't care for nice gods. They were bad; she shifted to poetry. Her verses about southern sunsets and beautiful rebels were so corny that she deleted the files from her battered laptop, and she wished she had written by hand so that she would have something to burn.

(Or this is what she says – we doubt that. Becca has a knack for doing everything at the highest standards, and we are sure that was the case with her writing as well. If those works had survived, they'd surely be hailed as masterpieces.)

Art was not the way forward. She told herself that it didn't matter. Nothing did – we are starlight and dust in the end.

Liquors and weed were the only lullaby that could put her to sleep. Her drink of choice was *Strega,* the Witch's liquor, an intensely yellow spirit which was considered an old man's choice. It was sweet and strong, and not as expensive as whiskey. Half a bottle of that and a strong joint were what she needed after a long day's work. It did help to have something to look forward to: the first sip and the first smoke of the day, the blessed numbness they brought. She looked forward to them so much that she started having them a little earlier every day, until a glass of liquor and a joint became her morning routine, where other people had coffee and a cigarette. She did not have a problem. She only needed something to help her chill while she considered her next move. And besides, we are starlight and dust in the end.

That is what led to the falling-out with Ric.

(It's unbearably sad to think of that, Becca and Ric being broken, divided. As if Planet Earth had cracked in half.)

She promised – against her will – to be with him on his graduation day, and she did force herself to go all the way to Portodimare, with her boyfriend, a bass player fifteen years her senior who lived off his dad's state pension. While Mum spent the night in Lecce, the university city where Ric was getting graduated, Becca and her boyfriend slept in Portodimare, at Mum's place. But they found Mum's drinks cabinet, and they had some strong skunk.

A phone call woke Becca up. She had a thumping headache. She reached out for her phone, bumped into it with her hand and made it fall, and rescued it from the floor. It was Ric.

'Becca!' he said. 'What happened?'

She yawned. 'Sorry, bro, I overslept.'

'You...'

'We had a bit of a party last night.'

'I should be with my friends, celebrating my fucking degree, and instead I'm driving back to Portodimare with Mum, to check on you.'

Becca giggled. 'Just go to the restaurant, we'll meet you there.'

'Don't bother.'

'But, Ric...'

'I don't want to see you or your boyfriend.'

'Don't be a prick.'

'No, Becca, we're done, you and I.'

'Ric!' she said, but he had already hung up on her.

By the time her boyfriend woke up, Becca had wiped her tears away – not that he would have noticed, anyway. They broke up the next week.

(He was an idiot. A scumbag. We hope he suffered.)

Becca and Ric wouldn't talk again for three years, years in which Becca kept sliding steadily down. Ric had been her only connection to her younger years, when life was good. She thought back to those days, and she remembered them as always sunny, always filled with hope. Sometimes she wondered how she had gone from that to this, how had she screwed up so massively after having been gifted with the vision of beauty she had in the pinewood. But then this or that pressing matter required her full attention – she had to put together enough cash for a room, or find a new boyfriend or girlfriend so as not to drink alone.

She spent six months in an ashram in the Po Valley, until the venerable teacher was arrested for running a human-trafficking ring which furnished cheap, expendable prostitutes to half the pimps in Lombardy. In the ashram she met her new girlfriend, with whom she moved into a studio flat in a rundown estate on the outskirts of Milan. The girlfriend was known as Snow White not for the hue of her skin but for the coke she sold and liberally snorted. Her kiss had an acid taste which prickled Becca's tongue. Snow White also dealt a vast array of other drugs, and every now and again Becca worked clubs with her. When they had sold most of their load, they would party with the leftovers: a snort of coke, an MDMA pill.

One night the MDMA was bad.

Becca would always remember the music dying out after she swallowed the pill, and the voices too. Only the humming remained. Above it rose a strange new melody, a horrible sound of fiddle music, which for some reason that she could not articulate terrified her. *There's nothing to be afraid of,* she told herself. *We are starlight and dust in the end.*

The room spun, and it went black, and Becca went down.

7

While Becca's life had gone down, Ric's had gone up. Mum was doing surprisingly well with the farm, better than Dad ever did. They were not rich, but they were okay. He enrolled in a Psychology course in Lecce, in the conviction that Becca was unwell and if she did not want to seek help, it fell to him to help her anyway.

His university years were some of the best of his life. He missed his sister, very much so, but everything else was easy. He read voraciously, a lot of the same books his sister was reading, in the search for words that could help him understand her. He read William Blake; he grabbed everything he could find on Joan of Arc, who heard voices and let them lead her to be burnt at the stake at nineteen. He studied William James's *The Varieties of Religious Experience*, Emile Durkheim's *The Elementary Forms of Religious Life*, T. M. Luhrmann's *Persuasions of the Witch's Craft*, along with works on neurochemistry, attachment theory and Lacanian psychoanalysis, with its focus on the unquenchable thirst that moves our every action.

Among the perks of being a Psych student was that Ric found

himself one of the very few men in a largely women-attended faculty. He had been awkward with girls at school, but now he flourished. His ways, on the verge of rudeness but still polite, made him a hit.

(His handsomeness helped: Becca and Ric were the two best-looking people you would ever meet.)

First he found in himself a healthy appetite for women and no shortage of ways to indulge it, then, after a drunken experiment with a teaching assistant, his appetites grew to include men.

Books and sex were not a bad way to spend his early twenties. If only Becca had been more present in his life, his world would have been complete. He could barely talk to, or about, her without getting angry, but he still wished she would see reason, one day, and allow him to help her.

Anger was, he would be the first to admit, his main problem. Not that he was ever gratuitously violent, but he did have a temper, and having been raised in open countryside, doing small jobs since a very young age, he had the meat to make his temper dangerous. When a young priest was outraged that Ric kissed a boyfriend in front of the Basilica di Santa Croce, one of Lecce's dazzling baroque churches, Ric punched the priest so hard he spat a tooth with the blood; when a tourist's hand fell as if by mistake on Ric's girlfriend's ass, Ric grabbed the hand and twisted it until it broke. The tourist was with friends, and they might have beaten the crap out of Ric, but at times like that he had a madness in his eyes that convinced people that discretion was the best part of valour.

He wrote a dissertation on the psychology of belief, and after reading the last draft, the professor who had been mentoring him praised it highly, and assured Ric an academic career was his to have.

(Like with Becca, Ric's intelligence was off the charts. Those who say their teachings were nothing much are simply unable to understand their depth.)

He could not wait to defend his dissertation and see what the future held. Nor could he could wait for Becca to be with him and Mum that day. Maybe she would get inspired and go back to studying. It was not too late – it is never too late in life.

But on the day that Ric had to defend his dissertation, Becca and her loser boyfriend were nowhere to be seen. When Mum called home, they did not answer. Ric was sick with worry for her, which made him stumble once or twice while discussing his dissertation; Mum's head was elsewhere entirely. Ric called her again the moment he was finished, and still didn't get any answer.

He got a first, as everybody expected. The plan had been to go to a nice little Jewish cuisine restaurant to celebrate, but Becca had vanished and neither he nor Mum felt in the mood. So they left Ric's friends and his girlfriend, and they drove back to Portodimare to check on Becca. It was a fifty-minute drive, but Ric was a good driver and could cut it to forty, if they didn't meet any police.

Ric called Becca when they were midway there. He took his phone in one hand, keeping the other on the wheel. 'What happened?' he asked.

She yawned. 'Sorry, bro, I overslept.'

'You...'

'We had a bit of a party last night.' Her voice was slurred.

'What is she saying?' Mum asked, from her seat.

Ric pulled over to the side of the road.

'I should be with my friends, celebrating my fucking degree, and instead I'm driving back to Portodimare with Mum, to see if you're alive.'

She giggled. 'Just go to the restaurant, we'll meet you there.'

'What is she saying?' Mum repeated.

Ric said, 'Don't bother.'

'But, Ric...'

'I don't want to see you or your boyfriend.'

'Don't be a prick.'

'No, Becca, we're done, you and I.'

'Ric!' he heard her say, as he hung up on her.

Ric and Mum went back to Lecce. Mum cried a lot during the drive and didn't say a word in the restaurant. Ric had to grimly pretend he was having a good time.

Awful as it was to say, cutting off Becca did him a world of good. His worry for Becca had been a nagging presence at the back of his mind, and by deciding she was not his business anymore, he had freed a huge amount of bandwidth. He started a career as a lecturer, poorly paid but satisfying, and found time to help Mum. In turn, she helped him buy a flat in Lecce, a tiny one-bedroom thing, but in a listed building close to the centre of town, with high ceilings and carved railings.

On some dark nights he did have to keep guilt at bay, and there were times when a memory of Becca – the way she would talk him out of trouble with Dad, the excitement with which she had shared the secret of her voices, the ring of her bangles – would come unbidden, and stab him. Soon enough life reasserted itself, and there was some new cute stranger to kiss, a book to read, a paper to publish. He did not miss the real Becca; he missed the girl with a bright smile and a zest for life who had died when her brain had misfired after a lifetime of small problems, and given her full-blown hallucinations.

One day Ric got a phone call from an unknown number.

'Riccardo Abbracciavento?'

'Yes?'

'It's about your sister.'

8

Ric drove through the night, one-thousand kilometres from Lecce to Milan, stopping only for petrol, alone. His sister had died.

She stayed dead for three minutes and twenty-seven seconds before a junior doctor managed to bring her back by an alchemy of willpower and dumb luck. For three minutes and twenty-seven seconds Ric had lost his sister, and he hadn't known it. He hadn't felt a shiver, he hadn't seen a ghost – nothing.

(Can you believe that? Our world was left without Becca for three minutes and twenty-seven seconds. The most dangerous minutes and seconds in humankind's history.)

The loneliness of the long drive gave him time to think, a time he had not allowed himself lately. The late-night conversations; the shared memories; Becca's unique way of curling her lips slightly askew when she laughed. All that had gone up in smoke, for three minutes and twenty-seven seconds. The thought that it could have gone for ever made his head spin. He had to stop by the kerb side and be sick. Someone had given her some shitty drugs, and she wouldn't have been taking shitty drugs if he had been with her. Becca must have felt inconceivably alone. It was entirely his fault. He should have been by her side. It was immense luck, to be able to stand by the side of someone like Becca. And he had renounced it – what for? Pride? God, what a moron.

He reached the hospital by early morning. A briskly kind nurse guided him to Becca's room. He had read of people turning into *a shadow of themselves,* and before seeing Becca in her hospital bed, he had thought it was a dead metaphor, but this is exactly what she looked like – a projection of herself, all her features blurred and darkened. She had lost weight, her hair had lost its shine, the hollows under her eyes were like unsettling wells. A thin woman sat by her bed. She was bad news. Ric had seen enough bad news to recognise them.

Becca smiled at him, and that smile had the power of rearranging her whole face, her whole body. It was like time had never passed, and she was still carefree and young. 'Ric,' she said. 'I'm sorry.'

Ric bit his own lips. 'I was a dick.'

'Undoubtedly,' she said, without reproach. 'But it must not have been easy for you either.'

'How are you?'

Becca asked the woman to leave the room. She did – not with good grace.

'Girlfriend?' Ric asked.

Becca nodded.

'And she brought you here.'

'Let's not talk about that.'

Ric sat in the chair, still warm from the woman's touch. 'You're the princess today.'

'I had to die to get crowned.'

'I said *princess*, not *queen*.'

Becca smiled again. 'I was stupid.'

'Me too.'

'I needed that, Ric. I needed to touch rock bottom in order to...' Her voice trailed off.

'To what?'

'I'd love to go back home for a while. Stay with Mum. Do you think she would be okay with that?'

'She'd love it.'

'Can I ask you something? Seeing that I'm the princess today.'

'Whatever you want.'

'When I'm home, I want you to do something with me.'

'What?'

'I'll explain when we're there. For now I only want you to promise me you'll do it.'

'Becca...'

'It will last only for a little while, okay? Only for a little while. A week. Ten days, maximum.'

'And you can't explain to me what it is.'

'Surprise, surprise.'

He kissed her on the forehead. 'Whatever you want.'

The thin woman was waiting just outside the door. When Ric came out, she made to go back in, but he asked, 'May I have a word?'

'What?'

'Are you Becca's girlfriend?'

'What did she tell you?' she asked.

Ric kept his voice level, and his body language relaxed. 'I want to say this very clearly, so that there are no misunderstandings between us. If you go back in that room, I am going to kill you, making such a mess that no strapping doctor will be able to put you back together. If you see my sister ever again, if you call her, if I as much as get a whiff of your presence close to her, I am going to kill you. I won't say this again. This is not a threat. This is a bare fact of life, a matter of action and reaction. You go close to Becca, you die.'

'Bullshit.'

Ric shrugged.

She put her hand on the handle. Ric didn't move, only looked at her. She let go of the handle and walked fast to the elevator, and that was the last time either Becca or Ric ever heard of Snow White.

9

Mum was overjoyed to have Becca at home and swore repeatedly that she would feed her daughter back to health. Food was, in Mum's view, the one and only panacea for all the illnesses of humankind. Ric visited them a few times, but he had to wait until the end of term to be able to come and stay for longer. He arrived on a Thursday night, to find a feast of home-made orecchiette with tomato sauce and meatballs, then sautéed mussels, swordfish cooked with cherry tomatoes, olives and capers, and as a side, a salad of bitter wild herbs Mum had gathered that day. She was not as strong as she used to be, but she was plenty strong.

The next morning Ric woke up before sunrise and went outside with a cup of hot coffee. Exciting as his life in Lecce was, in the last couple of years he had come to miss Portodimare. He could always jump in his car and come, but it wasn't the same as waking up surrounded by trees, a stone throw's away from the beach. He liked the lazy light of early morning, how it seemed to rise from a deep chthonic place of roots, making its way up the trunks of trees, reaching to the highest leaves and finally shooting up in the sky, turning it from black to rose to blue.

Later, he went for a walk on the beach with Becca. She breathed the salty air with the joy of a kid scoffing candies. 'I can't believe how good it tastes.'

'Best flavour in the world.'

Becca's face had already acquired a healthier light. 'So. Your promise.'

'It's the reason I came.'

'I appreciate your taking time off for me.'

'You said you needed ten days.'

'That should be enough to teach you the hum.'

'Hum?'

Becca squatted to look at a tiny crab, no larger than a thumbnail, who was hurrying to hide under a wet rock. 'No questions,' she said. 'Just follow my lead.'

'It has to do with your vision?'

'What did I just say?' she asked with a smile.

'I need to get a broad sense of this thing, to gauge if it's good for your healing process.'

'Going back on our word, are we?'

'I'm a psychologist, this is what I do. It's a matter of professional ethics.'

'You are a psychologist, but you *were* a dick. You said so yourself.'

'That I was.'

'Which costs you ten days of humming. You got away cheaply, if you ask me.'

'Ten days of humming,' Ric sighed, after a moment's hesitation.

But it did not take ten days.

They started that afternoon. They sat by the fig tree, wrapped in blankets, lit a small fire to keep warm, and Becca showed Ric the hum.

'That's easy,' he said, and tried the same tune.

Becca shook her head. 'Almost, but not quite. Also, you and I need to hum as one.'

'We need to hum as one *why*?'

'You cannot hum if you talk.'

Ric thought he would get there before dinner, but after an hour of fruitless trying he came to admit it was trickier than he had expected. He had to modulate his hum on Becca's while she adjusted her own tune slightly to make it easier for Ric to match, without changing it beyond recognition. He thought he got it, once, but he was actually trailing behind her, humming a fraction of a second too late.

That night Ric couldn't sleep; he was worried for his sister. He had no clue what she was trying to demonstrate, but whatever it was, it was insane. He told himself that there were far worse scenarios than spending time humming with her in the family pinewood. At least she was safe.

After another day of abject failure, Becca proposed to synch their breathing first, and then move to the hum. That was easy – it was only a matter of timing, and Ric had known Becca for literally all his life. He knew intimately every little clue her body language gave, every little noise of her normal breathing. It took only one day for them to start breathing in synch.

(Aren't you breathing with them, knowing their fight is over once and for all? We just cannot bear the thought of them being apart.)

There was another thing that worried him about Becca, and he told her that night after dinner, when Mum went to bed, leaving them to sit by the fire's dying embers. She had poured two glasses of Strega. 'You sure it's a good idea?' he said.

'What, you suddenly got sober?'

'For you, I mean.'

Becca sipped her drink. 'I drank wine at the table. Today, yesterday too, the other times you came.'

'I was waiting for the right moment to broach the subject.'

'The subject being my alcoholism.'

'In a not-judgemental way.'

'I was an alcoholic. I got better.'

'I'm going to say something, but I want you to know I'm only trying to help you, okay?'

She gestured him to go on, with a gleam of amusement in her eyes.

'You *cannot* get better, not really. You can only keep it under control. There are no former alcoholics. That's why people who had a problem with alcohol usually don't touch any of it.'

'I know.'

'But?'

'I'm alive by miracle, Ric. *Literally* by miracle.' She took another sip. 'This is the least of it.'

'I'm worried.'

'And I love you for that.'

The next day they went back to humming, fortified by their easy success with the breathing. The task felt achievable in a way it hadn't at the end of the first attempt. They slipped into an easy routine. Ric would wake up every morning before dawn, have breakfast, and get some work done for university, while Becca helped Mum with the million chores required by a small farm. Then, in the afternoon, Becca and Ric would go in the pinewood, wrap themselves in warm blankets, light a fire, and hum. Ric would sit with Becca, watching her while she watched him, synching the movement of his chest with hers, synching the vibration in his throat and the tiniest quiver of his lips. He was giving himself up to her completely, at the warmth of a scented fire of olive tree logs. They went to a secret place, only theirs, and Ric was vaguely ashamed of how much he enjoyed that. He was nine years old again, when his big sister knew everything and would protect him from any danger. A regressive pleasure, but pleasure nonetheless.

10

He felt it happen one moment before it did, the last piece falling snugly into place, the final curl of cream on a wedding cake, the one right word that turns an average paragraph into a glimpse of beauty. He raised his voice a smidge while Becca lowered hers, and they met at the exact right spot for an explosion. Ric felt the change on his skin, on his tongue, on the tips of his fingers. The sky turned to black and it filled with strange stars. The trees became larger, thicker, darker, with their canopy fading into starlight. It was only a moment – Ric jumped and screamed and the spell was broken.

It was the eighth day, at dusk.

Becca looked at him with an amused face. Ric whipped his head from her to the pinewood, which had reverted to normal. 'What was that?' he asked, when his heart slowed down enough to allow him to string three words together.

'We'll do it again tonight.'

'Can't you just...'

'Later,' she said. 'It is easier at night.'

Becca suggested they ate lightly at dinner, and after Mum retired to bed, they went back to the fig tree and lit a fire on the ashes still warm from the afternoon. 'There's one last thing we need to do,' Becca said. 'It is not necessary, but it's going make the rest easier. Don't freak out, okay?'

She unzipped her jacket, took off her sweater, then her shirt. When she brought her hand to the clasp of her bra, Ric asked, 'All the way?'

'All the way.'

'It's freezing cold.'

'Chuck some more wood into the fire.'

'But why?'

'If you want the unusual to happen, you must start from yourself.'

They undressed and wrapped themselves under one blanket, standing by the fire. They hugged each other to keep warm. It was not awkward as Ric had feared – he felt he was the piece falling into place, the curl of cream, the right word. He had found his place.

Becca rested her forehead against his, closed her eyes, and hummed. He followed her into the hum, and he had a sense of walking down a winding path made of sounds, hand in hand with his sister, until he felt the same sweet vertigo which had caught him in the afternoon. He opened his eyes.

They were under another sky, and the pinewood had shifted too. It was closer to the pinewood that had always existed in Ric's imagination, the endless place when, as a kid, he had been playing the pirate, the cowboy, the monster. He had to keep humming or the vision would break. Becca led him for a little longer, then gently brought the hum to an end. The stars went out, and the pinewood dimmed.

They put their clothes on again, fed the fire, and took out the Primitivo wine and the almond biscuits they had brought in a backpack. 'I needed you to see it,' she said, when they were sitting, 'or you wouldn't have believed me.'

'Nobody would.'

'Nobody sane,' Becca laughed. 'Are you ready? It's going to be a lot.'

Ric pointed his thumb at the sky. '*That* was a lot.'

'I took a bad pill and I died, Ric. I died for real. It's dumb luck that I made it to the hospital. When I did kick the bucket, I was among people who knew their deal rather than with a bunch of kids high on cheap chemicals. Had I died five minutes earlier, we wouldn't be here. It was, and I use the word in its more literal sense, a miracle.'

Ric munched a biscuit. 'I cannot think of it.'

'No, but you should, because that's when everything changed. When I died and a miracle happened.'

'Did you have a Near-Death Experience? Did you see a tunnel, a light, someone waiting for you…'

Becca laughed. 'The only vision I ever had was in the pinewood. No, I was in that horrible club with a stink of stale vomit and knockoff gin, my legs gave way, then— Then I woke up in a hospital bed, head fuzzy, a bruise on my leg, a bigger one on my bum. No visions. But when my mind cleared, I *remembered*.'

'You remembered what?'

'That you and I, with the help of a group of friends, did something important. Something *momentous*, Ric.'

Ric fed more wood into the fire. 'Nothing comes to mind.'

'Because we did not do it in the past, we did it somewhere down the line. In the future.'

'We *are going* to do it, you mean. A prophecy.'

'No, no, not at all! I wasn't seeing the future, I was *remembering* it.'

'You can't remember something that hasn't happened yet.'

'Of course you're right, but still, I know how memory feels, and these are memories I'm talking of, memories of the future. Can you take my word for it? I can't demonstrate anything, all I can do is ask you to trust me. Will you do that?'

Ric nodded.

'My hypothesis is, what we did was so fuckin' *big* it sent ripples in every direction, backward as much as forward.'

'That's impossible.'

'Says who?'

Ric smiled, remembering the conversation they had had the first time Becca told him about her voices. It had gone pretty much the same way. 'Everybody...?' he answered now as he had answered then. Becca grinned and bumped his shoulder with hers. She remembered too. Ric added, 'Seriously though. What is it that we are going to do?'

'We *did*. Somehow, we already did it.'

'Fine – what is it?'

'We saved the world. I know how it sounds, I know, but I promise, Ric, I promise – we saved the world. If you can believe only one thing I say to you, this is it.'

Ric let those words sit in his mind. He observed them from every angle. 'What from?' he asked.

'I cannot remember for the life of me, but it'll come back. It's like piecing together your actions on a very, very drunken night. I've got figments, words, images flying through my mind. I didn't remember you were part of it until I saw you in the hospital. Other pieces will come.'

'And why do you have these pieces and I don't?'

'You didn't die, did you?'

'You were strange way before that,' Ric teased her.

'Also that. I may be more attuned to certain psychic waves.'

'You still believe your voices are real.'

'You still believe they aren't?'

Ric took another biscuit. 'Are they making sense, after you... came back?'

'They're humming,' Becca said. 'This is what they have been doing for my entire life – humming. Preparing me for here and now. When we got the right pitch, they were humming with us. I wish you could hear the sound they made, Ric! It was beautiful music. If I'm right, the voices are echoes from the future. They may be us. Echoes of us, I mean.'

'What's with the hum?'

'We were humming when we did this thing in the future. We were humming, all of us. I just remembered it, when we hummed together.'

'And the hum is...'

'Your guess is as good as mine.'

'You've had more time to think this through.'

'An echo of the music of the spheres? A riff on the sound the universe makes? I have nothing better to offer.'

'When we *got the right pitch*, as you say, we went *somewhere else*.'

'No, I don't think so, I don't think we went anywhere. The hum doesn't shift us in space, it shifts our consciousness. Some music can make you cry, some can make you dance. Ours can make... this.'

'That lush sky wasn't only in our head.'

'Perhaps our consciousness isn't, either. I'm just thinking out loud, Ric, figuring things as I go. All I have is, I came back from death with these memories and there must be something to them, because I remembered we could do the impossible, and we just did, you and me. I need you to figure out the rest with me.'

'I'm with you,' Ric said, 'till the end of the world.'

'Help me gather the others then.'

11

Becca moved in with Ric. He gave her the bedroom and took to sleeping on the sofa. She pestered him to do it the other way round, but he was adamant it was his house, his rules (the sleeping arrangements were, in fact, the only rule he ever made). Becca had no intention to go back to university. 'It's not my path,' she said. She was not in Lecce to study or to start a career, she was there to find her people, an easier thing to do in a bustling cultural city than in a secluded pinewood. She went back to temp jobs, which did not make Ric particularly happy. Then again, his sister had died and come back, and could work miracles. She could take care of herself.

Living and hanging out with her, Ric came to believe that she had gone the same way the pinewood did when they hummed. It would be inexact to say she had changed, but she had turned up the volume of herself. The light in her eyes had always been intense and now it was almost unbearable; her gait had always been decisive and now she walked as if she was the queen of bloody heaven and hell; her voice had always been husky and now it played like one of those drop-dead gorgeous gramophones that only existed in films. She found a part-time job as a bartender in one of the trendiest bars in Lecce, and another as a bookseller in an independent bookshop, famous for catering to a crowd of impecunious writers and artists who spent a lot of time browsing and very little money buying. She was casting her net wide.

(The whole city must have been transformed, in those days: more vibrant, more alive. Becca and Ric were walking her baroque streets, and the world was waiting to be changed.)

Every now and again, they would hum. It was immensely more difficult to do in Lecce than in the pinewood. The one time they managed to get the pitch, the effect was more subdued. They could see the starry sky and also the ceiling, as if the first was a projection on the second, but their visions were fading even in the pinewood. Becca thought it was because they were getting too used to each other: magic dies, she said, in routine. They decided to stop the humming entirely until they found the ones they were looking for.

Becca clicked with Ric's friends, and made some of her own. The first was a curly-haired poet who wrote spectacularly bad lines but was, beneath all his airs, quite a sweet guy. When he wrote *the summer heat / sees the world through your eyes*, everybody knew he referred to Becca. She slept with him, out of sympathy, but made it clear that was that, and he was a good sport about it. Others came. A gym-obsessed young woman with a couple of black belts, a thirty-three-year-old who was still an undergraduate and smoked prodigious amounts of dope, a film-maker who was trying to get a black-and-white silent film financed, a pagan singer-songwriter whose every song sounded like 'Nottamun Town', a tarot reader in transition, another film-maker who was more about B-movies, a thirty-something who had been a nun for three years before becoming a rock climber, a self-styled witch who would go on about both her psychic powers and her cats, a PhD student of mathematics whose research questioned that reality actually existed, and many others.

One night, an underground legend came in, a gaunt man in his thirties with large ears and bottleneck glasses, called Art. Apparently he was from Casalfranco, the next town over from Portodimare, and all sorts of rumours flew around him. He was passing by Lecce, and would soon leave again, for Malta. He told stories about his life that nobody could make head or tail of. He said he had been to another world; he said he had knowledge of hidden things and was going to write a book about it, and he said he was *ready*, though for what, that wasn't clear. Becca and Ric both found him fascinating – but after that night, they never heard of him again.

(Art, the mysterious Art. We have heard so many rumours about him, and we could not tell what is true and what is not.)

The doors of Becca and Ric's flat kept revolving most nights. When Becca was working a shift, she would go back home late at night to be cheered the moment she stepped in. Sometimes people kept coming until well after midnight, for nightcaps that lasted until the crack of dawn. They'd shoot the crap about poetry, philosophy, bad movies and football; they did impromptu readings and showed the films they were working on; they traded books, spliffs and bodily fluids. One night Mikka walked in.

12

He was a friend of the pagan musician. They had met at a relentlessly rainy festival in Scotland, where they shared the tent of another friend they had in common. Mikka was much older than the usual crowd, and didn't speak a word of Italian. Both things conspired to make him a hit – people felt cosmopolitan getting to speak in English to this seasoned hippie with an outlaw's face, and Mikka had a bag full of stories which were less wild than Art's, but more relatable for that. Becca asked him how long he would be in town. 'Couple of weeks,' he said.

'He's one of us,' she told Ric, when everybody left that night.

'*That one?*'

'I remember his face, I remember his voice.'

Ric passed a hand through his hair. 'This is so fucking strange.'

'It was like seeing an old friend, Ric. I don't have a doubt.'

'And what do we do now? We set him down to hum?'

'You and I have been close for our whole life, that's why it took so little for us to synch. A new dude, it may take weeks, possibly months, to get there.'

'So he needs to believe before he hums.'

'I guess.'

'Okay: we need a hook.'

And just like that, the idea of the self-improvement workshops was born. Ric said that, in order to convince people to believe in something, you only need to give them a group they want to belong to, and a course of action enforced by the group. Make them act first, together with other people, and they will believe later.

Between the two of them, Becca and Ric had read enough to quickly hatch a philosophy of sorts, and a set of spiritual exercises. They slapped together a little Plato and a little Bergson, some Gurdjieff, a touch of Crowley, whisked with their own ideas, and they were ready to go. They spread the voice among a select number of people that they were organising a weekend retreat at their place in Portodimare, for free, to play with some philosophical ideas. Then they told Mikka.

They made music, smoked dope, listened to Becca's teachings in the pinewood, while Becca and Ric's mum cooked for them. They barely slept for three days, they were having so much fun.

At the end Ric and Becca played their card and told Mikka he was special. They recognised something in him and they did have a message for him, but they couldn't tell it just yet. He had to stay, if he wanted to find out.

Mikka was intrigued.

(It was not the first time he had heard similar lines, but the difference was, Becca and Ric were obviously special themselves.)

The tricky point was, he had no money, no job, and without speaking Italian, no way to find one. Becca and Ric couldn't believe they hadn't factored in a problem so obvious. They tried to come up with a solution, but meanwhile Mikka had to go. Philosophy and friends were all good, but he'd run out of cash. With him leaving, it seemed that Becca and Ric's plan would never lift off the ground.

Three months later Mum died, the way she had lived, without making a fuss.

13

Becca found in herself a hitherto unsuspected love for her mother. True, Mum had been passive in front of Dad's abuse, and true, she had left Becca high and dry in Becca's most difficult years, but she had also taken her back home without question, she had run a farm on her own, and cooked, when she was asked, for the offbeat characters her children brought home. People are complicated – Becca would never forget that moving forward.

Becca and Ric's friends all came to the funeral. Portodimare had never seen such a bright ceremony, which did not please some of the locals. Rosa Pastore, the dentist's wife, commented that the Abbracciaventos used to be respectable, but this last generation was destroying the family name. Becca especially – who would wear bangles at a funeral?

(Rosa Pastore: we cannot think of her name without wanting to scream.)

When the dust had settled, Becca and Ric talked next steps, although, as is often the case, it was more about talking themselves into doing what they had already decided to do than about weighing options. Our nature was unfolding.

Ric quit his job – the money was bad anyway. He and Becca threw one last memorable party in their Lecce flat, then put it on the market and went back to Villa Abbracciavento. 'Full circle,' Becca said, when she dropped her luggage in her once-and-future room. Ric felt an intoxicating sense of freedom. He felt as if he were riding a motorbike speeding up on a straight stretch.

It was three months before they sorted the nuts and bolts of running the farm, and six before they were ready to call Mikka with a job offer. He accepted on the spot. 'I'd seen crazy in my life,' he would say later, laughing. 'But these two were another thing. I cannot say I was completely bought yet. Damn sure I was curious.' A job with friendly hippies by a Mediterranean beach was better than what he had at the time, a zero-hours contract as a docker in an oil port in Scotland.

Mikka moved in with all his worldly possessions, which fitted in a scruffy duffel bag. 'It's a pretty large duffel bag, though,' he said good-humouredly when he confirmed to Ric that yes, this was all he had.

He fit in at the farm with ease. He was handy with the tractor, he would not squirm at killing animals or helping them give birth, and he was a quick study. He learnt enough Italian to get by with the hired hands and the Portodimare people.

It took four months to hit the pitch and when that happened, Mikka cried. 'It's so beautiful,' he said. 'So fucking beautiful.' He was not a crying man. For Becca and Ric, the experience had never been this intense again after their first time. The three of them spent that summer night messing about around the fire, starting a tradition. Mikka went as far as tongue-kissing Becca – and he was not at all keen on women, sexually. They drank and smoked and promised to each other they would save the world indeed, whatever the cost. 'We're going to be this universe's last bastion,' Ric drunkenly proclaimed. That's how we got our name.

Some things were looking up, others, not so much. Becca's main concern was that no new people were coming in. She, Ric and Mikka would throw open parties, and they kept meeting interesting characters, but not the ones she was looking for. Becca circled back to the workshops idea. 'Let's light a candle in the dark,' she said. 'Those who are meant to see it, will do.' She sat down with Ric to polish their teachings, with one eye on making them fun and one on making them useful. Mikka brought to the table his decades-spanning party experience. The goal was to create something people would want to join, something that would make their heart sing and blow their mind.

Becca and Ric advertised the workshops discreetly, but widely, and they took off like wildfire. Sam found his way to us with the second workshop, the Nameless with the fourth. That time Mikka said, 'Hey, another Swallow flew back home,' and the word remained. It was better than *newbie* – more respectful.

The workshops were an informal, cash-only affair, and much better for that. They had that easy feeling of friendship that would make the Open Feast such a success. When Becca recognised one of us, we asked them to stay, never explaining why, only offering an intriguing mystery and a longer holiday. A job on the farm too, if needed. Nobody ever refused. The more we did our patter, the more we refined it. We grew in numbers and confidence; we took over the work on the entire farm, without need for any hired hands. We became a family.

We became complacent.

Every Swallow made it so we had to start all over again with the hum, and every time it was harder, because the more of us there were, the more people each of us had to synch with. One person questioned the soul of all, which was, Becca said, exactly what kept us changing, and thus alive.

We had a good few years, before the stream of new people trickled to a stop.

We were not getting any new Swallows from the workshop, and (unmentionable truth we couldn't voice to ourselves) we were growing bored of the workshops themselves. To the participants, they were a blast; to us, they were more of the same. The same activities, the same games, the same ideas, the same show of enthusiasm, five or six times a year. Magic dies in routine. Even the hum started losing its lustre. Becca and Ric noticed that, and as was their custom, they did not wait for the problem to fester. They acted immediately.

One morning, out of the blue, Ric told us we were to start a new exercise. It was called the Receding Wave and it would be, he promised, one of the most intense experiences of our life. He was not lying; he never did. Each of us remembers our first Receding Wave. We are not sure it is possible to understand how life-changing it is without going through it – the silence in your mind, the clarity, the sex, the odd dreams. The Receding Wave refashions your reality, and opens up new spaces of possibility for you as a human being. It makes away with all the masks you wear, all the shields you hide behind, and shows what lies at the core of you. Becca drew it to a close after a month.

When she spoke to us, her voice was milk and honey. 'We're done with the workshops,' she said. 'That part of our life is over.'

We asked what came now.

'A festival,' she said. 'It is going to be fun.'

4

OUR NATURE, UNFOLDING

LILA

It was a sturdy branch. Galen, hanging, did not curve it at all. Ric brought his hands to his head and said, 'Fuck.' Becca was breathing hard.

I asked them if we could bring him back. I had seen magic at work, why not this?

'Can we?' asked Ric.

Becca shot him a look which made him raise his hands in apology.

'Get Mikka,' she said. 'A knife too.'

Becca sat down on the damp ground with me and took me in her arms, while Ric went to fetch both. I had not shed a tear yet. I put my head on Becca's breast, and heard her heart beat. *So strange,* I thought, *that Becca has a physical heart, like any of us.* A heart that could stop.

Ric and Mikka took the body down, hauled it between the two of them and took it towards Villa Abbracciavento, with me and Becca in tow. Imogen saw and spread the word. We gathered inside. Sam let out a cry when Ric and the others entered, and turned his head to one side, not to look.

We lay Galen on the floor. We covered him with a green blanket.

'What happened?' Imogen asked.

Becca opened her mouth to answer, but this was on me. 'Galen was scared, badly scared, and I didn't listen to him. He didn't want to fight in the coming battle.'

'Battle?'

'How do you think we're going to save the world?'

Ric searched for Becca's eyes, but hers were trained on us. Sam was taking out his phone.

'Please,' Becca said. 'Don't.'

Sam asked, 'We're not calling the guards?'

'They don't bother us while we keep a low profile. This comes out, we're done.'

'But that's our friend there...'

Becca reached out for my hand, squeezed it. 'Galen did what he did because he could not take the truth. But *he knew* it was the truth. What good would it be, to throw away all that we've built? How would that serve his memory?'

'You cannot ask us to *hide a body*!' the Nameless shouted.

Mikka unfolded his arms, ready to fight, if it came to that.

I said, 'Galen hated his parents,' and everybody shut up. They accepted that, if anyone had a right to having the last word, it was me. 'He hadn't seen them in years, he didn't know if they were alive and didn't care. We were his only family, the only ones who are going to miss him. We call the guards – what for?'

The Nameless grumbled and mumbled but even he couldn't argue. He had a soft spot for me.

Becca looked at me with pride, then looked at the others. 'You called this a *body*,' she said, disgusted. 'A body! This is not a thing, this is not *dead meat*. This is our beautiful Galen, our friend. And just to be clear, we aren't going to hide him. No, we are going to bid him farewell the way he deserves. Does anyone have any objections to that?'

None of the others did; not openly, not yet.

We set down to work immediately. Sirocco brought a warm spell, which quickly made the body simmer with a strong odour. Mikka guided a group to one of the fields of the farm's estate, to build a pyre. Becca and Ric had decided we would not burn Galen in the pinewood. A body makes a thick smoke which leaves an unsettling residue on everything it touches, and a scent like copper. We wanted open fields to set the smoke free, so that Galen would stay in our hearts, yes, but without haunting us.

The field had been a fig orchard, now left to its own devices for the benefit of shrubs, birds and bees. It was beautifully eerie, scattered with moon-pale fig trees, their stately branches naked this time of year, reaching now upwards, now downwards, in a prayer which went at once to the skies and the chthonic powers. In February the trees were bare, but the land was green with clumps of yellow flowers. They made the ground bright, even while the heavy clouds bore down on us like a death sentence. A round drystone hut with a cavernous mouth, a *trullo,* was the only building in sight. Herbs and plants grew in the gaps between the jagged rocks it was made of.

We built a tall pyre, which we filled with dry pine cones and twigs. It would catch fire quickly. The pine cones were releasing a balmy scent.

Back in Villa Abbracciavento, another group took care of the body, under Ric's guidance. Lila insisted on being part of it. 'You don't have to,' Ric said, to which Lila answered, 'I know.' We undressed the body, washed it and cleaned it thoroughly, and threw away the soiled clothes. We did nothing to conceal the red trace on Galen's neck. 'We don't hide what we do,' Ric said. 'We're not ashamed of our actions.' But we did comb his curly hair, and we anointed his skin with a scented rub of oil and pine. We placed in his mouth a coin for the Ferryman. We debated whether to dress him in fresh clothes, and in the end we decided he would leave this world the way we all come into it, naked. Ric and Lila were the only ones who were not sick while they worked on the body. We admired them for that.

Becca shuffled between the two groups, talking to us, working with us. Some of the things she heard gave her pause for thought.

'Headaches are coming,' she said to Ric, in the privacy of a bathroom. While he took a shower, she sat on the bathroom's floor, leaning against the wall outside the cabin.

'The usual suspects,' Ric said from the shower.

'Mh-mh.'

'I heard him too.'

'What do you make of it?' Becca asked.

Ric mentioned the Nameless. 'He's been gunning for a fight for, how long now? This could be his chance.'

'Can't say I'm going to miss him if he leaves.'

'He tells stories, we're fucked.'

Becca sighed. 'Don't I know.'

Ric turned off the tap, grabbed a towel and wrapped it around himself. 'This is on us. You and me.'

'Ric...'

'What were we thinking?'

'We're doing our best.'

'We pushed a man to take his own life!'

'How could we imagine?'

'How could we not? It's a band of outcasts that we've got here. Matches and kindling, fires will happen.'

'We're no less outcast than them.'

Ric sat down next to Becca. 'All the more reason why we should have known better.'

'We are learning on the job.'

Ric passed a hand through his wet hair. 'Do I sound terrible if I say, better Galen than another?'

'You were never fond of him.'

'He was holding Lila back.'

'And Lila can soar.'

'Lila can soar.'

'I don't disagree. Still, I liked Galen.'

'Course,' Ric said, with a grin.

Becca pushed his shoulder with hers. 'Oh, shut up. As if you didn't sleep with him.'

'Seriously, he wasn't a bad man, not by a mile. It's more that he was weak, the weakest of us. Too much life got at him too early, and damaged him beyond repair.' He shook his head. 'How did we miss it?'

'We're going to do better from now on.'

'You still want to go on with the Open Feast.'

'You screw up, you learn, you try again – that's how life works and that's what we are going to do. Well, if,' and she mentioned the Nameless, 'doesn't bring us down.'

'I'll take care of him,' said Ric.

LILA

It was a starless, moonless night. Plump clouds made the sky into a dark mush. Galen's body lay on top of the pyre, and I stood by it with Becca. Four torches burning at the four cardinal points, around the pyre, were the only light. Although the fields were empty, and private, I did feel exposed, with the wind coming in damp gusts to remind me how big and full of mystery the world was.

Ric drummed a solemn beat while we made a circle. It was the first time we came together like this – to mourn and not to party. One of us was dead, and that gave our mission a focus it hadn't had so far. It was the first time I was afraid. I had known, intellectually, that our task was real, but that night I realised what that implied.

I turned my head towards the pyre, and all of a sudden I couldn't hold it anymore. I wailed. A primal shriek burst out of my body like an alien creature and took over the fields and the clouds. When it died out, I flopped on to Galen's body, sobbing. I kissed his face, his forehead, his lips.

The others gave me time to talk to Galen. I didn't say anything coherent. There was no need to. 'My love,' I was saying. 'My sweet, sweet Galen.' My voice was small in the bleak fields. I kissed and caressed him, until I drew back, gave him one last look, wiped my eyes, and nodded at Becca. 'Sorry.'

Becca hugged me tight.

The others walked to the body one by one and gave Galen their personal farewell: a kiss, a caress, a word, a gaze. Then four people grabbed the torches and lit the pyre, while I drummed. One of the torch bearers was the Nameless, who did not make a secret of being unhappy. We went on drumming and humming while the fire consumed Galen's body. Our hum was awkward – Galen's voice was missing from it. We would need time to readjust.

When the last cinder died and only blackened bones remained, we dropped our hum, and I brought my drumming to a stop. I walked to the ashes and took the skull in my hands. I raised it; the coin rattled and fell. 'Can I keep it?' I asked, and after a moment's hesitation Becca nodded.

We put the other bones in a burlap sack and took them with us.

We would feed them to Napoleon, so that Galen would be, by next year, a part of us once again.

Back home, I cut the walnut and coffee cake we'd baked for Galen's birthday. It was our holy Communion at the end of that long night, and I felt better after it. I'd miss Galen every day of my life, but I did have many more days to live, a mission to accomplish, and a family to accomplish it with. Galen was a fallen soldier in our holy war.

THE BASTION

Our sadness degraded into peevishness, and soon we were at each other's throats. Malcontent spilled from the Nameless to spread quickly, the way bad coin does. He always had something to object to when we distributed tasks at morning call, he tried to get us to talk about Galen even though we didn't want to, he would find excuses not to pull his weight. It all came to a head one night, when Ric called us to the kitchen for a chat. He came straight to the point and said to the Nameless, 'You have a problem, which means we all do.'

'We don't have a problem,' he said.

'Speak up, man.'

'Why are you putting me on the spot?'

'I'm trying to keep it polite here. Speak up. Please.'

'Looks like you're the one having a problem with me.'

We had had rows before (there had been a few blazing ones while we organised the first Open), but this was different.

Ric said, 'You've been busting our balls, and twice as hard since Galen's funeral.'

He was speaking out loud what we all had been thinking.

'You call that a funeral?' the Nameless said.

'Why, what do you call it?'

'Hiding evidence?' he said, in the faux-witty voice of someone who pretends they're joking because they are too cowardly to own up to the fact they're not.

Becca said, 'You're still sore we didn't go to the guards.'

'*We burned a body!*'

'You were first in line with the torch.'

'Ric asked me to.'

'And you didn't refuse,' Ric said.

'I couldn't.'

'How come?'

'You'd have made a big deal.'

Ric asked us, 'Did Becca, I, or anybody really, ever make a big deal of someone saying no?'

'You're making a big deal now.'

'Of you busting my balls? Hell, yes.'

'I think it was bad business, okay?'

Lila said, 'I asked then and I'll ask again: what good would it have done, calling the guards?'

'I don't know, Lila, to keep us out of jail?'

LILA

The little creep. I wanted to gouge his eyes out on the spot.

THE BASTION

Ric scoffed. 'And we get to the point at last. Fuck what Galen would have wanted, fuck what Lila wants, fuck our mission. Just as long as your ass is safe.'

'*Our* asses,' the Nameless said. 'The Carabinieri would've given us a hard time, the press an even harder one, okay, fine. But now?' He looked at us. 'Do you guys realise what we did?'

'Do you?'

'What if Galen didn't tell us the truth about his family? What if he had friends who start wondering where the hell he is?'

'We're happy to take risks,' Mikka said, in an icy voice. 'Not you, apparently. Not for your family's sake, not for the world's.'

'The world!' the Nameless scoffed.

'Come again?'

'Can't we just be upfront and say what we all think? *We are going to save the world* – come on. From what? *Saving the world* as a, I don't know, a metaphor, a life goal, I get that. But Galen took it literally, and look how it ended! Do you actually believe we're going to save the world? Us? Between a foursome and a joint?'

'Yes,' Ric said.

'We're a bunch of superheroes, meant to save the world from fuck knows what?! I don't know about you guys, but Galen seemed pretty human to me. It's time we grow out of the comic-book stuff.'

Ric stood up, calmly, got closer, and hit the Nameless with a right hook in the face. We gasped while the Nameless stumbled and his nose bled. Ric grabbed the Nameless's balls and squeezed; the Nameless cried. 'Don't you dare make fun of our mission,' Ric said, above the Nameless's whines, before letting him go. The Nameless fell into the arms of two of us.

Lila spat at his feet. 'And don't you dare use Galen's name.'

A frisson of delight joined us all. It was dawning on us how powerful we were, how much we could do, when we came together.

Ric took a bunch of napkins and threw them at the bleeding one. 'I can't stand to see your face, but I don't call the shots.'

The Nameless blocked his nose with the napkins, which immediately reddened.

'We're going to have a vote, and I promise – I *fucking* promise – I'll abide by whatever the Bastion decides. A show of hands, please. Who wants,' and he mentioned the Nameless, 'to go?'

LILA

My hand shot up first, then Mikka's. Becca's too, more slowly. We all raised a hand. I'd never felt so powerful. We were rising to our first challenge. Together, we were invincible.

'It's done,' Becca said, and turned to the Nameless. 'You are leaving tomorrow. I trust that you are not going to tell tales, that you will have that decency at least. But in case you need it, let me remind you that you were burning Galen with us. That you were with us the whole time.'

'And let *me* remind you,' Ric said, 'that anything that comes between us and our sacred duty is fair game, as far as I'm concerned. You make problems for us, we will find you, and we will take full responsibility for any action necessary, no more and no less than we do with Napoleon. Am I clear?'

The Nameless did not answer, but when Ric clenched his fist, he made a small nod.

He left early next morning. We decreed we would cross his name from our mind, purge him from our life. He had never belonged with us in the first place. 'We made a mistake,' Becca admitted. 'It wasn't the first, it won't be the last. I remembered him being with us, but I didn't remember him doing what he did, as I didn't remember Galen...' She trailed off. 'Only liars can say they're perfect.'

THE BASTION

February gave way to March, and from there to June time ran fast. The organisation of the Open Feast left little space for sorrow. That year's Feast was the most fruitful we would ever have, as if the cogs of a secret symmetry were turning to compensate for our losses: three Swallows joined us. Life was good once again, and so it remained for many years, until a monster found us, and our war began.

ZOEY

She called my name: 'Zoey!'

I'd fallen into the habit of going for a run before breakfast. We all found ways to carve out some alone time, and running was mine. I would wake up early and go through the streets of Portodimare at an easy pace, pushing myself, not too much. The voice made me stumble and stop. I knew that voice better than my own.

Janis was sipping cappuccino at a table of the only café on my route which was open in the heart of winter. The baby was snug in a portable highchair which had the threatening look of an insectoid robot one bad line of code away from starting an uprising. There was a stark contrast between the futuristic gizmo and the worn plastic chairs of the café – there was a contrast between Janis and Portodimare – yet my first instinct was to find her presence completely natural. In my adult life I'd never spent more than three weeks apart from her, and that had been only once, when she went on her fucking honeymoon. Now the universe was sliding back into order.

Or not. 'You stalked me,' I said.

'Pleasure to see you too.'

'Seriously?'

'Why don't you sit?'

'No, thank you.'

'I changed three flights with a baby in tow just to see you.'

'Did I ask you to?'

Janis looked at me.

'I was working out,' I said. 'I'm sweating. I can't stop.'

Janis reached into the spacious mum-bag at her feet to fish out a blanket, which she offered to me. I knew defeat when I saw it. I let myself fall into a chair.

'What are you having?' Janis asked. 'Orange juice?'

'You know.'

'Keep an eye on Ellie.'

Janis went inside to place the order, leaving me alone with the baby. Ellie had grown stratospherically in the months since I had seen her, and she looked now more like a person and less like a bug. I still had no idea what to do with her though. She was starting to produce alarming sounds when Janis came out with a bottle of orange juice and a glass.

'The fuck?' I asked while Janis sat down.

'Please don't swear in front of Ellie.'

'She's too little to care.'

'She's impressionable.'

'I'll rephrase: what's going on?'

'*You're* asking *me*?'

'I just did.'

'Last time we talked, you told me to fuck off.' She turned to Ellie. 'Sorry. Don't repeat everything Mummy says, okay?' She turned back to me. 'And then you slipped off the face of the Earth. No Facebook, no Instagram, no WhatsApp, no nothing.'

I shook my head.

'What?' Janis said.

'Is that the law, now? That you have to be on socials?'

'It's just what normal people do.'

'*Normal* was the last thing we wanted. Remember? We hated *normal.*'

'We also hated cults.'

'You've become like the people we used to fight against! Knocking down what you don't understand.'

Ellie did not like the escalation; she was getting upset again. Janis took her in her arms to calm her down and asked me, in a patronising tone, 'Help me understand then.'

'How did you find me?'

'It's my scene. *Our* scene! I put out feelers, I called in favours, I asked around.'

'And some idiot broke the NDA.'

'The Bastion has skeletons in the closet.'

'Because SoulJo doesn't.'

'Not literally, no.'

That hit too close for comfort. Was that a reference to Galen? I changed tack. 'I made it very clear I didn't want you here.'

'Yet, here I am.'

'And you don't see how disrespectful this is.'

'I was worried sick.'

'The excuse of every controlling freak out there: *I'm worried! I'll be checking on your every move because I can't help it!*'

Janis turned to her baby again, to tie up her clothes. 'What did they do to you?' she asked. Her tone was concerned now, which sent me off the roof.

'They did more *for* me than anyone ever did before.'

'I've missed you, Zoey. Immensely.'

She almost drew a tear, with those words. 'I've missed you too. You know that.'

'Come back home.'

'I will! Some day. For now though, this *is* home.'

'I'm doing my best here, but you've got to give me something.'

I started feeling cold; the light breeze coming from the sea was drying up my sweat. I hadn't touched her orange juice yet – now I poured it into the glass. 'I found it, Janis. That thing we've always been looking for, that thing we couldn't even name. Magic, wonder, a deeper meaning of life... I still don't know what to call it. I don't know if it even *has* a name, but one thing I know is, I've found it.'

'With the Bastion.'

I nodded.

'These Becca and Ric – they seem to be remarkable people.'

'They are.'

'When am I meeting them?'

'Yeah, dream on.'

'Why, what's the problem?'

'We were keeping our location a secret to outsiders. It was our choice, our *right*.'

'I'm an *outsider* to your life now? *Me*?'

'You made yourself one!'

'We have SoulJo together.'

'I told you, keep it! Have your lawyers send me the papers and I'll sign everything you want.'

'I don't want you to sign a thing.'

'What were you thinking, Jan? You stalked me from New York to Southern Italy, you called me to account for how I live my life, and I should, what? Say thank you and buy you coffee? You're coming over as creepy. If you were anybody else, I'd be calling the police.' I made a show of checking my watch and stood up. 'I've got to go.'

'I'm talking to Becca and Ric.'

'I wasn't kidding about the police.'

Janis shrugged. 'Call them,' she said. And after a while she added, 'Go on.'

CHARLIE

Ever since the Receding Wave, we had been living between worlds. Oddballs would wake us up in the morning, and sunshine would make rainbows on giant bubbles. We would hear the barking of long-gone pets, smell the skin of lost lovers. We did our best to ignore the faint fiddling from the dark side of the sky, and the occasional banging. But none of that showed up for the stranger.

She wore loose harem pants and a half-moon on her nose. Her baby was tied to her chest with an ocean-blue shawl. She was one of us, but not really one of us. I knew she was trouble as soon as I saw her, with Zoey walking a step behind. Zoey in thrall to another human being: it was not a scene I believed I would ever see, nor one I particularly cared for.

We knew everything about Janis, Zoey's friend and one true love. Janis, who had gone and got married, breaking Zoey's heart. Janis, who had discarded Zoey like a used condom. Janis, who had been judgemental and aggressive when Zoey had tried to make a life of her own.

We were not fond of Janis.

Still, I made her coffee and offered her biscuits and cold cuts. She was aggressively polite, and kept insisting she had to talk to Becca and Ric alone, until Zoey snapped, 'Do you realise how patronising this is?'

'I'm sorry you feel that way,' was the stock answer she gave.

Becca said, 'We're happy to do whatever will make you feel better, if it is okay with Zoey.'

She made a dismissive gesture. 'As long as you shut her up.'

'We can go to the beach,' Ric proposed. 'It's nice and quiet.'

Janis started unwrapping her baby. 'Zoey, would you keep Ellie?'

'You're trusting your brainwashed friend with your baby?' Zoey said.

'I must love her very much.'

Zoey did not have a ready answer. Lila stepped in, saying that the baby would be fine. Janis gave her a smile which was more like a bite and left her daughter in Zoey's arms.

THE BASTION

The beach was empty, and the sea was as clear as love. Janis took off her shoes to feel the sand under her feet. 'I've never been on a beach like this,' she said.

Becca said, 'The Mediterranean is her own kind of creature.'

'Shall we talk openly?'

'That's the only way to talk,' Ric said.

'I'm worried for Zoey.'

'What is there to be worried about?' Becca asked.

'She left her home, her friends, without as much as a word of explanation.'

'How odd – she says the opposite. She says she tried to explain herself, but you cut her off.'

'She wasn't making any sense. Not last summer, not today.'

'So it's not that she didn't explain, it's that you didn't like what you heard.'

'If you want to put it that way, no, I didn't like it one bit.'

'Does Zoey look unhealthy to you?'

'She's throwing her life to the wind!'

Ric asked, 'And did her life make her happy?'

'Listen to the *psychologist*.'

Ric hadn't expected Janis to know about his past. He put on a stony face and said, 'Yes, listen to him, he knows what he's talking about.'

'And does Zoey know what you did for a living, before you came up with this cute set-up of yours?'

Becca said, 'We don't keep secrets from our family.'

'You must have spent a good deal of money and time researching us,' Ric said. 'What makes you so obsessed?'

'I don't give a fuck about you.' Janis walked to the shore, where cold winter water lapped her feet. 'But you stole my friend.'

Becca said, 'She came to us and we gave her a place to stay. You felt the need for a baby, Zoey felt the need for this. How can you not understand that?'

'The two things are not remotely the same.'

'Once more, this is you judging her. It's your problem, not Zoey's.'

It was remarkable, Becca would admit later, that Janis managed to keep her voice even, although she was obviously fuming. 'I've got to ask – what are you guys up to?'

'Our business.'

'If it harms Zoey, it's my business too.'

'And if she wanted you to know, you would know. It's up to her to decide what she's comfortable sharing with whom! We don't have a right to do that for her.'

Janis shook her head. 'You're good.' She squatted to touch the water with one hand. 'But I know you guys, I've met you so many times. So many! I've met you as activists, I've met you as the guards beating the crap out of activists, I've met you mapping birth charts and I've met you peddling books against astrology. You're just another group of people who think they have found the Truth, capital-T, and will do everything – everything – to ram it down other people's throats.'

'That's rich,' Ric scoffed. '*You* stalked us, *you* came to our place, *you* went ballistic the moment you saw us. We didn't say a word if not in self-defence, and *we* are the ones ramming truths down *your* throat?'

'I'm not here to pick a fight, okay? I'm not.'

'That's good to hear,' Becca said, 'because an argument with you is the last thing we want. Zoey loves you, which means a lot to us, believe it or not. All we wish is for her to be happy.'

'Help me out then.'

'How?'

'I was thinking, Zoey could see someone. A counsellor, a therapist. Just a one-off, to check she's okay.'

Ric said, 'I'm a trained psychologist, as you pointed out yourself. She's fine.'

'With all due respect, Ric, you're involved. I'm asking for a third party's help. I've known her for longer than you, and the way she's acting – it's not her.'

'Your friend doesn't do what you think she should be doing, and that means she's insane?'

'You're twisting my words.'

'I'm laying them bare.'

'Fine, gloves off. You have, how many people here? Fifteen? Twenty? I'm asking you to let one leave! Only one. You can keep the others, do as you like, only, help me convince Zoey to come back home. I promise – I swear – I won't bother you again. You'll never see my face, you'll never hear my name. I will give you some money too.'

Becca said, in her coldest voice, 'Zoey's not a farm animal to be sold and bought.'

'This is a business you're running. You let her go, you get something out of it.'

'We're not a business any more than we are a cult, or a labour camp! What you see is what you get – a family. We don't keep anybody against their will, and we definitely don't take bribes to sneak behind our people's backs. You want to suggest Zoey sees a therapist? Go ahead and do it yourself. We're not going to stop you. Of course we aren't, what do you think? That we will jump on you, kill you and burn the body? But neither are we going to help you gaslight one of us – or anyone else, for that matter – into believing she's unwell.'

Two seagulls came screeching. Janis watched them fly closer and then away. She said, 'I have resources.'

'So do we.'

'From what I gathered, no, you don't. Your finances are kind of shady, and you don't have one good connection in the industry. I will use every penny I have, I will call every favour I'm owed. I'm not letting this go.'

Ric said, 'Do as you wish. We will too.'

'Is that a threat?'

'Whatever you say.'

CHARLIE

We would have asked Janis to stay for the day, awkward as it was going to be, but Zoey wanted Janis to leave, and Janis showed no inclination to argue. 'I'll be in Portodimare,' she told Zoey, talking to her and to her only, before heading out with her baby and her bag. She refused a lift to her B&B. I found her insufferable. Zoey deserved better than that.

That day was a bad trip we just wanted to see the end of, and we went to bed soon after a quick, mostly silent, dinner. But I couldn't sleep. The irruption of Janis into our sanctuary had broken a spell; it had reminded me a meaner world existed outside our walls, with teeth and talons, and that world could lash out at any moment, the way it had lashed out against Bertrand. What we had was fragile.

Dark thoughts. I threw a coat on over my pjs and went for a walk.

Outsiders never could understand – never tried to understand – how deeply the Inner Pinewood came to be enmeshed with the Outer in our last weeks, after our breakthrough. Every night I would go to the spot where I first had heard Bertrand's music and, not always but almost, a saxophone would play for me.

That night the music was already playing when I arrived. I sat down. Giant bubbles floated around me, reflecting starlight. I lifted my head to the other sky. I still had no clue what that sky was. None of us did, not even Becca. We acted as if we did, but we didn't. Becca and Ric said it was another way of looking at the same old sky, but those were words which sounded meaningful when they were in fact meaningless. I had used similar words, in my professional life, when I couldn't get the hang of what was wrong with a patient, to reassure them until I figured it out. And we did not have the hang of it, none of us. We had punctured reality, but we had not figured out yet what we had found. All we knew – all I knew – was that it was beautiful. The music went on rising and falling, wrapping around me like a warm shawl.

I am not sure what happened, *what to call* what happened. It is a trope of old crime stories to have a crackpot composing anonymous missives by cutting letters from magazines and gluing them together to form words. That was the closest analogy that I could use – Bertrand had sent me a message with his sax, by gluing moments of our life together. No vision came to me, nothing so flamboyant, just memories. But I did not need visions, and Bertrand was never a flamboyant man. The music was bringing back those moments.

It started with a sax rendition of 'Let's Do It', and on its notes the first memory came, of the first time Bertrand and I had slept together. He had played that song that night, as a present for a common friend's birthday party in a warehouse in Marseille. We had been casually friends for three years, give or take, and neither of us thought we were particularly attracted to the other. But there was a fun set of people, there was champagne, and there was the spry air of spring. Ending up kissing someone was inevitable, and we ended up kissing each other; the kiss was unexpectedly good, and when Bertrand's hand wandered down my back, I didn't say no, and when it wandered inside my skirt, I didn't say no either. No dallying, I liked that. 'Come,' he asked me, and I followed him to his van, where we undressed among music gear and food wrappings, like teenage lovers out at a gig. When Bertrand cupped my breasts, I had to laugh – it was cheesy, awkward, and perfect.

The music changed, and now Bertrand was playing Paul Desmond's 'To Say Goodbye'. It was the song I found him playing when I came back late one night, after an awful day at work. A cancer patient I had grown fond of, a girl of sixteen, had taken a sudden turn for the worse in the morning, and was dead by the afternoon. When the girl's parents had left the room I'd cried, and fuck what the nurses would think. That night Bertrand made his signature fish soup, and listened to me. 'Do you believe there is life after death?' I asked.

'You want me to answer that?'

'Don't sugarcoat it.'

'No, I don't believe there's life after death. There's something stranger.'

Here's what Bertrand was trying to tell me: there's no life after death – there is something stranger. That was part of his message. Not all of it, though.

The saxophone moved to 'Body and Soul', and my memory brought me back to another long day at work, marked by a fight with an emphysema patient who was refusing what he called *big pharma poisons* in favour of a homeopathic treatment that, by having absolutely no effect, would kill him. I was talking to the hospital receptionist about this or that when I heard Bertrand saying, 'Hey there.' Before I could answer, he added, 'Don't turn. Whatever you hear, whatever you feel, please don't turn your head.'

I stopped mid-movement. 'Why?'

'If you turn your head, I will disappear,' he said, in an amused voice.

'That may be a bargain.'

'Just don't. Please?'

'I'm working.'

'Not for the next five minutes. Don't turn.'

I exchanged a look with the receptionist, a woman who some said was older than the oak tree in the parking lot, and twice as hard. The receptionist shrugged. There was a commotion behind me, a sound that I'd learnt to recognise – the sound of musical instruments getting taken out of their covers, being prepared, cats ready to roll. The cats played 'Body and Soul'. I felt frustrated at not being able to turn. I was never happy to do what I was told. It was the same frustration I felt now, in the pinewood, listening to Bertrand's music but never being able to see him. Was that the message? Was he confirming for me that the music was real, regardless of what I did or didn't see?

'You can turn now,' the receptionist said. 'The big handsome man is nodding.'

And when I remembered turning, the music changed for the last time. It was 'Flamenco Sketches' now, Bertrand's go-to piece when he was not having a good day. That was one of the worst of his life, the day he found that his best friend, his manager, had been stealing from him for years, possibly for ever. The owner of a jazz club in Paris had slipped the wrong word, in good faith or so it seemed, and Bertrand had joined the dots. 'It's not the money that stings,' he told me, over a drop of gin. 'Or the betrayal. It is knowing that I was such a fool I *allowed* him to take me in. It was obvious he was up to something, I should've got a whiff ages ago. I didn't because that would mean I had been wrong about him. I was the one fooling myself, he only made my stupidity work for him.'

That was not the first time someone had hurt Bertrand that way. He was incapable of duplicity. In the days before that time at the hospital reception, when he was preparing a surprise for me, he had been so clumsy I'd noticed he was going behind my back. I would have believed he was cheating on me, if I hadn't known better. When I turned, in the hospital, I saw this surreal scene: a quartet playing for me in the middle of the waiting room, with doctors, nurses and patients stopping to take pics. I had an insight of what might happen – Bertrand was nervous, and I'd never seen him nervous before. He was, by profession and inclination, the epitome of cool. When he stopped playing and went down on one knee, offering me a slim white ring, I burst out laughing. Why was he so nervous? Of course I'd say yes.

The music stopped.

I opened my eyes to an empty pinewood. I could not make head or tail of the message Bertrand had tried to convey, but *there was* a message. It left me ill at ease. I stood up, wiped the dirt and pine needles, and made my way back to Villa Abbracciavento.

I found my phone vibrating with notifications. *Ping. Ping. Ping.* I thought it was an issue with the phone. We did not keep any personal profile on social media, just access to the shared ones we used for the Open Feast, and we had not updated our socials since last summer (Zoey and I were the last Swallows – Open Feasts were over). Now they were going crazy, all of them.

I saw notifications from Instagram, X, Facebook, TikTok, a deluge of tags and private messages rushing like water from a breached dam. I tapped on Instagram. The followers count was going through the roof in real time. I opened a message at random, and after reading it, I dashed to wake the others up.

THE BASTION

It was that trite meme with a guy who, while walking hand in hand with his girlfriend, turns to look at another girl passing by. Over the girlfriend's head was written *my life,* over the guy's was written *me*, over the passing girl's, *sex cult on the beach*. The stuff of great comedy, it was not.

Janis had doxed us on SoulJo's socials. Reading her bloated post gave us the feeling of loss that you get from a bad diagnosis – the life we knew was over. We re-read the post obsessively. We learnt it by heart.

Hi folks, it read. *It's Janis here, from SoulJo HQ. I'm posting stuff today which is going to make me a bit of a party-pooper. I promise it's important. So. You know that Zoey, I, and all the SoulJo crew stay away from drama as much as possible. We do our thing and we let others do theirs, right? No judgement. But it would be disingenuous to hide the fact that the wider community of spiritually minded folks has always been attracting, among the many amazing friends that we know, some people who are, how can I say? Less than wholesome (Rasputin anybody?). It's always the same story – they pose as gurus, teachers, enlightened beings, and abuse others for sex, money, or simply the high of a power trip. At SoulJo we make a point of keeping these crooks away from our gatherings, and so far we had thought we didn't have any responsibility other than that. We tend to our garden and let others tend to theirs, that was our policy. Well, you cannot do that when awful stuff is happening in other gardens. You cannot just sit and watch.*

I know for a fact that a nasty sex cult is hiding behind the cover of a cute European festival you might have heard of – the Open Feast. Two siblings, Rebecca and Riccardo Abbracciavento, the minds behind the festival, have set up a system by which they convince some of their clients to stay with them for a little longer after the festival is over, for no charge. They have an amazing (truth be told) site in a pinewood by the beach, in Southern Italy, and who'd say no to a free holiday by the beachside? But then they start to methodically erode their new recruits' willpower, chipping away at it with techniques which are well-known among cult experts, until the recruits come to consider Rebecca and Riccardo (almost?) infallible and (nearly?) divine. Their recruits call them Becca and Ric – harmless-sounding nicknames. The recruits leave their families and friends without as much as a farewell to move in with Becca and Ric, and afterwards they rarely leave the pinewood at all, if not to work in Becca and Ric's nearby farm. Sounds grim? It does to me.

Mr Abbracciavento knows how it's done. He holds a PhD in psychology. The research which gained him his doctorate focused on (guess what?) mind control in cults, specifically on Jim Jones's Peoples Temple. Yes, the suicide cult to which we owe the very expression 'drinking the Kool-Aid' (the Kool-Aid they drunk was poisoned and they knew it). Mr Abbracciavento was briefly a university lecturer, until he changed career to self-styled spiritual teacher.

Ms Abbracciavento, well – look, we are not judgemental. Everybody has their history. Rebecca Abbracciavento has a particularly colourful one of drifting, alcoholism and substance abuse. There is nothing wrong with that, per se, and we are all working on ourselves, but her idea of working is making people worship her, and that is more of a problem.

Becca and Ric use a smorgasbord of manipulation techniques to keep their followers close: sex, drugs, all the stuff we love, turned in the service of systemic abuse. Just one pearl among many: they practice animal sacrifice – FORCING VEGETARIANS TO TAKE PART! I kid you not.

I personally visited Becca and Ric in Portodimare, the Puglian costal village where they set up their commune, earlier today. I am still in the village. I tried to start a conversation with them, for reasons which shall be clear in a moment, and they answered with not-so-veiled threats. That rubbed me the wrong way. I don't care for cults and I care even less for bullies, so here I am, sharing what I know. And I do not mean only this post – watch this space. A full exposé is coming, where all this little cult's secrets will be revealed.

Will the Abbracciaventos try a libel case? I pray to the Goddess they do! That'd give me a chance to prove what I'm saying in a tribunal. Or will they try to get at me with more direct means? We'll see. If I get as much as a burglary, or a bad look by a stranger in the street, rest assured you guys will know, and the police too.

I'm here for anybody willing to reach out, from inside the cult – if you want out, I'll help you. I'll give you protection, anything you need. I promise that.

And I'm here to ask a dear friend of SoulJo, a sister in all but blood, who fell in with this crowd: please, we are begging you. The SoulJo community is begging you. Come back home. These crooks are not your family. We are, thousands and thousands of us. They are not the good guys. You are.

Love you always. Xxx

ZOEY

'How dare you?' I said on the phone.

And Janis answered, in that neat voice of hers, 'I understand you're angry.' She was not groggy even though it was late at night. She must have been expecting a call.

'I'm not angry, Janis. I'm heartbroken.'

After a beat, Janis said, 'I hate to put you through this.'

'You hate to spread lies about me and my friends?'

'Was anything I wrote less than true?'

'Everything you wrote was twisted to give an impression that we are the Puglian version of the Manson Family.'

'It could go that way.'

'Why can't you just leave us alone?'

'*Because you're my friend*! Look, the exposé doesn't need to be published. I will delete my post. Apologise. Humiliate myself in public.'

'For the price of...?'

'Come back home with me. Now. Pack and come to my B&B, and we'll be out of here tonight. Not for ever! Only two, three weeks. Take some time to chill in NY, maybe talk to a couple of old friends, and then, if you want to go back to these guys, nobody will stop you.'

'Not that you could.'

'I promise that, whatever your choice at that point, I'll be good with it and I'll stay your friend, if you allow me. I'll apologise to you, I'll apologise in public, I'll do whatever it takes to make you forgive me. Your love, Zoey, matters to me as much as my baby's love, you understand that, don't you?'

I did. I had missed her voice so much. I was tempted to give in, to do everything Janis said, only to have her back in my life. But I closed my eyes, and imagined Janis's face, in some empty B&B better suited to summer months, with dusty shells on some white shelf and a faded surfboard against the wall. Every time I doubted our magic, I only had to close my eyes to witness it all over again. 'I cannot believe – I literally cannot believe – that you're blackmailing me.'

'I'm trying to build some common ground.'

'You're hurting me more than I thought possible.'

'And I'm so, so sorry for that!'

'Please, Janis, let it go. Don't hurt me anymore. I'm not coming with you.'

'You don't have to answer now,' Janis said. 'Take forty-eight hours.'

‘Blackmail and an ultimatum. And *you’re* the good guys?’

‘I’m here for you,’ Janis said, ‘I’m always here for you.’

LILA

It was a reboot of the crisis with my parents, only this time the enemy had acted before us. I was angry in a visceral way, angrier than I’d ever been. I was not the only one. Ric left a dent in a fridge with a punch. ‘Fuck!’

I wish we had savoured those last moments with him – he would be dead before ten days were out. Most changes in life happen like that, without notice. Your GP calls you after a routine check and by the end of the call all you know will be wiped out.

Zoey was sitting in a corner, twisting her hands. I’d never seen her like this. I didn’t know she could be like this. ‘I’m sorry,’ she kept saying. ‘I’m so sorry.’

I said, ‘My parents came after us, when I first arrived. It’s not your fault.’

‘It’s not,’ Mikka confirmed.

‘No, but whose fault is it?’ said Becca. Her skin was pale like sea-foam, and her eyes were burning with rage. ‘How come Janis knows this much?’

‘Brains and deep pockets,’ Ric said. ‘That woman has both.’

Sam was pouring limoncello into shot glasses. ‘She must have talked to the Nameless.’

‘Or one of us,’ Mikka said.

‘No. Just… no.’

Ric said, ‘We should consider all possibilities.’

‘Not if it means fighting amongst ourselves,’ said Becca.

Zoey's voice was faint when she said, 'Perhaps I should go.'

Ric grunted. 'We won't give in to blackmail.'

'What's the harm? I spend a couple of weeks in NY, make Janis back off.'

'She'll keep pushing and pushing with new requests.'

Zoey nodded slowly. 'We hate her right now, but I've got to say this, she's not a bad person, trust me on this, she's not. She's doing what she thinks is right.'

'Same as everyone,' said Becca.

CHARLIE

We gave magic a go, short as we were of mundane options, though our magic seemed to have deserted us when we most needed it. For the whole day we had not seen one Oddball, nor a single bubble. No music played in the pinewood. 'We are on edge,' Becca said. 'We need to refocus on what really matters.'

That night we lit five fires, one in the centre of our circle, the others at the four quarters, and we brought with us jugs of strong red wine.

It had been an endless day of doom-scrolling; it was impossible to resist the temptation to check our social media profile. For most of us it had been years since we had felt that temptation. It tugged me out of our heaven into the dull reality I had left behind. The trolls kept coming thick and fast. Ignoring them was a mistake (we should have acted immediately, mercilessly). All I can say is that life is easy to navigate in hindsight.

Before the end of the day the comparatively benign first wave of comments, jokes and pleas for attention was morphing into a nastier crowd of bigots defending moral values and their upholding, and of religious nuts calling for our damnation. Right on the dot the rape and death threats started pouring in (it is a truth of the Internet, Ric used to say, that every disagreement, big or small, will lead to rape and death threats). And this was before the exposé was published.

LILA

I called my parents for the first time in six years, to check they hadn't talked to anybody and would keep it that way. They denied any involvement and any desire to get involved, and they sounded sincere, the bastards. They sounded as if they had no use for me anymore.

CHARLIE

By early afternoon the local rag – a two-pence operation run by a well-known drunk – had picked up the news. They had simply cut-and-pasted Janis's post, with a few generic words of introduction. Ric's phone rang, then Becca's. They turned them off. By late afternoon, the news had graduated to the page of a medium-sized national paper. Was this a prank, the paper wondered? Would the exposé be a real one, or a product launch? The story was getting bigger the way the bad things do: quickly. All that was creating tension among us. I was not used to being tense anymore.

Even with the fires surrounding us and the wine burning in our belly it was a cold night. We came from a light dinner of raw tuna and salad – anything heavier would get in the way. It was a sad show, and we knew it was sad while we were at it. Lila and Ric started a perfunctory drumming. We danced half-heartedly, passing around wine and joints with fake smiles and no joy. I was there but not fully there. My mind was busy with the trolls, Lila's parents, the story Ric had told us about the early days of the Bastion. My eyes were tired after so much looking at screens. When I started undressing, I did it because I was supposed to, rather than because I wanted to. Getting naked was part of the liturgy, so to speak, and I got naked. I felt the cold acutely. I started humming.

It did not work. We made all the right moves, we pretended to have a wild good time, we tuned in to each other and got our hum in synch, but there was no spark. It started drizzling, and while my mouth and throat hummed, I was thinking of the cold water prickling on my skin, every drop like a needle, and couldn't wait to just go inside. It had never occurred to me how silly we must look, a bunch of hippies bumbling around naked in their backyard. We jumped, pathetically, but we didn't fly.

Ric stopped his drumming, and Lila followed a fraction of a moment later. 'We're done for tonight,' he said.

Zoey said, 'We were almost there.'

'Bollocks.'

'Ric is right,' said Becca, 'there's no point.'

'What's going on?' I asked.

'Our magic has left us,' Sam said, under his breath.

Becca gave him a kiss. 'It will come back after we regroup.'

'Janis will publish the exposé,' Zoey said.

'We have nothing to be afraid of.'

We gathered our soggy clothes, smothered our sad fires and went back inside, the drizzle now turning into rain. I had forgotten I could feel so lonely.

A video, and no cheap Zoom production.

Janis sits in a green velvet armchair, the Nameless in a grey one. Between them is a coffee table, a French design of glass and steel, with two bottles of San Pellegrino and two plain glasses on it. The Nameless's face is blurred, his voice electrically modified. The effect is terrifying – you feel for the guy sitting in that comfy chair, for his need to hide even when surrounded by comforts. It is upsetting to hear that artificial voice, and you cannot help thinking, *imagine how upsetting this must be for him*. Janis knows how to play the media. It has been part of her job since she has had a job.

It opens with her saying, 'Let me start with a heartfelt thank-you for being here.' She wears a black tailored suit and a silky white shirt. She looks sensible, respectable, reassuring. Perfect. 'It takes a lot of courage.'

'It takes some, yes,' the Nameless replies, with an endearing modesty. He wears jeans, a plain blue shirt, battered sneakers: clean, but rough around the edges, the look of a dignified fugitive. 'I cannot stay quiet anymore, or I'd be as bad as Becca and Ric. They're putting vulnerable people in danger.'

'We're cutting to the chase then.'

'We're cutting to the chase.'

'Who are Becca and Ric?'

'Rebecca and Riccardo Abbracciavento – we called them Becca and Ric. The cult leaders. Though at the end of the day, Becca is boss.'

'*Cult* is a loaded word.'

'It's the appropriate one. They call it a community, the word *family* gets thrown around a lot. But it's a cult, really. Just another horrible doomsday cult.'

'You were in this cult for how long?'

'Three years, three months and two weeks.'

'And does it have a name?'

'The Bastion.'

'Sounds ominous.'

The Nameless laughs uneasily. 'I suppose it does. Yeah, it does.' He sips a drink of water.

'How did you get involved?'

'Social media.'

'Care to say more?'

Even through the blur, the Nameless looks uneasy. He squirms in his chair like a kid at the dentist's. He is charming, a lost soul, like any of us. 'Have you ever felt at a dead end? Nothing specifically wrong with your life, only, everything. Say, you make enough money to get to the end of the month, but not enough to have any savings, and that makes you slightly anxious, but also, you feel guilty for being anxious, with all the people who cannot even get to the end of the month. You've got a good job, not bad, but boring, repetitive. I was a graphic designer with a car manufacturer, which is not as creative as it sounds. A well-trained monkey could do that. You're in a relationship, and it's fine, but the last time you were properly excited, dinosaurs were roaming the Earth. You've got friends, but God, are they boring. Always the same faces, always talking the same shit: jobs, tax, kids. What I'm saying is, you know your hamster wheel is comfortable, all considered, but it's still a fucking wheel you're running in. You don't have any problems you can put your finger on, so there's nothing you can actually *solve*. You can't find a way forward, 'cause you already are on the way forward, and it sucks. You're unhappy and you're stuck, and you end up doing something stupid. Well.' He pauses. 'If I could say there was some major disaster, some huge trauma to justify me fucking up my life, I'd jump on the chance, but no. I was just not very happy to be alive.'

'I've been there,' Janis says. 'And I've done stupid.'

'The Bastion had this Insta profile where they put all sorts of amazing photos. Folks laughing, meditating in the shade of some large trees, messing around with body paint. Pretty folks, guys and girls. Then an endless blue sea, a pristine beach. And that hashtag, always the same, *#nofilter*. Who wouldn't want to be there? In a world with no filters. From my room in an ex-council flat in Munich, it looked like paradise. They did not run the place as a business, but in their posts they dropped the hint they were open to, quote unquote, 'guests'. They said you could just DM them and ask if they had any space in one of their informal, friendly gatherings of minds.'

'Sounds like a tax avoidance scheme for a company selling workshops.'

'Spot on. They make it a part of their hippy, stick-it-to-the-Man act, but really, it's tax avoidance.'

LILA

Such a small mind! Taxes, can you believe it? That's as far as the Nameless's imagination stretches.

THE EXPOSÉ

Janis nods. 'Sorry for digressing. Go on.'

'I DMed them and forgot about it. I wasn't expecting an answer. I didn't get any for two weeks.' The Nameless massages his blurred forehead. 'It's hard to think back to those days. I DMed them on impulse – if I hadn't...' His voice trails off.

'We can take a break if you want,' Janis says, ever thoughtful.

The Nameless sips some more water. 'No, thank you, let's get it over with. So, I DM this Insta account, and after a while they write back saying they have a last-minute opening for a workshop next week, if I want to go. Three days, no charge, but a donation is encouraged. Cash is better.'

Janis makes a forced laugh.

'These guys,' the Nameless says, 'are Italians through and through. The timing is tight, the cash thing is dodgy, but I tell myself, *I wanted carefree, I got carefree*. And then, *what the hell, I need this*. I take a few days' leave, I kiss my girlfriend goodbye, and go.' The Nameless makes a pause here, before saying, 'I wouldn't come back for three years.'

'You leave for a holiday, and never come back?'

'Most of us got sucked in that way. See, Becca and Ric honed this strategy by which they give you a great time, then they make you feel good about yourself and promise you a freebie, and then... and then you're in, shoes and all. They were still developing the strategy when I joined. They got better.'

'Go on,' Janis says.

'The workshop, because that is what it was, was a lot of fun, and I'll give them that, it was packed with interesting ideas. Whatever else they are, those two are smart. The key notion of their philosophy, if we want to call it a philosophy, is that we live trapped in our own mind and in order to liberate ourselves we need the help of others. What many spiritual paths get wrong is that they think of personal freedom as something you can achieve on your own, but no. *Nobody escapes from prison alone*, to quote Ric.'

'An interesting choice of words. Did he have first-hand knowledge of prison?'

'Not him, no. For all his tough talk, Ric comes from a fairly uninteresting background. There was an actual ex-con with us though, a tall Finnish bloke, Mikka Koskinen. He was one of the reasons I stayed after the workshop was over.'

'Let's not jump forward.'

'Okay, sorry. I said the workshop was fun. I should also add it was sinister, in retrospect. I've read a lot about mind control since I left, and I know what they were doing. Slowly, gradually, they were making us trust them. And once you give trust to a person, you keep trusting them more and more. Lend someone five euros today, it's more likely you'll lend them fifty tomorrow. It's hardwired in our brains.'

'Could you give an example from your time there?'

'Yeah. There was this thing we did on the second night, where we gathered around a bonfire and we had to confess a secret we had. In theory, it was so that we could let go of our baggage. Makes sense, right? But you know where they did public confessions? In Communist China, that's where. In Jim Jones's Peoples Temple. It's a mind-fucking technique. It is supposed to make you whole, but the opposite is true: it makes you vulnerable. You open yourself and you feel scared and grateful in equal measure; the next time, they ask you to open yourself a little more, and you do just that. Every step you take is small, reasonable. You start doing a little something you don't really want to do, and you end up doing much, much bigger *somethings* you don't really want to do.'

'And you couldn't say no?'

'You were perfectly free, in theory, but everybody was being a good sport and if you disagreed, you would be the odd one out. It was all very gradual, and once you noticed you were in, you were in the deep end. There was the mask thing. You would put on an animal mask, and Ric would incite you to behave like the animal. I know… I know it sounds silly, but you needed to be there, people around you leaping and croaking and laughing, and you weren't going to be the spoilsport, so you started acting crazy too.'

'To be honest with you, I don't see the harm in jumping and laughing.'

'A guy came and pushed me. I pushed him back. I was wearing a gorilla mask and gorillas don't back off. He had an eagle mask or whatever. He comes and hits me in the face. And I start… I start on him. A proper number. I kick him in the shins, I punch him in the face.' The Nameless's voice lowers, his head bows. 'I can't believe that was me.'

'Nobody came and stopped you?'

'After a while, yes. What you need to understand is, I'd never been in a fight in my whole life. It felt magnificent. When it was clear I'd got the upper hand, after the second or third punch, it was like I'd found I had super-powers, you know. I could get shit done. That night at the bonfire the bloke and I made it up, and I felt *good*. I had gone to war, and I'd won.'

'I understand the allure of it. I also understand how some would find this… distasteful.'

'See, this is the thing. Those who found stuff like that distasteful, they were not material for the Bastion. Those who were perfectly okay, maybe. The choice cuts were those like me, those on the fence. The curious, the undecided: you could work on us. Becca and Ric pushed us outside of our comfort zone, just a little, and what we found there was Becca and Ric again, holding our hands. We grew grateful. We grew attached. We became unable to deny them anything – favours, sex, anything. They said they were liberating us, while actually they were trapping us with them.'

'Why did you stay after the workshop was over? You mentioned an ex-con.'

'Mikka, their oldest convert. You could say he's a henchman. He's charming, soft-spoken, and good-looking, though he must be in his late sixties. He saw something in me I didn't know was there. Even with all that happened, I'll always be grateful to Mikka for that. Not all the lessons you learn in the Bastion are bad. You become unable to sort out the good from the bad, and the fact that there *is* good stuff makes you go along with the bad too. Mikka showed me that I could like men as much as I did women. He was the first guy I slept with, thirty-odd years older than me, and that's one of the things I don't regret. It was the first time I cheated on a girlfriend, too.'

'Did you fall in love?'

'No. When I say that he was one of the reasons I decided to stay, I don't mean him personally, I mean what I learnt from him. The possibilities that opened up. In three days, I'd been in my first fight – coming out on top – and I'd slept with my first man. What else was there to find, deep inside my soul? Shame I wouldn't have another chance, because it was time to go home. I was having the mother of all end-of-the-holiday blues, when Becca came to me and said they'd recognised me as one of their own.'

'Meaning?'

'That I could stay for however long I wanted, free of charge. She didn't say more, for the time being.'

'And you stayed.'

'A free holiday, a chance for personal growth, and a mystery, rolled into one? Of course I stayed. I asked Becca if my girlfriend could come too, and she said, not really, because they didn't know her. She said that in a way that made me feel awkward for having asked. She apologised, looking taken aback. And I thought, these guys are giving me free rein over their place, and I'm the one making requests? I called home and said I would stay for another week. Just a week.'

'It wasn't a week.'

'There were two people who stayed, me and a girl, and the first night after the other guests left, well. We went to the sea for a midnight swim. You guess.'

'You were having a lot of sex, apparently.'

The Nameless scoffs. 'Yeah, sex. That's the main pull, you know? Behind the metaphysical bullshit, the self-improvement platitudes, it's about sex. There is so much of it going on at the Bastion, you wouldn't believe. I'd slept with my first man and I'd cheated on my girlfriend twice. Before the end of the first week, I'd also been in my first threesome, and my second. Sex was the main pull, and the drugs were the second. Mostly marijuana, but Mikka could always find a reservoir of LSD, mushrooms. The spiritual stuff. It's easy – it's easy to lose yourself in a scene like that. You fuck, you do drugs, you spend the night at a bonfire, you never leave this pinewood. It does your head in. It's part of the shtick. It's addictive. The workshop had been good, but that week? All that happened afterwards couldn't taint the memory of that week for me. It still feels like a dream. This is how much they fucked me up.'

'And when the dream was over...?'

'It got weird. The day before I was meant to leave, Becca and Ric explained why they said they *recognised* me. Becca heard voices, in her head, and those voices had ordered her to gather people to fight in an upcoming battle. Fight *how*? We didn't know. Against whom? We didn't know that either. But together, we were supposed to save the world. I know it sounds insane. I know, okay? Ridiculous. But it was how they said it – as a plain fact, not a thing to believe or disbelieve, just the way it was – and you could make of it what you wanted.'

'What did you make of it?'

The Nameless refills his glass of water and takes a sip before answering. 'Tell me you don't want to be the good guy, the hero of the story, and you will tell me a lie. They were promising me that I could be that, and all I needed to do was stay there in Paradise. I had a choice between a life of fun and sex, with a deeper meaning, or one of bills and drinks at the weekend, ending in a cheap coffin and crisps down at the pub.'

'Still, uprooting yourself on the spur of the moment...?'

'In my case, that was part of it. I was looking for a reason to fuck up everything and start again. They gave me a great one. I want you to understand this – when you're there in that pinewood, your old life seems far away, a dream of somebody else. The first thing they did, at the workshop, was take our phones. They gave them back to me and this other girl when they asked us to stay, but they also begged us to deactivate our social media profile for the time we were staying with them. We had very little connection with the outside world, and the inside world was a never-ending party. There was the grey outside, and every colour of the rainbow inside. It didn't feel like I was renouncing anything. All that I needed, all that I wanted, was there, with the Bastion.'

'Let me recap. First they recruited you through social media, then they hit you with sex and drugs, then they told you a story about saving the world. Did you consider yourself a part of the cult, by that point?'

'Of the family. Not yet, but I wanted in. Indoctrination proper began. Becca and Ric have another set of exercises for the inner group, mostly visualisation, singing, mind-fucking techniques which cults all over the world make use of. The promise is that if you only do as they say, follow their routine and trust the process, you will become more than human. You will learn – again, this sounds ridiculous, but there you go – how to work magic.'

Janis lets those words hang in the air, to give them time to make an impression on the listener. Then, when the silence becomes too much, she asks, 'Did you?'

The Nameless speaks in a self-deprecating tone, 'With my next words, I'm going to ruin everything I've said so far.'

'Just be honest. Nobody is going to judge you.'

'I've seen things,' the Nameless says, in the cautious voice of someone who is observing their thoughts while expressing them. 'A strange sky, with different stars from the ones we know. I've felt the presence of my grandma, who died when I was little. I saw, or I think I saw, Milou, my Jack Russell from when I was a child. My dad ran him over when I was eight, while leaving the house after a fight with Mum. I felt… I felt at times as if I'd slipped out of this world, literally out of this world, into another one, with a different shape and different rules.' The Nameless shakes his head, frustrated. 'I don't know, I just don't know. It may be all in my mind. With the booze, the drugs, the sex – even after so many years, I am not sure what's going on in that pinewood.'

'But you think that magic may be part of it.'

'Of course I don't buy the apocalypse bullshit, not anymore if I ever did, but there may be some parapsychological effect to what they do, why not? We only use a small part of our brain, that's science. But when I go there, then I think I could still be a victim of Becca and Ric's manipulations. They make you doubt yourself, so you have to rely on them. They kept raising the bar of what you were willing to believe, and do, to gain their approval. They made me kill a pig, you know.'

'A pig?'

'Yeah, a pig.'

'Why?'

'Have you ever killed an animal?'

'I can't say I have, no.'

'I'm vegan. Didn't stop me from slaughtering Napoleon, the pig.'

'Wow.'

'Yes, wow. It's wrapped up as a lesson in responsibility or something, but they're just fucking with your mind. There is this large bonfire, and drums, and they take this living pig in front of you, and they hand you a knife. You can refuse to do it, but I never saw one person back off. Not one. And when you do it, when you kill that living, screaming thing, when you feel the blade go through the skin – I won't try to embellish it – you feel like crap, but you also feel so very *powerful*. I guess some children torture animals to feel that rush of power, the illusion of being in control.'

'Drugs, sex, ritual violence, peer pressure: from what I'm hearing, Becca and Ric use every manipulation tool in the box.'

'Yep.'

'What I'm wondering is, what's the endgame? Do they believe in their end-of-days story, or is that a gimmick?'

'To this day, I don't know. They seemed earnest, but even if they were, so what? It's possible Charles Manson was earnest. You don't need to go down the magic route to see what's in it for them – everybody in the cult works on their farm, for free. And everybody would jump off a cliff if Becca and Ric asked them to. Money, power, sex, the Abbracciaventos have a nice set-up there. Whether they actually believe it is coming or not, the apocalypse is working pretty well for them.'

At this point, Janis makes a scene of checking her notes. 'This cult, this self-appointed last Bastion of humankind, organise a festival every year.'

'The Open Feast.'

'Those who have heard of it only know it as a boutique festival, very exclusive.'

'I know all about it – I helped create it. When I arrived at the Bastion, it was early days. The workshops were an experiment, Becca and Ric were still working on their, so to speak, recruitment and retention strategies. The Open Feast was the result of that work: a conveyor belt to get new people in. Becca said that magic, spirits, or whatever, would send the right people our way, but we needed to keep the door open. We cleaned up all our profiles and relaunched under the brand of a mind, body and spirit festival, a legit commercial enterprise. Becca and Ric even paid taxes on it. But it's a front. The Bastion gather vulnerable people to have their pick of the most vulnerable ones. They ask those ones to stay behind, same as they did in my time. We – and I say *we* because I was part of it, to my shame – refined the process down to an exact science. It's clever. Nasty, but clever.'

'A close friend of mine fell into their trap,' Janis says, in the soft voice of someone making a confession. 'I wouldn't have thought of them as vulnerable.'

'You can be outwardly strong, and still be easy prey. I didn't consider myself a victim, either! I was a professional, with a good career, a relationship – a functioning adult. Everyone is unhappy about this or that part of their life, and when you're unlucky, you meet people who know what you're unhappy about, and how they can leverage that. You can be Achilles, but the moment you clash horns with a dude who knows about your heel, you're toast.'

'They aren't advertising the Open Feast anymore.'

'Yeah.'

'Could you guess why?'

'Becca and Ric must have decided they have enough recruits.'

'Enough for what?'

'Either to fight the good fight, or to keep their bank account fat and their bed warm for the foreseeable future. I don't know. What do you say?'

'I find the second option the less frightening.'

'Me too.'

'I have one last question.'

'Go on.'

'How did you manage to get out?'

'Ric got violent. I dared question their capital-T *Truth* that we were these elite warriors who would save the world from some supernatural beasties – and he beat the crap out of me.'

'For questioning him.'

'Yeah.'

'Was violence common in the Bastion?'

'Up to that point, not at all – psychological pressure did the job well enough. Mind, though, that was the first time any of us dared question Becca and Ric, as far as I know. They made it very clear what the consequences would be. It worked on most of the others, it kept them in line, but it had the opposite effect on me. I'd already started questioning a lot of things, now I questioned everything. But listen, I still wouldn't have left if it wasn't for the thought of my family. Ric's beating opened a dam. I had left behind the people I loved for *this*? And the pain I caused them…' He brings a hand to his eyes, as if to hold back tears. He is not a good actor, nor does he need to be with the blur on his face.

'Your family got you back,' Janis says. 'Your real family.'

'With open arms.'

Janis nods. 'I'll do the same for my friend.'

ZOEY

Watching the interview made me want to scream in Janis's face until it melted. It was our life seen through a glass darkly. Little of what the Nameless said was a lie, strictly, but with his tone and his choice of words he was twisting our life into a horror story.

I couldn't care less about him, though. I'd never met him. I knew what he had done, that was all. Janis – I cared about her a lot. She had violated my new family's most intimate secrets. The video she'd made was filthy, it was obscene, and it was out there. Think how it would feel to listen to a bully reading your private journal to a laughing crowd, and you will get a sense of how I felt. I was not the only one. Tears were rolling down Sam's cheeks, and Ric went pale and stiff.

'Are we just rolling with this without pressing charges?' Imogen asked.

Becca said, 'We don't want to start a media circus.'

'This is the circus! This right here.'

'Galen,' Lila reminded us.

'The Nameless has zero interest in mentioning Galen, to the Carabinieri or to Janis.'

'A lawsuit would mean an official inquiry,' Becca said. 'And once the Carabinieri start poking their nose in, you don't know what they may find.'

'We *do* know,' Lila said. 'That is the problem.'

I said, 'I cannot believe Janis is doing this.'

'Well, she is,' Ric snapped.

'It's not like her.'

'We cannot sit back and watch,' said Imogen.

No, we couldn't. I said, 'We must go into crisis mode.'

'Meaning?'

'This is a branding emergency, or, at least we can treat it as such. We publish a statement on all the Open Feast channels immediately, negating everything the Nameless said. Then we go silent. Like, we don't say another word, not one. We don't answer DMs, posts, requests for interviews, nothing, no matter how tempting the offer looks. Anything we say from now on will be fuel for the circus's fire, and we want the circus to leave town ASAP. We make our statement and then wait the storm out until something new and shiny comes up and people move on. With a bit of luck, it'll be a matter of days. The public is after blood. The moment we give them that, we've lost.'

Becca made a small nod. 'Go.'

I cracked my fingers and typed, *We have seen the interview. Apparently Janis Mackenzie, the co-founder of Soul Journey, has an axe to grind with us. A large corporate festival viciously attacking an indie one which has been on a steady rise – surprise surprise. The situation is not made easier by the fact that Ms Mackenzie's former business partner and the other co-founder of SoulJo, Zoey Lee, is now working with us. She is the 'friend' Ms Mackenzie ominously mentions, as if deciding on a change of job were an act of satanic evil. Ms Mackenzie has been repeatedly trying to convince Ms Lee to go back to work with her, to the point of stalking and harassing her. This video is just the last move in Ms Mackenzie's obsessive campaign, which Ms Lee was gracious enough to ignore, so far. Ms Mackenzie can speak about friendship as much as she wants, but follow the money and you will see that what she is after is the 50% share of the internationally renowned festival that Ms Lee legally owns. The story is noble, the truth is sad.*

The man Ms Mackenzie interviewed was, indeed, part of our community, but that is the one true thing about his words. We are a group of friends who organise a summer festival, and for the rest of the year bring forward a co-housing and co-working project. That is the most interesting thing there is about us. We wish we were as mysterious and charismatic as this man made us.

We do run a programme of mental and spiritual exercise, yes, but so does every mindfulness centre in the world. We like to think ours is one of the best, but you know and we know that this is what everybody think about themselves.

'Oh, this is good,' Ric said. 'May I add something?'

I said he could be my guest.

Ric wrote:

The mask exercise we borrowed from improv theatre, which admittedly can be spooky in its own right, is a far cry from some sort of highly advanced CIA-like mind-control tool. Then there is the crown jewel of the accusations, that we want to save the world. Well, so do you, we hope. One must be seriously troubled not to see that our world needs saving.

Ric asked, 'What do you think?'

'Brill.' I typed on:

And yes, we did press the pause button on the Open Feast. We have been growing fast enough to attract the attention of the big league players, as Ms Mackenzie makes painfully clear, and this is not a league we are used to. We need some time to reflect on how we want to grow. How to go on without selling out. It is all lost revenues for us, if you want to put it in these terms. Is that a sign that some heinous activity is going on behind closed curtains? Only folks who value money over integrity would think that.

We want to be absolutely clear that we are not going to press charges, although that would be only fair and, to say it all, would help us in terms of visibility. We don't care for visibility. We know for a fact that the man Ms Mackenzie interviewed has a history of depression, as he hinted himself, and other mental health issues. We will not pile on a fellow human we know is unwell, even less so one whom we used to call a friend. We are going to live by our values, and if we look shady for that, then what a sad world this is. It does need saving. We do our bit. What about you?

I was hoping that would be enough to end the story there.

As you know, it wasn't.

THE BASTION

Later at dusk, Ric reached Becca on the beach, where she was sitting alone, staring at the sea. He brought a bottle of chilled white wine and two glasses. 'Mind if I join?'

Becca pointed with her chin at the spot of sand next to her. The sky and the water were reddening with the fire of sunset. 'I wish I had better words than *beautiful*.'

Ric poured a glass and handed it to his sister. 'It never gets old.'

'Humans do.'

They clicked glasses. 'How are you?' Ric asked.

'Do I look so bad?'

'Only to someone who knows you like I do.'

'Only to you then,' Becca said, curling her lips in the hint of a smile.

Ric punched her shoulder lightly. 'What's going on?'

'I don't know, Ric, you tell me. The crazy lady who's determined to make our life hell? The apocalypse?'

'There's something else.'

'I hate you,' she said in the voice that means the opposite.

'I know.'

Becca drank from her glass, without looking at her brother. 'I don't know if I can say it.'

'Why?'

'Because I don't want to make it more real than it is.'

'You're worried about our magic.'

Becca smiled. 'What did I do to deserve you?'

'You survived an asshole of a father.'

'When we had our breakthrough at last, I thought nobody, *nobody*, could take that from us.' She paused. 'Ever since I died and remembered the future, I had this sense of purpose, this certainty that I knew where we were going. I didn't know how we would get there, I didn't know what we would find, but every step I took was in the right direction. I was dead sure of that.'

'As you still should be.'

'Where's the Inner Pinewood then?'

Ric shrugged. 'With all that's going on, getting to the right mindspace is tricky.'

'Fucking Janis. You know what I'm starting to believe?'

'What?'

'This is it. Our final battle, the huge thing I remember us doing – it's started.'

'The Apocalypse is coming and Janis the herald.'

'What better herald than a cunt.' Becca sipped her wine and didn't speak for a while, then she said, 'I need to ask you something unpleasant.'

'Go on.'

'Do you ever doubt me?'

'No.'

'You never think I'm making it all up?'

'Why should I?'

'You didn't ask *why should you make it all up*?'

Ric topped up the glasses. 'People make up stories for all sorts of reasons, and for no reason at all, sometimes. There are those who start fibbing for fun, or on the impulse of the moment, and then get wrapped up in their own lies.'

'And you're positive this is not what I'm doing.'

'You're my sister.'

'I may be deluded. What if I made it all up? What if those guys who made their voices into religions – what if they were deluded too?'

'They may have been,' Ric answered. 'I think most of them were, to be honest. All of them, perhaps. Not you.'

'What if we're making it all up together then?' Becca said. 'A collective delusion. One of us says something they think they have seen, another one follows, and we create this perfect shared vision of miracles which never were. Wouldn't be the first time in history that had happened.'

'It wouldn't,' Ric conceded.

'But not this time.'

'No.'

'Why?'

Ric shrugged.

Becca kissed him on a cheek. 'Thank you for being you.'

'My pleasure.'

'I'm on the edge, Ric.'

'I didn't notice.'

'I don't want journalists on our door. I don't want strangers poking their nose into our business, Portodimare folks talking about us... I don't want any of that. I just ask to be left in peace, in my home, with my friends, doing my thing. Is that too much? We didn't hurt anyone, did we?'

'Zoey thinks it may fizzle out.'

'I hope so.'

'You're not the only one who's upset. Imogen's fuming that we're not suing, Zoey is drowning in guilt, Charlie's positively *terrified* that Bertrand's music has gone away once and for all. The others are all distracted, worried, dubious, with their minds elsewhere. That is the one and only reason why we can't get there. We're afraid, disconnected. We're all clammed up on ourselves. Our magic happens when we come together, and we can't, not this way. We've got to chill. Have some fun.'

'The world is ending and you're planning a party.'

'What better time.'

LILA

That was our last party before the end. You know how memory amplifies the colours of the best and the worst nights of your life? It makes every red into a flame and every black into a cave. In this case I can promise they were as vivid during the fact as they are when I go back there in my mind.

One of the things I've learnt with the Bastion is that good parties have their own rhythm, rising and falling at their own pace. Some are smooth, some are slow, some burn quickly, some are wild. But then some, the very special ones, move seamlessly from one rhythm to the other, and you are commenting on French cinema now, jumping in a mosh pit later. Those rare nights turn so memorable that you can't remember whole chunks of them, and the chunks you remember are as vivid as if they were happening now, and for ever.

When Ric told us about the party, I was less than excited. I was far from being in the mood – the best I could say was that I was grateful, like Charlie, that we were not making another sorry attempt at bringing back the Inner Pinewood. We would spend the night inside Villa Abbracciavento rather than outside. We would not chill our bare asses in another winter night – that was the one upside I saw. It was only half-heartedly that Sam and I drove to the village to buy some provisions. We didn't mind the odd looks we received; we had expected them.

Zoey and I decorated the main hall with bunting and warm fairy lights, Mikka set up the sound system. Sam and Imogen cooked mountains of sautéed mushrooms, the deliciously bitter local ones, and shellfish, and tartare. We lit the fireplace in the morning, so that the room would be cozy when the party started.

While we busied ourselves with the preparations, we gradually forgot our bad mood. We started throwing jokes at each other, laughing, at ease together. The divine scent of baking filled the room and I had to refrain myself from polishing off the focaccia before the party started. At some point the preparations rolled into the celebration itself, and we were chatting, drinking, with David Bowie in the background. Sam told a dirty joke about Mickey Mouse that made me laugh so hard my drink spilled out of my nose, Mikka served the best weed-infused biscuits that were ever baked, Charlie and Imogen talked football, wine entered our bloodstream. Against all forecasts, I was feeling good.

We did silly things. I started howling with Sam, which led to putting 'Thriller' on the sound system and dancing like the monsters in the video. The dance was a success, Ric shouted 'more', and now the music was 'You Never Can Tell', with Becca and Mikka moving like Uma Thurman and John Travolta in *Pulp Fiction*. Then Mikka took his guitar and we sang along with him until our throats were sore. We did '*Volare*' (only the Italians knew all of it, but the others got by), we did 'Life on Mars', 'Stand By Me', and many others. And now, hours into the party, the biscuits started working their magic, making the harsh edges of reality into marshmallows.

Ric and I got down to drumming. There is nothing quite like drumming indoors – the sound bounces off walls, ceiling and floor, enveloping you as physically as the brickwork. The beats throbbed through our flesh and made our souls quiver. We were turning down the lights and lighting the candles. Mikka took off his shirt, and the tattoos on his body were dancing with us. Becca followed, and soon we were undressing.

Naked, the guys snapped their heads back and forth to our drums, they shook their shoulders, they held hands and danced in twos and threes. Becca gave the first kiss that night, to Sam. We looked at their tongues tangling together, we looked at Sam grabbing Becca's ass, and squeezing, making Becca laugh. Then Imogen kissed him too, and Charlie was dancing for Ric, and Ric skipped one beat or two, and I burst out laughing. Soon Ric and I stopped drumming, and Ric was on his knees, sinking his head between Charlie's legs, and there our memories become confused. We were... living, and life was good.

The next day the photographs were online.

THE BASTION

Becca bit her hand not to cry when she saw the one in which she is straddling Sam in a sea of bodies, her fingers intertwined with his. There were seven photos in total. The quality was not great. It had been dark, and the photos had been shot from outside the window. That was beyond the point though. In those photos were *us*, exposed for the whole world to see, our intimacy violated. It was terrifying. Someone had sneaked inside our pinewood, walked to our window, watched us, snapped photos of us, while we thought we were alone. While we *had the right* to be alone. They made us sick, physically sick. Sam had to run to the bathroom.

We gathered that the photos were first posted on Reddit and 4chan, and then spread through the usual channels. Hundreds of people were commenting on them on our socials, under Janis's post, under the heinous YouTube interview. A tragedy unfolded on our screens, the numbers of views and likes and comments going up, up, and we looked on in stunned silence.

Zoey's phone rung like in an empty cathedral. The name on the screen was Janis.

'It wasn't me,' she said, as soon as Zoey picked up. 'God, Zoey, I promise, it wasn't me.'

'You hateful little bastard...'

'How can you think for a moment that I'd do anything like that?'

'Because of what you already did!' Zoey shouted.

'It wasn't me!'

'We're done playing nice,' Zoey said, and hung up the phone. She couldn't believe she had been in love with that woman. She couldn't believe she had suffered on the day that woman had got married.

We had heard the call. 'Do we believe her?' Sam asked.

Zoey said, 'Does it matter?'

'Now we press charges,' said Charlie.

Mikka was not so sure. 'The less I've got to deal with the Carabinieri, the better I feel.'

Imogen said, 'Charlie's right, we must go to the police. These assholes snuck into our house!'

'And how do you think the local force will react to solid proof that we're having orgies in their cute little village?'

'It's not their job to have an opinion. Sex was legal the last time I checked, trespassing was not.'

'It's immaterial,' Ric said. 'People will never forgive you for the sex they're not having.'

'Well, the cat is out of the bag.'

'But is it?' Lila asked.

While we fought, she hadn't stopped looking at the photos on the old laptop we kept in the kitchen for all to use.

'The cat is out of the bag and has ripped the bag to pieces,' said Charlie.

Lila pointed at the laptop. 'You can only say one thing for sure from these: that some folks are going at it. The pics are grainy, you can barely make out features of the interior of the house, and that is if you know the interior of the house. Recognising our faces is even harder. You can kind of see Becca's, but we know her really well.'

We brought ourselves to look at the photos again. 'Good job we were by candlelight,' Sam said.

'If we sue, we're admitting it's us. We don't have to do that. It may as well be a party of swingers in Kentucky.'

'Can't we *deny* it was us, then?' Charlie said.

That was a momentous decision to take. We wonder if things would have played out differently had we made a different choice. Even Becca can't tell.

Ric said, 'It'd be grist to the *he said, she said* mill. We want this story to be boring.'

'I agree,' Zoey said. 'Don't feed the trolls.'

Charlie, who was talking less than ever, said, 'Whoever took those shots could come back.'

Ric shut the laptop. 'I'm praying they do.'

For eight days, they didn't. Our life got steadily worse. Strangers fought online about whether we were a cult or not, about whether it was us in the photos, about our right to exist and do our thing in our place. They spoke about us and over us. They dissected Janis's post, our own, the interview. They dug up photographs of Ric from his university days and compared him to the men in the obscene pics. They found many more of Zoey from SoulJo, and compared those too. They zoomed our photos and inspected every inch of bare skin.

Thousands of strangers were slobbering over my flesh, weighing me like dead meat. It was a disgusting thought. We were not our own people anymore, we were public entertainment. Everyone had a right to have an opinion on us, and no one cared about the simple truth that we could read their opinions too, that they could hurt us, make us feel bad about ourselves. We were afraid in our own home.

And we couldn't fight back. For the first time ever, I wished I could leave the pinewood, go for a trip, but even if I would, I couldn't. We were surrounded. The siege started on the day the photos were published, with a white van making the rounds along the road leading to our gate.

The white van parked by the gate overnight.

We were painfully aware how easy it was to enter our pinewood. There was a brick wall on the side of the road, but nothing more than a flimsy steel fence by the beach. None of us had ever had reason to feel in danger before. None of us had ever *been* in danger. The unwritten rules were, we went on with our life discreetly and the village let us be. We were in Portodimare, but we could have been anywhere in the world. We had our own bubble, and it had felt indestructible. Now there was a white van parked on the street in front of us.

The next morning the van was still there. When Ric and I left our pinewood to head to town, the van's door opened, and a woman in glasses and a bob haircut came out of it, camera in hand. The first thing she did was snap photographs in a quick sequence, before we could cover our faces with an arm. 'You can't do that,' Ric said.

'I'm a registered journalist and you made the news, Mr Abbracciavento. It's perfectly legal for me to take a photo of you in a public place. Publish it too.'

Ric shrugged and made to go his way.

She put herself in his way. 'Sorry, we started on the wrong foot. I'm not a paparazzo. Name is Antonia Gallo. I write for,' and she named that vile digital rag.

Ric made to step sideways, and she stepped too.

I was getting sick of her.

'I'd love to ask you a few questions.'

'No, thanks,' Ric said, and stepped sideways again.

Again, Ms Gallo stepped too. 'I'm writing a fair piece, but I can't do *fair* without your angle.'

I was exploding. 'Listen...' I started, but Ric gestured me to stop it.

'Please,' Ric said to Ms Gallo. 'We're not interested.'

Her head turned to me. 'And you are...?'

I told her to fuck off, which was much nicer than what I actually wanted to tell her.

'There's no need to be abusive.'

Ric sighed. 'You're the one being abusive here.'

'For doing my job?'

Once more Ric tried to go his way, and once more the journalist stopped him.

'Any comment about the photos?'

'Don't fret over orgies, sweetie,' I said. 'Nobody's going to invite you to one.'

Which admittedly was not what you want to say to a journalist.

My words went online quicker than grappa makes you drunk. In her telling of the story, Riccardo Abbracciavento was 'leery' and I was 'a manic pixie girl in the thrall of an older man'. We had joined forces to harass and scare off an innocent journalist asking legitimate questions. The Manson Family was name-checked again, and that was how the public opinion started to see us – as two chips off the same block.

There were photographs too, of both of us. I was sick thinking of those who would run back to the seven photographs and confront them with these, another excuse to wank over me and the others. It was barely disguised pornography, and they called *us* perverts.

THE BASTION

Another van joined the first one, and two cars. Since Lila's parents' irruption, we had kept the gate locked. Now we had to disconnect the bell, because they kept coming – journalists, students, idlers – and they had no notion of privacy or discretion. A magazine photographer turned YouTuber, a medium-sized local network which covered most of Southern Italy, an RAI personality, more podcasters than you could throw a rock at. Every Italian paper was covering the story, and we were getting some international traction too. A Welsh TikToker with just shy of a million followers shot a video in which she joins a cult on a fake beach (all the cult members are played by her), has some strange pretend-sex on a bed full of dry pasta, then wears a cape and runs off to save the world.

If we had a penny for every view it got, we could have bought our way out of trouble.

It got worse. An old friend of Lila recognised her from the photograph, and in no time her name was all over social media. Her father's too. It was the kind of notoriety we did not need. Journalists reached out to her family, who wisely kept hiding behind a *no comment*. The best thing we could do was nothing. Lila and Ric's spat with the journalist had demonstrated the wisdom of Zoey's original plan. The fairness Ms Gallo had bandied around had never been in the cards. The crowds, in their wisdom, had decided we were rotten, and everything we said, everything we did, would be further proof of that. The upholders of good family values called us perverts, the self-appointed open-minded ones called us abusers. It was painful to sit on our hands while dark forces gathered around us.

The next time we left the pinewood, we had to do it in one of our vans, our faces covered with scarves and sunglasses. We headed to a market out of town for some shopping, checking that we were not being followed. Thankfully we were not at that point yet, but a young man in the shop recognised us, and whispered to his friend, who took out his phone. We paid in a hurry and sped back home.

ZOEY

It was a mental time. I'd known crises with SoulJo – scandals, last-minute emergencies, troll attacks, and so on. This was on another level. The doxxing of Lila was like the opening of a dam, and a deluge of shit came through.

Others were doxxed too, by their own friends and families or by the villagers. The parents of some made desperate pleas for their children to return, one of Sam's cousins gave a long interview to *Vice* about Sam's difficult childhood, tear-jerker posts flooded Facebook and sepia photographs crowded Instagram. We became a hashtag: #thesecretfamily. We were celebrities, in the sense that perfect strangers got to decide what we were, and we had no control whatsoever over it.

CHARLIE

I didn't have a family waiting for me, or close friends who knew where I was. I was lucky enough that my privacy wasn't being violated. I never left the pinewood, not to be photographed.

ZOEY

A nationwide TV channel cobbled up a report from interviews with Portodimare locals. Some of them went on about what a piece of work Becca and Ric's father had been, others always knew we were up to no good. In the parade of cliché, the word *satanism* was now being thrown around.

The one lone knight coming to our defence was a Luca Saracino, a local entrepreneur who hadn't let his blindness get in the way of building a fortune from very little. 'You don't know what's going on in people's lives,' he said, 'unless you listen very carefully. I wouldn't hurry to strike judgements. When I was a kid, I was a victim of that, briefly. Rebecca and Riccardo have always been polite to me; that is all I can say.'

One afternoon we heard a buzzing noise outdoors, and we rose our heads to see a drone fly over our pinewood, its four hateful propellers rotating with spite. Without saying a word, Ric went inside and came out with his hunting shotgun. Nobody stopped him from pointing at the drone and shooting. The explosion reverberated through the trees and beyond. People online wondered. We never found out who the drone belonged to.

It was all on me; it was all on Janis. Love, hatred, I didn't know what I felt. I wanted to fall on my knees and beg her to forgive me, but then I thought, *her forgiving me*? She was the bitch in this story. And I wanted to sink a blade in her filthy hide the way I'd done Napoleon (I could feel the vibration of the knife in my hand, the sense of power). I wanted to kiss and hit her. I wanted to be with her, talk with her and ignore her until she would go away. Yes, that's what I wanted, more than anything – to put her out of my mind, and go on with my life. But she wouldn't allow me.

I slept little, by night or day. No one did. We were tired, anxious, tense. It would take little to make us snap, but what did make us snap in the end was not little at all. The boys, the fucking boys who had taken the photos, returned.

CHARLIE

We should have done something about the fence, or at least mounted guard, yes, I know. But when your life changes substantially, it takes a while for the magnitude of change to sink in. For a while you keep going like before, like a headless chicken. In some ways, we were still acting as if we had the luxuries of peacetime. We were like people who refuse to see war even while soldiers are fighting outside their window.

By luck or design, the boys chose a moonless night. I spotted them. I was heading to the spot where I first heard Bertrand's music, mindless of the cold. He had not been playing anymore, but I went there every night. Hope was enough to keep me going.

Instead of the music, I heard heavy footsteps, low voices I didn't know. They spoke Italian in the local accent. Whatever they were saying, it couldn't be anything good. These were invaders, brain aneurysms come to pull my world from under my feet again. They were sniggering like evil imps, impatient to bite the throats of humans in their beds. In the near-complete darkness, their torch shone with a sick neon light. I caught a glimpse of tall bodies, large shoulders. I was afraid. I turned on my heel and made my way back to the house, quietly, keeping myself low, repairing behind bushes and trees.

'There's someone in the woods,' I said, entering the kitchen, where a few of the others were sharing a glass and some chat.

'You sure?' Mikka asked.

'I saw two, there may be more, I don't know.'

'Where?'

'I thought they were coming to the house. I was… I was too afraid to keep an eye on them.'

Ric said, 'You never got into a fight in your life. You did the right thing.'

'I've been in a few scraps,' Mikka said.

'They'll be poking their noses around,' said Zoey. 'Hoping to bag some more nudies.'

Becca asked, 'Who's coming?'

I was in – there's strength in numbers.

LILA

As was common at that point, the few lucky ones who were able to get any sleep at all slept lightly anyway, so in five minutes we were all gathered in the hall. Ric asked some to stay behind, in case the intruders made it to the house, and others to watch the fence. He did not want the intruders to get away before he had a word. I went with him. I grabbed a bottle of wine as a weapon.

We were fighting back. Too many people mistake acting nice for being helpless, and that night, at long last, we were setting the record straight. I was not prey. I was a kestrel.

Their hyena voices guided us to them. We found them chuckling and tittering as they carved something in the fig tree's bark. The light of their torch jerked up and down. They were having the time of their life, playing around in our place. We headed towards them with slow, considerate steps.

One of them cried out. The other too.

A solitary Oddball was lumbering towards them, a swollen, feathered body with a mouse's snout, three sharp talons, five tails. I felt a jolt of joy. It was the Oddball Galen had given me the first time we'd met. It was a memory of good times, and I took it as a promise they would return. I'd missed the Oddballs with a ferocious intensity.

'Hey!' Ric called out.

The intruders' heads snapped in our direction. They had the smooth, puzzled faces of those who have just come to the other end of puberty and don't know what to do there.

'We've got people by the beach,' Ric said. 'Don't even *think* of running.'

The boys didn't know where to look: at the impossible little beast at their feet, or at the pissed-off army closing on them.

'Don't move another step!' the taller one shrieked. 'We'll call the guards!'

We burst out laughing, but the absurdity of what they had said was lost to them.

'I know you,' Becca said, in good humour. 'Salvo Ruggeri. How's your mum?'

'You were doing another satanic orgy and shit!' the other boy said.

Ric realised. 'You were the one who took the photos.'

'What if we did, mmh?'

'Why did you have to do that?' I asked.

The boys looked more puzzled than ever.

'I'm asking, *why*? Were we hurting somebody? Were we? You tell me, what did we do to deserve to be slut-shamed that way?'

'Satanic orgies and shit,' the shorter, squatter one repeated.

Imogen rolled her eyes. 'Oh goodness. These two are barely verbal.'

We were having fun, for a change. The strangers who had stolen into our home and taken those pics had grown huge in my imagination, but really, they were these clueless young men barely out of their teens. Virgins, I'd bet. Their faces were a show of their own. It was the last funny moment we had together.

It ended when the taller boy said, 'Fuck.'

A bubble the size of a person was wobbling and swaying in the night, reflecting starlight. Then another. I felt a change in the air, like the scent of the first flowers in spring – magic was rising again, like sap in a tree.

The Oddball was licking the taller boy's shoes. He jumped, and brought his foot down on the little creature. I heard the stomp, I heard a crack and a squishing noise. I gasped.

Ric had had enough. 'Hey,' he said, advancing towards the boy. 'You asshole,' he shouted. He pushed the boy. 'What do you think you're doing?'

The boy was a good head taller than Ric. He pushed back.

He should not have done that. Ric hit him with a punch in the face. He staggered, backed off, and Ric hit him again, in the belly. The stars overhead were changing.

It happened then.

The other boy, the smaller one, fished a shiny toy from his pocket. Mikka recognised it as a switchblade, and ran towards him. But he never had a chance.

The panicked boy plunged the blade into Ric's back, once, twice, then into his side. I doubt the boy knew what he was doing; some primal function of his brain, or a force older than that, must have taken over. Mikka bumped into him with his shoulder, shoving him away, while Ric moved one unsteady step and turned his head to Becca. He tried to speak, but he could only gasp.

He fell to the floor spitting blood in an obscene foam.

CHARLIE

I remember it all so very well. I remember my legs feeling as heavy as oak trees, impossible to move; I remember the banshee wail of Becca as she threw herself on Ric's body, pressing her fingers on his wounds to stop the bleeding, like a little girl trying to contain a storm with her bare hands. I remember her kissing Ric on the mouth in a desperate attempt to stop the bleeding there, and I remember her putting her ear to his heart. I remember her crying and shaking her head.

ZOEY

A few minutes earlier – *only a few minutes earlier* – Becca and Ric had been drinking Mikka's dreadful limoncello with us. Ric had been telling a story about a disaster of a first date with a girl who, sensibly, never became his girlfriend. Now Ric's body lay motionless, Becca's was rattling.

Mikka was holding the monster who had butchered the one real magician I'd ever met, in a lifetime spent among pretenders. The monster too was weeping, babbling, as if tears could wash away what he had done. Becca's hand felt the ground and closed around a heavy jagged rock. She stood up, the rock in one hand. She turned to Mikka.

The monster was pleading now, but Becca was lifting the rock, and none of us stopped her.

THE BASTION

Afterwards, she turned to the other. We had taken care of him. He laid on the pine needles, undone. The stars above us were thick and strange.

5

OUR STAND

CHARLIE

We carried Ric's body inside and left the other two where they were. We would deal with them tomorrow, and if in the meantime they became food for birds and foxes, they would have accomplished more after death than they ever did in life.

What can I tell you about that night? We had lost our sense of direction. Becca would weep and sob, and when she wiped her tears she would smear her face with blood. Mikka, strong Mikka, steadfast Mikka, was as much of a wreck, crying without shame. The only helpful thing he could do was hammer the killers' phones and then burn them. Sam rolled joint after joint, which he smoked alone in an old swing chair on the porch, Imogen shut herself in her room, I grabbed two people and took them to my room, where nothing much happened. They were on edge, like everybody else. Some conked out and slept as soundly as they ever did, sleep being the only escape at hand; others would only be able to doze at moments, to get woken up by memories coming back to them: the image of Ric falling, the crunch of our hands breaking bones.

If it weren't for Lila, we would have fallen apart. She tended to us all with a ferocious determination. She made tea and poured wine, she replenished the supplies of weed, she cooked a midnight snack of pasta with tomato sauce for those awake. She washed the blood from Ric's body, and the other wastes we produce at the time of passing. She changed him into clean clothes, as she had done for Galen, years before. 'I was too furious to sit down,' she told me later. 'Ric would have wanted me to soldier on. He said it takes two for a knockout: the one throwing the punch, and the one deciding they can't take one more.'

Come morning she was barely standing, but she was on her feet. I admired her no end.

ZOEY

We had half-expected the bodies would be gone the way of bad dreams at dawn (it is a mistake I make a lot, to confuse what I hope for with what is actually possible), but Ric was still lying on a table in the hall, under a blanket, and the two boys were still in the pinewood. Twin trails of ants were climbing on what little was left of their faces.

We were at a loss what to do. We drifted from the house to the bodies and back to the house; we smoked cigarettes; we made the smallest talk possible. Sam was sitting on a jutting root, lost in thought, when he suddenly started weeping. Charlie sat down next to him and hugged him tight, letting him cry against her chest.

I kept looping between the boys and Ric. The third or fourth time I went inside, I found Mikka there too, by the body.

'Still looks badass,' he said.

'It's on me.'

'It's not.'

'My friend is a psycho bitch.'

'Your friend is not you.'

'I should've gone with her. Two weeks of my time and we wouldn't be having this conversation.'

'Like Ric said, she wouldn't have stopped there.'

I pointed at the body. 'Ric. Here's Ric.'

'I'm going for a smoke,' Mikka said, after a moment.

'Coming with.'

We headed out. Mikka rolled a cigarette, and I took the tobacco pouch from his hands to roll another. I said, 'Do you ever wish this wasn't on your shoulders? This burden?'

'Not for a moment.'

'Never ever?'

'You don't know my story.'

'You never offered, I never asked.'

'It's so sad it's a little funny. My biological mother abandoned me in a trashcan when I was three months old, in cold, windy Finland.'

'Cunt.'

'I was found, I'm alive; that's luck in my books. When I was put up for adoption, the authorities were spoilt for choice. They picked this young family, he a surgeon, she a lawyer, lovely folks – when sober. Which, given enough time, happened less and less frequently. My adoptive father killed a patient when he was operating on a full bottle of whiskey. I was six. He lost his job and every penny he had, which pushed Mum to drink *more*. One year goes by and she kills him, and herself, and nearly me too, in a car accident. On Christmas Eve, think about that. My maternal grandparents took me on. Once again – lucky, right? They were decent, perfectly decent, but they'd never signed up for an adoptive grandson. It was nothing personal, you see, they just didn't care for me very much. They were never on board with the whole adoption thing, and all I did for them was remind them that the fruit of their loins had shuffled off this mortal coil. They gave me everything they could, but they had no love left to give; it just wasn't in them. At sixteen I started running with a bad crowd, at twenty my run led me to a first stint in jail. I read Rumi while I was there, and when I came out, I flirted with Sufism, which didn't last. I moved on to Buddhism. I kept chasing *something*, I couldn't say what, and I kept running with bad crowds. Before I knew it, I *was* the bad crowd. Not even bad enough to be cool, just generically shitty.'

I appreciated Mikka's utter lack of self-pity – the world had enough people who cried into their beer. Me, for example. 'Until you came to us.'

'I was good at taking care of myself. I could survive, mechanically, day after day. But real living is another matter. You have to live for something, or you're no better than a piece of machinery, blindly doing what it's built to do, without a *why*. It's a privilege to have that *why*, something to live and die for. Most people don't. They come and go same as us, but not much happens in between. They plod on for no better reason than killing themselves would take too much thought. We're the lucky ones.'

'Janis can't understand, and she's too stubborn to let go.'

'It takes one to know one,' Mikka said, with half a smile.

'She and I both are used to getting what we want.'

'But she's on her own. You're not.'

CHARLIE

The killers would make the news soon; meanwhile they made the socials. Their families (both young men lived with their parents) had found them gone in the morning, their beds unslept in. By noon they were asking on Facebook if anybody had a clue where they were. The obvious theory was that they were sleeping off a hangover or a high at some friend's, but a round of calls had returned no results. They hadn't taken one's car or the other's motorbike, so they couldn't have gone far, and they were strong lads, so a kidnapping wasn't likely. Then – what? 'Ask the sex weirdos,' someone joked in a comment. More comments in the same vein appeared. They were not funny.

Becca came out of her room at midday, and gathered us in the kitchen. There was a warm sunshine, but we couldn't meet at the fig tree, not with the bodies lying in its shade. Becca had dark bags under red eyes, a formidable light on her face. 'How are you all doing?' she asked.

'Like crap,' said Sam.

I said, 'We killed two people.'

'We defended ourselves,' Lila corrected me.

'They're still dead.'

Lila raised her voice. 'They killed Ric!'

'And we should have called the guards,' I answered. I didn't want to fight with Lila, but I was raising my voice too.

'You weren't so coy last night.'

'Last night was ...' I paused. 'I got carried away. I wasn't myself, none of us were. But what we did was a mistake.'

Lila was mad. 'The only mistake was not getting them straight away! We've put the world at stake – *the world!* – only because we were too squeamish to do our duty.'

'I'm a doctor, Lila. Butchering two boys is very definitely *not* my duty.'

'We took an unnecessary risk before, and Ric died because of that.'

That was true, and I had nothing to offer as an answer.

Becca broke the silence: 'We'll make his death pointless by fighting among ourselves. We need to bring the fight to our enemies.'

I saw the others nod at the wisdom of that. Hearing her voice so firm, after the events of that night – once again, Becca seemed unbreakable. None of us could claim a loss like hers, and we were more of a mess than she was. She was the only one who had found the strength to take a shower, do her hair, change clothes. While I felt defeated, she had the look of a warrior who is just getting started.

She said, 'Horrible as it is, I agree with Lila – we did what was necessary. The question is, what now? Journos and locals are already pointing fingers at us for the boys' disappearance.'

'The bastards,' Lila said, between her teeth.

I made an exasperated gesture. 'But they're right.'

'They're *wrong*!'

'It is a fact that we have two dead men in our pinewood.'

'And it is a fact that nobody knows that! They're saying it's us because they hate us, no other reason; they're complete strangers hating us only because we dare exist. They *want* it to be us, and that's where they're wrong, where their thinking is all wrong. They're saying things which by chance are kind of true, but they're still wrong.'

'How's that for twisted logic?'

Before Lila could reply, Mikka said, 'We've got to get rid of the bodies.'

'The pigs ate all of Galen's bones,' Lila reminded us.

'We wanted to keep Galen with us though. Do we want to keep those bastards?'

Becca said, 'Then we feed them to pigs we're going to sell.'

I jumped to my feet and left the room without another word. Becca followed me. 'Charlie, wait.'

I raised my hands. 'I can't. I just can't, okay?'

Becca didn't answer.

'We're having a discussion on *how to dispose of the bodies of two boys.*'

'What else can we do?' Becca asked, kindly. 'As things stand, right now, what else can we do? It's either that or the guards. Do you want, in all seriousness, to call the guards?'

'Fuck,' I said, after a while. She passed a hand through her hair. 'I don't like any of this.'

'Me neither.'

We walked outside. There was a pleasant sunshine, and the earthy scents of winter. I sighed and wrapped an arm around Becca's shoulder. 'All we wanted, Bertrand and I, was a good time.'

'Did you get it?'

'Time of my life.'

THE BASTION

A white-haired sociologist, one of the numberless know-it-alls who jumped on us to pry their fifteen minutes of notoriety from our handcuffed hands, went viral on X holding forth on what emerged about Ric's funerals. In a drawn-out thread he explained that Becca had forced us to an extreme action – eating human flesh – as a bonding strategy, so as to keep us together at a time of crisis. After going along with such an unnatural act, we could not go back; we could only stick together and double down on our shared delusion, because if we admitted it was, indeed, a delusion, we would have to reconsider what we had done, and ultimately, who we were. And nobody wants to reconsider who they are, the sociologist confidently said. Becca's order that we would eat her brother was, he concluded, a culmination of the same tools Ric had devised for the indoctrination into the cult.

That was a lot of rubbish. The truth was simple: we ate Ric's body to preserve his magic. 'By eating his flesh,' Becca explained us, 'by taking his body into ours, we'll keep his energy in our community. Ric is going to stay with us. He will *be* part of us.'

The one who had a question was Lila. 'Becca, I hate to say this, but…'

'Yes?'

'You don't see the problem?'

'What problem?'

'The drums, the music. The journos will hear.'

'Let them.'

We spent the next day preparing ourselves, our home and Ric's body for the ceremony. We worked on the fence, fixing the holes, and adding posts to make it stronger. We rigged it with a solar battery to electrify it, and we connected an old radio alarm system to a couple of sensors we took from the farm. Mikka and Lila, helped by two others, loaded the killers' bodies on a van which they drove to our little pigsty, passing in full view of the journalists camping outside. Pigs will eat the whole of a human body, except for teeth and hair, and it takes nothing to burn hair and hammer teeth.

We didn't check the news or our phones. We avoided doing anything that would take our mind away from the here and now. Whatever storm was raging outside, it could wait one more day. We barely spoke. We were nervous at the thought of what Becca had asked of us, although we understood it was for the greater good.

But in the end it was a lovely ritual. We gathered at dusk, and made a circle around the body. When the moment came, none of us hesitated, and none of us was sick (the secret fear of many had been that they would puke and look bad). Ric's strength went from our teeth and tongue down our throat, filling our belly, and there it erupted, belching lava through our spine, our legs and arms. It was a delightful burst which burnt to a cinder all doubts and fears. It was a purifying fire. It was pure energy and joy.

A crow with a rat's head and the tiny hands of a mouse flew down on to Ric and pecked one of his eyes. Other Oddballs came to us, flying, walking, squirming. We cheered when we saw the one the killer had squashed, whole again. The bubbles came too. There had never been so many, and they had never been so real. They reflected us like the mirrors in a carnival, making us taller and squatter, turning our faces into grotesques. We partied with the bubbles and the Oddballs, returning to the body, every now and again, to cut another piece of flesh.

Becca started the hum. We joined her, but without Ric we were jarringly out of tune. We had to adjust for his absence. We kept working at it.

Red dusk gave way to a black night. There was the tiniest sliver of a white moon, and only one tiny star, at first. As it got darker, the stars grew in number. They shifted and found new positions, rearranging the earthly sky into the other. We didn't drop our hum. We could hear an echo of Ric's voice humming with us. Becca grabbed the hems of her shirt and pulled it off. We followed her; she did not mind the cold and neither did we. Sam howled, we all howled back in one voice, moving from hum to howl and back to hum. Ric had given us magic the first time, in life, and now he had done so again, in death. We couldn't be more grateful.

There was the banging at the sky, louder than ever before.

Becca screamed.

We repaired to the kitchen. Sam heated up the mushroom soup we had prepared for after the ritual. 'What was that?' he asked, handing a steaming cup to Becca.

'Our mission.'

Imogen broke a piece of bread. 'Did you remember it?'

'I remembered Janis.'

Zoey asked, 'What about her?'

'Janis and her baby, Ellie – they're the ones banging from the dark side of the sky. It's them we stopped.'

'From doing what?'

Becca shook her head. 'I don't remember. What I remember is that we... took them and brought them here, to our sacred land. We were humming, and they were at the centre of our circle, by the bonfire. Tied up. Then... then I don't know yet.'

'I'm sick and tired of talking in circles,' I said. 'We're not being real.'

Charlie said, 'What are you suggesting?'

'They need to be stopped.'

'Like we stopped the boys?'

'That was personal. This is about saving the world.'

'The world is under siege,' Imogen said, 'and so are we.'

There was a pause. Then Sam said, 'There's a classic question sci-fi nerds ask. Say you go back in time to when Hitler was a baby, and you find yourself at his cradle. Should you kill baby Adolf or not? You know with absolute certainty that this baby is going to grow into a monster who'll kill millions of people, which means smothering this particular baby in the cradle may be the right thing to do. But you'd still be killing a baby. The options seem clear-cut. But if you ask me, they're not. Maybe it's not that you've got to kill or ignore baby Adolf; maybe you should, like, give him a good childhood, and he'll turn out sane. Or you could set the time machine to go back to when he was a failing artist, help him deal with that in a healthier way than launching a world war.'

'Make therapy, not war,' Charlie said.

Sam shrugged. 'Maybe we don't kill them. Maybe we heal them.'

I hated it when Sam was like this: wavering, undecided. 'But what if you only have one minute with Hitler and his fucking cradle?' I asked.

'How do you know Janis and Ellie are evil?' said Zoey.

'*Ask Ric*! But okay, let's say then that it's the cradle of a baby you're ninety-nine percent sure is Hitler. If you kill him and you're wrong, you took a life. But if you spare him and you're wrong, you took a *world*. What kind of psychopath would risk *that* in the name of their ease of mind?'

Zoey drew back her lips, bowed her head, and looked as if she was walking to the gallows, but did not argue.

Becca said, 'Let's just focus on getting them here.' She stood up. 'We'll talk more tomorrow. I'm wiped.'

I felt the opposite – full of energy, and ready to go – but I didn't say so. Whatever I'd lost, Becca had lost it ten times over.

ZOEY

I was exhausted and I couldn't wait to crash, but before going to bed I checked my phone, for the first time that day. I found a voice message from Janis.

Her name on the screen, just after the discussion we'd had, made me deeply uneasy. When is a coincidence not a coincidence at all? I hesitated before pressing play, and letting Janis's voice fill the space.

'Zoey, you've got to call me back. This is important. I know you don't want to talk to me right now, and I promise, I swear, I won't bother you after this one, but please, *please*, if you ever loved me, call me back, okay? Any time.'

I tapped on Janis's name, and she answered immediately. 'You can't sleep either,' were her words.

She spoke as if we were still close. Janis, the *friend* who had caused my naked body to end up on a million screens. Who had caused Ric's death. 'What's up? Make it quick.'

'Face to face tomorrow?'

'No.'

'Only this once.'

'Janis, I'm living under siege, my face is on every rag in the world – my tits as well. Because of you.'

'Give me one last shot. Give me this and I'll go back to NY, disappear from your life, take over SoulJo.'

'What do you want to talk about?'

'Stuff I won't touch over the phone in a village full of tabloid journos. Oh, by the way, if any of you scavengers are listening to this, fuck you.'

I had to suppress a chuckle. 'That, too, is because of you.'

'One last chat and I leave. Deal?'

LILA

Come morning, the siege had intensified. Hikers passed by the windswept beach. They had chosen a blustery day, funny that, for a seaside walk. Some had cameras unashamedly hanging around their necks. We had learned our lesson and we were guarding the fence, letting the concerned citizens see us. I flipped the bird to a couple of them. They should know we would not allow any more intrusions in our life.

After last night's drumming, social media was on fire with theories on what unholy rituals we were surely carrying out. Satanism was taken for granted. And orgies, you couldn't mention our name without mentioning the orgies. I could feel their eyes on me, like insects crawling on my skin.

Social media was also on fire with theories about the missing kids. Most fingers pointed at us.

I started to feel that the world was not worth the hassle. Here we were, putting our lives on the line for *them*, and all we got in return was suspicion, hatred and dirty jokes.

'We don't do what we do to get something back,' Becca reminded me. 'We do it because that's the right thing to do.'

ZOEY

I left through the front gate, and the vultures swarmed on me the instant I was out. I had to make my way out pushing and pulling while Lila and Mikka guarded against people sneaking in. The famous photo in which I seem to be attacking a journalist – the scumbag had grabbed me and *demanded* me to answer a question or two. I was defending myself against an aggression, but you look at the photo and what you see is a crazy-eyed cultist shoving a bespectacled man for no reason at all. I understand why the world got the wrong impression about us. I'm not happy about it, and I cannot say I forgive it, but I do understand it.

I took a long walk to shake off the vultures, and in the end I had to shoo away the last one by threatening to call the police. In the process he bagged a few photos of me in which I looked like a madwoman. There was nothing I could do about it.

Get this: we were being hounded, bullied, made to feel powerless. Each moment of those last days was horrible.

It wasn't fun being behind enemy lines. It wasn't fun having to talk to Janis. My hand was not firm when I knocked at her door.

Janis opened the door and she made to hug me. I jumped back. 'Come on in,' she said, embarrassed.

I followed her in, telling myself there was nothing to be afraid of. *Nothing to be afraid of,* I repeated when Janis shut the door. I was relieved that Janis hadn't locked it, and I thought that was silly, but also, was it?

'Coffee or wine?'

'I'm not staying long.'

'You can drink quickly.'

'Wine, then.'

'White?'

'It's early for red.'

I followed Janis to the kitchen, where Ellie sat in her alien-looking travel highchair. She turned to me and grinned, for a split second, like an adult who is planning nothing good for you, before making her face innocent again. She giggled. I held onto a chair. My heart was beating fast. How much danger was I in, exactly? I was with Janis, my friend, my sister, the woman I'd loved. I was in the lair of the monsters who were crashing the universe.

'Are you all right?' Janis asked.

'What? Oh... yeah, I'm okay.'

Janis was setting crisps and olives on a tray. She took a bottle of wine from a pastel-blue fridge. 'Proper cork, not the screw-top shit we get in NY,' she said, rummaging in a drawer for a corkscrew. 'That's what we drink here.'

Janis put both bottle and corkscrew on the tray, and took the tray. She asked, 'Would you mind getting Ellie?' Before I found a way to refuse, she was out of the room.

Ellie had stopped giggling or making any noise at all – she just stared at me, challenging me to come any closer. I was never one to refuse a challenge. I rushed to the highchair and grabbed Ellie, not sweetly. It was all I could do not to throw her to the ground.

'Are you coming?' Janis called from the other room.

I sat the baby on one arm, and with the other took the baby's head to touch my chest. I was expecting to be bitten, or worse, at any moment. I held one of the most dangerous creatures in the world in my arms.

I forced myself to take one step, then another, to the living room. Janis was sitting on the sofa, piercing the cork with the corkscrew. It was a small room. I would have to sit close to her.

'Where should I put Ellie?' I asked, in what I could only hope was a casual voice.

'Just hold her. Look, she's so happy with you.'

I sat down with deliberate movements (I felt like I was handling a rabid dog which was not to be startled) while Janis poured the wine into two glasses. 'I'm not comfortable with babies,' I admitted.

'Fine,' Janis sighed, extending her arms. I handed her the baby and started breathing again.

'You're shaking. Are you sure you're okay?'

'I *was*, before you came and blew everything up.'

Janis was rocking Ellie on her knees, with the baby's tiny hands in hers. Ellie did a good act of looking just like any little girl. 'Everything I did, I did for you.'

'Well, you could've spared it.'

'Like it's easy for me! I'm losing sleep over this story, Zoey. You should hear the nightmares I'm having.'

'*You* are the nightmare I'm having.'

'Can we try and keep it civilised?'

'What do you want?'

'Galen Pantazis.'

Shit.

'Rings a bell,' Janis said, and it was not a question.

I drank.

'I know what they did, Zoey.'

'Good for you, because I don't have a clue what you're talking about.'

Janis mentioned the Nameless. 'He told me everything. He was a wreck. He's been holding on to this guilt for all these years... I cannot imagine how hard it must have been, to have this thing gnawing at him every day, every night. He didn't stop crying one moment when he told me the story.'

I replenished my wine. Janis hadn't touched hers yet, and the thought crossed my mind that it might be spiked. 'He could've told it the first time you talked, if it was so dear to his poor broken heart.'

'He was afraid of what his former friends would do to him.'

'But then he just couldn't keep it to himself anymore.'

'The Bastion is under the spotlight, he's got me in his corner. He feels safer. Not *safe*, mind, but safer.'

'And what are you going to do with this?'

'I already did. I went to the Carabinieri.'

'The fuck, Janis?'

'Not in front of the baby.' Janis sipped from her wine. Not spiked, then. 'If you were in your own mind, you would know that was the only thing I could do.'

'Calling the guards on me and my friends with the story a random dude made up?'

'With a detailed account featuring names and dates, and involving people I have every reason to be wary of.'

I shot to my feet. 'We're done here.'

'It was before your time, you've got nothing to do with it.'

'So it's only my friends who are in deep shit?'

'Your friends induced one of their own to suicide, and then they *burnt his body and fed his bones to pigs*, for Chrissake!'

'Have you noticed?'

'Noticed what?'

'You're always asking me not to swear in front of Ellie, and you're always doing just that.'

'Can you sit down, please?'

'Goodbye, Jan.'

'I'm not the only one who reached out to the guards.'

I sat down. 'I'll bite. Who else?'

'There's a crazy-eyed woman in your group, Lila Brasca. Her father. A powerful judge.'

'A crook.'

'Dr Brasca says when he tried making Lila see some sense, after Becca and Ric brainwashed her, they threatened him with trumped-up evidence. His daughter *beat him up* in front of her mother. He was keeping it in the family because he was hoping to reconnect with her, one day. Well, he thought this was the day.'

'A fucking *judge*, Janis. When did we come to this? Authority, power. I thought we didn't trust The Man.'

'Becca and Ric threatened me too.'

'*You* threatened them – *us*! And you're following through.'

'*That's not how it went.* No, you know what, let's stop it there, you don't have to convince *me* anyway. Dr Brasca is pressing charges. No judge will take the word of a sex cult over that of a colleague, less so when the cult has been hiding actual bodies.'

'*We are not a sex cult*!' I shouted.

Ellie burst out crying. Of course she did.

When the crying subsided, Janis drank another sip of wine. 'She's never seen me fight with her dad. She's not used to this.'

'Because you two are the golden couple.'

'Because we're adults! Take your head out of your ass, Zoey. You're better than this.'

'So I came here to be insulted, threatened, and patronised again.'

'Why don't you ask how I know that Dr Brasca went to the guards?'

'You're the ringmaster. The mighty and powerful judge will have come to your court.'

'The guards did.'

'Oh yeah?'

'Oh *yeah*. Yesterday. The problem with Dr Brasca was well before your time. You may get some minor charges, but in the maelstrom the process will be, it's going to be small beer. It could be no beer at all, the guards promised.'

The process. There had been a day when a twelve-year old me had had a weekend planned with Dad. He was always scrupulously on time, but on that occasion he hadn't shown up at the door of the little crappy flat where I lived with Mum. I called his phone, he didn't pick up. I started getting worried and Mum, who had better plans for her weekend than taking care of a little girl, started getting upset.

A phone call came two hours later, from the police. Dad would not come to pick me up after all. He had been sitting by the window, reading one of the fantasy novels that were always with him, at the exact same time a fifteen-year old had been playing with a gun in the street. The kid shot in the air, for fun. A stray bullet came through Dad's window and his head, killing him on the spot, with no rhyme or reason. What fun. That was my first experience of a point of no return. When Mum told me *your Dad,* even before she said any other words, I knew life had taken a turn towards a new normal, and the new normal sucked.

This was such a moment. *The process.* We had pretended we could deal with the press and go back to our life, our troubles just a blip, but the truth was this was not a blip, this was the start of a new normal. There would be a process. There would be an investigation. There would be disruption on a scale large enough to stop us from completing our mission. It dawned on me that Janis did not need to be in cahoots with any dark force, she could just be her normal stubborn self, and the world would still be damned because of her.

'But they need to find the boys,' said Janis.

I looked at the baby, and the baby, I promise, looked back, grinning. 'The boys?'

'The boys the whole village is talking about. The *whole country.* What happened to them?'

'I won't descend to answering that.'

'Zoey – *this is not before your time.* The Carabinieri have seen the interview and they know I have a friend inside. They asked me to reach out and propose a deal: help them with the boys and you'll come out clean. This whole thing – not just the boys, but the Bastion situation in general – is exploding in their hands from one day to the next, and they're aiming at closing it. The mayor has been weighing in. Portodimare is a family resort – this is not the kind of publicity it needs.'

'So they're trumping up charges to shut us down.'

'Nothing trumped up about two boys disappearing.'

'What do you think we did, killed them and hid the bodies?'

'Or you're fucking their brains out – how would I know?'

'You know I'm not a killer.'

'Your friends, though? Whatever *you* know, this is the time to talk.'

'Or?'

'The guards are asking for a warrant, and the judge is going to give one, *hey presto,* as a professional courtesy to Lila's father if nothing else. Once they've got it, they'll track the boys' phones, or their last known location. There's the story of Galen Pantazis, the Brascas' testimony, and if the guards find the smallest hint of malfeasance with the boys, that too. It's over, Zoey; one way or another the Bastion is over. A witness from within the group would save everybody time, money and would made the case stronger, but it's not like the guards *need* one. The law, the journos, the locals, the public opinion, everybody and everything is against your cult— sorry, your group. You personally, though? You can save your life. Take the chance, Zoey, I'm begging you. Don't go down with a ship that's not yours.'

I closed my eyes, pinched my nose. I felt immensely tired. 'How long do I have?'

'The guards wanted an answer by tonight.'

'Buy me until tomorrow,' I begged that awful stranger who had been my friend.

LILA

If we needed any more proof that Becca was right about Janis, here it was. Just when we zoned in on her, the bitch made another move against us. We argued for reasons why the situation *could not* be as bad as it looked. Nobody could prove that Galen had ever even been with us; nobody could prove we had done anything to the boys either. We could undermine the credibility of Dr Brasca by publishing the evidence we had of his corruption.

But we were disrespecting Ric's memory by doing that, sticking lies like plasters on a painful reality. We had to be real to the end, and reality was that we were done for. Fighting our way in court would take years, and it would also take all we had, financially, mentally, spiritually. Meanwhile the world would fall. These were the facts, and the facts were bleak.

I'd never realised the power of time until we had run out of it. We are twenty, time-rich, and we throw it around without a second thought, and then we're forty, and we wish there was a bank to loan us some more, and then we're sixty, and never found that bank. We had squandered weeks and months and years, until suddenly all that we had left was a bunch of hours.

'Time's up,' I said, and this time even Zoey found nothing to argue with. I loved her for it. I couldn't imagine how difficult it must have been for her.

We spent the evening preparing. Then, that night, we went back to Janis.

ZOEY

By nightfall the vultures had fled the beach. The weather was too inclement for them to hover in the hope of catching some small shred of drama, and we'd made it very clear there was no way in anymore. We slipped out at the edge of the land and walked to Janis's apartment through empty streets. The wind was biting, the humidity from the sea had the heft of bad news.

The others hid. I knocked at Janis's door. My knuckles were

steady, my face was blank. I had a knot in my belly and I had to make an effort to breathe, but that was all hidden inside.

'Zoey!' said Janis, jumping to hug me. This time I did not draw back. I let Janis kiss me on one cheek. 'Thank goodness. Thank goodness!' She took me by the hand to draw me inside, and shut the door.

LILA

We kept close, our ears trained for the smallest noise. We were nervous for Zoey. For all we knew, Janis and Ellie were ready to eat her up alive.

ZOEY

I was inside for the second and, I hoped, last time. Janis whispered, 'Why didn't you call?'

'Caution? Paranoia?'

'You're here, that's all I care about. I... I don't know what to say. I promise it's going to work out, Zoey. Everything's going to work out. Gosh, I'm so relieved.'

I was too; I was feeling calmer. There was no going back now, and that made everything easier. It was like the opening ceremony of SoulJo, when, after months of phone calls, emails, last-minute cancellations, the party started, and the only way was forward.

'Ellie's sleeping?' I asked.

Janis nodded. 'What do you want to do? Shall we go to the Carabinieri now, or...'

'Tomorrow, first thing in the morning.'

'Did you talk to your lawyer?'

'Not yet.'

'It's just past 6 p.m. in NY.'

'I'll call tomorrow. If I've got to drag him out of bed, so be it, I pay him enough. Sorry, Jan, I... It was a long day.'

'Of course.'

'Can we just go to sleep? We'll talk over breakfast.'

'Whatever you want.' Janis kissed me again on one cheek. 'We'll get to the other side of it together, I promise. I'm not leaving you alone.'

Janis gave me a clean t-shirt and the bottoms of an old tracksuit, and offered me the other side of her double bed. Lying side to side brought back memories. Janis and I had shared beds in college, in the flat that was the first SoulJo HQ, in countless B&Bs during the meagre years in which we were getting the festival off the ground. I had never dared risk our friendship making a move. Not at first, when I wasn't sure how I felt, not later, when I was.

Ellie's toddler bed stood out like a little jail in the half-light of the room.

I had never been so afraid in all my life. A part of me indulged in the fantasy that I may be colossally deluded. The woman in bed with me was Janis, my best friend, and Janis had been right about all of it: I'd become a killer for no reason, the Bastion's magic was smoke and mirrors, the Inner Pinewood was a hallucination, and my own healing not a miracle, but an effect of placebo. Silly fantasies, but terrifying. They made it all the more important to act, if only to keep them at bay.

Time passed, and now a light snore came from next to me. I rose up slowly, fetched my clothes, and tiptoed out of the room. I changed back before opening the front door.

Lila and Mikka were there. They slipped inside, clicking the door closed behind them. They handed me the sharp work knife I'd used at Ric's passing rites and took out theirs.

I headed to the toddler bed, with them in trail. I scooped up Ellie.

'Zoey?' Janis's sleepy voice came from the bed.

'Whatever happens, don't scream.'

'What's going on?'

'Don't scream,' I repeated.

Lila turned on the light.

I had the awful baby perched on one arm, the knife's edge pointed at her throat.

'Ellie!' Janis shrieked, and made to throw herself towards us. She saw the heavy knives and stopped. I think she saved Ellie's life, in that moment. Her breath became heavy; her eyes whipped from Lila and Mikka to me and Ellie, to Lila and Mikka, to me and Ellie again.

'I know how it looks,' I said. 'Forget it. Forget what you think you're seeing. For once, forget those fucking prejudices you're holding to. We're not here to hurt you. We're trying to save your life! But you must play your part. You need to do as I say, Jan, exactly as I say, or Ellie dies.'

'How could you...'

'Are we on the same page?'

After a beat, Janis gave the shortest nod ever given.

'Good. Now you're going to make a couple of calls: hubbie, PA, whoever may be expecting to hear from you. Tell them you're going off radar for a bunch of days and there's nothing, absolutely nothing, they've got to worry about. Say that you're up to something with me, you're halfway to rescuing me or whatever. Say what you like, as long as they leave us be. Then you're coming with us.'

'Please, Zoey…'

'I get as much as a vague suspicion you're passing some coded message, Ellie dies. Your voice goes up while we walk, Ellie dies. You have a go at running, Ellie dies. You make a funny face – you get the gist.'

'You wouldn't do that.'

I shook the blade. 'Say that again and Ellie dies. Go on, say it. Put your money where your mouth is.'

'You…' Janis started. She didn't go further than that.

'So now you believe me.'

'What happened to you?' Janis asked, barely loud enough for us to hear.

I had tried to explain, so many times. She had never listened to me.

CHARLIE

When I saw the others come from the beach, I drew back in the shadows. They pushed the net to one side and entered the pinewood. I kept quiet, watching. It was a grim procession, with Janis in the middle and Ellie in Zoey's arms.

One thing I can say for sure, none of us ever took pleasure in any of the awful things we did. This is one of the ways we have been misunderstood. The media made it look like we revelled in violence, when everybody there was constantly striving to steer clear of it.

After they passed, I sat again in my spot. The craving for Bertrand had returned. I thought I had worked through my grief, but here it was rushing back to me, becoming a physical ache in my bones and joints. I felt as if my skeleton had turned into a knotted marionette whose strings only Bertrand could untangle. I waited there for a while longer, but the music didn't come.

It came later that night, in my room, rousing me up. It was faint, Bill Evans' 'Here's That Rainy Day'. I was half-awake and half-asleep. Bertrand would only play that piece when he meant business. He used to say, *it goes too deep*. And then he used to add...

'It cuts to the bone.'

In my dozing state I couldn't tell if I heard the words, spoken in a barely audible whisper, or remembered them. But the music was still playing, and not even ghosts could blow into a saxophone and talk at the same time. I felt a weight sit on my bed, Bertrand's weight, as if he were alive, as if our life was still full of promise. His scent – tobacco and nutmeg – brought tears to my eyes.

I did not open my eyes, to not spoil the dream. I wished he would put his large hand on my cheek, the way he would do every morning, when he told me coffee was ready for his Queen of Heaven.

The music shifted to 'Flamenco Sketches' again, the piece that had been playing when Bertrand had opened his heart about his friend double-crossing him. The memory from the other night came back, stronger, detailed. I walked through the memory as if it were a Punchdrunk show, with an actor playing me and one playing Bertrand. I looked at myself hugging Bertrand, with my arms barely closing the circle around his large chest. He had said something in a voice so vulnerable that it had made me wish to protect him from duplicitous bastards, from the shady deals, from all the evils of the world. What he said was...

'You never think you're the one being played.'

I felt a tug in my head, like a dislocated shoulder snapping back in place. A new thought formed, wild enough and strong enough to make me open my eyes.

The weight on the bed was gone; the music had stopped.

THE BASTION

There is a key difference between science and spirituality, and it is that science is an exploration of things we should understand, spirituality is an experience of things we cannot understand. Not because they're forbidden, but because understanding them is beyond our reach, the way jumping a thousand feet high is beyond our reach.

LILA

We woke up to an amplified world. Overnight, pine needles had become greener and sharper, tree trunks thicker, the reds and browns of the soil were more intense than ever before. While we cooked breakfast giant bubbles came through the walls and up from the floor, like ghosts who had lost their way, and the Oddballs fluttered and skittered around. The Inner Pinewood was surging – the end was really coming.

We could hear the shouting, angry voices taunting us and calling us out from the gate. We wanted to ignore them, but they grew louder and more threatening, until we couldn't take it anymore. Becca asked me and Mikka to go with her.

An angry mob had joined the usual vultures. They had dark, tensed faces, and some held signs reading stuff like *Protect the Children* or *Ban Pornography.* A young man with an angry face was, for reasons that to this day I don't get, wrapped in the national flag. Another kept blowing a red plastic whistle. Two Carabinieri were leaning on their car, doing conspicuously nothing.

The mob leader was a bald man with a big frame, a big belly and the red wetland of broken capillaries on cheeks and nose that a lifetime of heavy drinking earns you. 'Here they are,' he screamed, when he saw us arrive. He grabbed the bars of our gates and shook them. 'Where are our children?'

Becca said, 'Good morning, Mr Ruggeri.'

'Our children!'

'They are not with us.'

A woman hurled herself on the gate, screaming, 'Bitch!'

I was ready to have a go at her; Becca stopped me.

'Monica, please...'

'You fucking whore, give me my Mimmo!'

Another woman joined her, smaller and thinner. 'Give back our sons *now*, or I swear to God, I'm messing you up, whore.'

'Whore,' the crowd repeated. 'Whore.'

'You've got a fine piece of ass,' someone shouted from the back. 'Show us more!'

We looked at the Carabinieri. 'And you're just letting this happen,' Mikka said, disgusted.

One of them brought a hand to his ear to signal he couldn't hear, though obviously it could not be true. He stood there with a grin that made me want to bash his face in and extract his teeth, one by one, calmly. I was not sure I agreed with Becca's strategy. I am still not. With some people you can reason, others, you must squash before they hurt you.

'This is unfair,' I said.

The guard shrugged.

'May I have a word, please?' Becca asked the crowd. She had to raise her voice slightly to be heard, but the crowd did hear; everybody always listened to Becca. The clamour abated.

'Thank you. It goes without saying that I am losing sleep over the two young men. I share your worry, and pain. If they were here, or if we had any clue as to their whereabouts, I would tell you in a heartbeat. But they are not, and we don't, and there's nothing else I can say. Some of you have known me for all my life, you know I'd never hurt a living soul.'

'You're doing orgies in there!' someone shouted.

'We're doing our business in here!' Lila shouted back.

Becca was going to say something, but the mob leader cut her short, asking, 'Where's Ric?'

'Ric's not here.'

'Where is he? The man of the house.'

Becca turned to the Carabinieri. 'I'm being harassed at my gate.'

'So move away from the gate, sweetie, and let us in,' the guard said. 'We'll sweep the place and put these good people's minds at rest.'

'Do you have a warrant?'

'Do we need one?'

'To get into our house, yes.'

'Enjoy, then.'

Give them back, the mob started chanting. *Give them back*.

ZOEY

We tied Janis to a chair in the washing room we had in the basement (Mikka knew one or two things about how to tie people, and he had plenty of soft rope we normally used for happier pursuits). It was a windowless room, with damp patches of mould here and there, as is to be expected in the basement of a house by the sea, but clean and tidy, nothing like the torture dungeon the media have depicted.

I went to see her alone in the morning, bringing a tray with cappuccino, orange juice, a slice of almond cake, bread and scrambled eggs. As soon as she saw me, Janis said, 'I need to see Ellie.'

I locked the door behind me. Better safe than sorry.

'Ellie's okay. I'm going to turn my phone's camera on. Someone'll be watching. You do anything wrong – she's not okay anymore. Good?'

She nodded.

I set the phone on the washing machine and undid the knots. 'I'm pissing myself,' Janis said.

'I'll come with.'

I took Janis to the tiny basement loo, keeping the camera on. She didn't complain. She did what she had to do and let me lead her back to the washing room.

It felt unreal, like a play. I was not really holding Janis prisoner – that would be ludicrous. We were both playing a part, a bonkers therapeutic role-play devised by the latest New Age quack, and come dinner, we would laugh it out together. 'We're still family, you and I,' I said, to reassure her.

'You've lost touch with reality.'

'I know more about reality than I ever did.'

'You kidnapped your best friend and her baby on some strangers' say-so.'

'And you're speaking in the third person.'

'Is the breakfast for me?'

'Both of us.'

Janis sat on the floor with her back leaning against the wall, and I sat with her. She threw herself on the eggs. She stopped after the first bite. 'Pinch of paprika,' she said. 'The way I like them.'

'I'm not the beast you make me out to be.'

'Beasts can cook eggs.'

'You used to say I did the best in the world.'

'Still holds.'

I tried some of the eggs, though I wasn't hungry. 'Yup, not bad.'

'They taste like the first day of SoulJo.'

It was a small ritual of ours that on the first day, before opening the gates, I would make eggs for Janis and our immediate crew. My scrambled eggs were legendary, partially because – I was aware – they were the only food I could cook halfway decently. Janis was the cook; I was the coffee drinker.

'How's it going? Doing the festival without me.'

'A mess.'

'Not to worry, you're going to master the secrets of Excel spreadsheets.'

'So we're coming out of this alive.'

'Of course, Janis, come on!'

'You're saying *of course* but your voice means *I hope so*.'

'If that's what you believe, why aren't you more afraid?'

Janis used the fork to cut the almond cake in two halves, and pushed one towards me. 'I'm holding on for Ellie.'

The pain in her voice stabbed me deep. 'We don't want to hurt anybody.'

'The boys are dead.'

'No.'

'Your voice means *yes*.'

'Here you are again, knowing what I mean better than I do.'

'It's the same voice you had when you were defending that loser girlfriend of yours, the Hekate devotee who made off with $40k from your account.'

Zoey sighed. 'You're implying I'm not the best judge of character.'

'Let us go. You've got my word I won't go to the guards.'

'The guards are already on our case.'

'I can help you with that.'

'Pray, tell: how?'

Janis finished her eggs in silence. 'What's the plan then?'

'That depends.'

'On?'

'On what *your* plan is.'

'Come again?'

'You need to come clean with me. What is this all about, Jan?'

'*You* are asking *me*?'

'You're doing something, or you're going to do something, which is going to end up badly for every last person on this planet.'

Janis seemed to be gasping for words. 'This is insane.'

'What are you planning?'

'A festival! Raising a child! Growing old with my husband!'

I sighed. 'Have you been approached by somebody? Or – or, have you felt a dark force pulling at you?'

'Oh my God,' Janis said, in a low voice.

'I'm not crazy!' I shouted, making Janis recoil. I closed my eyes, took a long breath. 'You're not yourself, Janis. There's something evil about you, and it's not *you*. I'm thinking there is *something else* acting through you.'

'Okay,' Janis said.

'You know I love you.'

'Me too. Even with all of this – me too.'

'Not as my best friend. Not *only* my best friend. When you went and got married, you broke my heart.'

'Oh,' Janis said. Then: 'That never crossed my mind.'

'Who's being a hypocrite now?'

'You should've said something.'

'Stop telling me what I should and shouldn't do! Other people's lives are easy to live. On the day you got married, I lost something. A spark? Joy? After the wedding party, I was back at the hotel, getting one last drop by myself, and I was looking back at my life. You know what I saw? A string of disappointments, that's what. I'd gone looking for magic and found bad theatre, I'd gone looking for teachers and found maladjusted narcissists, I'd found love without looking for it and love had kicked my butt. But whatever it was I lost that day, the Bastion gave it back to me, times a million. I've seen magic in action. I've seen... I've *done* miracles.'

Some colour had returned to Janis's face. 'But *did you* though?' she said, in a voice kind more than challenging. 'Faith healing can work, but it's nothing more mysterious than placebo. Every day people get over cancer, diabetes, terminal illnesses. Suggestion is the most powerful drug there is, you and I know that better than anybody. Remember SoulJo '16? When a bunch of kids swore they'd seen a UFO land behind the main stage? They weren't making it up; they believed what they said. Still, no UFO. They'd convinced each other that something that wasn't there was, in fact, there.'

'A wiser woman would shut up, in your place.'

'Whenever have we been wise, you and me?'

I kissed her on the forehead. I told her not to worry, we were going to sort her out that night.

CHARLIE

I felt displaced. *You never think you're the one being played.*

I kept clear of the bubbles. An Oddball, a toad with magpie wings which looked enormous, made to perch on my shoulder, and I shooed it away. I did not like that the colours were getting brighter and stranger. The physical world was inching closer to the Inner Pinewood, as if the consequences of our plans for the night were rippling to the present, but I was not so confident that the Inner Pinewood was where I wanted to be. This sacred land was sacred to *whom*, exactly?

Our magic was not all bad. Not a single word Becca said was hateful, not even after her brother died. But there was something Bertrand said after returning exhausted from a tour with a band well-known for being first in line fighting whatever the good fight of the moment was. 'Some of the nastiest narcissists I met were preaching peace and love.' The Bastion did preach peace and love, and yet here we were, with blood on our hands, pondering whether to kill a little girl and her mum. I remembered all too vividly my fists hitting the boy, his eyes emptying out. That memory was not old.

I only managed to catch up with Lila in the early afternoon, when our turn came to watch the fence. 'I wanted to talk to you,' I said.

'About what?'

'About tonight.'

'I'm scared stiff too.'

'You never look scared.'

'Hey!' Lila shouted to a bloke on the beach. 'This is private property, mate. Keep going.'

The guy mumbled something and made as if he was only minding his business.

'I do my best to act the way Ric would,' Lila said, 'but it's hard. That baby, Ellie...' she shrugged. 'I don't think she's a baby at all. To be honest with you, I wouldn't be surprised if we found she's an *it*. Not human.'

'I wouldn't be surprised if we found out we're wrong.'

'About what?'

'Everything.'

'I don't follow.'

'When I came here, I thought Becca and Ric were crooks, then I had a change of heart.'

'I know. I was there.'

'What never crossed my mind was that they might have been conned in the first place. That they may be in good faith, and still not be doing what they thought they were doing.'

Lila scoffed. 'It never crossed your mind for a reason.'

'It may go back to the very beginning, to when a little girl was born with the gift of hearing voices. Those voices – are we sure they are the good guys?'

'Yes,' Lila flat-out answered.

'I don't know, Lila, hurting a baby?'

'We're working hard not to hurt anybody!'

'That work would be easier if we didn't have a mother and daughter prisoner.'

'We do what is necessary.'

'I believe that too. But necessary to what end? You say we didn't hurt Ellie yet, and that she may not even be human anyway. Let's say you're right. We already murdered two boys. Weren't they human either?'

'They killed Ric. I don't give a fuck what they were.'

'Do you remember how it went?'

'I remember every moment.'

'It was going smoothly, until the Oddball popped up.'

'Until that dickhead squashed it, you mean.'

'Focus, Lila. Think back to what happened. The Oddball startled the boy, and the boy reacted the way a lot of scared boys would. So Ric lost it, so the other boy got even more scared and drew the blade. It's a neat chain of events that starts with the Oddball. They'd all be alive – Ric, the boys, everybody – if the Oddball hadn't popped up at the worst possible time – after no Oddball had shown itself in days. You could think they'd been holing up on purpose, to rile us up and make us paranoid, so that we would overreact at the first opportunity. You could think we'd been set up.'

'You could, if you were paranoid. The boys were scum who acted like scum one time too many and got their payback.'

'You never have doubts?'

'I used to be made of doubts. Sub-zero self-esteem, sky-high anxiety, and me in the middle, your run-of-the-mill product of my kind of family; a therapist would've found me uninteresting. Here I found a strength which I'd never thought was in the cards for me. Becca and Ric saved my life, and only asked for one thing back: that I trusted them.'

'And I do! Becca's well-meaning, we all are. But well-meaning people can still be wrong.'

'Not tonight,' Lila said, after a while. 'We cannot afford doubt tonight.'

'Say we're not saving the world. Say we're doing the opposite.'

'It's simple: would you trust Becca with your own life?'

'Yes,' I answered immediately, and I meant it.

'Then why not the world?'

THE BASTION

Becca hit the pillow with her fists until her muscles ached, clenching her fingers tight enough for her nails to dig moons in her palms.

She had been barely getting any sleep since Ric died. The bed next to hers, Ric's bed, was empty, and she couldn't fall properly asleep without the white noise of his breath. She hadn't managed to face changing his bed just yet. Ric had been rolling in those sheets on his last night on Earth, which made sacred relics of them. Ric's last razor left in the cup at the bathroom sink was a relic too, so was the book on his bedside table, a collection of Umberto Eco's writings on politics. He had been raving about it, and he never got to finish it. 'All readers die in the middle of a book,' he used to say. He had a knack for being right. He was a holy man.

She was so alone.

The voices went on whispering relentlessly, but they hadn't offered one word of consolation, or advice. She had been praying to them, cursing, begging, cajoling them, and got nothing, absolutely nothing. 'Fuck you,' she'd screamed to the sky. The sky had not answered.

She had to carry it on her own, the weight of the world and the weight of the family she had built with Ric. But she couldn't take care of herself, let alone everybody else. She had lost her way. She'd been Becca of *Becca and Ric,* and without Ric, what was left? What they formed together was more than the sum of their parts, and with one part gone, everything else had dissolved too.

Since the night Ric died she had felt hollowed out, beyond petty emotion like despair, hope or fear. The one thing she could find within herself was rage, a white-hot fury of a kind that was completely new to her. She and her family had been doing their thing without hurting a living soul, until the American cunt had got some superhero rescue fantasy in her head. Cunt, cunt, a thousand times a cunt. That monster tied up in the basement had as good as killed Ric herself. Who knew what else she would do, if the Bastion didn't stop her.

'Ric, come back to me,' Becca implored. She was in her room, sitting on her bed, facing her brother's. A circle of seven bubbles floated up from the floor around her, like the standing stones of a henge, but in rainbow colours. Each of them reflected her face, and her face only.

LILA

'Here we go,' Becca said.

She had gathered us outside, and asked us to raise our heads and look at the sunset. It was cold weather, but not windy. The pinewood was still.

'This moment, this night, is what we have been preparing for for the entirety of our lives. Think back to every friendship you had, every heartbreak, every turn of luck and every twisting road you went down, and you will see they all inevitably brought you to be here, now, together. This is when our nature unfolds, the very reason why we were put on this planet.' She paused. 'It feels sudden, but it is not. The stars have been aligning for decades, and tonight they fall into place. Things happen quickly when you prepare them slowly.' She gave us time to reflect on what she had said, before adding: 'So let us bask in this sunset. The wolves are at our door. However it goes tonight, it may be the last one we see together.'

We watched the sun fall in a blaze of glory.

'I love you all,' Becca said.

ZOEY

I'm not heartless. I do appreciate how terrifying it must have been for Janis to see me and Mikka open the door with stony faces, letting inside a distant hum and Sam's theremin. She must have felt utterly powerless, tied to a chair with two people looming over her and an otherworldly music in her ears.

But whatever she felt, she could still feel something; Ric couldn't.

'It's time,' I said.

'What are you going to do to me?'

'Please, understand this, Jan – we're done taking risks. Some of us believe we're going too far, trying to do this thing rather than just…' I was trying to find a way to make her understand we were doing our best to make the best of a bad situation. Her casting us in the role of the villains did not help. 'At the first hint of trouble, bad things are going to happen to Ellie.'

'Okay.'

'Literally the first hint, Jan. I'm not kidding.'

'Okay.'

I saw the tears in Janis's eyes and almost started crying myself. 'You've got nothing to be afraid of.' A lie; but a white lie.

'Okay,' Janis repeated for the third time.

We untied her and led her up the stairs and outside, deep into the pinewood. I appreciate the confusing mixture of awe and terror she must have felt when she saw the stars overhead multiply, and when she felt the dirt underfoot give way not in the way it should, not as dirt, but as the flesh of a giant. She pretended not to see the Oddballs, which buzzed and slithered and bumbled towards the fire, answering to our call, but she couldn't have missed them.

When she arrived at the fire she must have thought I had spiked her food. The flames bifurcated and trifurcated before joining back, drawing circles and ovals which stood a moment against the night sky before falling down in cascades of sparks, and rising again. The flames were dancing to our tune. Their colour was to yellow and orange what the sea is to a puddle.

'Ellie!' she called.

We had tied a soft rope around the little girl's belly to secure her to a tree stump, a natural altar, not far from the fire. Lila was standing close with a knife in hand.

'She's going to be alright,' I whispered in Janis's ear. 'Everything is going to be alright.'

Janis's eyes were very wide.

Zoey and Mikka took her to the fire, close to Ellie, but not too close. We had set a mat on the floor.

'Sit,' Mikka said.

He worked quietly on her with a long rope, binding her wrists and legs while we kept humming and Sam kept waving his hands around the theremin. Mikka's bindings were beautiful, like lace, but they were also strong. No matter how much she wriggled, Janis would not be able to get free.

How strange it must have been for her to lie like that, tied by the fire, straining her head to see what came next. Was it strange to me? Not anymore, not so much. That was my life now.

We took our clothes off. We didn't drop the hum as we undressed. Janis saw and heard Ellie cry, and could not reach out and take her baby in her arms. This must have been not strange, but terrible, I know. But, like Charlie said once, to crack a skull open is a terrible thing to do, and yet it must be done when you've got to scoop out cancer from a mushy brain.

I felt the good warmth of the fire on my skin. Sam waved

his hands around the theremin with a manic energy. We started dancing wildly, in twos and threes and alone, leaping, beating on our breasts.

'Please!' Janis implored. 'Please let us go!' She was barely coherent. 'Please,' she sobbed. 'Please.' She did not dare yell. Not that it would have made a difference; her voice could not reach the wolves at our gates. We were going deeper into the Inner Pinewood, a place inconceivably far from them and their concerns. Janis and Ellie may as well have been screaming on Pluto. We hummed.

We did not know what would happen, we were trusting the process. We were trusting that, if there was a way to stop Janis and Ellie without killing them, our magic would show the way. Sometimes you can plan, and sometimes you just have to accept what comes through.

The shift started with the trees, which quivered in and out of focus at the same pace as our sway, like a channel which is being tuned. Then the fire blew a bubble. It came from the tip of a flame, starting small and growing into the largest ones we had ever seen. More followed. The Oddballs were a swarm of hundreds and hundreds, many more than Galen had ever conceived, enough to fill the ground and the sky.

Janis had stopped pleading now, and was just bellowing and yelling without words. I felt pity for her; she didn't understand how beautiful it was. Now every rosemary shrub, every white rock, the land itself, was quivering.

Fixed shapes were gone. Nothing was any more set than the bubbles. The hard edges between things, the borders separating an Oddball from the other, a rock from the bushes growing on it, were blurred. A dizzying watercolour had replaced the usual stodginess of the world.

The change went further.

Wood, flesh, dirt and rocks transmuted into starlight. The transmutation started from their lower parts and rose up, shooting to the sky. I thought it must be like Becca's experience after her father's death. I could see that trees were still trees and rocks were still rocks, but at the same time everything was starlight. There was no firm land, only starlight. In the air was the scent of jasmine and fire. A spiced flavour, like ripe figs laced with ginger and cayenne pepper, filled my mouth.

And my nose and my mouth were starlight too. My body – my limbs, my tongue and throat – had changed, or perhaps had become itself at last. I couldn't tell anymore which voice was which; if I was feeling my arm on another's shoulder or their arm on my shoulder. All was light.

Only the fire in the centre remained very much itself. It grew taller, reaching out to the sky, and reaching down below as well, beyond what my eyes could see. I knew, with an absolute certainty which was like a new sense I had gained, that the fire stretched in both directions, reaching the point where directions end. There, the flames touched, forming a circle which encompassed the universe.

Janis and Ellie were not part of it.

Becca was the first to notice: I saw her lips curl in a disgusted expression, and I followed the direction of her gaze. While the pinewood shone in beauty, they were dull and smooth. There was a wrongness in them, like piss in a pristine stream, which made me gag. They came from some alien shore. They were not like us.

The banging at the sky started. It was getting louder and louder. Whoever was trying to smash the sky would manage soon. The unholy fiddles were playing, their music too close for comfort. What is it that Lila said?

Time's up.

CHARLIE

I thought of myself as a healer, always have. I was the little girl who takes home not only the sickly cat and the abandoned puppy, but also the misshaped bug and the wounded spider. I was the friend you go to after your first heartbreak. I took care of my brother during the terrible time of his illness, when my parents fell apart. I could never forgive the doctors who couldn't save him, and I swore I would do better when I became a doctor myself. But then, of course, I didn't. I had to learn that some people are beyond saving, and also that, awful as this truth is, the best doctor will make mistakes, and hurt patients. I understood that you've got to make tough calls, remove organs, cut off limbs; I also understood that you might be wrong.

I made an effort to observe the ritual with a clinician's impartial eye. I set apart what I had been taking for granted about our mission, I set apart my rage against Janis for destroying what fragile happiness I had found with the Bastion, I set apart myself, and just looked at the situation for what it was.

And my diagnosis was that we were working ourselves up. We were beating our chests, literally, and bouncing our rage and frustration between us, making it grow bigger, until it would grow big enough to allow us to do the unthinkable. We had killed the boys on the spur of the moment, and now we were engineering another moment, to give us the courage to kill again. Behind the bollocks we told ourselves about finding a better way, we knew how this would end. We were thirsty for our enemies' blood and what we were doing, what we were really doing, was pushing one another to drink.

The others were saying they heard the fiddles, but I didn't. I thought I could hear Bertrand's saxophone.

In a matter of heartbeats I had to take the most difficult decision of my life.

THE BASTION

We still love her. We know she did not betray us light-heartedly. It must have been gruelling for her to decide to turn her back on us and run towards the gate.

We didn't notice her going. It was unthinkable that one of us could do that to the others.

CHARLIE

I stopped by a tree close to the gate, keeping out of sight. 'They're killing a baby!' I screamed. 'Come! They're killing a baby! Oh God, please, come in!'

They had been drooling after a moment like that, those monsters, an easy chance to display their bravado by aiming at an easy target. What they saw was a naked woman in hysterics. There was a commotion, a rumble of excited voices and engines starting. Then came the deafening clang of iron against iron, when a pickup crashed through the gate and into our world. The Bastion had been breached: the wolves poured in.

THE BASTION

The Battle of Portodimare, some gamer on too much sugar christened it on Twitch, and the moniker remained. By and large, the story comes off as a black-and-white morality tale about good (them) defeating evil (us), at a price. We do have our fans and defenders, but they are not, for the most part, the kind of fans and defenders who really do you any favours.

The story, as it is told, is one of brave citizens who heard a cry from inside the pinewood telling them a baby was getting killed, and decided that enough was enough. What followed was violent and confused, and some of what happened in the heat of the moment was not ideal, the public opinion is ready to admit, but on the whole the citizens were in the right. We have filed as many lawsuits against those who violated us that night as the State and various families did us, but public opinion does not care about truth, nuance or fairness. Public opinion only cares about volume: the louder, the better. Public opinion is idiocy weaponised.

The real story of that night is unlike the one you know. To begin with, it was no battle. It would be ridiculous to define any of us, or any of them, as a fighter in any physical sense. It was an awkward, gory mess. And the *heroic* citizens – there was not a shred of goodness, of basic human decency, about them.

Take the mob leader, Piero Ruggeri, the heavy-handed father of one of the boys who killed Ric. This man had been beating his wife regularly for twenty-one years, and his son for the nineteen years he had been on Earth. When his son was ten, this man found a stash of male fitness magazines under his bed. The man called his son *fucking poof*, and duly went on to beat any trace of poofness out of his son. This man, when he and Becca both were teenagers, had wanted to go out with her, never succeeding. Once he had cornered her and forced her into a kiss. Becca never told Ric, because she knew Ric would have killed him. This man was convinced he was upright and strong. He was wrong on both fronts, and he was long due a rude awakening.

He was not the worst; others were far more dangerous. Take for example Rosa Pastore, the woman who stabbed Zoey. Normally she would have not wished to be seen dead with Ruggeri. She was of a much better class, married to the only dentist in Portodimare, and a personal friend of the chief priest. She dressed demurely and had always condemned, loudly, Becca's piercings, Becca's bangles, Becca's colours. She had been praying to God that the moment would come when the slut, her brother and their deviant friends would be eradicated from Portodimare. She had a violence in herself which was ten thousand times that of the boy's father, and she had more means to put that violence to use. When she had seen the photos of the orgy, she had been sick (she must have felt a warmth in her womb which she couldn't quite name, but that she wouldn't admit even to herself). In her world perversion calls for punishment, and she was the one deciding what perversion was, and what the punishment should be. She was thin, fragile, easy to tears. She was the sort of bully who turns their own weaknesses into a tool of oppression.

Or take Simone Gennari, the student whose head was smashed against a tree. He knew all about mind control – he had watched the TED talks. He was a free thinker, and in order for thought to be truly free, he argued online, there needed to be strict rules about speech, and it was up to the good guys (like him) to set them. What we were doing in the woods, he had been writing on his Substack, misquoting more than one philosopher, had nothing to do with *real* freedom. We were bending vulnerable people to our will. He was not the first sexually frustrated man who saw himself as a knight on a white horse, riding to the rescue of those who could still be rescued. He too had seen the photographs. He too had dreamt on them, and we could swear he was thinking that maybe, just maybe, if he was knightly enough, some of those he rescued would be grateful, and fuck him as joyously as they fucked each other.

But more than any of its members, take the mob as a whole. They say there is a wisdom in crowds, but this is one of the biggest lies ever told: crowds are mindless, and brutal. Ric would always say that being right is not compatible with being righteous, and that night we understood what he meant. The crowd that descended on us were made of the same people who burnt witches at stake, the people who sold their neighbours to the regime *du jour*, the people who chased strangers out of their job because of something someone had alleged on X. They were hateful, they were heartless, they were, in their own mind, absolutely *just*. The story of the Battle of Portodimare is the story of a witch hunt, only, one where the witches fought back.

That, they will never forgive us.

ZOEY

The wolves were taking photos, shooting videos, even as they irrupted inside. They couldn't wait to see what was going on behind our doors. This was the ultimate reason why they hated us so much – they couldn't bear not being us.

One famous video, illegally but widely shared, shows them making their way through the trees. The video is dark, difficult to decipher, which only makes it more powerful. It has been dissected, analysed frame by frame, turned into a society game. It doesn't show the starlight, but it makes it clear that the wolves were seeing *something*. 'The fuck is that?' one says, in Italian. 'Fuckin' psychos,' decrees another.

The fact that none of the videos and photos show anything definitively odd, except for a tendril of light here, or a shadow there which may be an Oddball, has been taken as proof that our magic is bogus. But we know what the intruders saw, we know what Janis saw. So what if the cameras didn't capture it? Miracles refuse to happen on record. No camera has ever captured how it is to die, and yet death, stubbornly, continues to exist.

The video shows the wolves slowing down to look at the trees. The camera zooms in on a pine tree, then a carob tree, for no apparent reason. A giant bubble does show, and some of the wolves stare at it with an open mouth. Then there is the glow of our fire, and Janis's screams get piercingly loud. The camera gets past the last tree and there it stops. It shows us, the way the wolves saw us – naked, humming, some of us with knives in hand, and a woman and a baby tied by our fire.

I noticed the starlight dim, as if weighted down, and when I looked at the trees, I saw a mob armed with sticks and blades come out of the darkness. The camera jerks from us to the mob to us again. It shows the moment in which we stare at each other, us and them, both parts quite unable to believe what they see.

Every hope was lost, that much was clear. They were forcing us towards the violence we had been trying so hard to avoid.

Becca looked at Lila. 'Run.'

'But...'

The mob was awakening from their stuporous state, taking their first steps forward.

'We're going to need someone on the outside.'

'On the outside of what?'

Becca ordered: 'Run!'

Lila obeyed.

That was the trigger the mob needed. You can't hear the exchange between Becca and Lila in the video, but you can see something going on between them, then Lila running away, and at that, all hell breaking loose. Each member of the mob, alone, would have fled from us, but together they felt invincible. You see them flock to our circle. That's when the camera falls. From then on, it shows only dark shapes. You can hear the screams though: ours, theirs, Janis's.

Other invaders were taking snapshots – even in that moment, they were taking snapshots. Can you believe people? There is one of Becca raising her knife, with something like a smile on her lips. There is one of Mikka, muscular and taut, with his teeth bared, throwing himself at a wolf. There is one of me looking feral with my knife, close to Janis, ready to strike. These photos twist truth out of shape, making it another falsehood.

The mob leader headed straight to Becca, and before anyone could stop him, he had hit her in the face. It was as if he had hit all of us. As one, we turned towards him, and he was hitting her again. Becca ducked, and slashed her starlight knife at his throat. Light poured out where the blade cut the flesh. Everybody was shouting, screaming. The spilled blood called for more.

I won't give yet another blow-by-blow account of the so-called *battle*. What for? There are too many retellings of it, from when the wolves came in to when, a handful of minutes later, two Carabinieri pointed their guns at everybody. Suffice to say that we never stood a chance.

I could tell of the five people it took to subdue Mikka, of how the man Imogen killed had tried to do the same to her, whatever lies to the contrary his friends have been spreading, but it would be nothing that has not been already told countless times, in courts of justice, on papers and television.

I managed to get close to Janis, like the photo shows. I was making my way to her and I still did not know how I would use my knife: to kill her or cut her loose. I never found out, because when

I was almost there, the dentist's wife came at me screaming, 'Slut! Slut from hell!' and plunged a blade, one of ours that she had got hold of in the mayhem, into my side.

There was a sharp pain, a wet sound, and for a confused moment, I thought I was back in the circle, in happier times, when we butchered Napoleon, only I had been wrong, I was not the hand with the knife, I was Napoleon.

The hurt made it difficult to breathe, to see.

When I got a measure of my senses back, Janis was looming over me, free. She kicked me where the woman had stabbed me, sending another wave of pain through my body.

'Janis…' I said.

She hit me once more, and the pain was too much to speak.

LILA

I ran through dimming starlight. I knew everything that happened to the others, the same way as I knew every step I took and every jutting root I leapt upon. The stars overhead were vanishing. At first I headed towards the beach, but then I felt a tug, and a solitary Oddball appeared, with a mouse's muzzle, a feathered body, three bird's legs, five tails. It was the first Oddball Galen had given me. It flew around my head once, and then turned towards the pinewood. I followed it deeper into the woods, to our sacred fig tree.

All starlight trailed there.

I saw it for what it was, at last: the Tree of Life, seed and source of all that breathes and throbs and dies. A hum came from the tree, the same pitch as ours. Every white branch was humming. The tree was heaving and swelling like a living organism, the way the hut had done in the vision I had had during my first pathworking, so many years ago. I had been afraid back then, but this was now, and I was fearless.

I touched the bark. I found it warm, like flesh. The tree opened herself to me. I felt Zoey's pain, I felt Sam becoming smaller and smaller, and then disappearing, under the kicks he was being pummelled with. I felt it all and promised I wouldn't forget one single thing.

The tree was shimmering.

I walked in.

6

THEM

FROM THE PODCAST *IT'S A CULT!*, EPISODE 3X4

(The host, former Bikram Yoga teacher Sarah Harrington, interviews Prof Enrico Giannarelli, Chair of Social Psychology at La Sapienza University, Rome, who spoke for the prosecution as expert witness in the process for The Bastion).

EG: What you need to understand, Sarah, is that at the core, these people were looking for parental figures.

SH: They joined a cult because they wanted Mum and Dad?

EG: Basically, yes. A British scholar and dear friend of mine, Alexandra Stein, has written extensively about cults and attachment theory. To simplify massively, this theory says that the way we build relationships throughout our life – with lovers, friends, colleagues at work, employees, bosses – is largely dependent on the kind of relationship our parents, or our primary caretakers anyway, built with us. The healthier that relationship was, the healthier the relationships we are going to build in the rest of our life will be.

SH: Could you give an example?

EG: You might come from a very strict upbringing: your mother never scooped you up when you cried, or she would tell you to buckle up and stop complaining, and when you told her you were afraid of the dark, she would only order you not to be stupid. Under these circumstances, you may develop what we call an *avoidant attachment style*, which means that, as a grown-up, you never ask for help, you have trouble expressing what you want, and so on.

SH: And you say this can help us understand The Bastion.

EG: This is *key* to understanding The Bastion. From what we have learnt about the members, none of them had what we call a *secure base*, that is, a healthy family that would allow them to grow up as fully rounded human beings, knowing they could always go back to a safe place. With the Bastion they created what they dreamed of: an ideal loving family, in an ideal home, better than anything that could ever exist in reality. And it was imperative they kept the external world out, so as to preserve the delusion.

SH: Becca and Ric were Mum and Dad.

EG: It is very common for cult leaders to take on a parental persona. Sometimes they are actually called 'mother' or 'father', and they refer to the cult as a *family*. Charles Manson put a capital-F to it, but he was by no means the only one going down that route. Political parties, terrorist cells, all groups that require your unquestioned loyalty work along similar lines. But then, beneath and behind that loyalty lies a darker truth. The attachment styles these groups foster are profoundly unhealthy. Their members must show their loyalty continuously. No divergence is accepted. Look what happened with that brave man they call *the Nameless*. When someone disagrees, the very memory of them gets annihilated.

SH: With all the sex that was going on, though...

EG: Sexual fantasies involving parents are part of the normal psychological development of any human being. In the Bastion, people were acting out those fantasies.

SH: And many more.

EG: And many more, yes. Sexual fantasies, fantasies of transcendence, saviour fantasies. It is no surprise they got to the point they could not distinguish between fantasy and reality anymore.

SH: The whole 'saving the world' bit was *a lot.*

EG: Again, nothing new there. Apocalyptic cults are a dime a dozen. Charles Manson's Family was one, and so was Heaven's Gate, and so were the Branch Davidians in Waco. When you want to keep people together, you must give them something to *do*. That goes for a cub scout summer camp as much as for a terrorist cell. An ideal, a meaning to their life. Give people a *why* to live, and they'll follow you to hell and back. And what better ideal than being the chosen ones to save the world? In this respect, at least, the Bastion is slightly unusual. Most apocalyptic cults don't maintain that the world can be saved, they maintain that the cult members can be saved.

SH: And where do you think this angle comes from?

EG: Superhero and fantasy series. Yes, don't laugh, I am serious. Cults use the cultural materials they have at hand in their time and age. Apocalypticism could take a Christian tone in a time marked by Christianity. In ours, pop culture has taken the place that belonged to myth. Superheroes save the world. Fantasy heroes save the world. And so did the Bastion. The very name, The Bastion: doesn't it sound as if it came out of a Netflix series?

SH: A part of me is kind of jealous of them. Believing you're a hero, you're going to save the world!

EG: Consider though that apocalyptic cults rarely end well. It's usually suicide, or a violent confrontation with the external world. You can live in a delusion only for so long. Sooner or later reality will ask you to pay the bill.

SH: Am I right in thinking the Battle of Portodimare will become a historic moment for cult scholarship?

EG: You are quite right, yes. It is remarkable. Up there with The Peoples' Temple suicide in Guyana and the Waco siege.

SH: I mean, we've all seen the scenes. They were – I've seen scary stuff, but this was the scariest I've seen. I don't know how the Portodimare people didn't just run the other way when they saw these crazed obsessives, stark naked, brandishing knives...

EG: Quite remarkable.

SH: With a baby tied to a tree.

EG: We need to understand the Bastion's mindset. They were not killing a mother and her baby. They were *saving the world*. In their mind, those were not human beings anymore, they were monsters which needed to be disposed with, for the greater good.

SH: And of course it is only by chance that *the monster* was the same person who was calling them out publicly.

EG: Once you accept their reality, everything else makes perfect sense. In their paranoia, they were not taking it out on a woman who was causing them problems. On the contrary, the fact that the woman was causing them problems was proof they needed to take care of her for a greater good. They had been told they were going to save the world, so anybody who stood in their way had to be the puppet of some sinister master. Their thinking is topsy-turvy. They were the good guys by definition, so everything they did was *good,* because their intentions and their goals were good.

SH: And this isn't even the weirdest thing about them.

EG: They haven't told us a whole lot about their cosmology yet, but the little they let slip is fascinating. They believe they can work magic collectively, by coming together. You know where you've got to go to find similar ideas?

SH: Where?

EG: Maxim Gorky, in early twentieth-century Russia. He wrote about people coming together and developing psychic powers. His works had some influence on early Bolshevik thought, even in circles close to Lenin. They called it *science* rather than *magic,* but it is a matter of wording. It is interesting that the idea cropped up again in the twenty-first century, in the West, in a capitalist, individualistic culture. I don't think it is by chance that it cropped up in Southern Italy, where capitalism was never fully realised, and families and communities are still comparatively prominent, rather than, say, in London or Milan.

SH: So you don't believe the Bastion can actually work magic.

EG: (Laughter) Goodness, no. Once again, it is not surprising they believe they can. The area Becca and Ric grew up in is ripe with superstitions. In the nineties a local woman, Concetta Pecoraro, made a flourishing business of her visions of the Blessed Virgin Mary. She saw Mary every month at the end of the month, right at a time when the faithful got their salary and had fresh cash to donate. There was a tragic episode in which two professionals, husband and wife, developed a religious mania after the death of their first daughter, and started abusing the second in the name of God. It ended up in a homicide-suicide. There are rumours about a manuscript written by a local eccentric which should open the doors to communication with the Saints, no less. This is the milieu the Bastion come from.

SH: Superstition.

EG: Exactly.

SH: Of the two cult leaders, only Becca remains. Nobody knows where Ric is.

EG: I think we all know.

SH: You mean...

EG: Like the boys. Those poor, poor boys.

SH: The Carabinieri traced the phones of the two young men, which did stop functioning in the pinewood, on the night the boys disappeared.

EG: Exactly.

SH: But nobody has been charged yet. Nobody has found any bodies, either.

EG: It's tricky.

SH: Ritual murder?

EG: I'd rather not comment on that.

SH: Yeah, the Bastion has good lawyers.

EG: You say that.

SH: What about Lila Brasca? Do you think she died too?

EG: She left on the night the Carabinieri disbanded the cult, this is the one thing we know for sure. There are two scenarios I can see. In one, she is hiding, and perhaps, far from the clutches of her former gurus, she'll be able to clear her mind and go back to her real family. In the other scenario – it is what I just said about the way apocalyptic cults often end.

SH: Death.

EG: You either kill yourself because that is how you fulfil the prophecy, or you kill yourself because you cannot live with the prophecy failing.

SH: I hope she's alright. She looks so young.

EG: This is a complicated situation. Lila was brainwashed into committing some terrible actions. She did commit those actions, undoubtedly she did, but she also was under a tremendous psychological pressure which could have broken any of us. She is both a culprit and a victim, like most cult members.

SH: Even Rebecca Abbracciavento?

EG: You could write a whole book about the Abbracciaventos.

SH: Which is what you are doing, if I'm right.

EG: Yes, I signed a contract with...

[...]

JOHN ANDERSON-CAMPBELL, WRITING FOR *THE GUARDIAN* OPINION:

> [...]
>
> Everything about the Bastion is bad. This must be stated loud and clear – everything about the Bastion is bad. Especially the things that seem fun, those are the worst. What is fun about coupling with every one of your

friends, hanging naked outdoors among mosquitoes, chanting and drumming all night long? I am not a prude, as my readers know, but all this does not sound fun to me.

I am suspicious of 'free' sex. Every time someone has called for free sex, it was, in the end, about men wanting to sleep with as many women as possible, and women demurely accepting. The freedom is always one-way. The members of the Bastion swear it was different with them; excuse me if I don't take the words of cult members at face value.

And yes, this group of creeps was led by a woman, but 'Becca' is the worst of the whole bunch. I couldn't see a trace of compassion in her eyes. She comes from a well-off family, doesn't have any excuses for the money-grabbing, brainwashing scheme she put together with her brother. She is, let's say it, a bad apple with a good-looking face. The fact that she has her defenders speaks loads about the problems of our current cultural climate.

Don't get me started on the Bastion's greenwashing. With all their solar panels and septic tanks, they were still living by the beach, and when has it ever been the case that living by the beach is sustainable? For heating, they would burn logs in fireplaces, which as we all know is highly polluting. Only one of them was a vegetarian, and eating meat is a surefire way to destroy the planet.

This is not how you save the world, definitely not. I'll tell you what we need to do if we want to save the world. It's very simple…

[…]

A TWITTER/X THREAD

MsLuisa: In the end, the Bastion were victims of political correctness gone mad, nothing more, nothing less.

DarrenPhD: They were killing babies!

MsLuisa: No baby was killed.

LUK: That we know of.

MsLuisa: @LUK, by that reasoning, you didn't kill any baby either – that we know of!

DarrenPhD: Are you accusing those who disagree with you of killing babies?

MsLuisa: This is not what I said.

LUK: It is though.

AndreaD: I'm with @MsLuisa. What did these guys do wrong?

DarrenPhD: Kidnap a mother & daughter...?

Ms Luisa: After a targeted campaign of bullying.

LUK: You call _that_ bullying?

Ms Luisa: @LUK, fuck off.

A TIKTOK VIDEO

The video is shot in night-vision, like the spooky segments of ghost-hunting shows. Ms Sallybum, who has over 700,000 followers, is humming under a fig tree, dressed like Super Mario. She suddenly snaps her head up.

On the fig tree there is Ms Sallybum, dressed like Columbus. She says, 'I'm your magic, baby.'

Ms Sallybum/Super Mario says, in an Italian-with-thick-New-York accent, 'Mamma mia!'

Ms Sallybum/Columbus magically produces a pizza.

Both the versions of Ms Sallybum eat together. Writing appears: *Pizza Bastion, call now, we deliver magically.*

EXCERPT FROM AN INTERVIEW WITH DR BRASCA PUBLISHED IN MAJOR ITALIAN NEWSPAPER *CORRIERE DELLA SERA*

DR BRASCA: No, to this day, I have no clue where my daughter is.

CORRIERE DELLA SERA: There have been sightings.

DR B: Nothing reliable.

CDS: You are fighting the Bastion on multiple fronts. They levelled some accusations against you.

DR B: It would be more correct to say they started a smear campaign. They weren't happy with taking my daughter from me, no, they had to do this too. I represent all that these people despise – integrity, a sense of the institutions, solid values. If they could, they would destroy me. But they picked the wrong target. I'm tougher than them.

CDS: Do you have a message for your daughter, if she is reading?

DR B: Same as always. Come back, Daniela. We are your real family. We forgive everything you did. You have a chance to start anew. Don't waste it.

7

US

At sunset today, we heard Lila's drumming.

Some of us are behind bars, others live under surveillance. The judge tried to demonstrate that Becca and Ric practised some form of financial abuse, but she couldn't find the smallest shred of evidence. She had to drop the sex angle too: none of us was a minor, none of us was forced into doing anything. Dr Brasca has been very vocal in deprecating the filth we had lured his daughter into, and the vast majority of the public opinion agrees, but filth is not an offence yet, the best efforts of the respectable ones notwithstanding.

Our situation is as bad as it looks, but not as bad as it could be. Although everybody believes we killed the boys – and for once everybody's right – that has been hard to prove without bodies. Even if we got unlucky and some evidence surfaced (say, a fragment of a tooth), in legal terms saying that *we* killed them means little. *Who* of us, exactly? We are ready to support and contradict each other as needed, muddying the waters until they are as thick and dark as quicksand, and you know what happens to those who venture onto quicksand.

It is going to be a long battle in court; for every new suit we receive, we make two countersuits. We sold movie and book rights to our story, and there is no shortage of lawyers who want to work on a high-profile case like ours. We can afford a long battle.

The kidnapping of Janis and Ellie is the sticky point. Lawyering up is not helping much about that, and that is the only reason why the judges could keep Becca, Zoey and some of the others in jail. That, and the violence that happened on our last night in the pinewood. Two of the invaders died – the father of one of the boys and a student. But Sam died too, many of us had to be hospitalised, and Zoey took five months to stand on her legs again. We were defending ourselves against trespassers, but the trespassers were there because they had good reason to believe two people were in danger. It's complicated, and we are making it more so.

They wonder where Ric and Lila are. We say Ric and Lila left, which is true, in both cases. They are adults and we don't know their whereabouts – is that a crime?

We have been humming every night. Wherever we are, in our cell or in our house or deep in the woods, we hum, catching the echo of each other's hum, and slowly synching together. We have been banned from our home, but nobody can take the Inner Pinewood from us. Dispersed as we are, it has been hard to hum in tune together. But we have been getting closer every night. Alien stars flashed overhead for a moment, in jail as much as outside. We caught a glimpse of an Oddball from the corner of our eye.

And today at sunset we heard Lila's drum.

She is ready and she is calling to us. We are ready too. Tonight we are going to break through. We will burst out of our cages, and head to the place Lila has made for us, and start again. Janis and Ellie walk free, the banging at the sky continues, the world is on a knife edge. We went through a crucible, and we came out stronger than ever before.

But taking care of our enemies is not the first thing we are going to do. Family is more important. Charlie made a terrible mistake, but we love her and forgive her. She did what she thought was right – we would expect nothing else from any of us. So the first thing we are going to do tonight, when we reach our breakthrough and free ourselves once and for all, is go find her. We know she is in trouble. We are going to help her out, and envelop her in our hum.

And then you'll see.

8

HER

Eighteen months and a lifetime have passed since the Battle of Portodimare. I spent the first weeks in hiding, fearing that my name would come out, but it didn't, and I could go back to my life. I was one of the few of the Bastion who had not been doxxed before that awful night, and remarkably, none of my old friends gave my name. They were loyal to the end.

Unlike me.

On this spring sunset, I am facing once more the gates of the pinewood. It is the first time I feel it is safe to return since fleeing that night. The gate has not been replaced. The two crooked sides are kept together with a chain, but no lock. Behind the gate, the pinewood is overgrown, and silent. I miss everything about it. I undo the chain and walk in.

Everything is how I left it, more or less. Kids have come to play: there are spray-painted inverted pentagrams on some trees, empty beer cans and food wrappings. Someone stole the solar panels (of course they did), and almost all of the hammocks. These are details. Irrelevant.

I walk to Villa Abbracciavento, which still stands exactly the same as when I first saw her, patrician and timeless, beyond the petty squabbles of humans. I walk inside. It's a wasteland of broken windows and upturned tables. I can smell Sam's breakfast, I can hear Ric's decisive voice, Lila's laughter. I hope Lila is well. I hope I will see her again one day, although I doubt it would be a happy meeting.

I move through the ghosts of the family I betrayed. Everything

I have lost comes back to me: the colours, the conversations, the bonfires, the parties, the sex, the magic. I gave it all up, for what? I do not always have an answer to that.

I never hear Bertrand anymore, after fleeing the pinewood that night. I had hoped he would reach out to me in Saint-Malo, but no. Perhaps, cutting myself off from the Bastion, I've cut myself off from magic. With the raindrops dispersed, no rainbow will ever form again. Or perhaps there has never been any magic, only broken folks finding some consolation in playacting and stories. I know what I remember, but memory is a fickle thing.

Or perhaps there is some magic left here, in this sacred land.

I stand before the fig tree for a while, then I go to my usual spot and sit down, as I have done so many times, to watch the beach and the endless sea. I can hear from afar Lila's drum and Sam's theremin, but it is only my imagination.

I will never forgive myself for what happened to Sam.

Night comes.

I bite into the sandwich I brought. I bide my time, I wait.

Until saxophone music comes, soft, then more decisive. 'Body and Soul', the song Bertrand and his band played in the hospital when he asked me to marry him. *Don't turn*, he had said, before he started playing.

'Bertrand,' I call.

I feel his presence behind me. I hear a rustling, then two hands rest on my shoulders. Bertrand is touching me again. This is bliss, unadulterated bliss. It lasts only a moment.

A terrible certainty dawns on me.

This thing was able to fake Bertrand's sound, his attitude – but it could not fake Bertrand's gentle touch. Its fingers are burning hot.

I can't breathe. *You never think you're the one being played.*

This thing here, this abominable thing that is touching me, is not Bertrand.

'You can turn around now,' it says.

AUTHOR'S NOTE

One night in my twenties I found myself in the woods of a secret Eastern European location, surrounded by cultists. I had three friends with me; everybody else – everybody for miles – was in the cult. They were called the Raelians. Following their prophet, a former journalist, they believed it was their duty and privilege to prepare humanity for the return of the aliens who had created us in the first place. I had been hanging with the cult for a couple of years, getting to know them, listening to their voices. We were shooting a documentary.

I have had nights which were more outwardly strange (the story of the Black Mass is for another time), and yet that one stayed with me. Imagine two hundred cultists dancing to Britney Spears and you will not be far off the mark. They were not swaying by savage drums, shouting invocations in Latin. No: pop music. The prophet, a man with a genial smile and a mischievous face, sat in a chair. He was dressed in white, and the chair was draped in white too. Women were dancing topless around him, feeding him grapes. He was the half-brother of Jesus Christ, as his own teachings went. He deserved some joy.

The cultists were – they were people. Some were nice, others less so, some were smart, others sweet, some were well-educated, some well-travelled, some starry-eyed. They were nurses, biologists, stall-holders, antique dealers, dance teachers. Just people. You could have a perfectly pleasant conversation with one of them over a dinner of pizza and beer (this was, in fact, my way in), and they wouldn't appear any odder than the screaming family sitting at the next table. Except, they were laying the groundwork for the return of alien gods. That was the strangest thing about them: that they did look perfectly normal until they didn't. The question I started asking myself was – who gets to decide what *normal* looks like?

I grew up in Southern Italy in the Eighties and Nineties, which left me with psychic scars I bear with pride. The Church was everywhere, in every office, in every hospital, in every school, in every house, in every bedroom. When I was a kid, I was afraid my parents wouldn't make it to Heaven, because they both did like their food, so they were gluttons, so obviously they were on a highway to Hell. Not that my household was particularly religious: Mum and Dad didn't even go to Sunday mass (they sent me). This was just the *terroir* of everyday life. A life where bodies could physically come back to life, demons had the power to possess humans, and Heaven and Hell were real places on a supernatural map. Nothing strange here, nothing to see. Not like those cultist weirdos.

In sociology of religion, the word *cult* is not a pejorative. It is used for minority spiritual groups. Christianity itself was a cult before it went viral. And most cults are harmless. The Raelians teach meditation and preach free love, offering, for a reasonable fee, meaning and community to thousands. The satanists I met were considerate chaps. The only reason why people in my hometown are not classified as 'cultists' is that their belief system won. It is a matter, not of what they believe in, but of how many people believe in that. The brute force of numbers gets to decide what is normal.

There are many reasons why cults are endlessly fascinating. A key one is that they show us normality fraying at the seams. The things *we* believe, the values *we* hold dear, are no less strange than *theirs*. Believing that everything is matter requires as big a leap as believing that everything is mind: the New Age nutter and the New Atheist wisecracker play the same game, in different teams. Yes, there are some technical truths (paracetamol does work), but anything more than that, is anybody's guess. Alien gods are strange, sure. But I'm reasonably confident the whole universe is conscious, which, I'll be the first to admit, is not less strange. Hardcore materialists believe that consciousness doesn't exist at all, not even in humans, and that we are deluded into believing it does, which is a guess as good as any, only, don't try to sell me *that* is not strange.

They are not the weirdos. *We* are.

I have spent a lot of my life around spiritual types, like Zoey in *The Dark Side Of The Sky*. I still do. I've met all the folks she mentions, and more. I was around scientists as well, and philosophers. My one take, for what it's worth, is that nobody has a clue what's going on. There is only people doing their best, day by day, and sometimes their best is different from ours. *They* don't have a clue, and *we* don't, either.

How beautiful is that?

TOASTS

It was an honour to be able to shed some light on the strange story of the group called The Bastion, and their downfall. It was also a lot of work. I would have never made it to the end on my own; it would be ungrateful not to raise a few glasses to those who have been helping me along the way. I'm going to toast to four people in particular. In a book where the end of times features so prominently, these are the Four Horse Riders of whatever Apocalypse may be coming.

The first toast goes to Enrico Pozzi, who, when I was eighteen, initiated me into the twin pleasures of Social Psychology and cult studies. I owe to his lectures and his book *Il Carisma Malato* (an extraordinary account of the life and death of Jim Jones and The Peoples' Temple) an interest in cults which never abated. These days Enrico lives in a scorpio-shaped castle, which would be a great place to start a cult, but he swears he's not going to do that anytime soon. We'll see. Meanwhile – here's to Enrico!

My second toast goes to Piers Blofeld, my agent. Putting your agent in your acknowledgements may feel like something you just have to do, but seriously, Piers deserves it every time, and every time more. In the years we have been working together he has been unwavering in his support, his publishing wisdom, his trust, his tough love and sense of humour. He is a full-fledged creative partner, and I know I'm a lucky bastard to have found one of those rare beasts. So – here's to Piers!

The third Horse Rider is my editor, George Sandison. His ideas and comments and suggestions turned this book on its head, in a good way. He managed to help me tell an intelligible story without renouncing my aesthetic obsessions. The ideal editor should be able to listen to authors and help them make their voice *more*. George was the ideal editor. I hope he won't transcend our plane of existence, now that he got to such a quasi-Platonic stage. Malkuth still needs great editors. Here's to George!

And then, as always, Paola Filotico. I don't like the person I would be without her, and I don't like the books I would write without her. She saves my life every day. She is the kind of person you wouldn't believe actually exist until you met them; a living proof that reality is stranger, and sometimes better, than any fiction. Here's to Paola!

Till next time, folks.

ABOUT THE AUTHOR

Francesco Dimitri is a prize-winning writer of fiction and nonfiction, a comic book writer and a screenwriter. He published eight books in Italian before switching to English. His first Italian novel was made into a film, and his last was defined by *Il Corriere della Sera* as the sort of book from which a genre 'starts again'. His first English novel, *The Book of Hidden Things*, a critical and commercial success, has been optioned for cinema and TV. After his second, *Never The Wind*, the *Fortean Times* called him 'one of the most wondrous writers of our time'.